THE DRAGON'S RAGE

❧❦❧

"You will stay!"

Now a transformation came over the Dragon King. His arms and legs twisted, his hands curling into claws. He swelled in size, and as he grew, leathery wings burst from his back and a tail sprouted from below. The vestiges of humanity quickly slipped away. The dragon head crest slid downward, remolding itself into the true visage of the reptilian monarch.

Within seconds, a huge emerald dragon had taken the place of the scaled knight. The dragon unfurled wings that nearly spanned the entire width of the great cavern. "Think what you do, Yssa! This is no game!"

"For once I agree with you, Father." The enchantress pointed at the massive dragon. Light flashed before the dragon's crimson orbs. He roared, startled.

"Goodbye, Father . . . "

❧❦❧

Books by Richard A. Knaak

THE DRAGONREALM SERIES

Firedrake
Ice Dragon
Wolfhelm
The Shrouded Realm
Shadow Steed
Children of the Drake
Dragon Tome
The Crystal Dragon
The Dragon Crown
The Horse King

King of the Grey
Frostwing
The Janus Mask
Dutchman

Published by
WARNER BOOKS

THE HORSE KING

RICHARD A. KNAAK

WARNER BOOKS

A Time Warner Company

For Barbara Puechner
In gratitude for
many years of guidance
and assistance

WARNER BOOKS EDITION

Aspect® is a registered trademark of Warner Books, Inc.

Cover design by Don Puckey
Cover illustration by Matt Stawicki

Warner Books, Inc.
1271 Avenue of the Americas
New York, NY 10020

Visit our Web site at
http://pathfinder.com/twep

Ⓦ A Time Warner Company

Printed in the United States of America

First Printing: March, 1997

10 9 8 7 6 5 4 3 2 1

CHAPTER I

He was sorry, but the king had to die.

Miklo Vinimus respected, if not liked, the king of Zuu, but for the sake of peace, Lanith had to die before his ambitions grew to fruition. It was not that the muscular, graying monarch was so terrible a ruler. But he had begun gathering forces that Miklo and a few others understood would eventually overwhelm Lanith himself, then spread unchecked over much of the Dragonrealm.

Back in the quarters of the Order, all the others save for Hysith would be sleeping now. Miklo did not fear that particular would-be mage. Hysith only had a shadow of Miklo's power, just enough to become a member of the king's Magical Order, and most of the time the aged figure could not even recall his own name. He had been drinking heavily tonight and Miklo had left him even stronger drink on his way out. Hysith would definitely be no danger. Lanith only kept him around because human sorcerers were still very scarce. Zuu could now claim a dozen, but most were little better than Hysith.

Miklo had only been a baby when the Dragon Emperor had perished, a death that had opened the way for a new generation of human mages like himself. The last generation had been hunted down by the draconian emperor and his servants after the drakes had nearly lost a war against the Dragon Masters. The human spellcasters forming that legendary group had been out to free their kind from the oppression of the drakes. They had nearly succeeded, failing more because of betrayal in their ranks than because of the Dragon Emperor.

A few spellcasters with resources or, more often, no discernible power had escaped the hunt. Meanwhile, more newcomers with potential appeared every year. However, Miklo would be old and wrinkled before mages became more than legend to most common folk. Only in Zuu and perhaps far-off Penacles did common folk see sorcery on a daily basis.

But not much longer, if I succeed. It'll all crumble without Lanith to urge it on. Clad in robes the color of the night that made his rather trollish features look even less human, the short, swarthy Miklo stalked quietly through the corridors of the palace. The Magical Order had its living quarters in a converted stable next to the palace . . . near enough if Lanith desired the presence of his mages but far away enough for when he did not. The place still smelled of the memory of sweaty mounts, but then, so did the rest of Zuu as far as he was concerned. The murals Miklo passed were illustrations of the natives' great passion. Each one represented some scene of equine majesty, the animals gamboling, racing, or charging into battle. The kingdom was renowned for the horses it bred, horses purchased by eager folk from every corner of the continent. The horse folk earned a good living from raising and running the animals. It should have stayed that way, but Lanith was too ambitious a monarch. With most of the Dragon Kings dead or their power in disarray, he had decided that the time to expand his lands was near at hand and his grand Magical Order was to be one of the weapons he would use to achieve that desire. Even horses seemed now a secondary passion to the king.

Torches lit the corridors through which the self-appointed assassin silently moved, but Miklo left no shadow as he passed. The trick that *she* had taught him worked well, even better than either of them could have hoped. Although he had started learning to use his gifts just shortly before reaching adulthood, he had quickly proven himself a capable and fairly powerful sorcerer. Not at all as powerful, say, as the great Bedlams, but powerful enough. His abbreviated training had been enough to gain him entrance into Lanith's Magical Order and a position of some trust. He was one of the Order's more competent mages and, therefore, one of the more well treated.

Of course, without her quick training, he would never have made it to this point, the assassination of the king. She was the reason he had finally dared to take this great risk, even if she had not actually wanted him to make such an attempt. However, Miklo's home in the independent barony of Adderly lay just to the north of Zuu and was an attractive first target for the horse king's campaign. For that reason alone, Miklo had to stop Lanith.

Adderly consisted of rich farmlands barely defended by a few large towns and one castle, a land that had prospered since the death of the Dragon King who had lived there. Miklo's parents, his sister and her family, and his younger brother all lived in the heart of the barony, near the castle itself. Although he had not seen them since leaving for Zuu a year before, their possible fates if Zuu went to war were always on his mind. Adderly could not hold out against the horse king. It would be trampled by his armies in one day, two at most.

There would be no aid. Gordag-Ai, the nearest other great kingdom, lay much farther north, too far away to be of assistance. Besides, Gordag-Ai had a marriage treaty with far-off Talak, and Talak a treaty with Zuu from over twenty years ago when both had fought for freedom against the drake lords. Neither of those kingdoms would likely risk their treaties simply for his home. They would probably be preparing their own defenses instead, waiting for the day when the horse king unveiled to all his mad crusade.

Miklo's own people could not believe that their neighbors to the south, neighbors with whom they had traded for generations, would suddenly turn to war. Frustrated at their lack of comprehension, he had finally come to Zuu on his own with only the intention of seeing if his notions were simply delusion. However, his chance meeting with her two days after his arrival had introduced him to revelations so great and terrible that had he not seen proof Miklo would have not believed them himself.

Lanith has opened the way to a future darker than the one the Dragon Kings once intended for our kind, she had informed him that first night. *There's something already alive in the palace that should not be a part of our world. I can feel it.*

He had not seen that thing, but he had seen evidence of its existence, evidence that frightened Miklo yet steeled his resolve to kill the horse king.

A guard stood before the doorway through which Miklo needed to pass, but the bronzed, braided figure neither heard nor saw the mage slowly walking toward him. Miklo allowed himself a brief, satisfied smile. His potential had both stunned and pleased his mistress. Miklo knew very well that his ability to perform sorcery had been the reason she had also chosen him as a lover; she herself was quite accomplished in sorcery, not to mention a few more fascinating fields, and more than once she had spoken of how the marriage of Cabe Bedlam to the legendary Lady of the Amber had produced offspring reputed to be even more powerful sorcerers than their parents. Knowing nothing about the Bedlams save from tales passed on by visitors to his village, Miklo took her word on the abilities of the children, but he was also aware that each time she spoke of them, she did so with envy. She clearly desired a similar union and the results thereof and he was the prime candidate. Once this was over, there would be time . . .

When he was next to the guard, Miklo reached up to the man's chest and tapped it. The guard immediately went rigid. Impressed by his success so far, Miklo paused a moment to admire his work. True love had not been a part of the relationship between the northerner and his mistress, at least not where she had so far been concerned. Miklo was already hopelessly her slave and had been so from the moment he had first stared into that perfect face. Only on one other had he seen such beauty and that beauty belonged to one who would flay him alive if he was captured. Saress was very protective of her royal lover and her power of sorcery was as great as that of Miklo's mistress, possibly even greater.

They will both be in the bed, asleep by now. One simple tar-

get. She said that even Saress would have no defense against this attack. How his mistress knew so much about the horse king's devil woman Miklo did not know, but everything had so far worked to perfection. The guards he had passed were now ensorcelled, the Magical Order slumbered on without knowledge that their protective spells had been temporarily negated, and King Lanith and Saress had only a few steps left worth of life.

He tried the door, but found it locked. Reaching into his robe, Miklo removed a small vial from an inner pocket. For some reason, locks remained impervious to his skills no matter how much he practiced. Miklo would have stood a better chance of breaking the door down with his shoulder than of opening the door with sorcery.

Miklo poured some of the contents into the lock, then leaped back as the liquid immediately began eating into the metal. A low, sizzling sound accompanied the process, but other than the would-be assassin the only one within earshot was the frozen guard. Miklo Vinimus counted to twelve as he had been instructed, then pushed against the door. It resisted at first, but with a little more effort, he at last opened it. The slight groan of the joints was not enough to worry him. As soon as the door was open wide enough, he slipped through.

"Almost there . . ." he whispered. Miklo gazed around the chamber, somewhat disappointed at the dust-encrusted but otherwise bland decor of what had once been a royal bedroom. Dark shadows clung to the farthest corners of the room. The dust made his nose itch, but Miklo held back his sneeze as he stepped farther inside.

It had once been the chambers of Lanith's brother Prince Blane, but Blane had perished years ago in some old battle against the forces of the long-dead Dragon Emperor. The previous king had ordered the chamber sealed up and guarded after his son's death and Lanith had carried on his father's eccentric desire. Miklo felt a touch of guilt at the thought of utilizing the room of one dead son in order to eliminate another, but for the sake of his homeland and the lives of many, it was best that Lanith walk the Final Path.

With one last glance down the hall, Miklo closed the door.

Slowly his eyes adjusted to the darkness. The details of the decor did not interest him save that the center of the chamber had to be clear of any objects. He saw that this was so, something that pleased him immensely, for a sudden nervousness had spread over him. Miklo had been anxious from the start, but this near to his goal the ramifications of what he was about to attempt now became overwhelmingly clear. He was about to assassinate the monarch of one of the leading kingdoms of the Dragonrealm. He was about to change the course of the land, save the lives of countless innocents.

Almost Miklo Vinimus turned to flee, but her voice echoed in his head, almost as if she stood in the room with him. *If you're going to do it, do it then, Miklo! There's no hope for any of us otherwise.*

His brow furrowed as he briefly thought over the last, but the urge to complete his task again took precedence, pushing away the fear and all else. The horse king had to die for the sake of the Dragonrealm.

Moving to the center, Miklo dropped to his knees. Lanith's personal chambers were directly overhead. Surely the fact that providence had supplied Miklo the perfect location from which to cast his spell of death meant that he was destined to succeed.

If all worked as planned, the spell would come up from below the horse king's bed and envelop its occupants before they had a chance to stir. Saress no doubt had set her own defenses, but Miklo's mistress had insisted that what they plotted would work, defenses or not. It was clear that she knew Saress reasonably well.

He coughed once because of the dust, then began to concentrate.

Like many sorcerers, he saw the power as lines of force crisscrossing everything. Even here, it cut across the darkened room, creating a strange glow visible only when he used magical sight. The sight was useful when one had to draw upon substantial levels of power, but otherwise interfered with normal vision. Miklo was still amazed that more competent spellcasters such as the Bedlams could shift into and out of magical sight in the literal blink of an eye. It always took him a few moments to adjust, both when shifting into and out of the phase. Perhaps those like the Bedlams did things differently than he did. If he survived this, he would ask her.

Tendrils of power—thin, misty things that only he could see—floated with purpose toward the ceiling. They paused there, as yet unable to penetrate the man-made barrier, but Miklo was not perturbed. He still had to bind the power a bit more. Her instructions had been explicit. If he wanted to slip past Saress's defenses without disturbing anything—

A sudden shifting of forces made him pause. An oddly foreign presence briefly touched his mind. It vanished before he had a chance to try to identify it, leaving him only with an unsettled feeling. Miklo waited, but when it did not return, he finally shrugged it off as nerves and decided to push on with his effort.

He raised one hand toward the ceiling.

A giggle escaped him—no, he realized, the giggle had come from somewhere in the chamber.

"You've been very amusing, very amusing indeed, little Miklo. I watched and waited with anticipation as you wended your way despite all obstacles to your moment of destiny," piped a voice from the shadows surrounding him. "Very amusing it was, but now I can't let you go on. I've so many plans, so many things to do, and if I let you go through with this, it'll just take that much longer for me to achieve them!"

Gasping, Miklo rose from the floor. The forces he had been gathering he now turned toward the darkest shadows in the chamber, those being the only place he could imagine the source of the voice hiding. Green and red flashes of energy momentarily illuminated dead Prince Blane's room and stirred up so much dust that despite his predicament Miklo Vinimus had to pause to cough and sneeze.

A massive hand seized him by the collar and raised him into the air.

"Don't fret, though, little Miklo. I shall find a place for your name in this great epic I'm creating. A small place, to be sure . . ."

The hand released the hapless, would-be assassin. Instead of the floor, a huge maw of darkness now opened beneath his feet. Miklo Vinimus found himself falling and falling and falling without end in sight.

His scream grew distant.

In the hills overlooking the city, the golden-haired enchantress stirred from her self-induced trance, sweat suddenly enveloping her. She blinked and looked around as if afraid that something terrible now stalked her. Then, her somewhat elfin features twisted into an expression of annoyance, frustration, and not a little guilt at having used a loyal if very naive man whose magical potential was now lost to her.

"Damn . . ." she muttered. If what she had sensed before breaking contact with Miklo was true, there was no hope left for the ugly little northerner. "Damn . . . damn . . . not another one . . ."

Lanith stirred from his slumber, slightly disgruntled at having lost the thread of his dream. He had been breaking in a magnificent stallion, a creature more elemental than animal. He dreamed such dreams often, for in his mind there was only one mount worthy of him.

A giggle from nearby pushed away the last vestiges of the dream from the graying, bearded king's mind. Lanith blinked, allowing his eyes to grow accustomed to the darkness. He saw that the giggle could not have come from Saress, for she still slept deeply. He admired her long, flowing mane and the curves of her body before sitting up and looking around for the true force.

"What is it?" he asked.

A part of the darkness blacker than the rest coalesced into a tiny figure much like a puppet without strings. It had no mouth or nose; in fact, the only discernible features were a pair of ice-blue, narrow eyes that lacked any sort of pupil. The presence of the macabre nighttime visitor did not disturb the horse king. Lanith was too familiar with the thing by now.

Despite the lack of a mouth, the figure had no trouble speaking. "Are you sleeping well, my great king?"

"I was until something woke me." Lanith's craggy features

twisted into an expression of annoyance. He liked being woken by no one in the middle of the night.

The thing, now perched on the end of the bed, giggled. "I think that you will find one of your Magical Order missing, O King Lanith."

"What's that?" The monarch stiffened, dark piercing eyes fixing on the inhuman orbs of his companion. "What have you done, imp?"

"He was about to send you to join your brother Blane. I thought you might not want to do that, but if I was wrong, then I do apologize."

"An assassin? Where are the guards? What about the defenses? They should have been sufficient—" Lanith started to rise, but the puppetlike figure shook its head. To his surprise, the king obediently sat back down. Beside him, Saress continued to sleep. She had not so much as shifted since the creature's arrival.

"He was naughty, so I've sent him away. You'll have to inform Ponteroy that the amusing little Miklo has decided to forgo the rewards of the Order."

"Miklo Vinimus?" Lanith had nurtured hopes for Vinimus. With a little training from Saress, Vinimus would have been able to replace Ponteroy, something of an egotistical popinjay, as second in the Order. Saress had been hesitant to teach the northerner, however, and now Lanith saw that her judgment had been sound. "You sent him away? Bring him back! There may have been others involved. He'll have to stand for questioning."

"Oh, dear . . ," Even devoid of features, the ebony puppet somehow physically displayed comic dismay. "I'm afraid that he won't be coming back from where I've sent him." The thing giggled. "They never do."

Lanith frowned. "Nevertheless, this does not end here. If a member of my Order attempted an assassination on my life, there will have to be some changes made. Fewer privileges. More proof of respect and loyalty to the one who feeds them and pays them good gold. I will have to draw a tighter rein on them."

"A tighter rein." Another giggle. "You're right, of course,

and I shall help you achieve that, but not yet. Let them have their freedoms, their rewards. When their loyalty is demanded, good King Lanith, I'll make certain that they pay their due. Have I failed you thus far?"

"No . . ." Sleepiness once more touched the monarch of Zuu. Vague images of the magnificent black stallion again began to sprint through his thoughts. "No, you've not failed me, although I do not know why you—"

"Because I *like* you, good King Lanith! Because I want to do things for you! You've given a poor, lost soul a home and hearth! That's why soon you'll have the mount a conqueror and emperor deserves . . . because I want to do it for you."

The horse king leaned back, eyelids barely able to stay open. He did not question how swiftly sleep was overtaking him; he never did. A grin tried to spread across his face, but he was already too exhausted to complete it. "The shadow steed? You'll . . . help me . . . capture him?"

"Help you snare him, saddle him, and break him. Oh, especially *break* him . . ." The shadowy puppet rose from his perch and completed a comic bow of obeisance that King Lanith barely noted. "Rest easy now, my lord and master. When all things are in place, I will tell you what to do and you will do it, won't you?"

"Tell me . . . to do . . . do it . . . yes . . ." The warrior king drifted off to sleep.

"And no one but you and I will know that I'm helping you, will they?" As he spoke, the thing on the edge of the bed began to grow and as he grew he became more diffuse. Only the eyes remained strong.

"No . . . one . . ." spoke Lanith even though he was now deep into his slumber.

"You will be my puppet, great king. You'll serve me, bring me glorious battles and wonderful chaos for my epic, and in return I'll give you a most disobedient and ungrateful child, an offspring who has long been due a lesson."

"Shadow . . . steed . . ." mumbled the horse king. "Dark-horse."

"Yes . . . oh, yes, indeed . . . nothing will give me greater pleasure . . . well, *one* thing, but that can wait . . ."

King Lanith of Zuu did not respond this time, for no response was desired by his visitor.

Ice-blue eyes studied the horse king a moment longer, then the thing giggled once more and faded from the bedchamber.

CHAPTER II

Penacles. The City of Knowledge. A place of wonders. It was the location of the magical libraries, a fount of history and information older than the kingdom itself. It was the land ruled by the Gryphon, sorcerer, shapeshifter, and warrior. Here the first victories against the centuries-long reign of the Dragon Kings had been won. Here humans had finally gained the chance to be truly free.

It was a kingdom that had witnessed many astonishing events and played host to a variety of unusual guests throughout its long history, but for those gathered in the royal court, there was one guest who ever unnerved most of them simply with his presence.

His arrival tended to do even more.

A crackle of thunder. A burst of wind. A flash of light.

Someone screamed. Someone generally screamed, even though it was likely they had witnessed the same entrance a dozen times or more. The shadow steed did not try to hide his amusement as he trotted onto the marble floor. The brightly decorated chamber, newly renovated in the year since the Gryphon's reascension to the throne, contrasted greatly with his ebony color. The clatter of his hooves echoed throughout, the only sound now other than the gasping of one courtier or another as he passed among them.

He resembled a huge black stallion, although everyone there knew he was much more. How much more, even his dearest companions did not understand. He would have been hard-pressed himself to explain all that he was and was not.

There was nothing else in the Dragonrealm that was at all akin to Darkhorse.

The last humans scurried out of the way. Darkhorse cared little about any of them. Only the three figures ahead were of great importance to the steed. The one seated on the throne, sharp beak clamped tight in an obvious attempt to hold back his laughter, was the Gryphon. He was a humanoid variation on the traditional winged creature, a being as unique and as fascinating in his own way as Darkhorse was. The face was that of a bird of prey, although the feathering at the back gave way to a mane of hair more akin to that of another predator, the lion. A loose robe of crimson and gold covered most of the Gryphon's form, but Darkhorse knew that although the monarch of Penacles seemed perfectly human in body, the knees bent backward and the feet were taloned. The Gryphon also had vestigial wings, although as with the legs and feet, he kept those differences well hidden.

Standing alongside the Gryphon and looking slightly uncomfortable was the sorcerer Cabe Bedlam, Darkhorse's truest friend. Cabe Bedlam was a plain man by the standards of humanity, save for the silver streak in his dark hair that marked him as a spellcaster. However, his plain demeanor hid a sense of fairness and honesty achieved by very few beings that the shadow steed had met over the centuries. It also hid power such as few had ever attained. Cabe Bedlam could have laid waste to much of the realm just as his father Azran had attempted once, but where the elder Bedlam had been a monster, the son was a protector. It was he more than any other force that had helped shape the peace effort between not only the kingdoms, but also the races.

But there is still much work ahead, Darkhorse thought. *And some kingdoms will never accept a peace they have not achieved through war.*

The other figure standing near the throne was the sorcerer's mate, the fiery-tressed Lady Gwendolyn. Like Cabe's, her hair possessed a streak of silver. Unlike her husband, she was by no means plain. Accenting her beauty most were her emerald eyes, eyes that perfectly matched the sleek gown she wore. Those very eyes now fixed on the newcomer, dampening some of Darkhorse's humor. Lady Bedlam somehow had the ability to make him feel embarrassed, an emotion he otherwise rarely experienced.

Darkhorse had expected the two sorcerers to be here, having stopped briefly at their abode before journeying to Penacles. Their daughter, Valea, had informed him that her parents had transported themselves by sorcery to the Gryphon's palace only a few hours before. He was glad that they had done so; it would save him from having to repeat himself.

Just a few yards from the throne, the shadow steed dipped his head. It was as close as he ever came to bowing. "My greetings, Your Majesty! I apologize if my coming has greatly disturbed things!"

The Gryphon briefly flexed one clawed hand. "No. In fact, you are quite welcome this day. We had just begun discussing some matters that you may be able to lend a . . . hoof . . . with at some point. That can wait, though. To what do we owe your visit, my friend?"

There had been a time when *friend* would have been the last word the monarch of Penacles used to describe Darkhorse. There had been a time when the only one who had really trusted the demon steed had been the faceless warlock Shade, himself hardly the most trustworthy of characters. Shade was long dead now—*supposedly*—but over the past two decades, Darkhorse had gained for himself more friends than he had ever had before. Not only the Gryphon, but the Bedlams and their remarkable children. He was also good friends with the queen of Talak and her daughter, although the king of that mountain realm would never be too comfortable with him.

"I have the news you wanted about the drake confederation."

Everyone in attendance quieted. The Gryphon fixed one avian eye on his fearsome guest. "And what news is that?"

"Sssaleese appears to have strengthened his position. Two competitors seem to have . . . disappeared. The drakes have solidified their holdings in the northwestern region of the continent. They presently hold what used to be the northern half of the Iron Dragon's old domain. They've not moved on the hill dwarves to the east, but I suspect that is coming soon."

"Just as we suspected," commented Cabe Bedlam. "Sssaleese intends on becoming a Dragon King even if the others will not acknowledge him so. He probably believes that if his confederation grows large enough, Kyl will have to give him such rank."

"Do you think the young emperor will do that?" The king rubbed the underside of his beak. "He might lose the support of the other Dragon Kings. Storm and Black will certainly not accept Sssaleese as one of them."

Both the Storm Dragon and the Black Dragon were neighbors of sorts to Penacles. The Black Dragon had already tried to seize the kingdom and although his forces had been repulsed, no one believed that the lord of Lochivar was not constantly watching for weakness.

"I can't say. We're due to visit Kyl very soon. I'll try to put the question to him then." The Bedlams shared a unique relationship with the young emperor of the drake race, having raised him after his predecessor's death. That relationship had not always been easy, Kyl not always liking the human way of life.

"I could pay a visit to Sssaleese." Darkhorse stared at the sorcerer, one of the few who could look into his pupilless, icy blue eyes without flinching. "I could suggest new options to him if you like."

"That would not be wise, Darkhorse," Lady Gwen interjected. "Don't underestimate Sssaleese's power. We suspect that he has gotten his hands on some artifact. Certainly his success so far has been astonishing."

"I still say he had some hand in Toma's efforts to subvert Kyl to his cause." Darkhorse snorted. Toma had been a renegade drake, half brother to the new emperor, who had tried to control the throne to which he had not had any right. First he had attempted to manipulate his sire, the former emperor, and then, masquerading as a human teacher, he had sought to twist Kyl's mind. Toma was dead, but some believed that Sssaleese had given him refuge during the many years the renegade had remained hidden.

The Gryphon nodded. "Perhaps." He looked around at those gathered in the court. "My friends, please forgive me, but I must delay all other requests for an audience at this time. I apologize for letting you wait. Tomorrow, those of you who had business set for today will be first. Now, if you'll excuse me."

While those gathered still attempted to digest his words, the lionbird departed from the high-backed throne. He did not look at anyone as he hurried away, but the Bedlams followed him as if given some signal. Darkhorse paused only a moment longer, then proceeded after the mages. The shadow steed heard much whispering behind him, but nothing that sounded angry. The people of Penacles knew that their inhuman monarch, however brusque his manner, worked constantly for the benefit and safety of his subjects. He did not cut an audience short without good reason.

Guards came to attention as the Gryphon passed through the hall. At last they reached an open area in the palace where the sun could shine through onto a small inner garden. Benches circled the garden. To one side, a small pool populated with a few golden fish added to the feel of nature.

"I never know how to end audiences," grumbled the monarch of Penacles. "I never did. Toos was always more at home with the trappings of state, even if he was a crusty old soldier like me." The Gryphon looked to the heavens and raised a fist in frustration, a maimed fist missing two fingers. "You should've remained ruler, Toos, not me."

Toos had been an invaluable comrade and friend to his former commander, and Darkhorse, who had lost his share of friends, sympathized with the Gryphon. He turned his gaze toward the Bedlams, unable to keep from wondering what he would do when they, like all the others he had known, would fade into the past.

"I'm sorry." The Gryphon shook his head as if to clear it. "I think I would rather face the hordes of a Dragon King than sit on the throne, but the people refuse to see that others would be better fit to reign. They won't even let me very far out of their sight for fear I'll go running off to fight in some far-off war again."

"Troia might have something to say about that, too," remarked Lady Gwen. "Especially now that you have a child to raise."

Life and death, thought the shadow steed. *Everything always comes down to life and death.* Darkhorse could die, but he had lived so long that such a concept always seemed distant to him. However, such was not the case for his companions. Besides his old comrade, the Gryphon had also lost someone even dearer to him . . . his son. The lad had died in that same far-off war that the king had just spoken of. Of course, if the Gryphon had not journeyed across the sea to fight the wolf raiders, then he would have never met his mate, the cat-woman Troia, in the first place.

Life and death. It was a never-ending circle, the one villain Darkhorse could not defeat.

Which was why he sought other, more earthly foes. At least he could achieve some sense of satisfaction from overrunning a drake war party or barreling into a flock of arrogant Seekers. "My Lord Gryphon! You mentioned something else you wanted of me! What might that be?"

"It can wait a moment, Darkhorse," interrupted Cabe. "There is something we need to finish discussing with the Gryphon."

"Which is why I decided to bring us here instead of remaining in the court. The fewer ears the better, my friends." The lionbird glanced at his companions. "But my manners are slipping. Please, be seated."

Darkhorse noted the tension mounting in their host. Whatever topic he had missed because of his late arrival greatly disturbed the monarch.

"I've forgotten if you answered me earlier, Cabe. How many does that make?"

"Three. Two might have been coincidence, but the third one makes it all too clear that someone is hard at work here. The last was named Ilster. Fairly promising younger man."

"They've all been younger men," Gwen commented.

"And what do you mean by that, milady?"

She frowned. "Nothing. Just an observation. It might mean something more, but I can't be certain."

Darkhorse had to break in again. "Would it be possible for someone to clarify what is happening? I gather from what I hear that this has something to do with the school for mages?"

"That's right." Cabe's expression was a mixture of worry and puzzlement. "Three of our students have vanished over the past few months. No trace whatsoever."

"Three? They did not just simply give up their attempts and go home?"

"We thought of that, Darkhorse, but no one has seen them. If they left, then they didn't head for their homes."

"Aah! Then that leaves only one place where they could possibly be! They have gone to . . . Zuu!" Darkhorse uttered the name of the southwestern kingdom with the expectation of surprising his companions with his quick thought, but his pleasure faded as he saw that his announcement was far from a shock to them. "You know that, then . . ."

"It's what we *suspect*," returned the Gryphon. "There is a difference, my ebony friend."

"Well, then, we simply have to go there and find out!" Darkhorse backed up to give himself some room. "Come, Cabe! You and I will ride there now and be back with them before King Lanith can even blink!"

The Gryphon bristled. "With all due respect and for the sake of peace between Penacles and Zuu—at least for the moment—I'd prefer we handle things a little differently. This calls for treading a little more carefully, if you don't mind, Darkhorse."

"Are you suggesting that I cannot be delicate, my Lord Gryphon?" He looked from the monarch to the spellcasters, read their answer in their expressions, then dipped his head. "Well, perhaps you have a point."

"Zuu has been building up its strength for years, Gryphon," remarked Cabe. "Especially where mages are concerned. These disappearances have to be related to that."

"I agree, but we need proof. I have agents at work on it now. I'd prefer to hear what they've discovered before we move against Zuu. I—"

The clatter of metal made the entire group look around. A guard raced down the hall toward them, his face pale.

"Your Majesty, my pardon! Lord and Lady Bedlam! Your son! He's—"

"Aurim!" Gwen was on her feet. "What is it? Has something happened to him?"

The guard paused to catch his breath. "Not . . . not to him, my lady! He was showing . . . you just have to come, my lady!"

Cabe held on to his wife. "His sorcery. He was using sorcery again, Gwen."

"Where is he?" demanded the Gryphon.

"Your practice field, Your Majesty."

"Not far. Everyone with me."

With the Gryphon and the guard in the lead, the band hurried through the palace. Although the royal guard had a vast practice field by their quarters, years ago the king had usurped part of the royal gardens for a walled practice yard specifically designed to test his own unique abilities. Most humans would have found themselves hard-pressed to successfully navigate some of the features the Gryphon had added over time. To him, practice did not just concern swordplay; it also involved gymnastics and problem solving.

Just moments before they would have reached the field, a scream reached them.

"Is there someone with him?" the Gryphon snapped.

"He was with the daughters of Baron Vergoth of Talak." Vergoth was one of King Melicard's chief advisers and often played ambassador to Penacles. He had been good friends with Toos and also got along well with the Gryphon. Vergoth had many children, and Darkhorse vaguely recalled that two of the daughters were only a few years younger than Aurim Bedlam.

"I suspect that he was trying to show off." Cabe shook his head. "Not again."

No one else had an opportunity to comment, for they were suddenly standing outside facing the Gryphon's private field.

It was a living nightmare.

The ground rose and fell as if something huge were trying

to punch its way to the surface. A series of poles, originally set up for gymnastics, popped up and down at random, rising at times with such force that they surely would have badly injured anyone who happened to be standing too near. Climbing bars set in one wall seemed to believe that they were snakes, to coil around whatever object was within reach.

At various points around the field, weapons darted about of their own accord. One long blade buried deep into one of the poles was attempting to pull itself free.

"Animation," Gwen whispered. "He should know better than to try animation."

In the center of the chaos huddled three frightened figures. The daughters of the visiting baron—pale, tiny women clad in wide gowns—clung to Aurim's side. Aurim Bedlam was a golden-haired youth who might have escaped the pages of an epic tale, so physically did he resemble the handsome, noble heroes of such stories. At the moment, however, the younger Bedlam did not act the part of the epic hero, his face almost as terror-filled as those of his companions.

A pole shot up from the ground. It was close enough to strike one of the females a hard blow on the arm, but at the last moment, the pole bent away. Despite his fear, Aurim had at least put together a protective shield, albeit one that did not allow for much movement.

"They're all right." Lady Bedlam breathed a sigh of relief. Darkhorse knew that she had not only feared for her son, but for anyone near him. Although Aurim's difficulty with sorcery extended back to when he had been a small child, there had been surprisingly few injuries and none of those serious. Still, considering the lad's great potential, Darkhorse and the others still feared that one day the unthinkable would happen.

"He is not without some control of his abilities," the shadow steed offered, trying his best to soothe the Bedlams' worries.

Cabe stepped forward, arms outstretched. Darkhorse felt him summon up power. The sorcerer stood motionless for several seconds, then frowned. "I can't put a halt to it."

"Let me try." The Gryphon's eyes narrowed. Again, Darkhorse felt power build up . . . then nothing.

"It's Aurim," decided Cabe Bedlam. "He might not have complete control of his abilities, but that doesn't make him any less powerful." The sorcerer studied the mad scene. "I'll have to go in and get them out before we can put a stop to his spellwork. He can tell us what he did."

"I'll do it, Cabe. This is my practice field and although it's a little more lively than even I prefer, I stand a better chance of reaching them."

"Neither of you should go running into there." Lady Bedlam anxiously clenched her fists. "If I thought it was safe to just go in, I'd do it myself. You know that. Aurim's abilities are unpredictable. They're safe so far because he cast both the spell that caused this chaos and the protective one now covering them. Our protective spells might not be so effective in there."

Darkhorse tired of listening to them discuss their options. He understood their fear, but could not fathom why the obvious solution had escaped them. "Never fear, my friends! The answer to your dilemma stands before you! I am not as fragile as you! I will not be bothered by a few enchanted blades or some dancing poles! Allow me!"

Before they could say anything, he had entered the pandemonium. The two females had their faces buried in Aurim's rich red mage's robes, but Aurim saw him immediately. The fear turned to relief and the youth opened his mouth to say something.

One of the serpentine bars wrapped itself around the stallion's neck.

The action was so startling that for a moment Darkhorse could not react. The bar should not have been able to touch him; his will alone should have made him a ghost, a phantom, which the enchanted bar should have passed through. The shadow steed concentrated, willing himself even less substantial, but the thing's hold did not slip.

Darkhorse reared, pulling the bar from the wall. It squirmed around his neck, seeming unable to tighten its hold but unwilling to give up. The stallion moved forward again, but found his hooves sinking into the stone surface. He pulled one loose, but the other three sank deeper. Try as he might,

Darkhorse could not make himself light enough or insubstantial enough to completely free his legs.

His power is astonishing. Many had said that Aurim had the potential to be a spellcaster several times stronger than his parents combined. His deficiency had lain in his concentration, not his actual skills. Darkhorse had not understood just how powerful his young friend was until now. Aurim *was* much stronger than his parents . . . strong enough that this enchanted practice field could injure, possibly even kill, his would-be rescuer.

Darkhorse was an eternal creature, never aging, but he could be destroyed. He had faced death many times for those he considered worthy. Aurim had been the accidental cause of this sinister chaos, but that was certainly not reason enough to abandon both him and the two females.

He surged forward, pulling his hooves free, then burying them again as he moved closer and closer to the trio.

Only at the last minute did he see Aurim pointing frantically behind him. Ignoring the futile movements of the serpentine bar, Darkhorse twisted his neck at an angle all but impossible for a true equine. A buzzing sound passed over him.

An ax buried itself in a wooden pole to his side. It had been aiming for his head and although Darkhorse was fairly certain that it would not have actually harmed him, he was grateful for the human's warning.

At last reaching the three, Darkhorse found that he, like the animated weapons, was unable to pierce the protective barrier. "Aurim! Disperse your shield, then help them mount up! I will protect all of us!"

Aurim closed his eyes and concentrated. Several seconds passed without any discernible change to the shield and Darkhorse began to fear that the three were trapped within. Then, just as he was about to give up hope, he sensed the shield fade away.

To his credit, the young mage moved the moment the defensive spell faded. He dragged both women forward. Darkhorse adjusted his form, growing longer and shorter. Aurim helped both of his companions to mount, then proceeded to do so himself.

A pole burst from the ground, knocking the mage backward. One of Baron Vergoth's daughters shrieked and it was all the magical stallion could do to keep both from falling off. He heard Lady Bedlam call out, but what she said was lost amidst the pandemonium.

Again one of his passengers began to shriek, but Darkhorse, both impatient and anxious, twisted his head completely around and roared, "Be silent!"

Both clamped their mouths shut and stared wide-eyed at their rescuer. Darkhorse turned his attention back to Aurim, not caring at all if the females were now frightened to death of *him* so long as they stayed put and quiet. Up to now, he had been able to keep his footing, but his luck was certain to fail soon. He had to take hold of Aurim and get them away.

"Darkhorse!" Beside him, seeming to materialize from nowhere, was Cabe. "Take them! I'll get Aurim!"

The ground gave way more and more. A pole shot up just before the shadow steed's muzzle, startling him. He wanted to help Aurim, but arguing would take too long. Darkhorse trusted the master sorcerer to rescue his elder child. If anything went amiss, however, he would come back.

Twisting around, the ebony stallion fought his way back toward the opening where Lady Bedlam and the Gryphon waited. Several others had gathered in the short time since he had entered the enchanted practice field and one of those was Baron Vergoth. The Talakian aristocrat stood poised by the very edge, as if debating whether or not to go charging in after his daughters. Darkhorse knew that he had to escape the field quickly lest the man do such a foolhardy thing. Vergoth already sported two ragged scars on his right cheek; if he entered the practice field while Aurim's spell still held, the baron risked losing his head.

The Gryphon had one hand on Vergoth's shoulder. Gwendolyn Bedlam stood before him, shaking her head and pointing in the general direction of the ebony stallion and his passengers. *No doubt she is assuring him that his daughters are safe with me!* For some reason, though, the baron did not seem convinced.

The going was still slow. Darkhorse silently cursed as he pulled back before what appeared to be a dancing sword. He did not fear for himself—he rarely did—but human life was precious to him, more so because they lived so few years in the first place. Whether his passengers had been aristocrats or beggars would have made no difference to him; Darkhorse would have protected either with equal effort.

At last he reached the end of the field. The humans parted way for him as he leaped the final few feet and landed silently on the marble floor.

Vergoth retrieved his daughters. The two young women clung to him. "My gratitude, Lord Darkhorse."

"I am lord of no realm, Baron! I am and shall always simply be Darkhorse! No gratitude is necessary! Besides, there are still others in danger—"

"Not any longer." The voice was Cabe's. With him, still very pale, was his son. This near to one another, the two humans looked more like brothers than father and son, but mages aged very slowly. Cabe Bedlam might have seemed only in his mid-twenties, but he was nearly twice that.

"Thank you, Darkhorse. I'm . . . I'm sorry." The last comment appeared to be directed at everyone, not simply the shadow steed.

The baron, his expression neutral, ignored Aurim, instead turning to the Gryphon. "If you will excuse me, Your Majesty, I would like to take my daughters back to their quarters. They are understandably shaken up by this and I am certain that they need to rest."

"By all means, Baron Vergoth. If there's anything you need, please let me know."

"I will." The aristocrat bowed. His children attempted to curtsy, but Vergoth steered them away before they could finish.

"That is going to require some diplomatic work," the Gryphon quietly commented. "I'll have to have some of my best wine sent to his guest quarters . . . along with some of the young women's favorite flowers and treats."

A tremor shook the hall, followed immediately by a loud clatter. Everyone glanced back at the practice field. The flying weapons had dropped to the ground. The poles and bars were motionless. The entire field looked normal once more.

The monarch of Penacles looked relieved. "Thank you, Aurim."

The golden-haired sorcerer looked sheepish. "I didn't do it, Your Majesty. It just . . . stopped."

"Well, I'm sure you tried your best to make it stop."

This only seemed to make Aurim feel worse. Darkhorse knew full well that such statements had flooded the boy's ears for most of his almost twenty years. People were always consoling him over this mistake or that. The eternal could identify with his situation. Despite his great age and power, Darkhorse was often reprimanded for his impetuousness. He did not see things quite in the same way as humans even though he had lived among them for lifetimes. Even now, he did not understand why some of the things he did worried his companions so.

Many of those who had gathered were now drifting away, aware that this situation was one the king would prefer to handle more in private. Darkhorse carefully kept from saying anything, wanting to hear the decision of both the Gryphon and the elder Bedlams before adding his own thoughts. He hoped that they would not be too severe with Aurim. The spellcasters' children were most dear to him.

"What happened?" Gwendolyn Bedlam asked.

Aurim refused to look at anyone. "They wanted to see me perform some sorcery. Just something little. Queen Erini has power, but she doesn't use it unless necessary and there's really no other spellcaster in Talak. I . . . I didn't think I'd have any problem with something so little, but I brought them out here just to make sure there was enough room."

"What did you try to do?" The Gryphon's tone had softened.

"I took a chess piece from your set and—"

"From *my* set? The set that was sitting in the palace library?"

"Yes." Aurim tried to back away, unnerved by the Gryphon's sudden anxiety.

"That set is ancient. Possibly magical in some ways. Very intricately carved. I was a fool to leave it out like that, but I never thought—"

Darkhorse recalled the chess set and although he had suspicions concerning its lost origins, he decided now was not the time to mention them. What was important was that the Gryphon did not realize how his words were cutting deeper and deeper into the young mage. Even Darkhorse, who would ever observe the workings of humanity from far away, could see that the more Aurim's confidence sank, the worse it would be for him in the long run.

Perhaps the king saw this also, for he then added, "But I can hardly condemn someone for something so little when I consider some of the things that I did during my life. What did you do with the chess piece?"

Brightening a little, Aurim explained how he had taken the chess piece and led the two young women outside. From the way he talked, Darkhorse gathered that Aurim was attracted to both, but more to Vergoth's elder daughter. Cabe's son seldom had the opportunity to associate with one attractive female near his age, much less two. He had grown a little reckless, telling them how he had animated things before, including, once, a number of stick men. Of course, Aurim had failed to mention that they, like so many other things he had animated, had gotten out of his control. This time, however, he had been certain that he had the proper concentration.

Everything had gone well at first. The power was his to control. He had fed it into the chess piece as his two admirers had watched in fascination. The figurine, which he had chosen at random, had started to shiver as if about to move.

Then a backlash of energy had thrown Aurim to the ground. That was when the practice field had suddenly come to life.

"I don't understand *what* went wrong! Everything was going just as it should have!" He looked at his parents. "I swear I kept my concentration perfect. It should have either moved just like I wanted or stood still. I don't know why the spell backlashed into the practice field."

"It may have been your choice of items," his mother answered. "If, as you said, Gryphon, the chess set contains some trace of power, then perhaps that's what caused Aurim's spell to go awry."

The lionbird rubbed the bottom of his beak. "You may be right. I'll investigate it. I've always meant to, but I just never got around to it. Perhaps the time's overdue." To Aurim, he added, "In the future, though, I'd like to be asked for permission before you attempt to dazzle attractive young women with your magical skills."

"Yes, Your Majesty."

"Where is the chess piece now?"

"I . . . don't know." Aurim looked around. "I don't see it, but it must be somewhere in the yard. I'll look for it—"

"Never mind. I'll hunt for it myself later. If you did succeed in animating the piece, it could be anywhere." To the elder Bedlams and Darkhorse, the king remarked, "I still need to discuss those other matters with the three of you, but I think it might be good if I first talked to my queen about what else can be done to smooth things over with Baron Vergoth. Troia's become quite friendly with Queen Erini and through her has come to know the baroness. She should be able to give me more insight on what to expect from Vergoth's wife. I know that the baroness has much influence with her husband. In the meantime, I'd like you all to stay as guests. Your usual chambers are available for you and your family, Cabe, if you'd care to use them."

"We'd be honored, Gryphon," returned the sorcerer. "Valea is overseeing the Manor while we're gone and I think she's been looking forward to proving that she can do as well as her mother and me. She's not often had the opportunity to oversee things on her own."

"I'm certain that she'll do an excellent job. She's grown up quite a bit since Kyl's ascension."

Unspoken but understood by all, including the shadow steed, was that there had been some fear that the Bedlams' daughter would have a difficult time shaking off the emotional turmoil caused by the young Dragon Emperor's attempt to seduce her and then his brother Grath's betrayal of her to

Toma. However, instead of caving in to the damage to her heart, Valea had turned around and seemed to grow to adulthood overnight. Her power was already at a more advanced stage than her mother—who knew better about these things—had predicted, and her handling of her skills was already superior in some ways to that of her older brother.

Thinking of that, Darkhorse cast a quick glance at the youth. Aurim frowned slightly, but the moment he realized that someone was watching him, the frown disappeared. The younger Bedlam suddenly found the ceiling of the hall diverting.

There is more turmoil in the lad than we have suspected. Should I mention this to Cabe?

While he was trying to decide what the proper human course of action would have been, the Gryphon and the Bedlams evidently came to the end of their conversation. The king bowed to the spellcasters, something he did for few others, then departed.

Cabe sighed. "Aurim, I—"

"I'm going into the city." The golden-haired figure started to walk off.

"Wait, Aurim!" The elder mage reached out.

His wife took hold of his arm and whispered, "No, Cabe. Let him go. Let him burn away some of his frustration. He's been like this before. You know that he won't do anything foolish."

"I don't like to leave him alone, though, Gwen. I know what it's like to be so uncertain about one's abilities. Maybe if I walk with him—"

"And what if you only succeed in reminding him that your abilities and your handling of them were enhanced by the memories that your grandfather Nathan instilled in you? You had some benefits to your training that few ever had, you'll have to admit."

"I did at that, but I still don't like leaving him alone."

Darkhorse brightened. He had wanted to help his friends, but until now had not known how to go about it. "Have no fear, my dear companions! There's no need for your son to be

on his own! I will join him, be his companion during his trou
bled times, and, coincidentally, keep him from any mischief!"

Both spellcasters immediately opened their mouths, no
doubt to express their gratitude to him, but now that the decision had been made, Darkhorse wanted not to waste a single
moment. He wanted to join Aurim before he left the palace.

Darkhorse felt a surge of power and recognized it immediately as the work of the younger Bedlam. Aurim had decided
to transport himself out of the palace rather than walk or ride.
The shadow steed immediately followed suit. When focused
by a great desire, such as escaping his parents after a debacle
like today's, the golden-haired mage's ability to properly
complete his spells increased dramatically. *If he could only
focus as well when not so upset . . .*

The hallway of the Gryphon's palace faded away, to be replaced immediately by a busy street in the market district of
Penacles. People whirled around as Darkhorse materialized,
some screaming and others turning so pale they might have
been denizens from the realm of the Lords of the Dead. The
crowd around him melted away, leaving only one other figure
besides the huge ebony stallion.

Aurim turned around and looked up into the pupilless, icy
blue eyes of his friend. "Get away from me before I kill you."

CHAPTER III

"What's that?" The eternal could scarcely believe what he had heard. "What are you saying, Aurim? You are distraught! You cannot mean such a ridiculous thing!"

"Don't I?" Aurim approached the shadow steed heedless of the spectacle the two of them were creating. "Look at me, Darkhorse! Look what I did! I nearly killed Adelina and Mersi and all I was trying to do was show off for them! I should have known better. I can't control my powers; I'll *never* control my powers! Better I stay at the Manor for the rest of my life before I injure or even kill someone I care about . . . including you!"

"I am a bit more durable than you think, my friend."

"I saw how you had to struggle in the practice field. I *could've* killed you. I know that."

Darkhorse looked around at the still startled crowd. Penacles was an enlightened city, thanks in great part to the efforts of both the Gryphon and the Bedlams, but watching a sorcerer argue with a creature out of legend was too much for most of the folks around them. He tried to think what Cabe would do.

"Aurim, there is an inn nearby run by a man named Gullivan. It is a place where the students from your parents' school often go and one where even I am considered . . . less of a curiosity now. Let us go there and talk this out. You can find some drink and I . . . I can listen."

The human calmed a little. He looked around at the rapt audience, then visibly pulled himself together. "All right, but you better take us there. If I try another spell, I could leave a gaping hole in this part of Penacles."

That was hardly likely, but Darkhorse did not want to become entangled in another argument concerning Aurim's fear of his own powers. That could wait until they were at Gullivan's.

It took the slightest effort to transport the pair of them from the street to the interior of Gullivan's inn. A few faces looked up at them in surprise and one serving woman gasped, but the overall reaction to their astonishing appearance was far more reserved than it had been outside. Months of dealing with the students of the fledgling school of sorcery, not to mention visits from the shadow steed on rare occasions, had steeled most of the regulars. The Gryphon also paid Gullivan a fairly good amount of money to tolerate the antics of the students and their possible effect on other business, although any serious incident was to be reported to either the king or the Bedlams immediately.

Cabe had once informed Darkhorse that Gullivan's inn had actually benefitted from its unique clientele in an unexpected way. Many newcomers to the city found the thought of seeing the students or even possibly Cabe Bedlam himself enticing enough to risk any magical mischief the practicing spellcasters might unleash. Even now, a pair of Irillian merchants, their bluish, wide-legged sea garb the newest rage in their kingdom but rather out of place here, watched with open fascination the arrival of the two newcomers. Feeling a bit mischievous, Darkhorse looked at them and winked. They stiffened, then leaned forward and whispered to one another rapidly. The shadow steed studied them, deciding that they were what they seemed and not actually spies for the Blue Dragon. While a treaty existed between Irillian By the Sea and Penacles, it was not unheard of for agents of both kingdoms to circulate around. One never knew what information might be needed if a treaty was later broken and war was declared.

Of the other five or so humans in the room, two were students he had noted several times. They watched with interest until a look from Darkhorse made them return to their own conversation. The remainder consisted of two serving women, one of them Gullivan's niece, and the innkeeper himself. While Gullivan's niece was used to strange sights and only smiled at the new pair, the other woman, obviously new, was already retreating to the back room.

Gullivan, a former soldier, as were many in his present trade, was a muscular man just beginning to thicken at the waist. He was only slightly older than Cabe Bedlam, but, lacking the sorcerer's abilities, looked more like the master mage's father. What little hair remained on his head made him resemble a monk until one noticed the scars on his face and his arms.

"Darkhorse . . . and . . . it's Master Aurim, isn't it?"

"Greetings to you, Gullivan!" The first time the ebony stallion and the ex-soldier had met, they had, by mutual consent, dispensed with the titles they generally used for all others. No Lord Darkhorse or Master Gullivan. Darkhorse liked the man although they did not see one another that often.

"Hello, Master Gullivan." Aurim turned from the innkeeper and, after a study of the interior, located a booth far away from the rest of the people. It was a wide one, but hardly wide enough for Darkhorse in his present form. Nonetheless, the eternal made no attempt to either transform himself or request Aurim to change booths. The youth was still sensitive. The stallion settled with standing next to the table.

The door to the back room opened and a brawny but younger version of Gullivan walked out. "Zaysha said that there was a *horse* in the place, Father! What could she mean—" His eyes alighted on the shadow steed. "Gods!"

"It's all right, Pietr. You haven't been here for any of his visits. This is the legendary *Darkhorse.*"

"Darkhorse, but he's just a . . . no, I guess he isn't, is he?" Pietr shook his head. "I never know what to expect in this place. I'm sorry, M-Master Darkhorse."

"Simply call me Darkhorse, young human, and I have taken no offense."

"My son, Darkhorse. Been away for a few years. The other woman is his wife. She's from a coastal village to the south where the weather's been the most she ever had to worry about."

"I'd better go explain," Pietr added, already retreating into the back.

A brief smile lit Aurim's features. Darkhorse chuckled. Aurim quickly looked down.

"Come now, Aurim! Surely there is no reason to continue feeling so terrible! It was a minor thing. No one was hurt. The baron has kept his daughters under his protective arm for all their lives; a little adventure is good for them."

"A little adventure? Is that what you call what happened? It could've been a disaster . . . it *was* a disaster!"

"Hardly that, but the point is, it is over and all is well, Aurim! You need not worry. You simply need more time!"

Aurim slammed his fist on the table, causing the Irillian merchants to briefly look at them again. Gullivan immediately blocked their view, asking them if they required anything else, then came over to his new customers.

"Did you care for anything, Master Aurim? On the house for you and your family; that's the way I set things. I owe your folks for a lot of business."

"Nothing, thank you."

"If you change your mind . . ." Gullivan retreated without asking Darkhorse if he desired anything. By now he understood that Darkhorse did not eat.

"Now perhaps we can talk a little." The shadow steed paused, however, noticing a peculiar expression on his young companion's face.

"I'm sorry. I don't really want to talk. Why didn't you just leave me alone? All I wanted to do was walk around for a little while until I could bring myself to face my parents or the baron's family. Is that asking too much, Darkhorse?"

"Your parents were concerned about you, Aurim, and as both their friend and yours, I thought I would join you on this walk! Surely I am no great bother! I will walk or stand quietly by as you work matters out in your head. You will hardly even notice that I am nearby!"

"I think the fleeing crowds would keep reminding me," the youth snapped. A moment later his expression became apologetic. "I didn't mean it to sound so severe, Darkhorse, but you know how most folks react to you. They didn't have the fortune to grow up knowing you as I did. You're still the demon steed of yore, the monster only their king and the wondrous wizards Bedlam can control."

"Is that what they think of me?" He laughed. "I would have been disappointed if they thought any other way."

"The point is, I can hardly relax if you're with me. I need time to wander around, think for myself." Aurim's tone grew more imploring. "Darkhorse, I hardly ever get to see anything other than the Manor unless I'm with Mother and Father in Penacles or Talak . . . and I rarely get to see much of either kingdom save the royal grounds. My parents have been through so much, seen so much—"

"And I daresay they would like you to avoid much of what they had to fight through, young one. You and your sister have also had your share of excitement. Let us not forget that Toma lived among you and your family for a long time without anyone realizing that he was not your tutor Benjin Traske. I am not completely versed in the desires of humans and I doubt that I ever will be, but most would find your adventures more than sufficient to last them their lifetime . . . even if it may be a sorcerer's lifetime of three hundred years."

"I've been doing some thinking, though." The young spellcaster paused and glanced briefly at the two students.

Darkhorse followed his gaze and saw that once again they had been studying the two newcomers. Darkhorse supposed that they were in awe of him, not an uncommon event. He decided that some time soon he would visit the school again and give all the students the benefit of his centuries of peerless wisdom. Surely no one had a view of Dragonrealm sorcery to equal his . . . even if his own abilities followed a different path than those of a spellcaster native to this world.

"I think I do need to be on my own for a time," Aurim continued. He leaned nearer. "All the teaching, all the tutoring, can't do for me what being out in the real world can. If I was on my own for a little, I think that maybe I would be better able to focus. I'd be less nervous each time I attempted some spell. I *would*."

Aurim on his own. Did his parents know of this desire? "And how long have you had this notion? Did you come to this conclusion after the incident in the practice field?"

"Actually, I've been thinking about it for some time on and off. It came back to me while you were talking with Gullivan and his son. I realized that I shouldn't be dwelling in pity, but trying to overcome my difficulties. That's what Father and Mother have always preached and I know that Great-grandfather Nathan believed the same as Father. Even . . . even Grandfather Azran would've agreed with them on that."

"I would prefer to keep Azran Bedlam out of this conversation just as I suspect your parents would. If this notion is at all influenced by your grandfather's foul memory, then it is a notion best dropped!" Even Cabe rarely mentioned his father. Azran would forever be a bloody stain on the Bedlam name.

"No, I just used him as an example." Aurim shuddered. "I would never want to be like my grandfather. You can see what I mean, though, don't you? If I could just spend some time on my own, maybe visit Gordag-Ai in the northwest or Irillian By the Sea, I might gain the confidence and will I need to set myself straight."

Darkhorse's quandary grew. He was certain that neither of the lad's parents would agree to something like what Aurim desired, but he himself was almost willing to agree with his companion. Why was it not possible? Gullivan, he knew, had started as a soldier when he had been at least two or three years younger than Aurim was now. What was so dangerous about visiting either of those two kingdoms? Both were relatively safe. Gordag-Ai had always been a peaceful land and since the treaty Irillian and Penacles had come to trade with and respect one another. Surely Cabe and Gwen would see that, too.

They might agree if they knew that I would secretly be keeping an eye on the lad . . .

The door to the inn swung open. Aurim looked up, eyes widening with interest. Darkhorse shifted his gaze to the entrance. A young woman with dark brown hair that flowed down over the back of her bright green cloak looked over the interior as if uncertain that she was in the correct location. Her eyes grew especially round and questioning when they fixed on the black stallion.

"Greetings, my lady!" Gullivan hurried up to the young woman, hands folded together. "Looking for a room or simply a meal? You'll find the finest of both here at Gullivan's!"

"There's . . . do you usually allow your customers to bring their horses into your place of business?"

"Him? My lady, that is not an animal there; that is the legendary Darkhorse, friend and companion to the Bedlam sorcerers and the king of Penacles himself!"

She either did not understand or did not believe him. Darkhorse decided that he had to intervene before the innkeeper lost a customer because of him.

"What he says is true, my lady." The shadow steed paused while the newcomer registered his words. Her expression tightened and her hands trembled, but otherwise she remained calm. Darkhorse was impressed by her reaction; most women of her station—her flowing, colorful clothing indicated that she was the educated daughter of a wealthy merchant from Gordag-Ai—tended to gasp, back away, and possibly even faint in his presence. Others simply fled.

"I've heard . . . you *are* real, then."

"Some would still say unreal, my lady, but yes, here I stand, in the . . . well, *flesh* is perhaps not quite the proper word!" He chuckled, in part hoping it would ease the situation.

"You rescued the princess once." She walked toward him, fascinated.

Erini. Before becoming King Melicard of Talak's queen, she had been Princess Erini of Gordag-Ai. He had rescued her, but she had also rescued him. There was a statue of Darkhorse, or at least a statue of what the sculptor believed he looked like, in the royal gardens of Gordag-Ai, a tribute from her parents. He had never journeyed there to see it, although Erini had always insisted he should. "Queen Erini is a good friend of mine."

Her gaze abruptly shifted to Aurim, who had remained speechless so far. "The silver streak in your hair. You're a sorcerer? I've never seen a powerful one."

"I'm . . . I'm Aurim."

"My name is Jenna."

Darkhorse did not have to be human to understand his companion's slow reactions. Cabe Bedlam had reacted much the same during the first days after meeting his future mate. Aurim was fascinated by the young woman. Jenna had large, expressive brown eyes and a small but sloping nose. Her lips were full and her mouth seemed always to be smiling. She was, the shadow steed suspected, very attractive by the standards of any human male.

Perhaps here is a different and possibly safer adventure to take the lad's mind off of his difficulties. Jenna seemed attracted to Aurim as well. Perhaps if the young sorcerer gained more confidence in his dealings with others outside his family, he would gain more confidence—and therefore more focus—concerning his powers. Even if it did not help Aurim in that respect, what was the harm in a little flirtation? The boy needed to enjoy himself.

"Are you a powerful sorcerer?"

"Aurim is the son of Cabe Bedlam!" Darkhorse proudly announced, certain that such news would impress the woman. He saw immediately that he was correct, but for some reason Aurim did not appear to appreciate his aid. "And a fine sorcerer himself, although he, like his parents, has promised to keep their use of power to a minimum while in the city. Most folks are not used to such skills."

"Darkhorse—" Aurim looked even more frustrated. He rose and bowed for Jenna. "Aurim Bedlam, at your service. It's a pleasure to meet you."

"And you, too." Her smile grew wider and as it did, the sorcerer's countenance turned faintly red. Jenna looked around. "My father's stayed here on occasion while he had business and he said that this was a fascinating place, but I never dreamed he was telling the truth about those he met here." Her attention focused on Aurim again. Darkhorse might not have been there for all the interest she now had in him. He was both amused and pleased. "He told me I should try to find a room here. Father thought that I might like it because . . . because I have a little magical skill myself."

The eternal stirred. Although Darkhorse had not actively

tried to sense power within her, he generally noticed such, anyway. It was surprising that he had not sensed her presence before she had even entered. However, now that the merchant's daughter had mentioned it, he could sense a trace of power buried deep within her. It was faint and a little peculiar in signature, but each spellcaster seemed to have a unique link to his or her abilities. What was odd was that she did not have any silver in her hair. Human spellcasters always had silver in their hair.

"You're a sorcerer, too?" Aurim's eyes lit up.

"Not a very good one." Jenna reached up and lifted her hat, revealing a tiny lock of silver hair. "Father likes me to keep it hidden." She replaced the hat, then held out her hand toward Aurim. "This is all I know how to do." Jenna stared at her hand. After a moment, it began to gleam. The illumination was not very strong, however. Jenna stared at it for a second or two longer, then blinked. The gleam vanished.

Curiously, Darkhorse noticed that he did not feel any tug of power as he did with other spellcasters. Jenna's skills, he decided, were so meager as to be nearly nonexistent.

"That's very good," Aurim assured her. "Most people can't even do that."

"But I want to do more. I've tried, but this is all I've been able to manage."

"Sorcery can be pretty difficult at times. I *know*."

The shadow steed watched both of them with growing interest. More and more he was certain that what the younger Bedlam needed most was time with a woman such as this, someone who he could confide in and understand. Humans seemed to need such relationships throughout their lives.

"Aurim." The cross expression with which Cabe's son briefly presented him was sign enough to Darkhorse that his assumptions were correct. "As you are in Gullivan's and in trustworthy company, there are some tasks that your father and the king require of me which I should deal with now. I trust you will return to the palace before nightfall?"

"I will."

"Then I shall bid you both fond farewell! A pleasure to meet you, Jenna! I hope to see you again soon!"

"Oh, I think you will." She smiled at Darkhorse, as if sharing some jest of which only she was fully aware.

Both of the young humans seemed to appreciate his departure. The shadowy stallion glanced at Gullivan. "Good day to you, innkeeper! My gratitude for your tolerance of my presence!"

"Come whenever you please, Darkhorse. Come whenever you please."

Darkhorse could not resist doing one more thing. He turned to the two students, who had ceased their attempts to continue their conversation and were now simply watching him, and added, "I trust your studies are going well! I may test you later!"

They both immediately nodded, evidently too dumbfounded to speak. He had no true intention of testing their skills, but he was certain that for some time to come they would study with more passion than they had ever managed in the past.

Darkhorse laughed, then, with everyone watching, vanished from the inn.

He rematerialized in the palace, this time avoiding a location where he might surprise a crowd. The palace library, not to be confused with the legendary magical Libraries of Penacles for which the City of Knowledge had earned its title, was generally utilized only by the Gryphon, his queen, and the Bedlams. Therefore, it was not at all surprising to discover it empty. The king was likely still trying to make amends to Baron Vergoth. What Cabe and Lady Bedlam might be doing, he could not say, but it would be easy to enough to find out.

It was a simple matter to reach out to them. It was something they did all the time, speaking to one another through thought. Only if a spellcaster had reason to shield himself did it prove difficult and for Darkhorse even that was often not a barrier.

Cabe . . .

He felt the first flicker of awareness.

A mind touched his . . . but it was not Cabe's. It was—

It was his *own*?

Darkhorse broke the link he had been trying to forge with

Cabe. What had just happened? It had been like touching his own reflection, viewing his own thoughts. He had never experienced such a backlash before, not in all the centuries he had journeyed across this world.

He reached out again, seeking to re-create the effect. There were many defensive spells surrounding both Penacles and the palace and although most of these had been attuned so as not to affect the Gryphon's allies, perhaps a newly set defense had accidentally caused the peculiar reaction.

What the shadow steed got instead was Cabe Bedlam. The sorcerer's mood was anxious. *Darkhorse! What happened to you? I felt your presence and then you broke off abruptly! Are you all right?*

I am fine, Cabe. Something . . . it was nothing, simply a curiosity. I will tell you about it some other time. Perhaps you or your grandfather may have come across its like in your research.

Where's Aurim? Is he back in the palace?

Carefully, the ebony stallion explained the situation, playing up Aurim's interest in Jenna and how he thought it would benefit the lad. Cabe countered that it had been Aurim's attempt to impress Vergoth's daughters that had created the initial chaos.

Jenna seems different, Cabe. Besides, Aurim seems to understand that he needs to be careful. I think that he might need to see the outside more, meet those who have no affiliation with either the Manor or the palaces of Penacles or Talak. He has seen little. Besides, he should be safe in Gullivan's.

There was a pause. *Maybe. I'll see what Gwen thinks. You're in the palace now, aren't you?*

I was going to join you. The Gryphon had said earlier he had need of me.

The need is greater now. We're with him at this moment in his quarters. I should have told you to come directly here rather than waste time talking to you like this. Cabe seemed to grow more tense by the moment. *Aurim should be all right. It's probably better that he's enjoying himself for a while. We may be here for quite some time. You'd better join us now.*

What is it? What do you mean?

Again Cabe paused, this time for much longer. *Just come.*

Thought was action. Darkhorse transported himself to the Gryphon's personal quarters. The room was wide, bright, and somewhat reminiscent of the forest: the work of the queen, no doubt. The king was of a more militaristic bent, although he, too, was a lover of beauty. Several shelves lined one wall, shelves filled with books and scrolls. An elaborate writing desk stood nearby. Several paintings and statuettes depicting animals and scenes from nature decorated the rest of the chamber save for one wall where an elaborate tapestry hung. Illustrated on it was a very detailed image of Penacles, an image so intricate that one could have located every individual building. If one stared long enough, it was possible to see the image shift on occasion. Whatever happened to the structure of Penacles was reflected in the tapestry, although that was not its primary function. The tapestry was the only way to reach the magical Libraries of Penacles.

The queen was not there, but the Gryphon and the Bedlams were. There were two other figures near the closed doors, figures who were not in any way human. They were tall, broad, and unless they moved, one would have thought them simply iron statues. They were more than that, however. Both were golems, constructs created by the Gryphon through great effort. When the royal family slept, the golems watched over them. They also made certain that no one attempted to use the tapestry without permission. Two identical creatures waited on the outside of the chamber.

"Darkhorse." The monarch of Penacles nodded to him. In his hand he held a peculiar, avian-shaped artifact. From the manner in which he held it, it was obvious that it was of some great importance. "A timely entrance."

"I am ever timely, Your Majesty! Cabe made his summons sound urgent. What is it? Has it something to do with that constructed bird you hold?"

"This . . . construct . . . arrived only moments after I left you. One of my guards found it and the moment he touched it, he felt compelled to bring it to me." The lionbird turned over the object. Viewed up close, it proved to be an even cruder representation of a bird than Darkhorse had first thought. "As far as I've been able to discern, it *flew* here but lost control when it passed through the first defensive spells. The compulsion spell activated when the bird was touched."

"A clever mage."

"And there aren't too many of those," Gwen remarked. "Even if there hadn't been a message inside, it would've been pretty obvious from what region it originated."

The eternal's ears pricked up. "Zuu?"

"Zuu," repeated the Gryphon. "The message was sent to me, but it was also addressed to Cabe."

The sorcerer held up a small piece of parchment. "In fact, it's written almost as a personal note to me, although I don't know who it could be from."

"And what is it about?" Darkhorse feared that he already knew.

"According to this, Zuu marched—or rather *rode*—against one of its small neighbors to the north. The message doesn't say when, but I gather in the last day or two. More important, his forces include his Magical Order."

"He has begun his mad campaign, then?"

"More a testing of his strength, I suspect," the Gryphon interjected. "To see how his forces will do in battle. He will win, of course. The strongest foe he could possibly face is the Baron of Adderly, whose domain lies just north of Zuu's lands."

The shadow steed shook his head. "I have never failed to see the allure of conquering others! It has always looked far too complicated to maintain control afterward!"

"That it is," agreed the monarch of Penacles. "But that won't stop some from continuing to try. Once Lanith tastes a little victory, there'll be no stopping him short of full-scale war." The Gryphon looked up at the huge black stallion. "I have a favor to ask of you . . ."

King Lanith, clad in the traditional leather pants and jerkin of the brave Zuu warrior, pushed his short helm up by the nose guard and watched as his messenger returned at full gallop from the local baron's castle. He had sent what he considered a fair offer with the man. If the defenders surrendered, they would be relieved of all weapons and a small garrison would take over under an officer Lanith trusted. The baron's family would be transported back to Zuu where they would be hostages.

He could see that the offer had been spurned.

In his head, he heard the merry voice. *The brave baron insults you! He has the audacity to reject your kind offer. I suppose you'll just have to slaughter everyone inside.*

"Be silent, puppet!" Lanith muttered, ignoring glances from one of his officers. "When I want your advice, I'll ask for it!" Still, he had a point. Who was this country baron to think that he could resist an army of horsemen that blanketed the landscape for as far as the eye could see?

The messenger reined his mount to a halt and leaped from its back. Kneeling before his king, he said, "The man refuses to listen. He says that our riders will run their mounts into the ground and our archers will waste all of their arrows, but that we will never breach his defenses. He says that he will outlast us until finally exhaustion, frustration, and hunger send us riding back to our stinking stable of a kingdom."

Although the words were spoken plainly, they created a stirring among Lanith's officers. The horsemen of Zuu were respected warriors throughout the Dragonrealm. They had fought for a variety of causes since their nomadic ancestors had first chosen to settle in Zuu. The king's own brother had led a band that had fought hard to push back the Dragon Emperor's forces at Penacles. Blane had given his life and Lanith always pointed at the late prince as the example by which his soldiers, male and female, should live. There were a few who would have liked to point out that Blane had never believed in conquest, but they had wisely kept silent. However, no warrior of Zuu, whatever his or her feelings concerning the grand crusade, was willing to accept such insults from a country aristocrat.

"He's brought his destruction on himself."

"Do I send in the first wave, then?" asked his second, a graying warrior named Belfour. Like many of the officers but *unlike* the king, he wore the more protective padded metal vest and arm protectors common these days. In fact, with the exception of Lanith's special guard, the horse people were all better protected than their monarch. Bravery was one thing, but living to fight another day was preferable.

Of course, no one realized that the king was watched over by a hidden defender who would make certain that no weapon touched him. All they would see was that their ruler, self-declared conqueror of the Dragonrealm, was impervious to harm.

The image of a grand charge by his ready hordes enticed Lanith, but his unseen ally suddenly interjected. *The walls are strong. There are hidden pitfalls awaiting any of your eager riders who come in from the western side. What the human in the structure claims is also true. He could outlast you.*

"Then what—?" At the last moment, the king recalled that only he could hear the other. *Then what do you suggest? Why don't you just go in and deal with them?*

Oh, I'm not that powerful, great king, no indeed! Besides, if you wish to achieve your other desire, I must keep my presence as secret as can be . . . and where would the fun be without an epic battle? Did you know that there is a fault in the earth beneath the structure? A slight but significant fault?

I don't want to bring down the entire place! I want it fairly intact, you foolish imp!

A giggle briefly echoed through his head. *It will only cause a little damage . . . just enough to give you the time and entrance you need if your warriors are swift enough after the sorcerers do their work.*

The voice faded away, but Lanith needed no further explanation. "Ponteroy!"

A tall, overdressed man, narrow of face with a long mustache and thin, oily hair, rode up beside the king. He looked uncomfortable, probably because his clothing, while very elaborate, was more suitable to the cooler kingdom of Gordag-Ai than down here in the warmer southwest. Ponteroy performed a partial bow, then fixed beady eyes on his monarch. "Yes, my liege?"

"Prepare the Order. I've work for them. This is what they'll do." He signaled Ponteroy to lean closer, then whispered his orders. The officers tried to listen while pretending not to, but

Lanith spoke too quietly. When he was finished, he waved the newcomer away. "You have your orders. Leave us . . . and do not fail, Ponteroy. I don't like failure."

"Yes, great one. As you command, great one." The newcomer nervously removed what at first appeared to be a small riding crop from his belt. The upper tip of the short staff was a crystal carved into the head of a horse, a head that glowed slightly the moment Ponteroy touched it. The mage saluted Lanith with the staff, then with some awkwardness turned his mount and rode off.

"Why isn't Saress here?" growled one of the younger officers, a female. "I don't like that slippery little serpent!"

Lanith silenced her with a glance. "Saress has other matters to attend to. Ponteroy has been paid his gold; that's all that matters to him and that's all that should matter to you. He knows what'll happen if he fails me." The king looked over his officers. "I trust all of you know as well."

More than one warrior paled. Lanith ignored them, staring at the stronghold of his foe. So far, his legions had barely suffered a scratch; he had conquered a pair of villages and a good-sized town, but nothing significant. The baron here was, in fact, the first true resistance that he had encountered. He could have simply allowed his officers to conduct a siege of the place, eventually overwhelming the defenders at the loss of many lives, but Lanith was impatient to complete this final testing of his might. This place was merely in his path. It was a bump in the road to conquest that he had to smooth before he could prepare for the real campaign against the true enemy. Gordag-Ai.

Gordag-Ai. Their lands were rich; they would easily feed his armies. Once he had his hold there solidified, he could turn on Talak. From there, he could ride into the Tyber Mountains and seize the still inexperienced emperor of the drake race.

One of his former officers had insisted that such a plan of attack could only lead to destruction and chaos, that Talak would not stand for Gordag-Ai being assaulted because Talak's queen was the daughter of the rulers of Gordag-Ai. Talak, in turn, had treaties with Penacles.

But I have allies, too. In return for his aid, the drake confederation's leader, Sssaleese, would lead his forces in concert with the hordes of Zuu. Already Sssaleese had strengthened his hold on the lands west and north of Esedi, where Gordag-Ai lay. Talak could not stand against both and while the emperor nervously debated sending drakes against drakes, Lanith and his ally would crush the mountain kingdom ruled by half-faced Melicard.

Suddenly the thought of what he plotted began to overwhelm even the horse king. Gordag-Ai. Talak. Penacles. The drake emperor. So many powers and all of them against him. What could he possibly be thinking?

Victory is nearly yours, whispered his impish ally, scattering his anxious thoughts to the wind. *The first true step toward conquering the Dragonrealm takes place now. This is the test that shall reveal to your warriors their destiny!* The giggle that followed was loud enough to make Lanith wince in pain. *Your great sorcerers are ready to begin! All they need is your word!*

The last faded away just as Belfour informed him, "Your Majesty, there's a signal from Ponteroy. I think he's awaiting your command."

Lanith's fears vanished. There would be epic battles, tales to be told for generations to come, but they would be told by his descendants, the future emperors of the Dragonrealm. He would build an empire vaster than any the human race had dreamed of. There was no reason why the continent even had to be called by the worthless title of Dragonrealm once he conquered it. He could even name it after himself—

"Your Majesty—"

Stirring, the monarch of Zuu, future master of all that existed, nodded. It was the only acknowledgment Belfour needed to signal to the waiting spellcasters.

Lovely, oh, lovely, I cannot wait! came the voice in his head again.

At first, all that Lanith noticed was the restiveness of his many legions. His officers had primed them for war for months; now they wanted battle. Well, he would give them battle, glorious, victorious battle . . . but only a small taste of it today. As his invisible ally had more than once pointed out, it helped morale to know that you went into battle with victory a certainty. Once this day was over, they would be snapping at the bit to begin the actual move toward Gordag-Ai.

The horses suddenly shifted, growing uneasy. Several snorted and tried to back up. Some of the officers and soldiers had trouble keeping their mounts under control.

Lanith felt the earth below him tremble slightly.

Several heads appeared on the battlements of the castle. Someone raised a bow and shot at the surrounding force, but the single shaft fell short.

The tremor grew stronger. There were distant shouts of consternation from the stone fortress.

"Earthquake!" a young officer gasped. Others also looked shocked.

"Belfour, if anyone panics, I want them executed on the spot. Is that understood?"

"Y-yes, Your Majes-Majesty!" The senior officer's stuttering was not due to fear on his part, but rather the ever-increasing strength of the tremor.

"Ready our warriors."

"As y-you command."

A block fell from the battlements. Another followed. From within the castle came a cry, then another. Lanith smiled. Inside, panic had to be spreading like wildfire.

A crack opened in the ground just before the front gate of the castle, then another opened up toward the eastern side.

Moments later, a fault developed in the gateway. The high wooden gate, raised early on to prevent access to the attackers, came loose on one side, swinging open with a clatter that even the quake could not mask. Part of the gateway came crashing down.

"That'll be enough," Lanith remarked.

Belfour raised a hand. Almost instantly, the quake began to die down.

"Signal the advance."

Horns blared. Officers shouted commands. Inside the castle, people were still crying out. Only one or two figures still remained on the battlements and they appeared dazed.

They dared defy you, great king! They mocked you and cursed you! They should be punished! They should be . . . examples . . .

King Lanith of Zuu nodded. The imp was correct. The imp was always correct. This country aristocrat and his little army deserved to pay for their insult to him. "Belfour!"

"Yes, my liege?"

"Tell the officers that all inhabitants of the castle are to be executed."

The senior officer's expression tightened. "Are you——?"

You must not grow soft now! They must be made examples to those who would defy you in the future. A little fear goes a long way, doesn't it, O great one? More lives may be saved by the loss of these insignificant few.

"Yes, I can see that," the monarch of Zuu whispered. To his second, he roared, "You've been given an order by your king, Belfour. Are you questioning it?"

The warrior swallowed, then looked down. "No, my liege."

"Then go!"

The landscape between the king's position and the baron's stronghold had already become a living wave of roaring, eager riders, a mounted army that was awe-inspiring even to him. He thought about riding with them, but this battle was hardly worth his while. Let his men see that he had faith in them. He had already ridden untouched into the last town, killing more than half a dozen of the laughable defenders the elders had mustered from the inhabitants. Any weapon that had sought to mark him had been turned at the last moment. The imp had kept his promise then, just as he always did.

A pair of archers fired from the battlements, but they were the only visible defenders now. The first of Lanith's warriors reached the broken gate and rode their beasts inside, their swords raised high. Even though the first ones would probably die, there was no way that the defenders would be able to plug the gaps now. It was only a matter of time.

As he watched his forces swarm around and over the battered castle, his one true ally's voice worked to relieve him of any uncertainties concerning his chilling commands to his second. *So much death, but it will all be worth it, O great one!*

You will unify the land, bring it to a glory that others have only dreamed of! Generations will sing the praise of Lanith the Conqueror, Lanith the Horse King!

Horses. That reminded him again of the one promise that so far his unseen companion had failed to keep. Where was the mount he desired that would befit his glorious status? Where was Darkhorse?

Patience, Emperor Lanith! The shadowy presence giggled. *Already that is under way! Soon, very soon, you will have your wondrous, monstrous steed . . . and I will have my vengeance . . .*

CHAPTER IV

Jenna was already waiting for him. Aurim fought hard to control his eagerness, the dazzling smile that spread across her face as he entered not at all aiding his struggle. After checking with his sister Valea to make certain that all was well at the Manor, his parents had decided to stay longer as guests of the Gryphon. He had been given the choice of returning or staying, which, in the young spellcaster's eyes, had been no choice whatsoever. So long as Jenna was in Penacles, he wanted to be there, too.

He felt a bit guilty. His parents had stayed because of urgent news from the western reaches: the possibility of a war of some sort. Aurim had had trouble paying attention, more interested in when he would finally be able to see the merchant's daughter. She was the first woman that the mage felt he understood. There were few women his age at the Manor and most of those treated him with the same respect they did his parents. It made it difficult to truly know them. When he visited the royal families of Talak and Penacles, the situation was even worse. True, there were more choices, but they were generally the pampered, overly delicate daughters of men like Baron Vergoth. The baron's daughters had actually been some of the more tolerable females he had met.

Jenna was different. She spoke her mind, but respected his as well. She admitted to her shortcomings, but seemed to be able to turn those shortcomings into something useful. Everything she said or did seemed to reflect his own desires, his own dreams. Around her, he felt more confident, more independent from his famous parents. Independence was important to him.

"Aurim!" The beautiful young woman rose as he neared what had become their favored table. She was clad in a forest-green riding outfit with gold trim, a fairly conservative outfit for someone from Gordag-Ai. Her hair was done up behind her and on her head she wore a peaked hat with feathers on one side of it.

He sat down. "I'm sorry I'm late, Jenna. My parents—"

"Should give you more freedom, Aurim." She frowned. "You are a great mage in your own right. You're more than old enough to be on your own. They should have to understand that."

"It's not that simple. They often leave me in charge of the Manor and its grounds. That's a big responsibility. I have to watch over what amounts to a village."

The frown vanished. "Your home sounds fascinating. I'd like to see it someday. I can't imagine drakes and humans living together in such cooperation. I know they live together in Irillian By the Sea, but humans have always taken a secondary standing there. Where you live, they work as friends!"

"It started when my parents were asked to raise Kyl, the Dragon Emperor, and it just grew into so much more. Many of the drakes decided to stay after Kyl departed."

Her hand slid forward, just barely touching his. "Do you think that we could go there? Just for a few minutes, I mean. You can do that, can't you? Transport us there? I know you could."

When she spoke to him in the tone she was presently using, Aurim was nearly willing to believe that he could do *anything*. He almost agreed to bring her to the Manor there and then, but just as the words reached his tongue, Aurim recalled that no one was allowed entrance into the magical domain of the Bedlams unless his parents knew first. They had good reason for setting such a rule. More than once, foes had sought entrance using false identities. Spies for a few of the Dragon

Kings still sought to gain the secrets of the Manor for their respective masters.

"I'm sorry, Jenna. I've promised. Maybe if I introduce you to my parents and they got to know you—"

The hand quickly withdrew. "No, that's all right. Another time, perhaps. I understand if it's too much to ask."

Aurim knew that his face had turned scarlet. He had let her down. "I'm sorry."

"Please don't be." Her eyes appeared to sparkle. "I've an even better idea. Maybe you can help me. Would you teach me how to better control my abilities?"

Her request both flattered and worried him. Aurim wanted to help her, but then she might find out just how uncertain his own control was. Still, if he only had to make suggestions and didn't have to risk doing anything significant himself, then . . . "I guess that I could—"

"Oh, thank you!" Jenna leaned forward and kissed him lightly on the cheek. "Let's go to my room! We'll be able to work better there."

"Your room?" Aurim, raised to observe proprieties, shook his head. "That wouldn't be right, Jenna. I don't want you to get in trouble—"

"Oh, don't be silly, Aurim. I trust you . . . and you trust me, don't you?" She gave him a smile that would brook no dissension. "Besides, Gullivan speaks very highly of your family. I'm sure that he would see nothing improper about the two of us going to my room to talk, do you?"

Whatever misgivings he might have had, they were no defense against her beauty. Aurim finally nodded.

"Let's go now." Jenna practically had to lead him from the table. It was not until they reached the stairs that Aurim recovered enough to pretend that he was no longer concerned about what anyone might say. He did glance at Gullivan, but the innkeeper was busy with a customer.

Gullivan had a dozen rooms above the inn, most of them small but serviceable. There were two larger rooms, though, and one of these was where Jenna stayed. The furnishings were clean and well kept and the place in general was above the standards of all but the best inns. All in all, Gullivan provided something of a bargain, which was perhaps another reason why his business did so well.

Although there was some illumination from without, Jenna lit two oil lamps. Aurim now saw that other than one chair by a small table, there was nowhere to sit but the floor or the bed.

"We'll probably have more room if we just use the floor. Is that all right with you, Aurim?"

"Of course." Inwardly, he breathed a sigh of relief.

"Good." The merchant's daughter sat down on a wide animal skin that served as the only rug in the room. Aurim sat across from her, folding his legs as he generally did before beginning concentration exercises.

"I said I could only do this." She stared at her hand. It briefly glowed, then returned to normal. "But I can also do this." Staring at her hand again, she started to draw in the air with her index finger. A streak of light formed wherever her finger had been. In seconds, she had drawn the crude outline of what was possibly a horse.

Aurim blinked. The horse lifted its head, put one leg forward . . . then faded away.

"I can draw things like that and make them move a little, but that's all."

That's all? That she was able to do as much as this indicated that Jenna had more power than he had assumed. She was, in fact, what his father would have called a prime candidate for the school of sorcery.

Now there was a notion that appealed to him. Aurim wondered if he could somehow convince the merchant's daughter to leave her father's business for a time and study at the school. Not only would it enable her to better learn about the limitations of her skills, but it would put her nearby whenever he was able to get to Penacles. Although it was possible that he could transport himself to Gordag-Ai, his lack of knowledge of the kingdom coupled with his distrust of his ability to correctly perform such a long-range spell made it doubtful that he would ever see her again if she returned home.

It was too soon to approach such a subject. *After* they practiced a bit, perhaps.

"You're better than you think, Jenna. You could become an excellent sorcerer if you put your mind to it."

"You're just saying that." She smiled wistfully. "It would be interesting. The things you must be able to do. Can you show me something now? I know you don't like to show off, but it would really mean a lot to me."

What could he say? He wanted so much to impress her, but since the incident in the palace, what little confidence he had once had in himself was virtually nonexistent now. If he failed, Jenna might laugh at him and ask him to leave.

"My concentration's been a little off today, Jenna. Couldn't I try to help you learn a little more about your power? Maybe we can get your images to last longer."

"Please, Aurim? It would encourage me if I saw some of what you were capable of performing." She looked down. "Not that I could ever be as good as you, but I want to experience what it must be like to have such power under your control."

Under my control . . . if Jenna only knew. Still, looking at her, Aurim found he could not resist another attempt. He would keep it small and simple, completely avoiding animation whatsoever. Well . . . maybe not. There were some old concentration techniques that he had once been good at—*had* been good at until his debacle in the Gryphon's palace—and if he cast the spells exactly the way he had, it was possible he might keep on going for a few seconds. Just long enough to impress his companion before things fell apart again.

"All right. Watch closely. I'm only going to do this for a breath or two." As she nodded, the young mage held out his hands, palms upward, and summoned up power.

An indistinct haze formed above his palms. The haze quickly defined itself into several tiny forms. The longer Aurim stared at them, the more distinct each became until at last he had re-created what had once been one of his favorite practice spells.

Each harlequin was colored blue and red and stood about two inches tall. They floated counterclockwise in a circle, but that was not all. Each little figure also performed a somersault. Over and over they went, much to the delight of Aurim's audience.

Without warning, the circle collapsed and the harlequins plummeted to the floor, where they faded upon contact.

Aurim cursed without realizing it. He slammed a fist on the wooden surface, sending shock-waves of pain through his entire arm.

"Aurim! Are you all right?" Jenna reached forward and took his hand in hers, studying it closely for any cut or bruise.

He tried to pull back, but her grip was surprisingly strong. The merchant's daughter locked gazes with him. "You shouldn't do something like that. You startled me."

"I'm sorry. It's just that the circle should have stayed in motion until I dismissed it! I've gotten worse, not better!"

"You're having problems with your spellcasting?" A look of concern crossed her features. "But you're supposed to be even more powerful than your parents! You are, aren't you?"

"As my father keeps saying, I have the potential. It's there, but I just can't seem to concentrate properly. I thought I was getting better with my control just prior to Kyl's ascension to the throne of Dragon Emperor, but afterward it all began to fall apart again. I don't know why, but it did. Very little I do works right."

She leaned forward and took both hands. "You must have gone through so much during that time. I imagine there were also a lot of changes afterward, maybe more work, more stress. I can appreciate the pressure you've been under. It's not easy being a merchant's daughter, being taught the business because my father has no son to turn it over to when he gets too old. Your parents act as representatives to the Dragon Emperor's court, too, don't they?"

"Yes."

Jenna nodded. "And you are left with more responsibilities when they are away."

"So's Valea."

"But you're oldest. In general, you're the one left in charge, aren't you?"

It was true, and sometimes he felt that the pressure was overwhelming. Valea sometimes said that he tried too hard, that he could not make himself responsible for every single matter going on in the Manor. Most of the activities that took place in and around the Manor did not require his watchful eye.

"I think that you've tried to do too much at once, Aurim. That's all. You need to turn away from everything else and let sorcery be your entire focus . . . but in a more relaxed manner. You need to become your strength, your power."

He laughed. "I thought I was supposed to be the instructor."

"Even a teacher can learn," Jenna countered, smiling again. Before Aurim realized what she was doing, the beautiful young woman leaned forward and kissed him. It was a brief, light kiss, but it left him completely befuddled. "I've got an idea. First, I'll teach you how to relax properly, then you teach me how to better utilize my skills."

It certainly sounded enticing to him, admittedly for more reasons than one. "How do you plan to make me relax?"

"My father taught me a few techniques." Jenna slid back a foot or two. "Turn your back to me."

Aurim did. The next thing he knew, Jenna had slid forward again, nearly nestling herself in his back. His heart beat faster. If this was intended to relax him, it was having the opposite effect.

"Close your eyes. Good. Now breathe slowly and let me do the rest."

The mage obeyed, although it was difficult to breathe slowly with her so near. Suddenly he felt her hands slide past his shoulders. Aurim twitched without meaning to, but Jenna stilled him with a single word. She touched his temples with her fingertips.

A tingling sensation spread over him.

Darkhorse and Cabe materialized at the edge of the Dagora Forest just a few miles west of the barony of Adderly. The sun was fast setting, which was just what they wanted. At the Gryphon's request, the pair had come to investigate the truth behind the message, and Adderly was the appropriate place to begin. If the horse king was testing his might, Adderly was his nearest reasonable target.

"I still do not see why we do not just return to Zuu, Cabe! We've visited the kingdom in secret before!"

"Yes, and the last time we were nearly caught by Lanith's pet sorcerers. I think they've learned a little since then, Darkhorse, especially if their numbers include the missing students."

Deep down, the eternal knew that his companion was correct, but he still doubted that their present course of action would tell them anything worthwhile. Find Lanith, Darkhorse surmised, and one found the center of activity. They would learn more that way. The king of Zuu might have his own spellcasters, but Darkhorse doubted that any of them had skills worth fearing. Those that Cabe and he had encountered on their previous excursions a few years back had been as organized and competent as panicked sheep.

The shadow steed peered at the landscape before them. Adderly's eastern border seemed tranquil. There was no evidence of any battle. However, the castle of the baron was a few miles to the west and very much out of sight. If any struggle had taken place, the signs would be evident there, not here in this emptiness.

"Thank goodness there's no one here," the sorcerer remarked.

"Why would they bother to come here? There is nothing here, Cabe."

"True, but if they intended on invading the Dagora Forest, this entire area would now be overrun by more cavalry than I doubt anyone outside of Zuu has ever seen."

"I have witnessed the massing of hordesss far more vassst than what this human conqueror can gather," responded a harsh voice from behind them. "But I, too, am pleasssed that no such force camps jussst beyond my domain."

That Cabe was at least as startled as he was no compensation to Darkhorse. He did not like being spied upon, especially when he should have been able to sense this particular newcomer.

Cabe Bedlam's tone grew icy. "Lord Green. We were trying our best not to disturb you."

"Disssturb me?" The tall, armored figure walked closer.

The setting sun left much in shadow, but it was clear that the dragon-helmed knight was not human. With the exception of his eyes—bloodred this time, although not always—the warrior was emerald-green. His armor was scaled, save for the helm, the crest of which was the startlingly realistic head of the menacing dragon. The lower half of the helm was open, revealing a flat, lipless mouth and daggerlike teeth. The scaled skin perfectly matched the scales of the armor and with good reason, for they were one and the same, the tough hide of a draconian shapeshifter.

The master of the Dagora Forest, the Green Dragon, had been watching them all the time.

"We didn't intend on encroaching long in your domain," Cabe added, clearly uncomfortable around the drake lord.

Darkhorse did not care for the drakes himself, but the lord of the Dagora Forest had always been friendly toward humans. Something, though, had changed the once-deep friendship between the Green Dragon and Cabe Bedlam into a shade of its former self. They conversed when necessary and met together when circumstances required it, but where once the scaled warrior had been welcome in the Bedlams' domain, he now never visited.

"You are not encroaching, Cabe. I undersssstand the reassson why you are here. Asss the power of my people, mysssself included, has declined, thossse like Lanith of Zuu have taken full advantage of it. I have been watching, and my agents, both human and otherwissse, have also been well at work."

"And have they found anything?" Cabe asked, still maintaining his distant tone.

"Very little." The Green Dragon looked from one to the other. "I have lossst at least five spies, all loyal volunteers. They entered Zuu . . . and did not return. I am quite certain that they are all dead."

This intrigued Darkhorse. The drake lord before them was one of the great powers of the Dragonrealm. He had access to rare artifacts and knowledge. His predecessors for generations back had worked to gather these things, providing the present lord of Dagora with many options when it came to such business as investigating the activities of a human monarch who had once been his vassal. "Have you looked for them?"

"I . . . have. Of courssse, demon sssteed. I do not leave ss-such things unfinished."

There is something he fears about me. While fear was an emotion Darkhorse encountered often from those he confronted, the drake lord had never reacted like this. It had something to do with whatever had shattered the drake's friendship with the sorcerer.

"Did you find out anything?" the spellcaster pushed, clearly desiring an end to the discussion.

The scaly warrior looked away, obviously disconcerted. This time, however, Darkhorse surmised that it was because of the results of the drake's investigation.

"Nothing . . . no . . . almossst nothing, Cabe. Each one left no trace, but I did sssense twice a great emptinesss just before the link to me faded. I can't explain it. They were not agents without protection." The Green Dragon looked up, eyes locking on the sorcerer's. "Lanith controls sssome power, sssome *force,* that makesss his insssipid Magical Order redundant and yet I cannot fathom what it could possibly be! Only that it may be more than any of usss can deal with alone!"

The more he spoke, the more the drake's natural sibilance took over. The upper hierarchy of the drake race prided itself on speaking the common tongue perfectly, but whenever too emotional, they slipped.

"An emptiness," Cabe mused. "That's all you can tell us?"

"If I had more to tell you, believe me, I would. When I sssensed you, I debated whether to sssay anything until I knew more, but then I quickly realized that I have no idea how I *can* learn any more. Not without entering Zuu myself . . . and I do not think that would be a good idea."

"What about Adderly?" asked Darkhorse. "Has anything happened to this barony?"

The pause was far too lengthy for either Darkhorse or the sorcerer. "Adderly is no more. A laughable offense that Lanith callsss hisss first great victory. A tessst of hisss might . . . asss if Adderly had any defense of significance. The cursssed horse king did not even attempt to take the castle without the aid of his misssbegotten ssspellcastersss!" The Green Dragon clenched his fists. "They ssslaughtered the inhabitants even after they had sssurrendered! Monssstersss! They call usss abominations and thisss isss what they do?"

Such an emotional admission from a warrior whose race was known for its savage ways surprised even Darkhorse. It also made the shadow steed more eager than ever to return to Zuu. This Lanith had been allowed too much freedom; he had abused every notion of humanity. Darkhorse understood many of the reasons that the Gryphon and the Bedlams had given for no one having gone to war with Zuu, but he was now aware that such reasons mattered little anymore. There was no doubt now as to either Lanith's intentions or his methods for achieving them.

"I can't believe Blane's brother could be like that." Cabe grimaced. "I knew Blane for only a short time, but he was a good man, a brave warrior. He cared about people. Can Lanith be that different?"

"Lanith wasss alwaysss the ambitious one, Cabe. Alwaysss the more driven. Yet thisss is far more than I expected from him. The Lanith I recall did once have compassion . . . but not now."

"Talk! Talk! All we do is talk!" The eternal had had enough of talk. Everyone talked about how terrible things were and what a threat the horse king was. Well, it was time to take action, not continue treading softly. "We waste precious moments here! Lanith has moved, tested his power! He will move on from here, moving north, no doubt! If we do nothing, he will be at the walls of Gordag-Ai before very long! He may be marching there even now!"

The Green Dragon shook his head. "No, eternal, he isss not. Lanith returned to Zuu after this massacre and now awaitsss some newsss. I know not what, though. Only that his mistress, the sssorceresss Saress, is to bring it."

"Saress?" Cabe Bedlam looked up. "Do you know anything about her? Even the Gryphon can't find out much."

"Rumorsss, Cabe. Nothing more. Saresss is nearly as great a myssstery to me asss thisss power that Lanith wields."

"Could they be one and the same?"

"No. I can tell you that, at leassst."

"We waste time here!" Darkhorse kicked up earth with one of his hooves. "Cabe, we should go to Zuu ourselves!"

His companion looked down at him, then at the Dragon King. The latter made no sound, did not even move. "Not Zuu, Darkhorse, but I do want to see the baron's castle. There might be something we can learn there. Are Lanith's forces still there, Lord Green?"

"Only a small garrison. There are many patrols, however. The bulk of hisss forces are encamped nearer to Zuu. I believe he likely intendsss to attack Gordag-Ai, but on the chance that he will sssuddenly turn east, I have kept a careful eye."

"We'll look over Adderly first, then. Do you mind, Darkhorse?"

He still desired to journey dirctly to Zuu, but the eternal trusted Cabe's opinion. "Very well."

By this time, the sun was barely a glimmer on the horizon. The Green Dragon had become a shadow among shadows. He backed away in silence. Cabe seemed disinclined to bid him farewell. Darkhorse swore that someday he would find out what had come between them . . . and if the drake lord had betrayed his friend in some way, the ebony stallion would see to it that the master of the Dagora Forest paid for his folly.

"Have you been to Addcrly before, Darkhorse?"

He twisted his head around to look at Cabe. "I have passed through it. There is not much to see there. I have only seen the castle from a distance."

"There arc hillsss to the north and some wooded areasss to the west and cast," called the retreating drake. "Neither afford much cover, but for the two of you, either should be sssufficient."

Cabe stiffened, then twisted around so that he could face the nearly invisible figure. "My thanks, Lord Green."

"Take care, my friendsss . . ." The Dragon King vanished into the forest.

Darkhorse's comrade stared at the forest a moment more, then turned back to him. "Do you know those areas at all?"

"I recall them somewhat. His suggestions have merit. Cabe, what is the—"

"The darkness will help us. Let's go."

"As you desire, Cabe." Feeling subdued, Darkhorse reared, then started westward. His hooves made no sound as he raced, and in fact, he left no prints in the earth. Now was the time for speed, yes, but also for stealth. Even if he did not fear for himself, he always tried to watch over Cabe.

The castle of the baron of Adderly was at first a black hill jutting upward just a short distance from the true hills that the drake lord had mentioned. One or two tiny points of light flickered near the battlements, but as Darkhorse and Cabe moved nearer, other lights materialized around the castle grounds. It became obvious that besides the garrison, there was at least one band of cavalry, likely a returning patrol, camping nearby.

"The structure looks unsettled," Darkhorse commented after a brief study. "As if someone had tried to crack it in two."

"Lord Green did say Lanith utilized sorcery. The baron and his people probably expected a more conventional battle." Cabe inhaled sharply. "Lanith killed them all . . ."

The shadow steed was about to remark on the last when he felt the slightest tug of power. Some sort of spell was at work and it had a familiar feel to it, although he could not say exactly how. It did not strike him as a major undertaking, but he nonetheless grew curious to study it.

"Do you feel something, Darkhorse?" his companion suddenly asked. "A spell of some sort?"

So Cabe felt it also. "I do. Shall we investigate? I sense nothing extraordinary about it, but I find myself curious as to its origins! It seems to come from the wooded area just east of the horse people's encampment. We can be there and gone before any of them notice us."

Cabe looked up, Darkhorse following his gaze. Only one of the two moons was evident and that one was mostly obscured by cloud cover. The sorcerer acquiesced to his companion's suggestion. "I'm curious, too. We'll have to watch carefully, however. There may be some danger we can't sense from here."

"And what danger is there that the two of us cannot handle?" The eternal chuckled quietly. "Lanith may have his tame spellcasters, Cabe, but you and I . . . there is nothing we cannot overcome together!"

"I wish you'd quit saying that, Darkhorse," whispered Cabe with a rueful smile. "I'm not quite as invincible as you think I am . . . and come to think of it, neither are you."

Despite the other's words, Darkhorse still felt confident. This was so much like times past. He and Cabe against the villainy of such as the wolf raiders, the burrowing Quel, the treacherous Toma . . . it was in times of adventure that the eternal felt most alive. He could not tell this to his human friend, though. Even Cabe, who knew him best, would not have understood the sense of pleasure that always underlined the shadow steed's emotions during such dangerous missions. Darkhorse felt needed at times such as this.

They reached a position near enough to the enemy encampment that they could make out individual figures moving about. The horsemen of Zuu appeared restive; Lanith had succeeded in stirring his subjects to war. They would be ready to ride the moment he commanded them to do so. Darkhorse snorted. While he enjoyed adventure, he found no enjoyment in war. All it did was waste lives.

"Ahead, Darkhorse," Cabe muttered. "By that small open area behind those trees."

He was already aware of the location, having sensed even before Cabe the strong presence of the spell. Again, Darkhorse thought that there was a familiar signature to it. He had confronted the creator of the spell in the past . . . but where?

Then a feminine voice whispered, "Get *away!* Not here!"

Startled, Darkhorse turned toward the voice. As he did, one of his hind legs touched what felt like the branch of a tree, only there should have been no tree, not even a bush, at that location.

An intense pressure closed in on Darkhorse from all sides, squeezing him with such force that it grew more and more difficult to maintain his form. Darkhorse grunted, fighting as the incredible pressure threatened to squeeze him into a shapeless mass.

A cry alerted the shadow steed to his rider's plight. Cabe was caught in the same trap and he did not have the malleability of form to survive for very long. The eternal was not even certain that he could survive very long. This was like no spell trap he had ever encountered.

It was already futile to retain his equine shape. Darkhorse drew his legs inward and then collapsed his upper torso. His struggling companion fell with it. The shadow steed immediately enveloped the sorcerer, shaping himself into a soft, spherical cell that would, for the moment at least, provide Cabe with some protection from the spell.

His head was the last vestige of his equine shape that he discarded. The snout retracted quickly until only the pupilless eyes and a slash that had been his mouth remained. His new shape would afford him a little extra time, but unless he found some way to disrupt the trap, both he and Cabe were doomed.

There was *one* other thing he could do for the sorcerer, Darkhorse realized, but even a death as hideous as what the pair of them faced would have been preferable to the human. Cabe had witnessed Darkhorse absorbing his enemies and it was a sight that the spellcaster had clearly abhorred.

There must be something! I am Darkhorse! There is nothing from this realm that can hold me! Yet . . . that was not entirely true. There had been other traps, other spells, that had nearly done him in. Somehow he had always escaped. This time, though . . .

Despite his best efforts, the pressure continued to squeeze him into a smaller and smaller ball. Before long, he would be too small for Cabe to survive.

In the midst of it, Darkhorse sensed an emanation that made no sense. It was his own power, yet it worked against him. It was as if he had designed this trap himself. That was foolish, though, no doubt the product of his rattled senses.

The pressure increased. Unable to withstand the added pressure, the eternal shrank yet again. Now he sensed the sorcerer's new discomfort. Cabe had folded himself up as best he could, but that was no longer sufficient. Darkhorse felt Cabe make one aborted attempt to disrupt the trap, but it held firm.

And so I shall discover what death means to me! I shall see if I, too, am granted an afterlife! He doubted the latter. Having been created in the endlessness of the empty dimension called the Void, he was not at all like the creatures who were born in the world of the Dragonrealm. When he perished, Darkhorse suspected that he would simply cease to exist.

For being so foolish, for failing to save his dearest friend, he expected nothing better.

The pressure increased yet more . . . then *decreased* just as the eternal was about to collapse. Seizing advantage of the shift, Darkhorse expanded as quickly as he could, trying to wreak what havoc he could on the spell. It continued to weaken and as it did, he pressed harder.

As suddenly as it had been sprung, the spell trap dissipated.

Free at last, he remained still, not even attempting to reshape himself. The eternal shifted his gaze and caught a glimpse of long golden hair in the darkness. Again he sensed a familiar magical signature, but he was too weak to give chase. Besides, Darkhorse was suddenly very certain that it was through *her* doing that the deadly spell trap had abruptly faltered. Only from the outside could anyone have affected such a sinister snare.

But why had she saved them . . . or warned them in the first place?

Unfolding as an oyster might, Darkhorse inspected the still form of his companion. He knew that Cabe still lived, but what condition was the human in?

At first the sorcerer did not move, but when Darkhorse prodded Cabe's mind with a gentle magical probe, his companion immediately stirred.

"Dark—Darkhorse?" Cabe awkwardly rose to his knees. He blinked, then stared in visible amazement at the peculiar shape of the eternal. The latter made no attempt to resume his equine form. What mattered most was whether the human was injured or not.

"How do you feel, Cabe? Are you well?"

"Well pressed," muttered the sorcerer. He touched his side,

immediately wincing. "I think a rib . . . may be cracked. I could fix . . . this . . . eventually . . . but I'll need s-some time . . ."

A horn blared. Darkhorse heard men calling out and horses moving. "Time is not something we have, it seems! A wonder they did not arrive sooner than this! We were held—"

"No more than . . . a few seconds, although I agree that it seemed like much . . . much longer." Cabe grimaced. "If they have any more spells at . . . their command l-like this, I don't think that I can fight them j-just now, Darkhorse."

"On that I must unhappily agree, Cabe." The eternal attempted a limb. It was of the proper length, but rough-hewn, as if some artist had just begun work on a sculpture. It was proof enough, however, that Darkhorse could resume a shape capable of carrying his companion to safety. He adjusted his form immediately, gingerly raising his injured friend up.

Cabe seized hold of his mane. Given time, the sorcerer would be able to heal himself, but with Lanith's men approaching, all the pair could do was retreat.

His first movements were ungainly. Darkhorse had to struggle to recall the proper coordination of his limbs. The more he moved, though, the smoother his movements became.

Unfortunately, the delay allowed the first of the riders to reach them. Two warriors, one bearing a torch and the other a bow, urged their mounts toward the duo. A third horseman followed, sword in hand.

Darkhorse felt Cabe draw upon power. Dirt swirled up into the air, blinding men and mounts. The horses struggled against their masters, not at all willing to ride into the magical storm.

"Ride . . . Darkhorse!" Cabe gasped, his voice sounding more and more ragged. The spellcaster slumped against the re-formed neck of his comrade. "Ride!"

The shadowy stallion would have preferred to fight these first attackers off, but while he probably would have survived, he was not so certain about Cabe. He turned in the direction of the Dagora Forest, knowing that the best way to lose them would be among the thick foliage. Still weak, it was impossible for Darkhorse to transport the two of them away, but he had no doubt that he could outpace the patrol's mounts. They were, after all, only mortal steeds . . .

That thought came back to haunt him a moment later as a long row of flickering torches and dark, rapidly moving figures to the south warned him that a large patrol sought to cut them off from the safety of the forest. The riders moved with such precision and planning that Darkhorse wondered whether they somehow could read his thoughts. He increased his pace as best he could, but between his need to keep an eye on the injured sorcerer and his own weariness, the eternal found that outracing the horsemen of Zuu was a greater challenge than expected.

A fiery arrow shot past his muzzle, striking the ground no more than a few feet from him. His fear for Cabe's safety increased a hundredfold. Darkhorse sent a mental probe to his comrade, but the thoughts he received were jumbled. The sorcerer was alive, but barely conscious. It was all the human could do to maintain hold. Darkhorse shaped himself so as to better keep Cabe from slipping, but could do nothing to protect the sorcerer should the archer fire any more of the deadly bolts.

The riders continued to close. Everything appeared to be working as if someone had planned to capture or kill the shadow steed and his friend. Had they really known that the duo was here or had they simply *expected* them?

From somewhere ahead came the touch of another mind. A female. *Just a few feet more. I can help you, then. You must turn a little to the right, though! Hurry!*

To the right would take him even nearer to the oncoming riders, many of whom were evidently expert bowmen even on horseback judging by the increasing number of bolts that assailed him. Darkhorse almost demurred, but at the last moment decided to take the risk. He only hoped that he was not being played for the fool. The stallion altered course, at the same time pushing forward with what strength he had left. The spell trap had taken too much out of him; he had not felt so weak in decades.

Directly ahead, the woman informed him. *Only a few yards more.*

Her last words confused him. He was still far from the forest and there appeared to be nothing in sight. Darkhorse could not even sense any *sorcery*.

That was what made the hole that swallowed them a moment later even more surprising.

CHAPTER V

Darkhorse stood in the midst of a picturesque field of lush, high green grass that covered the sloping landscape to the horizon. Several trees of different species stood tall among the grass, islands in an emerald sea. Birds flew among the branches, singing and darting about without care. Overall, the pastoral scene was a sight that should have gladdened the heart of any who came to this place.

The shadow steed could only think of how much danger he and Cabe might be in from this supposedly tranquil land.

Where was the night? Where was the moon? According to the sun's position it was roughly an hour after dawn. The shadow steed did not like the abrupt changes. Only sorcery could have twisted his world so much, making night into day.

Yet even the shift from darkness to light did not bother him as much as the presence of the gently swaying grass. Each blade that touched his legs made him want to jump back.

"It won't harm you," said the familiar feminine voice. "It won't harm anyone but certain drakes. You can thank your sorcerer friend for that."

A human female now stood among the tall grass. Despite being clad in a simple brown and white peasant outfit, the newcomer was impressive. She filled the blouse and bodice in a manner that Darkhorse knew would have garnered the attention of any male other than a blind one. Her features were slightly elfin, but a bit more full, more human. She had hair almost as golden as that of Aurim, save that hers appeared natural whereas his had been altered by an early juvenile attempt at sorcery. There was no visible streak of silver in her tresses, but he could sense that she was most definitely a sorceress or witch.

Her eyes glittered, but when the shadow steed tried to identify the color, he found it impossible. Sometimes they appeared emerald, sometimes golden, and sometimes . . . sometimes they were as red and narrow as those of a drake warrior. Who was this woman?

"I'm sorry," she added, smiling mischievously. "The blink hole wasn't supposed to work like that. I thought for a while that I'd lost you, but then it finally opened on this side."

"Finally?" Darkhorse snorted. "If that was a blink hole, I do not think that I have ever seen another one that took hours to cross through!" He looked again at the sun. "Is it truly the next day?"

"Yes." The smile faded. "But we can talk about that after I've taken care of him. Let me get him off of you."

"I think not!" He backed a few steps away, glancing quickly around at the grass. It did nothing but sway gently in the light breeze.

"I know what you're thinking. These are no longer the Barren Lands, as you can see, demon steed." She smiled again. "Cabe Bedlam is responsible for that. It's known that he and the Brown Dragon, the savage drake lord who ruled here, rode into this desolate region and only one of them departed alive. Sometime shortly after that, the grass and trees sprouted from the parched soil and everything became as it had been before the Turning War caused the creation of the Barren Lands in the first place. Cabe Bedlam brought life back to this domain. He'd hardly be in danger from it."

"Perhaps, perhaps not, human! This may no longer be the Barren Lands, true, but this is hardly an idyllic field! Among the green hills and oh-so-lovely trees of this new wonderland lie the bones of most of the drakes of clan Brown! This grand pasture *strangled* them to death, little sorceress! Every one of them! It took from them to build this deadly paradise and I do not doubt that it hungers still! Where did you think that it got the sustenance to revive itself, hmmm?"

Now her eyes briefly flashed crimson again. "I understand what happened, perhaps even better than you. The spell worked against the drakes of clan Brown because it was their master who tried to sacrifice your friend. He wanted the same results, but by using the blood of the grandson of the Dragon Master who'd caused the creation of the Barren Lands in the first place. The land is at peace now, though." She reached out a hand. Several of the stalks twisted against the wind to gently caress her palm. "I know, I've lived here long enough."

"Then you are foolhardy." Nonetheless, Darkhorse knew that he really did not have any choice but to allow her to treat his companion. Hours might have passed for the rest of the realm, but for Cabe and him, it had only been moments. Cabe could not help himself and Darkhorse was too weak to do much more. He could neither transport them to Penacles nor safely attempt to heal his companion's injuries. The female had been helpful so far. Perhaps it was taking a risk, but the eternal had to trust in her.

He would be watching everything she did, however. If even her slightest action seemed questionable . . .

"Very *well*. Take care of him . . . but know that I will be watching!"

"I'm sure you will." She waited for Darkhorse to kneel, then, without the slightest sign of fear of him, she carefully pulled Cabe from his back.

The grass moved toward the sorcerer, but just as Darkhorse was about to act, he saw that the blades had massed under his companion and were aiding the female in lowering Cabe to the ground. Those blades that were no longer needed retreated while others slipped under to form what appeared to be a soft bed.

"It's fortunate that you shielded him when you did. He has at least two cracked ribs, but I don't think much more than that," she whispered. Her hands moved upward, the fingertips gently touching the spellcaster's chest. "But his body's strong. He's in very nice form."

The tone of her voice suggested that her comment was not

entirely clinical, but Darkhorse let it pass. Now that he saw her with Cabe, he suddenly knew who she was—and that knowledge disturbed him. Their previous encounter remained in his mind for one very good reason. It had taken place in Zuu.

"Step away from him"—the name she had used previously sprang to mind—"Tori."

She obeyed, not quite so confident now that he knew her identity. "We never really met. You shouldn't know me."

"I know you from a glimpse and also from detecting your presence when first you tried to seduce Cabe Bedlam. You are from Zuu, witch! You are one of Lanith's dogs!"

The last seemed to stir resentment in her. "I'd never be one of Lanith's puppets! I leave that to Saress and that popinjay Ponteroy! I'd never have anything to do with any of them!"

They might have sunken deeper into the argument, but then Cabe stirred. It was only for a moment, but it was enough to turn Darkhorse's concern to the more immediate problem. "I am taking him back to Penacles! Move away!"

"I won't. Look at you, Darkhorse. You might be able to knock me aside, but you're still too weak to travel by any other means than running. That spell trap was designed specifically for you. It *had* to be. I was trying to see what it and the others were for—"

"Others?" He had sensed nothing.

She gave him a knowing smile. "Others. The area around the castle is dotted with them, but I've seen riders and their mounts pass through the traps without disturbing them. Only when you came across a trap did it spring. It was meant for you, demon steed, even if it also caught your friend in the process." The sorceress returned her attention to Cabe. "Now let me take care of him before his injuries grow worse."

Darkhorse relented, but he watched closely as the female delved into her work. She appeared to be earnest in her efforts, her hands carefully running over the areas of the injury. He sensed subtle uses of power over the ribs as she worked to mend them. Secretly, Darkhorse was grateful that it was not his task; he had been concerned about his clumsiness. Human systems were so delicate, so fragile. He might have caused more harm than good.

Cabe's expression gradually relaxed and his skin, which had grown so pale, was now more pink. He breathed with less difficulty now. Darkhorse probed with his power and found no trace of the injuries.

"He needs to rest now." As she rose, the grass shifted to better comfort the unconscious figure. Other stalks caressed the enchantress's arms.

"Thank you . . . Tori." The eternal eyed the lively grass with lingering distrust. How could it know the difference between a human and a drake warrior? Why would it protect one and kill the other?

"I did it because I wanted to, so don't thank me. Besides, it's probably my fault you came here in the first place. You got my message, didn't you?"

"You sent the message to Penacles?"

"It was the only method by which I thought that I could eventually reach Cabe." She smiled wistfully at the slumbering mage. "A pity I didn't latch on to him before he met the Lady of the Amber."

Darkhorse eyed her. "You are not quite the same female that Cabe encountered in Zuu."

"Things have gotten worse in Zuu. I can't even stay there anymore. I like fun, not war." She pretended to pout.

The shadow steed judged that Tori, if that was truly her name, was a person of masks. She pretended to be frivolous when that served her, serious when the situation called for it. At other times, he suspected that she switched back and forth without warning, putting those around her constantly off-guard. That, combined with apparently substantial abilities, made her formidable.

"Why Cabe? Why him? What do you expect of him?"

She started to put a hand on the sorcerer's arm, but Darkhorse's sudden glare made her pull back. "Because I've never known someone with the power he has. He's amazing. I don't think that there's another spellcaster who can match him power for power . . . and yet he keeps it all under careful control." This time the blond woman defied Darkhorse, lightly caressing Cabe's arm. Her expression was not light, however. If anything, worry now dominated. "He's the only one I can think of who has the power to deal with the thing in Lanith's palace."

"Thing?"

"Yes, thing. I wasn't certain until . . . until recently, but there's a power, a force, in Lanith's palace . . . an intelligent force . . ."

A power, a force . . . It was almost the same description that the Dragon King had used. She might have been eavesdropping, although that was doubtful since among the drake lord, Cabe, and himself, Darkhorse did not think that even someone as clever as the woman who called herself Tori could have remained undetected. She had also added something to the description. *An intelligent force* . . .

Intelligent? What did that mean? He wished that Cabe would wake so that he could ask him his opinion. Cabe and his wife were so much better at puzzling out such things. So, for that matter, was the Gryphon. He needed to get Cabe to Penacles. By this time, Lady Bedlam and the king of Penacles had to be worrying about them. "Can Cabe be moved?"

"I'd wait a little longer, just to make certain that I haven't missed something. He also needs some rest. Give him a couple of hours at least, demon steed."

Hours? Darkhorse had to let the others know what was happening, but he dared not try to contact Penacles from so far away. If Lanith had some powerful unknown mage working for him—that was the only answer Darkhorse had so far come up with to explain the "intelligent force"—then such far-reaching communication could not be trusted to be private. Darkhorse saw no sense in alerting Lanith as to their present predicament.

"An unknown mage . . ." he muttered. Could it be that the warlock Shade was alive? Shade had been both bane and hero to the realm over his centuries-long life, depending on which of his incarnations had been active. Many had thought that they had killed the warlock, only to discover afterward that he had been immediately reborn. Shade was *permanently* dead, though. He had to be. It could not be him.

Could it?

"I have to go now," the female announced. "There're things I have to do."

"Such as?"

"I have to search for someone, someone important to Lanith who hasn't been around lately. That could mean trouble."

The shadow steed snorted. "Could you be a little more specific, Lady Tori?"

His use of the title amused her. "'Lady Tori.' I'd like that if Tori were my real name. Maybe I'll still use it sometime." She looked down at Cabe. "For him I'd have been Lady Tori for the rest of my life."

"You are evading my question, little one, and are also far too late. As has been pointed out, Cabe is married, happily, I will add, and has children, too."

"Yes, and one of them is now a man, isn't he?" Her eyes sparkled, reminding Darkhorse momentarily of a Vraad, one of the race of sorcerers who had been the precursors of the present human population. "I've heard he's handsome." She dimpled, a sight no doubt designed to melt the heart of a human male but which only served to intensify Darkhorse's distrust. "Is that true, do you know?"

"If things are progressing as I believe they are," the ebony stallion responded, "then you are probably too late to snare the younger master as well. He has recently met one that I think has caught his fancy." He pawed at the ground. "Now! Perhaps you might clarify what you said . . . and also, I think, you might tell me your true name—"

"He's recently met someone, you say?" The golden-haired woman's expression darkened. "Interesting . . ."

"I said—" Darkhorse got no further. The enchantress had vanished as abruptly as she had first materialized. He barely felt her depart. There was no sense trying to track her. In some ways, the female was more skilled than many of the other spellcasters that he had encountered over the centuries. There was also a peculiarity to her magical trace that he could not recall having encountered in another being.

Cabe shifted. The shadow steed wanted to wake him, but he

knew that there was merit in what the enchantress had said
about letting his companion rest. When Cabe was awake and
fit to travel, the pair would immediately return to Penacles . . .
and then Darkhorse would discuss with his friend their mysterious benefactor.

Aurim knew that his mother was anxious about his father's
return, but he had grown up watching one or both of his parents vanish somewhere on some important mission, each time
returning, and so he was less concerned than she was. He did
worry, but what was there that his father and Darkhorse could
not together defeat? They were two of the greatest powers of
the Dragonrealm.

What was more important to him was seeing Jenna. Aurim
was glad that his parents had not asked him to go back to the
Manor. He suspected that Darkhorse had told them of his
growing interest in the merchant's daughter, which was good.
At this point, if his mother had requested that he return to the
Manor to help his sister, the younger Bedlam would have refused. He was old enough to do so, too. They no longer had
any hold on him. Aurim was his own man.

Jenna waited for him, but not at Gullivan's. She had suggested a change of scenery, a place where the two of them
could better be alone. The river Serkadian, just a mile west of
Penacles, had what she said were some wonderful idyllic
spots, perfect for people trying to clear their thoughts and
relax. While Jenna had been speaking in terms of sorcery,
which was the supposed reason for the meeting, Aurim was
more interested in the romantic aspects. He already knew that
he wanted the relationship to blossom into something perma-
nent. It was already impossible to think of life without her.

As Aurim rode, he tried to think of the proper things to say
to her. She was a merchant's daughter, someone who had no
doubt grown up hearing clever, fancy words from everyone
around her. He, on the other hand, while somewhat familiar
with the courts of two major kingdoms, had never paid much
attention to protocol and such. Aurim knew few clever words
and even fewer fancy ones. Everything that had so far run
through his mind had sounded clumsy, oafish. His parents

were no help. They had been married so long that even the simplest words seemed to relay meaning between them.

"What can I say to her?" he muttered as he neared the river. Lush trees lined much of the edge. There was a settlement north of here, but far enough away that it was unlikely anyone would disturb them. Here there was nothing but wild fields dotted with yellow and blue flowers and the occasional song of a bird perched high in the trees. A perfect setting, but not if he could not say the proper words.

"What do you want to say?"

Aurim started, not having realized that someone else was nearby. Jenna rode up to him from behind a small copse of trees, smiling all the while. She was clad in a bright blue and red riding outfit, another typical statement of fashion from Gordag-Ai. Her beauty made it even more difficult for him to think. "Jenna! I . . . wasn't . . . you startled me!"

She giggled. "Silly, that's what I wanted to do! I saw you coming and couldn't resist. Now what were you talking about?"

"Nothing. Nothing." Aurim tried not to squirm in the saddle. "Did you find a good place to stop?"

"I did. Just over there by that open part of the riverbank. Have you ever been here before?"

"I've hardly ever been to the river at all. Mostly I've seen the city. We're hardly ever in Penacles for very long."

She did not reply to that. They rode to the location she had chosen and, after taking care of the mounts, sat down on the soft grass. Jenna smoothed her riding outfit, then looked at him expectantly. "Did you do as I suggested?"

Aurim nodded. "I didn't tell anyone what we were doing. I decided to keep my progress a surprise, just like you said."

"They'll be so thrilled when they see." The young woman took hold of his arm and squeezed gently. "Just think what they'll say when you show them how you can perform without losing control of your powers!"

"You've done well, too," he countered. "You've learned quickly for such a short time."

"I think we've got much in common, Aurim. We both just

needed someone who understood our lack of confidence. We needed each other."

He was certain that his face was burning. Jenna had shifted nearer as she had spoken and now only inches separated their bodies. The young mage grew more and more nervous.

"I want you to show me how well you're doing."

"What?"

The merchant's daughter rose without warning. She smiled down at him, then pointed at the river. "I want you to try something for me. Will you?"

Aurim struggled to his feet. "Jenna, I—"

"Look at this!" She cupped her hands before him. A moment later, a ball of blue light formed just above the palms. Jenna stared at it. The ball rose a few inches, then sank to its previous position. It then began to spin around. After a few rotations, Aurim's companion blinked. The sphere faded.

Her success thrilled him. In only a short time she had increased her control over her abilities far more than either of them would have thought possible. "That's wonderful, Jenna!"

"And I owe it all to you!" She hugged him. "Now, let me see how good you've gotten!"

"I—" He did not want to disappoint her. "What do you want me to do?"

"I want you to stop it." She pointed at the huge, rushing river.

The spellcaster was not quite certain that he had heard correctly. "You want me to . . . stop . . . the river?"

"Of course." Jenna moved closer until their bodies touched. She looked up at him, expectant. "I know you can do it. I really do."

Aurim's angle gave him a view of more than her arresting face. Embarrassed, he took a step back. Jenna did not let him completely escape, however. The young woman took hold of him by both arms and would not release him.

What could he do? He could no more refuse her than stop eating. His head tingling, Aurim finally nodded. "All right. I'll give it a try . . . but I can't promise anything."

"I know you can do it!" She leaned up and kissed him.

While he was still recovering, Jenna added, "Remember, you're the son of Cabe Bedlam and the Lady of the Amber! You're more powerful than *either* of them!"

For the first time, he actually believed that. In fact, the more he thought about it, the more his confidence grew. He *could* stop the river. Well, he would not actually stop the entire river, but what he had in mind would prove effective enough.

"What would you think if I created a dry passage through the river?" Aurim saw that he had her interest. "The water would keep flowing . . . it would just . . . um . . . miss the area where the passage would be."

"That would make all the time we've spent together worthwhile." She squeezed his arm, her eyes bright with anticipation. "Are you going to start now?"

In response, Aurim stepped away from her and faced the Serkadian. It seemed simple enough now. He looked beyond the normal world, reaching into one of the levels where the essence of sorcery was visible. The lines were everywhere. Aurim tapped into them, drawing up the power that was both in and around him. He stared at the onrushing water.

I will do it! If he had any lingering doubts, one last glance at her face was enough to douse them. Before his heightened will, even the powerful forces of the river had to obey. Slowly at first, then swifter, a strange depression formed. The depression spread from one side of the riverbank to the other for roughly four or five yards. The water level on both sides of the gap did not alter in the least.

The depression grew deeper and deeper. On each side a wall of swirling water stood firm. As far as the river was concerned, the gap did not exist. That was the way Aurim planned it; he did not want someone either upstream or down growing curious about sudden changes in the water level. Word would then get back to the king and his parents, none of whom would have approved of this spell even if they *would* have been happy that he had finally conquered his uncertainties. He could always tell them later, sometime after he had already proven to them that he was now capable of completely utilizing his vast abilities.

His spell squeezed the last of the water away. The river continued to flow smoothly along, sorcery enabling the water to leap instantly from one side of the depression to the other. Anyone standing between the two magical walls would hardly even get damp. Even though he had been certain that this time he would succeed, Aurim was impressed. Now his parents would be proud of him.

"I was almost afraid to hope," Jenna whispered, "but you did it. You *are* powerful."

"I know it's not quite what you wanted, but—"

"Oh, no!" Her face was aglow. "This is far better than even I expected! You've done excellently, Aurim!"

She wrapped her arms around him and kissed him hard. Aurim felt a tingle run through his body. He almost lost track of the world around him.

Jenna stepped back, eyeing him. Her expression was not one the young mage expected. The merchant's daughter looked slightly confused.

"Is something wrong?" he managed to ask once his voice returned.

"You *are* stronger than I thought." Jenna glanced at the river. "You'd better change that back."

"All right." It was easier to disperse the spell. The process took only the blink of an eye.

"I've outdone myself," his companion whispered.

"What do you mean?"

In response, the attractive young woman seized him again. The kiss that followed made the previous one seem short and indifferent. Again a tingle coursed through Aurim. However, unlike during the last kiss, it did not go away. Instead, it spread, growing stronger at the same time. The world receded. Aurim almost felt as if he were watching himself from outside his body.

Stepping back, Jenna nodded triumphantly. "That's better."

Aurim tried to say something, but found that he could not. It was not that he was still overwhelmed by her passionate kiss, simply that he could not *move*. He tried to raise an arm, but nothing happened. The only thing the sorcerer could do was breathe and blink and he suspected that he was doing so only by permission.

Jenna had to notice his predicament, but instead of helping, she seemed very proud of herself. She also looked a little different. Slightly older, more lush of form, and with a different cast to her features, a cast more akin to those of the southwestern continent, not the northerly climes from which she hailed.

"Raise your arm," she commanded.

To his surprise, he did. Aurim tried to lower it, but his limb resisted.

"Lower it now."

He obeyed. He had to. *What's happening, Jenna?* Aurim wanted to ask. *What did you do to me?*

Perhaps his companion saw the question in his eyes, for she then said, "You're completely mine now, Aurim. Isn't that what you wanted?" She laughed, a harsh, pitiless laugh. "Of course you did. You had no choice. You were stronger-willed than I would've imagined, but I like a challenge. The others were simple in comparison, even if none of them were quite as naive."

Others? She had done this to others? Something registered in his mind. Talk concerning students who had vanished from the school of sorcery his parents had developed in conjunction with the kings of both Penacles and Talak. At least two students, possibly three. Were they the ones that Jenna spoke of?

Jenna continued to change both in form and clothing. Her hair tumbled down to her waist and her features were transformed into something not quite human, as if somewhere in her lineage was included elfin blood. Her curves were more arresting, the kind that Aurim had only dreamed of ever seeing. She clearly knew that he could not help looking over her new shape, for she briefly posed, giving him ample view of her ample charms.

"He's talked about a new step in his plans, you know," Jenna whispered, pressing her body against his again. "Breeding the strongest of his Order to one another to give him a new generation of even more powerful sorcerers." The enchantress leaned forward and kissed him soundly. Had he been able to, Aurim would have pulled himself away in disgust. As stunning as this woman was, her manner, her attitude, revolted him. "I think I like his plan better now, dear, lovely Aurim. You look much more delicious than that perfumed jackal Ponteroy."

The clatter of hooves caught the attention of both although only Jenna, of course, could turn to see who was coming. Aurim's hopes rose. Perhaps the Gryphon had noticed him depart. Maybe his father had even returned.

"They're a little early. I was hoping we could have had a little fun before they arrived." Jenna patted his cheek. "I know you're disappointed, darling. If I'd had my way, we'd have had a bit more time to better get to know one another. Don't worry, though, there'll be plenty of time in Zuu."

Zuu! For the first time the depth of his dilemma struck him. Not only was he a prisoner, but they were going to take him to the land of the horsemen. There was no telling what they planned to do with him once they had him there, although Jenna's words hinted at least of one intention.

The clatter grew louder, then abruptly ceased. A faint wave of dust drifted past Aurim and his captor. The sorcerer wanted so badly to sneeze.

"You're early, Captain."

"Not by my reckoning, Saress. I'm right on time."

Saress. Aurim stared at the sinister temptress. Everything about the woman he had been infatuated with had been a lie even down to her name.

"Did you think I might get carried away? Was that it?" she teased. "Come, Captain, you know Lanith has both my love and loyalty, which is why you should be more careful what you say."

"It isn't that," the unseen officer suddenly protested, not nearly so arrogant now. Saress obviously had much influence with his master. "I just know how you like to be thorough. Sometimes that demands too much of . . . your quarry."

Saress winked at the captive spellcaster. "I don't think that there's much beyond this one, although we'll have to experiment further another time. Is our route planned?"

"Yes, we can skirt just south of the Dagora Forest. It's the most direct route."

"South of the Dagora Forest. Are you suggesting we ride through the Barren Lands?" The enchantress did not seem at all pleased.

Aurim heard the horse move forward. Out of the corner of his eye, he caught partial sight of a brown stallion and its rider, a tall figure clad in a simple brown outfit with a riding cloak. Strands of blond hair dangled from the rider's hood, but his features were otherwise obscured. "It seems the best way. The place is no longer desolate. Why should we avoid such an unpopulated stretch when it gives us the straightest route home?"

"Why, indeed?" Saress was still not pleased. Suddenly her gaze shifted to Aurim. "Then again, why take so long to get back to Zuu? Why not make use of new options . . . or at least test them out?"

"What're you talking about, sorceress?"

"He's strong, Captain. He's everything we thought he was and more. He parted the river to impress me, the dear boy."

For a moment the soldier was silent. Then, "He did that?"

"And I, for one, think he's capable of so very much more." The enchantress stared Aurim in the eyes. "Aren't you, Aurim? All you needed was a boost of confidence and I gave that to you with a few subtle spells and more than a few loving looks." She laughed lightly. "Yes, I think you can do it."

Aurim knew what she wanted of him, and knew that now he could probably give it to her. He did have the concentration and confidence, both of which had been built up by a serpent in human form. Yet if he was so powerful, how could he have been so easily snared? Why could he not escape?

It's not always a matter of power, his father had once said. *It's also a matter of using your power in the most effective manner.*

Saress was not as strong as he; he knew that. However, she had a far better grasp of her abilities than he did and she had used them to her best advantage.

"Gather the men, Captain. Our dear new companion is

going to take us back to Zuu in the best dramatic fashion. Lanith will love it!"

"You're not serious! I'm not going to—"

"I've had enough argument." Saress waved her hand in the direction of the soldier, who stiffened in the saddle. "You'll get your voice back after I've proved my point." To Aurim, she added, "You will listen to everything I say, won't you, darling?"

To his surprise, he answered her. "I will."

"That's a good boy. This is what I want of you. You'll take everyone here—the two of us, my friend the captain, and his three playmates *and* all the horses—all the way to the royal grounds of Zuu."

Again Aurim spoke against his will. "I've never been to Zuu. I don't know the kingdom."

She took him by the arm. "Don't you worry, Aurim. I will give you a destination."

Reaching up with her free hand, she touched his temple. Instantly, the image of an open courtyard materialized in his thoughts. A huge stable covered one side of the yard and the tall walls of what had to be the king's palace or castle made up much of the remaining view. In the walls were carved the images of men on horseback. A banner fluttering from the top of the stable bore the head of a charger.

"Is that good enough?" Saress asked him.

"Yes." It was. He wanted to deny it, but could not.

"Then take us there now, my darling Aurim."

Unable to resist, Aurim concentrated. He was finally the sorcerer he had dreamed of becoming . . . and now his dream had become his nightmare.

CHAPTER VI

It was more than three hours before Cabe stirred, three hours in which Darkhorse could do nothing but think and glare at the magical grass.

"Darkhorse?" Cabe's voice was weak, but in this quiet place carried well.

"Cabe! By the Void! I had begun to fear that you would never wake!"

"Dark—where are we?"

"In what was once termed the Barren Lands!"

"The Barren Lands?" The mage stared, taking in the trees, the birds, and, most of all, the endless sea of grass. He nodded. "Yes, I can feel it. These were the Barren Lands once. I've been here a couple of times since it changed; I'd recognize the sensations I feel anywhere."

The shadow steed felt nothing, but did not question his companion. He was simply overjoyed that Cabe was awake and well. At least, he *hoped* Cabe was well. "Are you all right, then?"

The human touched his side. "I think so." He shut his eyes for several seconds, concentrating. "Yes. Yes, I am. Thank you."

"I . . . I did not mend you, Cabe."

"No? Then who did?"

"It was . . . a female. A sorceress. In Zuu you once knew her as Tori."

"Tori?" Cabe's expression went from complete befuddle-ment to dawning recognition. "Tori. *She* was here? She mended my injuries? I don't remember anything other than escaping that trap."

"And that was done with her aid, too, Cabe. She assaulted it from the outside. Then, after you caused the earth to rise up and hinder some of our pursuers—"

"I did that?" The sorcerer shook his head. "I don't even re-call doing that. I think I may remember holding on to you for dear life."

"She called to us. Told us to ride in a certain direction. I did. A blink hole materialized directly before us, leaving me little chance to avoid it. When we finally exited, though, it was to arrive here . . . several hours later."

"Several . . ." Cabe looked up at the sun. "I didn't even pay attention to the fact that it's setting! Gwen! She'll be worried! Did you contact her?"

Darkhorse could scarcely look at his friend. "I feared to do so. There was good reason—"

"I think I understand. You can explain everything else later, then. We have to get back to Penacles." As Cabe started to rise, he seemed to lose his footing. The sorcerer immediately sat back down. "Maybe I'd better do this a little slower. Looks like I needed the rest after all. Thank you for watching over me, Darkhorse."

"I am sorry I could do no more. Tori said it was wise to let you rest and I agreed."

The spellcaster rose again, this time with more care. "We'll have to talk about her and everything else *after* we reassure Gwen and the others." He blinked. "I didn't even think to ask you how you were doing. That spell trap seemed designed for you."

"It was. As you said, though, that is something else we can speak of after we assuage the fears of your wife, Cabe. As for me . . ." The eternal rose up on his hind legs. The grass spread away from him as far as it could. Darkhorse laughed as he dropped down on all fours again. "I am Darkhorse! How could I be anything but perfect?"

Cabe did not question his answer although it was clear that

he did not entirely believe him. Darkhorse was still a bit weak, but not nearly so much as before. He had recovered enough that racing across the Dragonrealm would be a fairly simple task. They could be in Penacles just before sunset. Still soon enough as far as he was concerned.

The sorcerer mounted, groaning slightly in the process. "Maybe it would be best if we just rode back, Darkhorse. I don't think that I could stomach another sudden shift in location just yet. Is that all right with you?"

"Did the female miss some injury? Are you ill?"

"No, nothing like that." Cabe positioned himself for the ride. "It seemed to me that it would just be a good idea."

"As you wish."

"It really is a beautiful, peaceful land now," commented the human. "I'm surprised it's still empty. I'd think anyone would love to settle in a place like this."

Darkhorse held off comment. The sooner he was away from this land, the better. The grass still seemed too interested in the pair, constantly touching both of them whenever possible.

The grass, though, was hardly a threat compared to what they had already faced . . . and *would* face soon enough again. Lanith was indeed a danger to the fragile peace of the Dragonrealm if he had such power to control. Even Darkhorse was willing to admit that anyone who could set such a snare was a foe with which to be reckoned.

An intelligent force . . .

There was indeed much that they had to discuss after their return to Penacles.

Lady Gwendolyn Bedlam stood at the entrance to the Gryphon's palace, either relieved to see them or ready to throw something, Darkhorse was not certain which. Only when the sorceress finally met them at the bottom of the palace steps did her mood become more evident.

"Cabe! You're all right! Why didn't you contact us?" Her expression darkened. "What have you been up to?"

The sorcerer slid off Darkhorse's back. The eternal tried to quietly step back, the better to escape the brunt of any explosion, verbal or magical. He had a healthy respect for Cabe's wife.

Cabe tried to calm her. "It took longer than we expected to investigate the barony. We had to be careful, too, what with the possibility that any of Lanith's mages might be in the vicinity. I'm sorry we had to keep you anxiously waiting, Gwen."

Her gaze darted from her husband to the shadow steed. "Is that all? Nothing terrible happened?" She folded her arms. "I don't think that I believe you."

"I assure you, Lady Bedlam—"

"Never mind, Darkhorse." Cabe sighed. "I can't lie to you, Gwen. I don't know why I tried to make it sound as if nothing had happened. We'd have to tell you everything soon enough, anyway. Something did happen. I don't even know all of it. There's much that Darkhorse still has to tell *me*."

"Then the best thing for all of us," declared the voice of the king of Penacles, "is to retire to my chambers and discuss this in privacy."

The Gryphon stood several steps above them, having arrived so silently that even the eternal had not noticed him. He was perhaps one of the few creatures who could consistently surprise Darkhorse, although, to be fair, Darkhorse was one of the few creatures capable of consistently making the monarch uneasy.

It did not take Cabe very long to relate his story. The others listened carefully, Gwen's expression turning darker as the tale of the spell trap unfolded. By the time the sorcerer was finished, her hands had folded into such tight fists that her knuckles were bone white.

"You nearly died, Cabe! If not for Darkhorse—"

"It wasn't Darkhorse, darling. Not exactly."

"If I may . . ." The Gryphon poured himself a goblet of wine. He had made certain that his guests had been given both food and drink, especially the still-weary sorcerer. The king raised the goblet and sipped, his features momentarily shifting to that of a handsome gray-haired man with patrician features. The Gryphon could completely shift form for long periods at a time, but preferred the one with which he was most familiar. "Let us simply hear Darkhorse. Then we can take it from there."

The Bedlams nodded. Darkhorse debated leaving out some aspects of the adventure, especially the part concerning their feminine rescuer, but knew that Cabe would never allow him to do so. That in mind, he threw himself into the telling, making certain that no part of it, however small, was left out. Darkhorse even related his own sensations during the struggle in the sinister trap and his mistrust of their rescuer afterward.

His mention of Tori brought forth a variety of reactions from the trio. The Gryphon looked merely curious. Gwendolyn Bedlam kept her expression neutral but her narrowing eyes were a clear indication of what she thought of the mysterious woman's interest in her husband. As for Cabe, he first looked uncomfortable, then thoughtful, especially when the eternal mentioned that their benefactor had used a false name.

"I wonder who she is?" he commented after Darkhorse had finished.

"I would very much like to find out." Lady Bedlam gazed at her husband, who wisely kept silent.

"The identity of this goodwilled enchantress aside," interjected the Gryphon, "what she and the lord of the Dagora Forest have said worries me greatly. What sinister force is it that Lanith has at his beck and call? A mage of great power? Why is he or she not leading the horse king's Magical Order, then? That position, according to my reports, is still filled by a woman named Saress, who shares more than her sorcerous abilities with Lanith."

"I had a thought earlier, Lord Gryphon." Darkhorse shifted uncomfortably. "I thought that perhaps it might be Shade."

"Shade is dead, demon steed. You saw to that yourself. He is truly and honestly dead. Do you think that he could have kept himself hidden for so long? That was never Shade's way, good or evil."

Cabe agreed. "Besides, you searched nearly every inch of the Dragonrealm. Shade was a Vraad, a last lingerer from their time. He had the most distinctive magical trace of any creature in this world, including you. One of us in this room would have noticed his presence."

Darkhorse did not entirely agree, knowing better than anyone how powerful the warlock had been, but he acquiesced. "I do not really think it was Shade, but I felt the need to mention it. However, it could very well be a Dragon King! Zuu is not that far from the domain of the Crystal Dragon . . . and none of us know much of his doings."

"No." Cabe's response was quick. "No, it's not the Crystal Dragon . . . take my word for that."

"But Darkhorse does make a good point, Cabe Bedlam. What about the others? Storm and Black to be precise." The Gryphon stroked his savage beak. "Better yet, Sssaleese. Yes, his fledgling federation would benefit if attention was drawn from it for a time by everyone's interest in Lanith's crusade. A treaty between the pair would also aid him. Sssaleese needs matériel, food. The Dragon Kings haven't been very happy with his presence and I know at least one has pushed Emperor Kyl to take some action against him. Kyl's held off. Sssaleese is strong enough to create a situation. The refugees from the broken drake clans believe in him. He gave them something that the Silver Dragon promised but then failed to deliver. Kyl is surely keeping that in mind."

"Sssaleese may be involved with Lanith, but I somehow don't think he's this force." Cabe sighed. "The Green Dragon didn't speak of the force as if it were one of his own kind. He talked as if it were something he could not identify. I think if it was Sssaleese, the lord of Dagora would've discovered that. The drake lord was honestly uncertain."

"So what we are left with is what we had at the beginning. A mysterious, intelligent magical force that may or may not be related to Lanith's Order of sorcerers." The king rose and began pacing back and forth like an anxious cat. "There were things I came across in the empire of the Aramites. Age-old forces left by the founding race of our world. I know that some of them *could* reach this land if they desired, but I've never noticed any sign. Lanith might also have made some pact with the Seekers or the Quel, but I doubt either the avians or the underdwellers would work with any human long."

Gwendolyn Bedlam cleared her throat. "Perhaps you should consult the Libraries."

"At this point, Lady Bedlam, that might be more trouble than it's worth. I wouldn't even know what to look under . . . intelligent evil forces? Mysterious entities? Even if an answer was in there, it would be in some godforsaken riddle or poem that we'd have to piece together. I don't have the patience for the Libraries of Penacles right now. However, I do have access to some other volumes that the last Dragon King here gathered during his reign. There may be something in them."

"There might also be something among the books and scrolls at the Manor," suggested Cabe. "Something that perhaps will help us detect and define this force without it noticing."

"So it seems we now know our next step." The Gryphon eyed Darkhorse. "You have no idea where this enchantress vanished to, do you? She's given us some information; I do not see why she just doesn't join us."

Cabe's mate did not look at all pleased with the suggestion, but only Darkhorse noticed. The shadow steed explained how she had vanished without leaving any discernible trace.

"Her powers seem almost as mysterious as this force working for Lanith," the lionbird commented. "Someday we'll find out more about her, but that can wait."

The Bedlams rose together. "We should return to the Manor as soon as possible, then." Cabe looked for confirmation from his wife before continuing. "We'll keep in contact whether we discover anything or not."

"I have agents out in some of the surrounding regions . . . and some other resources that I've yet to tap. Between all of us, we should be able to uncover some answers, Cabe."

"I, too, will do my best to ferret out some answers." Other than hunting for the enchantress, however, Darkhorse did not know what he could do short of invading Zuu. He sincerely doubted that either Cabe or the Gryphon would appreciate an effort like that, though.

"Aurim!" Gwen's outburst caught them all by surprise. "I nearly forgot about Aurim! We have to tell him what's happening so that he doesn't wonder what's happened to us!"

"Well, that's easily taken care of, darling. Where is he?"

"Not in the palace. I think . . . I think he's with the young woman named Jenna."

"She has been staying at Gullivan's, Cabe," the eternal added. "Shall I go retrieve him?"

"No, I'll simply link with him." The master sorcerer closed his eyes, but the look of confidence on his plain features gradually shifted to one of uncertainty and puzzlement. Finally breaking off his attempt, Cabe glanced at his wife. "That's odd. I don't sense him anywhere."

"That cannot be!" Aurim's mother shut her own eyes. After several long, silent seconds, she, too, gave up. "He should be in the city. He should be."

"He may be shielding himself from us, darling. After all, he probably wants privacy."

"Perhaps . . ."

Darkhorse stepped forward. "I will look for him, friends! It is likely, as you say, that he wanted privacy. Have no fear! I can cover Penacles much faster than either of you. You may return to the Manor if you so desire. When I have your son in hand, we shall return there."

"What do you think, Gwen?"

With some reluctance, she nodded. "Thank you, Darkhorse. I'm sure it's nothing, but with all that happened to Cabe and you, I cannot help but worry a little."

"Perfectly understandable!" Already the shadow steed wanted to be on his way. His preference was always action over discussion. Now, at least, he could do something important, however minuscule it was compared to the overall situation concerning Zuu. Darkhorse had no doubt that Aurim and Jenna were somewhere nearby, acting as all young human adults seemed to during the early stages of a relationship. That did not at all mean that he condoned the younger Bedlam's carelessness, however. Aurim's position and abilities demanded that he not hide his presence from his family even in a kingdom where they were very respected. There was always some risk.

"Please emphasize that we would appreciate it if he could come home immediately. We'll need everyone's help, including his and Valea's."

"I shall do so, Cabe. Have no fear!" He reared and, as they watched, vanished from the palace.

The ebony stallion rematerialized directly inside Gullivan's. He had thought of materializing outside, but that would have brought too much attention to him. Darkhorse hoped that none of the innkeeper's customers would take offense at his sudden arrival. Anyone who stayed at Gullivan's was warned about the possible sudden appearance of spellcasters associated with the Bedlams' school. Of course, nothing could prepare them for Darkhorse, but he hoped for the best.

The same serving girl who had been frightened so easily the first time took one look at him and screamed. Gullivan burst out of the kitchen, eyes wide. When he saw the cause of the scream, the human sighed.

"Oh, it's you, Darkhorse."

"My apologies, Gullivan!" The eternal glanced around. Two gaily-clad merchants from Gordag-Ai had been discussing business matters with the pair from Irillian and another pair likely from Penacles. The men from Gordag-Ai stared openmouthed while the others simply stared. One of the men from Penacles was trying to hide a smirk. He had evidently seen Darkhorse in the past and now was enjoying the foreigners' shock.

The innkeeper hurried over to Darkhorse. "How may I help you? Are you looking for Master Aurim, by any chance?"

"That I am, Gullivan! Very astute of you! Is he here?"

"I don't believe so. The young woman isn't here. That much I know. She stepped out earlier and hasn't returned."

"No?" This made Darkhorse's task much more complex, but he was undaunted. "Do you have any idea where she went?"

"Not me, but I'll ask in back. Maybe one of the girls or someone else saw her after I did." Gullivan bowed briefly and quickly retreated into the back room. A moment later, he emerged again, scratching his chin.

"Any word?"

"My son says that when he stepped outside earlier, he saw the girl riding off from the stable. She looked like she was packed for a trip."

"A trip?" What sort of foolishness had the young pair gotten into? If Jenna had packed for a trip, then it was likely that Aurim and she were meeting outside the city, possibly for a more private encounter. While the eternal did not begrudge his young friend such privacy, Aurim should have informed someone if he was leaving the safety of the city walls.

"Did your son say which way she rode?"

"She went north, but she could've easily turned another direction later on. Is there something wrong, Darkhorse?"

"Not as far as I know. Just two young ones with their heads lost in the clouds, I suppose." The eternal paused. "Tell me, Gullivan, where outside the city walls would a pair of young friends go to meet? What I mean is—"

The veteran soldier smiled. "I know what you mean, friend. I've watched the lad and lass. If I wanted privacy and I was willing to ride a little, I'd probably head toward the Serkadian. There's some lovely spots out there if you're interested in setting the mood."

"The river?"

Gullivan's smile faded slightly. "The river. It's very scenic in places. If one wanted a place to meet a young lady, there's some nice places along the river's edge, especially where the flowers are in bloom. Ladies like that sort of thing."

"Do they? Then I think that I shall go there and look." He dipped his head toward the innkeeper. "My gratitude, Gullivan, and if Aurim should return, please tell him that matters require his presence back at the Manor. Make certain that he knows that it is urgent."

"I'll be glad to do so, Darkhorse. If I may . . . is there something wrong?"

Darkhorse backed away a few steps from the innkeeper. "It is nothing to concern yourself with, Gullivan. Now if you will excuse me . . ."

He vanished from the inn while the proprietor was still nodding, rematerializing a moment later near the western gate of the city. Two sentries on duty inside the wall leaped to attack position before they realized just what faced them. A family passing through the gate froze in terror, the man and one of the three small children crying out. Behind them, another man on a horse struggled to regain control of his frightened steed.

With some effort, the guards restored order. The braver of the pair approached the eternal slowly, saluting. "My Lord Darkhorse! I—we didn't recognize you at first! Greetings! I am . . . uh . . . Haplin! May I ask for what reason you honor us?"

"Easy, Haplin! Forgive me for my sudden arrival! I am in search of someone! Are you familiar with Aurim Bedlam, son of the sorcerer Cabe Bedlam?"

"I've only seen him from a distance, my lord."

"Enough to recognize him if he passed through these gates?"

Haplin frowned, then glanced at the other sentry, who shrugged. "We've seen no one like that, Lord Darkhorse. Just the usual merchants, farmers, moving families, and riffraff."

The shadow steed caught the second man glancing at a young woman accompanying an elderly couple into the city. After pondering for a moment, Darkhorse decided to try a different query. "Have you perhaps seen a young merchant woman?" He described Jenna as best he could, attempting to emphasize those features that the guards might best recall. "It would have been earlier this day."

"I remember her," called the second sentry. "She headed straight west, which I thought kind of funny since when I asked where she was going she said 'home to Gordag-Ai.'"

"Indeed?" That struck Darkhorse as strange as it had the guard. Perhaps Jenna intended on returning to her homeland after her meeting with Aurim, but the eternal could not see the young woman making the journey all by herself. He also did not think that after the attraction the pair had shown for one another that she would separate herself from the young sorcerer that easily.

Something did not sit right. Darkhorse's uneasiness grew.

"I thank you for your time, friends!" The ebony stallion reared, which immediately caused a path to clear for him. Haplin saluted, but Darkhorse was already past him. Now more than ever, he wanted to reach the river quickly.

There was still no trace of Aurim. The boy had shielded

himself well. As for this Jenna, what little power he had sensed in her was not sufficient to track her down. That meant that Darkhorse would have to physically search the area until he located the prodigal pair. It was the only way he could be certain that he would find them.

The short distance to the riverbank was no difficult hurdle, but the winding, foliage-rich landscape threatened to be. Two young lovers would do their best to find a secluded location, of which there were far too many from the looks of things. The shadow steed paused, then turned south. As he traveled, Darkhorse studied the ground for recent tracks. He also continued to search on another plane, seeking any momentary lapse, any accidental sorcerous trace left behind by Aurim.

A short time later, he at last found some clues. The tracks could have belonged to anyone's mount, but he sensed also a slim hint of sorcery in the vicinity. Darkhorse followed the mild trace, noting that the tracks also led in that direction. Ahead of him was what looked to be a perfect location for his quarry, a quiet, private opening near the riverside. Colorful flowers even decorated the area.

He heard nothing but the birds and the rushing water, but that did not mean that the two were not nearby. It could be that they had even noticed his presence and were keeping silent. The shadow steed hoped that was the case although he doubted it.

A moment later his fears were confirmed. The area was empty. Still, Darkhorse was certain that they *had* been here. The longer he remained, the more he felt the past presence of Cabe's son. Aurim had performed sorcery of some sort, sorcery of a high degree. The trace grew stronger the nearer Darkhorse moved to the river.

What had the lad done? Had something happened to both of them because of some spell Aurim had been trying to cast?

Darkhorse shuddered, then rethought matters. The traces that remained of the younger Bedlam's attempt were too delicate to be the by-products of a magical disaster. Whatever spell Aurim had cast, he had completed without problem.

Which brought the eternal back to the question of where the two young humans were now.

He glanced down, seeking tracks that might indicate the pair had ridden off elsewhere. His eyes widened as he found the two sets of hooves met at least three more.

What company joined them? Bandits? Even at his worst, Aurim would be able to handle three bandits! All he would have had to do was reestablish his link with his parents.

Oddly, when Darkhorse looked for the newcomers' path of departure, he found nothing. According to the prints, the strangers had ridden up to the horses of the young pair and then all of them, Aurim and Jenna included, had simply vanished. There were no tracks leading away.

Doubling back, the eternal checked once more. Tracks led to the spot, but no tracks led away. Studying the river, Darkhorse wondered if perhaps they had somehow managed to cross it. Perhaps that was what Aurim had done, created a path or bridge across the river.

Had a fisherman been walking near the riverbank he might have noticed a wondrous sight. Unhindered by normal limitations, the huge, ebony stallion trotted across the vast Serkadian, his hooves not even touching the swift water. However, there were no tracks on the other side. Darkhorse searched for quite some distance in either direction along the bank, but found nothing, not even a trace of sorcerous activity.

He returned to the original site, mind racing. The evidence did not bode well. Aurim was nowhere to be found. Jenna had told the sentry that she would be returning to Gordag-Ai even though it was clear that she had indeed met with the young sorcerer. At least three riders had joined them and then the entire party had simply disappeared.

Disappeared. Spellcaster's work. Yet, Aurim's trace was the only strong one . . . although there was a very faint hint of something else. It reminded him vaguely of . . . of the female sorcerer who had rescued Cabe and him from the spell trap.

Something has happened to Aurim! His parents must be told!

The moment Darkhorse contemplated telling them, however, he found himself unable to move. The Bedlams were back at the Manor in the midst of important research, trying to puzzle out this sinister force working for King Lanith. By the time he retrieved them, there was no telling how cold the trail might be. It behooved him to try to track down the missing sorcerer first.

If they had not forded the river or ridden from this location, then the only logical assumption could be that someone had transported them away. That would require power and the longer the distance the group had to be transported the more power the sorcerer would need to expend. Jenna had not struck him as having that much strength—although Darkhorse was beginning to suspect that she had more than his cursory inspection had revealed—which left Aurim himself the logical choice.

But why would the lad aid his own captors . . . if that is who they were? The evidence was circumstantial for the most part, but the shadow steed was fairly certain that he was correct in his assumption. Now he needed to do something about it.

If Aurim had cast such a great spell, then there had to be some trace of his path. Travel by sorcery seemed instantaneous to most people, but the truth was that the spell still occasionally left a slight trace. At the very least, if Darkhorse was able to detect such a trace he might be able to follow the party.

It was a long shot even for him. Only because of the intensity of the young spellcaster's power did the eternal think that he might have a chance.

Steeling himself, Darkhorse projected his mind in a dozen directions. No human mage could have imitated his efforts, for their minds were restricted to a few petty planes of existence while the shadow steed, being a creature of the endless, empty Void, was open to many, many levels. However, he rarely looked beyond the ones known to most spellcasters of this world; there was always the danger of permanently fragmenting his mind. He was willing to risk some of that danger now, however, if only it would aid him in finding Cabe's son.

I allowed this relationship to grow . . . I allowed this to happen . . . I am at fault . . .

Again and again his probing failed. Somehow, Aurim Bedlam had gained such control over his abilities that he had used scarcely more than the slightest amount of power necessary to complete the transportation spell. There was no sign of a blink hole nor any evidence of any other method of magical travel. Nonetheless, Darkhorse did not give up. He could not. There had to be some sign, some bit of—

And there it was. The trace was so very minuscule, only detectable on the very edge of human magical senses. Neither the elder Bedlams nor the Gryphon would have likely noticed its presence. Darkhorse had already missed it twice. Only because of his stubbornness had he finally taken notice. It was too faint for him to decipher which direction the party had traveled, but not too faint for him to follow using a spell of his own.

Without hesitation, Darkhorse opened a blink hole. There were other, swifter modes of magical travel, but because he was not certain what lay at the other end, the eternal wanted to have that extra moment in which to prepare himself. He suspected he knew just where Aurim had been taken. Now he could verify it.

The hole floated before him, a wide oval rip in reality. Darkhorse took one last glance around him, then entered.

What existed within the blink hole was a question even the shadow steed could not completely answer. He stood upon a path floating through a vaguely seen dimension of mist. In some ways it reminded him of the Void, but where now the light mist floated around him, in his home there would have been nothing but a great, bright emptiness.

Darkhorse moved along the path, knowing that he had already crossed much of the distance between Penacles and his destination. He had created this blink hole carefully, forming it so that with his power he could manipulate its time span. He would reach the end when he chose and not a moment before.

The path before him grew more distinct, a sign that Darkhorse had nearly reached his goal. He slowed. The blink hole was not supposed to open until he reached the very end. The shadow steed tried to gather his thoughts. There might be a dozen different threats beyond the hole, but Darkhorse was prepared. For Aurim's sake, he had to be.

The shadow steed willed the gap to open.

Nothing happened.

Perplexed, Darkhorse tried again. The results were the same. The path ended, but no doorway formed.

He turned back. Something had blocked the way. He would have to return to Penacles and plan anew.

Only . . . now it was impossible to see the path back. All that lay behind Darkhorse was mist. Endless mist. The ebony stallion tried to trace his route, but without the path, he had nowhere to go.

He was trapped. Someone had set another snare, catching Darkhorse because of his own arrogance and overconfidence.

This time, there was no one to save him.

CHAPTER VII

Zuu.

Aurim had often dreamed of visiting the land of the horse people, but not as a helpless prisoner of the king and his vile, treacherous witch. He had no one to blame but himself, though. His father would have seen through her disguise, of that the younger Bedlam was certain. Only someone as simple and naive as Aurim would have fallen prey to Saress's masquerade.

As if sensing his thoughts, the enchantress turned and smiled at him. The two of them had been waiting here for the past half hour. Saress seemed not to care; whatever the king wanted her to do, she did. If he wanted her to wait, she waited. If he wanted her to trick and capture potential sorcerers for him, the woman leaped to obey. Worse, if what Saress had said of King Lanith's future plans was true . . .

"Patience, darling. He'll be along soon. Just . . . enjoy the sights."

She meant herself, of course. Saress was clad in a thin, low-cut outfit made entirely of leather. It covered little more than necessary. Aurim knew that it was a variation on the traditional jerkin and pants of the horse king's guards, but Saress had turned it from a piece of history to something with a much darker purpose. It was supposed to be seductive, and under other circumstances, he knew that it probably would have captured his full attention, but after what the witch had done to him, Aurim could only look upon her with revulsion.

Despite the spell that held him in stasis, Aurim still had use of his eyes. Rather than glare at his captor, the sorcerer chose to again study the room. This was supposed to be the throne room of the kings of Zuu, but it more resembled the interior of some old keep built in the days when Lanith's ancestors finally decided to give up their nomadic lives. Likely it was a reminder of that time. More than one palace had been built on the site of previous royal buildings. Perhaps King Lanith's throne room was all that remained of the original house of the first chosen monarch of the new kingdom.

There had been alterations since then, of course. High up the walls, someone had added barred windows. Someone else had added a number of torch holders shaped as astonishingly lifelike armored hands. They appeared to line the walls on both sides from end to end, but unable to move his head, Aurim could not be certain.

The dais before them was of the same dark granite as the walls, which meant that it, too, had probably been part of the original structure. The throne, however, looked new. Carved from what Aurim recognized as rare elfwood, it stood taller than even one of the Dragon Kings. The legs had been shaped to resemble those of horses, even down to the hooves. The armrests were the sleek backs of racing chargers, whose ferocious heads seemed ready to snap at anyone who approached too closely.

Forming the upper back of the chair were twin steeds who reared toward one another, forehooves clashing. Underneath them, a pair of swords pointing earthward completed the back. The entire throne had been painted a dusky brown, the most popular shade of the famous horses of Zuu. Only the leather seat of the chair gave it any variation.

It was the ugliest piece of furniture that Aurim had ever seen.

A door behind the throne suddenly opened. Saress immediately went down on one knee and, to his dismay, so did Aurim. A full dozen warriors of the king's special guard marched out in perfect order, then split into two equal groups.

The warriors, evenly divided between male and female, lined up across from one another, forming a corridor of muscle extending from the dais to the enchantress and her captive.

Only then did the horse king enter.

A chill wind seemed to precede him, as did a darkness that no one else in the chamber noticed save Aurim Bedlam. Despite the many lit torches, the illumination suddenly appeared muted. Aurim shivered, a spontaneous reaction that not only surprised him, but pleased him as well. The reaction had been independent of Saress's control. That meant that her hold on him was not perfect.

Lanith was the tallest of the horse people that Aurim had so far seen. He was older and graying, yes, but hardly soft and weak. The horse king's features reminded him of a mountain chiseled by time and weather. Not handsome, but impressive. Lanith was clad in garments akin to those of his guard, an outfit that hearkened back to generations of fierce nomadic warriors. He might have stepped through the centuries himself, so menacing did he appear. The shadow and the chill added to the effect, which made the sorcerer wonder if their presence was planned. Aurim tried to probe the darkness, but found his probe deflected by some magical force.

With no further ceremony, the horse king seated himself, the darkness settling several feet above him. He glanced first at the captured spellcaster, then at Saress. A thin smile spread across his features.

"My love!" the enchantress called much too loudly. "I have for you a very special prize!"

Perhaps it was only Aurim's imagination, but he thought the monarch of Zuu was slightly amused by Saress's obvious attempt to seduce him with her outfit. "I'd imagine he must be, considering that you were supposed to remain in Penacles for another week. How good is this one? Better than the last?"

She rose, each movement an invitation to her king. Aurim, who was forced to rise with her, was fairly certain that Lanith had accepted more than a few of her invitations in the past, enough so that now she was the puppet and he the master. "Better than any of them! Better than any you hoped to add to the ranks! I have *him*."

"Him?" The horse king straightened, studying the golden-haired mage closely. "Rich clothing for a student. A head of hair that almost looks like. . . ." The air of disinterest faded. Lanith grew eager. "He's Aurim Bedlam!"

"You see? I said that I could get him and I did, my love!"

"Yes, at last." King Lanith stared at Aurim, finally frowning. "But if he's so powerful, then how could you take him so easily?"

Saress leaned back, her body momentarily pressing against her victim as she touched Aurim's chin in mock tenderness. "A young man in love is apt to think of little else. It was easy to wrap him around my finger and lead him along. Power without thought is easy prey."

"So it is." Because Saress had her head turned toward Aurim, only the captive saw that Lanith's gaze briefly shifted toward his pet sorceress as he spoke. "But is he that powerful?"

Saress abandoned her captive, joining the king at his throne. She draped herself over his left shoulder, allowing his eyes to linger on her form before pointing at Aurim. "He can create passages through rivers, passages wide enough to cross an army! His might is such that he transported five of us, including our *mounts,* all the way from the Serkadian River to your royal courtyard!"

"Yes, I heard about that." King Lanith's eyes burned into Aurim's. "I could make much use of someone as strong as you, young sorcerer. Would you serve me willingly if I paid you well? You could have almost everything you wanted . . ." His hand rested on Saress's own.

Once more, Aurim Bedlam's mouth moved of its own accord. "I would try to escape the moment I could."

The tall warrior almost stood. His gaze turned darker. "Is that so? You arrogant, pampered little colt—"

"He must answer our questions, my king," the enchantress interjected. "My spell requires it of him."

"Has he no will of his own, then?"

"Only in the privacy of his mind. The rest belongs to u—to you, Lanith."

"To me." The horse king leaned toward Saress. "Make him perform . . . some trick."

"As you command." Saress smiled at Aurim. "Show him your little harlequins, darling."

Parlor tricks. He was being forced to perform parlor tricks for his captors. Rage overtook fear. Aurim did not want to perform for them like a trained animal. He was a free man and a sorcerer. His arms rose halfway, but the young spellcaster tried to keep them from rising farther. He would *not* perform.

His arms stayed where they were. Aurim could not lower them, but neither did they continue to move on their own. In one sense it was a stalemate; in another, it was a grand victory for him. Saress's spell did not have complete control over him after all.

Unfortunately, King Lanith also noticed his success. "The boy's not obeying. I thought he had to do every thing we said, Saress."

"He does!" Seeming more embarrassed than fearful, the sorceress abandoned her position and stalked toward Aurim. The look in her eyes was anything but seductive now. Her prisoner had succeeded in making her appear foolish before the man she obviously adored. "I gave you a command. Do the little trick with the harlequins!"

His arms rose an inch higher, then settled back to their previous positions. Aurim smiled triumphantly, then smiled more when he realized that he now had control of his mouth again.

Saress slapped his cheek before realizing that her captive was now partially mobile. The moment she understood her danger, the temptress immediately stepped back.

"What's wrong, Saress?"

"Nothing that I can't deal with, Lanith." Despite her tone of assurance, though, the expression on her face, an expression only Aurim could see at the moment, was anything but confident.

His hopes continued to rise. She still had enough control to prevent him from speaking or casting his own spells, but that control was rapidly fading. Soon he would be able to take matters into his own hands.

"Naughty boy! No man leaves Saress!" The woman thrust her left hand toward him.

Aurim felt a crackle of energy surge through him that briefly stole from him the movement and force of will that he had regained. The sorceress smiled at Aurim again, but with renewed effort, the golden-haired mage swept away her second spell and further weakened her first. Now he had enough control of his arms to slowly move them as he desired. Aurim still could not summon enough strength to cast a spell, especially one to transport him away from this evil place, but he only needed a few moments more.

Beyond Saress, King Lanith did a peculiar thing. He leaned farther to one side and raised his head as if listening to someone nearby . . . only there was nothing but the sinister darkness. Then the monarch of Zuu looked again at Aurim.

"Cease your efforts, Saress."

"Lanith—"

"You're dismissed. That goes for the rest of you as well. Leave now."

The guards looked as perplexed as the enchantress. Aurim, too. What made the man think that he could face a sorcerer of Aurim Bedlam's ability? It would only be a few moments before the spellcaster was free. Better that the horse king depart with his witch in tow than face his former captive's wrath.

Despite her obvious reluctance, Saress was the first to obey. The guards followed slowly, each of them glancing from the captured sorcerer to their lord. At the doorway, the enchantress paused while the warriors filed out. Only when she was the last left did Saress finally depart. Even then, her eyes lingered on King Lanith until she was out of sight.

Throughout it all, Aurim continued to struggle for freedom. His arms were his. Then his entire body began to respond, slowly, then faster. He was only seconds from complete control, seconds from escape.

All the while, the horse king merely sat on the throne and watched.

The last vestiges of Saress's spell shattered. Aurim briefly paused, wondering whether he ought to do something about the king of Zuu. The man had ordered his kidnapping. He was ready to begin a great war. Surely if Aurim had the opportunity to capture Lanith, then he had to try.

The sorcerer glared at the figure on the throne. "King Lanith, you should've run."

His adversary looked anything but fearful. The king slowly rose, arms crossed. Aurim could sense nothing, but Lanith's attitude put him on guard.

"I run from no one, especially a pampered little magician with high ideals and, until recently, no control over himself. You think that a few little victories win a war? You've no idea about the workings of strategy, the playing of the game, the writing of the epic—" Lanith broke off, suddenly blinking. "I want him under control now, imp. I've no more time to waste."

Aurim had no idea what Lanith meant by the last, save that it gave some indication that the pair of them were not as alone as he had thought. He looked around, assuring himself again that no one had remained behind, and finally came to the conclusion that perhaps Zuu's lord was insane.

It was definitely time to depart. Aurim assumed that if he could transport an entire party across most of the continent, he could still send himself back to Penacles. He summoned up the necessary strength—

—and felt his effort suppressed by another force.

He wanted to try again, but suddenly his body was once more a prison. Aurim could not move, could scarcely even breathe this time.

A giggle echoed through the chamber. Aurim found himself raising his arms in a dramatic gesture, then flapping them like a Seeker trying to take off. He knew that he was an absurd sight, but he could not help himself.

The darkness floating above Lanith drifted toward Aurim, slowly coalescing as it moved.

"Stop the games," the king commanded the air. "Keep him still."

"As you command, O great majesty . . ."

Despite its merry tone, Aurim found nothing amusing about the voice. It was the voice of a creature who had no concern for human life or death. There was something vaguely reminiscent about the voice, too, as if he had heard another akin to it before.

"You've got him secure? He can't use his sorcery against me?"

"Oh, no, no, Your Majesty! He is your puppet to command! You want him to dance"—Aurim performed a wild, clumsy series of steps—"and he dances! You want him to—"

"Enough of the theatrics, imp!" Lanith strode up to his prisoner. "Little brat . . ."

The spellcaster could do nothing as the warrior king thrust his face near. In truth, what concerned Aurim more than the man was the creature that served him. Only now did he sense something of its presence and that only because the shadow was now an indistinct yet swiftly solidifying blob. What was it?

"So, Aurim Bedlam. I made you an offer, but it's clear that you won't accept it. I can't trust you to join me. Should I have you then executed? You're a danger to me, boy. Maybe I should have your neck stretched . . . or better yet, toast you over an open fire so that I'm *certain* you're dead. I've heard a good sorcerer is hard to kill."

For the first time, the young mage was glad that the spell holding him did not allow him any movement. If it had, King Lanith would have certainly noticed his fear.

"It would be such a terrible waste, though, great majesty," suggested the voice. "He is, after all, an asset in more than one way! He would lead your Order in battle and also act as bait!"

Bait? What does he mean? They had to want his parents. That was it. His empty-headed romantic ideals not only threatened him, but his family, too. Lanith probably intended on making all of the Bedlams his unwilling servants.

Of course, Aurim's mother and father were hardly the simplistic fools that he was. Lanith might have some pet creature working for him, but it could hardly be as powerful as the elder Bedlams or, say, Darkhorse.

Darkhorse? Thinking of the shadow steed made him stare again at the mysterious form. Now it vaguely resembled a tiny, humanoid figure, a black, faceless thing.

"He escaped once, imp. His will's very strong. Admirable at other times, but not now. If his will's strong enough, he'll escape again. I can't take that chance."

"A sorcerer is a terrible thing to waste, *Emperor* Lanith, but rest assured, where there's a will, there's a way to *crush* it thoroughly!" The tiny figure giggled, "I can make your will his will, if you like."

This intrigued the king. "You can do that? You can make him do what I want?"

"It is *difficult* to do," replied the demon in a tone that made Aurim suspect that it was anything but difficult. Lanith appeared not to notice, however. "But I think that I can turn him to your grand cause, great majesty . . ."

The creature had completely formed now. He—for lack of a better pronoun—resembled a foot-tall, unfinished puppet. Aurim saw now that the king's imp had eyes and he was almost certain that he knew whose they resembled.

"Do it, then. With someone of his power to guide the others, my Order will be the greatest weapon of war ever."

The puppet floated toward Aurim, eyes fixed on the sorcerer even though his words were for the king. "And let us not forget: as bait, he will garner for you the other great prize you desire, my lord!"

The creature was barely more than arm's length from the captive—and now there was no denying exactly who he reminded Aurim of. It had to be impossible. There could not be two such astonishing beings, yet, the proof was before him. Coming for him. Burning into his soul with pupilless, icy blue orbs just like those of—

"Darkhorse," King Lanith whispered, responding to his companion's last words. "Darkhorse."

It was worse than being trapped in the Void, Darkhorse decided. Nothing but mist surrounded him. He could barely see his own limbs, much less anything that *might* have lurked nearby. At least in the clear emptiness of the Void Darkhorse had always been able to see that nothing watched him, nothing stalked him from behind . . . and nothing tried to reabsorb him, in the horrific process eradicating the sense of self that he held so precious.

At least I am safe from that! Any fate, any death, was better than the slow draining loss of his identity. It was one reason he had been so pleased when the Vraad sorcerer Dru Zeree led him back to the Dragonrealm. In the Dragonrealm, Darkhorse could hide from the one thing he secretly feared.

Such thoughts did not, of course, aid him now. It was possible that he might never escape this place, but the eternal planned to exhaust all options before giving in to such a fate. He could not re-create a blink hole from within the very nether region into which a blink hole opened, but there had to be a way of forming another exit. Darkhorse had traced his way from the Void to the Dragonrealm; this should be no more difficult.

Darkhorse soon regretted his confident thoughts. A scan of the misty nothingness with his senses revealed no trail to the dimension of the Dragonrealm. The place was a veritable blank in terms of sorcery. For the first time, the shadow steed grew anxious. His anxiety was not entirely related to his own fate, either. At this very moment, Aurim Bedlam faced possible danger. Worse, his family was ignorant of his disappearance, thanks to the eternal's mistake.

"I will be free of this place!" Darkhorse snapped out loud, more to shatter the unremitting silence than because he believed what he said. Without some path to follow, the eternal was at a loss.

He tried to review what had happened. The dissipation of his blink hole had been no accident. Some spellcaster had taken advantage of his travel spell and disrupted it at the most opportune moment. A very, very difficult form of attack, which meant a sorcerer of tremendous ability. It also meant a sorcerer who had some inkling of his plans or at least had kept a distant but careful eye on him.

But who . . . and why? One of Lanith's puppet mages? The missing students had promise. Perhaps one of them. Doubtful, but Darkhorse had no other answer.

A slight tingling in his head scattered all other thoughts. His magical senses came alive as Darkhorse realized that a thin tendril of energy now reached out to him from the mists. It was so very faint that Darkhorse kept expecting to lose it. Immediately he began tracking the tendril's path. The nearer he got to the source, the better the chance that he would find a way to return to the Dragonrealm.

On and on through the mist the eternal floated. The tendril never grew stronger, but neither did it weaken. Still, the longer Darkhorse followed, the more frustrated he became. Was this another trick? Was he cursed to follow this trail forever? Surely at some point the tendril would cease to be . . . and that would leave him once more stranded in the middle of nowhere.

Before him, a gaping hole burst into being.

Darkhorse was sucked through the newborn blink hole before he could even react to its presence. His equine form stretched like so much molasses, twisting and turning until little remained that resembled any sort of animal, much less a horse. The eternal cursed the multiverse, sorcerers, and sorcery in general as he fought to keep himself from tearing into several pieces. He dared not let that happen. The cost not only to himself but the Dragonrealm in general would be too great if even one fragment of his being separated too long. He knew too well what could result from such a disaster. If the fragment survived and, worse, thrived, it might become the monster people had often thought him to be.

Then, even as he began to believe that he could hold himself together no longer, Darkhorse fell into the Dragonrealm.

Unable to control his flight, the shadow steed plummeted earthward . . . but it was not earth he struck, rather water. Much water.

The splash as Darkhorse struck drowned out all other sounds. The eternal registered only that whatever lake or river he had landed in was very deep, for despite the speed with which he had fallen, he still did not touch bottom. Gradually the eternal's wild flight slowed until at last he floated, quite dazed, several feet below the surface.

Darkhorse slowly recovered, noticing only belatedly that he was drifting along at a good rate of speed. A river, then. The shadow steed regained enough control of his body to halt his progress, then, still underwater, started the process of re-structuring himself. The legs formed readily enough, but it took him several minutes to re-create his head and tail and a few minutes more to add fine detail.

Suddenly Darkhorse sensed the presence of a spellcaster, likely the same one whose probe had led him back to the Dragonrealm. The unknown mage searched the waters for him, probing closer and closer. Darkhorse decided to save the other the trouble of searching any longer. The spellcaster might be the reason that the eternal had managed to escape the nether realm, but he also might be the one who had trapped him there in the first place.

The shadow steed burst through to the surface, rising above the water. He saw now that he had indeed fallen into a river. A forest covered the landscape as far as he could see. Suspicions concerning his whereabouts grew solid.

His attention shifted to a figure among the trees: The spell-caster he had sensed. Not a man, but a woman. Not any woman, either, but she who had gone by the name Tori.

Darkhorse swooped down on her, moving so swiftly that the sorceress had little time to react. He came to a sudden halt directly in front of her, one foreleg raised up, and glared. The eternal still floated two or three feet above the woman, which meant that she had to crane her neck in order to look at him.

"I have had enough of your games, female!"

"What are you talking about? I saved you!"

"And how was it I became trapped in the first place?" From the way her expression altered, Darkhorse assumed that he was correct. The enchantress *had* been responsible. "I know not what your plan is, but you may consider it a lost cause!"

To her credit, she did not back away. "I don't know what you're talking about! I arrived at this spot, saw nothing, and was about to leave when I felt your presence. You were here but not here. I searched and found you . . . somewhere beyond. After that, I kept working until I was able to open one end of a blink hole for you! If not for me, you'd still be . . . wherever!"

"I do not believe you. I believe that you are in part responsible for the kidnapping of Aurim Bedlam!" The shadow steed descended to the ground. The woman did not behave as he would have expected. She should have attacked or, if she was sensible, retreated. Instead, the sorceress acted as if *she* were now the offended party. Despite her defiance, however, Darkhorse pressed on. "And after you kidnapped Aurim, you worked to assure I would not be able to rescue him!"

"Which is why I also helped you to escape, I suppose." The blond sorceress shook her head. "That makes no sense and you know it, demon steed."

"What makes no sense, unless you are lying, is your sudden appearance at so opportune a time! I follow the lad's trail, discover that he and his captors have seemingly vanished, and when I try to follow, I find my spell torn about and my path back no more! Then you appear and lead me out! Tell me that your timely rescue of me can possibly be due to chance, female!"

"My name, if you have to have one, is Yssa."

"A name as false, no doubt, as Tori!" The shadowy stallion took a step forward. Yssa, if that was truly her name, had the good sense to retreat an equal distance. "You are avoiding the subject!"

"Believe what you will." The enchantress steeled herself, even daring to stare him in the eye. "No, my finding you was no chance thing, demon steed. You mentioned Aurim Bedlam during our last visit together . . . and how he'd met someone. I came to . . . to see who it was."

"Did you? How very, very inquisitive considering you had never met either of them." Darkhorse snorted. "Or have you? Aurim, likely not, but perhaps you did know the young woman Jenna!" Her blank stare did not suit him. "A merchant's daughter, so she claimed." He described her in detail, but Yssa still gave no sign of recognition. . . . or did she? Yssa's mouth tightened slightly as the shadow steed added every bit of information he could recall about Aurim's lady. She knew *something.* "You still claim no knowledge?"

"I know no one who looks like that."

Darkhorse kicked at the ground, creating a tiny yet deep crevice. Yssa jumped. The eternal stepped forward. Yssa again retreated, but this time a tree trunk blocked her path.

She looked ready to do another vanishing act, but Darkhorse shook his head. "No escapes this time, human! You will find it impossible to depart, I promise."

"I've done nothing but help you, demon steed. You've no right—"

He reared, sorcerous energy radiating all around him. His eyes flared. "I am Darkhorse! I do what I choose to do for what cause I care to take up! Someone dear to me and dear to others I care for is missing! You know much, but you think you can keep it from me!" The branches of the trees nearest Darkhorse shook wildly. He thrust his head so close to Yssa's face that it filled her view. "I *will* have answers!"

"*Saress!*" the stunned and frightened enchantress blurted. "It was Saress! I'm sure of it! I know she's journeyed to Penacles in secret in the past and each time she's brought back a young spellcaster for Lanith. Someone . . . someone I knew within the palace walls told me that she brought at least two, both of them ensorcelled! If Lanith can't pay them enough to be his lackeys, he's more than willing to take them against their will, and the easiest way is through Saress!"

"So, you pretended not to know her when I described her as Jenna! I do not like being lied to, human!"

"I didn't lie to you . . . not exactly. That wasn't Saress. Not her normal appearance. She's good at casting illusion, though. If it wasn't her, then I can't imagine who it could've been!"

The tree limbs stilled. The shadow steed allowed the aura surrounding him to fade, but he did not back away. "You know this Saress very well, I believe! How?"

"I've encountered her before. She . . . she nearly made me one of King Lanith's forced volunteers. She also killed a friend of mine in the name of her master."

Her sincerity was questionable, but Darkhorse sensed some element of truth in her words. He took one step back, giving Yssa just enough space to let her relax a little. Darkhorse did not want her becoming too relaxed, however, not until he was certain that he had all the information he required. "How powerful is Saress?"

"Powerful?" Yssa seemed uncertain what the eternal meant by his question. "She's fairly powerful. Not like Cabe Bedlam. Better than the others in the Magical Order, but that's not saying much." A long hesitation followed. "She might be a little stronger than I am." Her expression hardened. *"Maybe."*

"Is she this intelligent force?"

"No." She said it with such confidence that Darkhorse could not doubt her answer. He had suspected that Saress was not the dark power behind the horse king.

Darkhorse came to the conclusion that Yssa was not an enemy in disguise but rather an unruly, self-reliant witch who preferred her own unorthodox methods over working with others. True, she had passed along information to Cabe and the Gryphon, but more because it suited her purpose. Darkhorse was amazed that she had remained hidden from both the Dragon Kings and human spellcasters for so long, but then, it was possible that she was even more skilled than the eternal believed. Certainly the peculiar pattern of energy within her, the magical signature, was unique. In some ways it was also harder to read than most. There was much about Yssa that remained an enigma, but Darkhorse would worry about that after he had rescued Aurim.

How he was to do that, Darkhorse still did not know. Best to talk it over with Cabe and Gwen, however unnerving the thought of telling them about their son's kidnapping. In desperate hope that he was wrong, the shadow steed asked, "You are certain that this Saress is responsible? You sensed her presence where the boy vanished?"

Her nostrils flared as if she had inhaled something repugnant. "I could mistake her for no one else. She was there. If your friend also was, then they were together. It couldn't be coincidence."

"No, I thought not." That was it, then. He had to break the terrible news to the young sorcerer's parents. Darkhorse looked around, trying to orient himself so that he could head the proper direction back to the Manor. "This is . . . the Dagora Forest, is it not?"

Yssa looked uncomfortable. "Yes."

"Why here? Why bring me to this place?"

"This is where I was when I sensed you. I didn't notice anything near Penacles."

"Indeed? How very peculiar." It was also very suspicious. What the woman had told him sounded like the work of a powerful spellcaster. There were very few of those. Of course, this *was* the Dagora Forest, but surely that did not mean— "Yssa, what brought you to this place? Why come here after Penacles?"

"Because she came to see me, demon sssteed," answered a figure suddenly standing among the trees.

"Lord Green . . ." The Dragon King bowed in acknowledgment of his identity. Darkhorse shifted to better face the drake. Again he found himself wondering about Cabe Bedlam's sudden withdrawal from friendship with the armored ruler and how that affected his own standing. None of the drakes had ever considered the eternal a comrade, but this one had at least acted respectful. Now, though, the Green Dragon's anxiety shone like a beacon. The drake lord was worried about something.

Darkhorse thought he knew what it was, and the knowledge made him furious. Small wonder that the Green Dragon might fear his wrath. "It was *you*, was it not? It was you who trapped me in the first place! It was you who prevented me from rescuing Aurim!"

"I'm sorry," Yssa called, but her words were not meant for Darkhorse. Instead, she bowed her head toward the Dragon King and repeated her apology. "I'm sorry. I didn't think."

The drake lord waved off her apology with one mailed hand. "You could not know. It doesss not matter, my dear."

"You know her?" It was a conspiracy, then. The woman had to have worked with the Dragon King to trap him. Darkhorse did not know why they had dared snare him, but he would have answers even if both of them had to pay. The ebony stallion reared up, energy crackling around him.

"Pleassse calm yourself, demon sssteed. No harm wasss meant to you. I only sssought to prevent you from becoming yet another of the horssse king's slaves. I wasss nearly ready to release you myself. I only needed to compossse myssself for what I knew would be a very . . . sssensitive . . . conversation with you."

Darkhorse was not at all certain he believed the drake, but

he dropped to the ground. "Then say what you must say, Lord Green, for I have a friend in peril."

"I will, but not here." Before the eternal could question him, the Dragon King raised one hand. As he did, their surroundings shifted. Gone was the forest, to be replaced by a cavern chamber, a vast natural room that Darkhorse recognized as the court of the Green Dragon.

The drake lord no longer stood before him, but sat on a huge stone throne. An arch formed from vines rose above the throne. The same vines coursed along the walls of the chamber, adding a sense of life to what might otherwise have been an empty, soulless place. Despite a lack of natural light, the vines seemed as healthy and fresh as if they had been growing outdoors.

"We risk no one listening in while we are here," explained the Green Dragon. "Not even whatever force it is that ssserves Lanith. I have also disssmissed the guardsss. There will be no ssspies of any sort."

All that might have been true, but Darkhorse still wondered about the presence of one other in the chamber. Yssa now stood to one side of the throne, as if she had every right to be there.

"What of her? What is her part in all of this, Lord Green? Too many questions have been dangled before me. Too many questions and not nearly enough answers!"

"Yssa is here by my permission. It isss too long since we ssspoke and that is a shame that I mussst bear. I am glad that she hasss at last come back to me."

"I had to," she responded. "I had no choice."

"Yesss . . ." The Dragon King seemed somewhat bitter, but his bitterness appeared to be directed at himself. "Of course."

"Yssa." For the first time, the name made some sense to Darkhorse. Many drake names had similar sounds. There had been Ssarekai, so loyal to the Bedlams, his human lords, that he had sacrificed himself in an attempt to stop the renegade Toma. Now there also existed Sssaleese, leader of the fledgling drake confederation. Yssa was a perfectly normal name—especially for a drake. "So . . you are not human after all, female."

She looked insulted. "But I *am*, Darkhorse! I am . . . at least in part."

"Yssa *isss* human, demon steed," insisted the drake lord somewhat uncomfortably. "Her mother wasss a very beauteousss woman"—the Green Dragon reached out a hand to the sorceress, who took it after some hesitation—"and I . . . and I am her *father*."

CHAPTER VIII

"You cannot mean what you say, Lord Green! Such a coming together is . . . has always been . . ."

"Unthinkable?" The drake lord removed his hand from that of Yssa and leaned forward, red eyes staring defiantly into the eternal's own. "Do you deny the possibility that at least once in the past the two races have come together? Do you think that *no one* ever thought of such a combination?"

Darkhorse snorted. "I am not so naive. There have always been those of both races who found themselves attracted by . . . shall we call it the exotic, my Lord Green? Yet, that does not guarantee that their union will be blessed. We are talking of drakes and humans, after all!"

"Two races not so dissimilar as you think, at least based upon my ssstudies. There are those who find the new emperor attractive, if you recall."

Darkhorse recalled all too well. Cabe's own daughter Valea had been attracted to the young drake, who, admittedly, looked nearly human. Many of the latest generation of drakes seemed more human than ever, which made the potential for human-drake relationships more and more likely. The eternal did not like the notion; the Dragon Kings and their people had always been adversaries, the masters who needed to be overthrown or, at the very least, taught humility. "I do not deny such things, Dragon King, but what you say—"

"Isss only the truth. Yssa is my own, the only legacy I have of her mother." The drake lord looked away, obviously reliving the past. "Humansss have ever had a more ressspectable place in my domain, demon steed. Not quite the level achieved by those in the Manor, but I and my predecessorsss have always known the value of their kind. Humansss have ssserved in positions of authority in my realm. Sssuch a one was Yssa's mother. Penelope wasss her name. She looked much like her daughter, I mussst say."

"You've no need to explain everything to him, Father," Yssa protested with a glare at the shadow steed.

"But I would like to tell sssomeone, if only becaussse I have kept your presssence hidden much too long. I have acted ashamed of you, my daughter, ashamed of one of my own." The Green Dragon leaned back. "Her mother wasss a woman of rank here, one who kept my research records in order and kept track of my ssstudies. She was a valuable sssubject." His tone grew darker. "My matesss do their duty, but we have long gone passst love. Now we work only for the sssake of raising a sssuccessor. Penelope, however, shared my passions, and having grown up among my kind, she sssaw not the monster outside, but the kindred sssoul inside."

Darkhorse did not want to believe the Dragon King. He did not want to think that such . . . hybrids . . . existed, but it explained Yssa's peculiar magical signature. He also saw no reason for either of them to make up what would have seemed to most a preposterous tale. It also perhaps explained a few encounters Darkhorse had had in centuries past with spellcasters whose abilities and style had matched nothing he had known. Perhaps hybrids were not so uncommon after all . . . just secretive.

Perhaps.

"It wasss only once, but that wasss enough. The unthinkable happened. Penelope wasss with child. No one dared sssay what everyone knew, not even when she gave birth." The Green Dragon looked at his daughter. "She wasss beautiful even then. Mossst human infants are so . . . so raw. Not her. I thought of her as her mother reborn . . . which proved prophetic asss her mother died but a day later."

Silence followed, a silence finally broken by Darkhorse. "I am sorry."

The figure on the throne straightened. "I do not ask for your sympathy, demon steed. I only tell you what happened. Yssa is my daughter and although we have been essstranged for quite sssome time, we are no longer."

"Then I am glad for you, Lord Green! However, we have diverged from the reason I have been brought here! Why did you do it? More important, how dare you entrap me, leave me to float in the world between worlds?"

His words seemed to strike the Dragon King hard. "I did what I did to protect you, Darkhorse, not becaussse I am your foe."

"Protect me?" Darkhorse laughed. "Protect me! From what could you protect me, Lord Green? I am Darkhorse!"

"Which doesss not make you invincible, demon sssteed," countered the master of the Dagora Forest. He pointed into the air. "Sssomething resssides in the domain of the horse people, sssome force whosssse powers and origins I have been unable to fathom. My daughter callsss it a creature, although I myssself have not even been able to verify that."

"It lives." The enchantress shuddered. "I felt it." Her eyes narrowed. "But now that I think of it, it reminds me of something else . . . I don't know what, but something else."

"That we can worry about later, daughter. Darkhorsssse, I know of Aurim Bedlam'sss abduction. I sssensed his presence in Zuu, and one of my few remaining spiesss verified it. However, shortly after his arrival, it wasss asss if the youth vanished. I sense that he isss in there sssomewhere, but it is asss if he is shielded from my sssight now."

"Which makes it all that much more important that I rescue him as soon as possible! If that is all you have to say to me, Lord Green, then I shall be off!" The shadow steed took a few steps back. He intended to create another blink hole from this very spot, one that would open up in the court of King Lanith if necessary.

"Wait!" The Dragon King's voice boomed throughout the chamber. He stood now, one open hand held high. "Hear me out, Darkhorse! Yesss, you mussst rescue Aurim, but to go charging into Zuu isss to court disssaster! There isss another way, a more sssubtle way! I can help you there!"

The shadow steed held off departing. Inwardly he knew that he was risking much. What he should have done was go straight to Cabe, but that seemed far too time-consuming at this point. The Green Dragon, however, was also a planner—and he knew Zuu better than either the Bedlams or the Gryphon did. If there was a way to work around King Lanith's defenses, then the Dragon King was the one who would know.

"Very well. I am still listening."

The reptilian monarch inhaled, his eyes growing a little less fiery. "The gatesss of Zuu are still open for busssiness despite the rumblingsss of conquesssst. Lanith still encourages business, although why ssso many fools would continue to go there, I cannot sssay. Merchantsss still bring their waresss to the city and othersss still come to purchassse the kingdom's fine sssteeds. That will sssoon change, but for now it worksss for us."

Darkhorse understood what he was suggesting. "I am to imitate a simple mount, thereby gaining access into the city. A reasonable suggestion, but surely Lanith's sorcerers will be watching for such a thing. If this woman who tricked Aurim was indeed the horse king's enchantress, then they will of course watch for me. I suspect that she is powerful enough to detect my presence. Better to leap in, rescue the lad, then depart."

"The matter of detection is not a problem, demon sssteed." The Dragon King extended his hand. He now held in it a medallion, the center of which was a green gemstone. "Thisss is a variation on the tokens all travelers who enter Zuu mussst bear. Unbeknownst to mossst, they are also desssigned to detect any newcomer with sorcerousss abilities. Thisss one, in turn, will act asss a damper, shielding your powers from the senses of Lanith's sorcerers . . . even Saress."

"I would look a little out of place wearing such a thing and I expect that I could not absorb it within me, could I?"

"Your rider will wear it. Asss long as the pair of you are

within range of one another, you will be protected. Once inside, you can contact a representative of mine."

It seemed a reasonable if still somewhat risky option, but Darkhorse had some misgivings. "Who is it who will ride with me?"

Yssa stepped forward. "I will, Darkhorse."

"Daughter, that wasss not—"

"I know Zuu better than even your spies, Father. I lived among the people." She spread her arms. "Look at me. I might as well have been born among them."

"Your mother's parentsss were from the kingdom, true. However, I cannot risssk having you —"

She would not be put off. "Who else could defend themselves so effectively?" Yssa turned to Darkhorse. "You've no choice but me, demon steed. Will you accept that or do I have to argue with you, too? The longer we wait, the more danger to your friend."

He was probably as leery as the Dragon King was of involving the female, but she was correct. Yssa was the one best suited to journey with him, the only one he could trust to also defend herself. Her knowledge of Zuu would be invaluable, too. "I accept your company, wo—Yssa."

"I do not," insisted the Green Dragon. "Yssa, I forbid you to—"

She snatched the medallion from his hand, then vanished, only to rematerialize a moment later next to the shadow steed. The Dragon King hissed, starting toward her at the same time.

Yssa leaped aboard Darkhorse, a riskier act than she likely realized. Darkhorse immediately shaped himself to better accommodate her weight, then turned to block the drake lord.

"She will not go with you, eternal! I have only regained her! I will not lossse her again!"

"The choice is mine, Father. You know how much I enjoy adventure!"

"You will ssstay!" Now a transformation came over the Dragon King. His arms and legs twisted, his hands curling into claws. He swelled in size and as he grew, leathery wings burst from his back and a tail sprouted from below. The vestiges of humanity quickly slipped away. The dragon head

crest slid downward, remolding into the true visage of the reptilian monarch.

Within seconds, a huge emerald dragon had taken the place
of the scaled knight.

Darkhorse backed several steps, but he was not daunted by
the leviathan. Powerful though the Dragon King might be, the
eternal had faced such strength before. If need be, he would
defend himself, although the shadow steed hoped it would not
come to that. The drake's concern was for the welfare of his
daughter.

"Good-bye, Father!" Yssa called. To Darkhorse, she whispered, "Be prepared to leave here when I say so."

The dragon unfurled wings that nearly spanned the entire
width of the great cavern. "Think what you do, Yssssa! Thisss
is no tryst! Thisss is no game!"

"For once I agree with you, Father." The enchantress
pointed at the massive dragon.

Light flashed before the dragon's crimson orbs. He roared,
startled.

"Time to go!" Yssa called merrily.

Darkhorse followed her lead. The cavern faded even while
the dragon sought to regain his sight. A moment later a vast
field of wild grass formed around them. Darkhorse silently
cursed his haste. He had transported both of them to the former Barren Lands.

The grass seemed to take note of Yssa the moment the pair
appeared, straining toward her like a pack of puppies yearning to be petted. The eternal shifted ground, trying to avoid
the tendrils.

"He always had such a temper," his companion remarked.
"I knew that he'd grown careless, otherwise he would've
never been diverted by such a simple spell. He'll give in now
that he knows there's no stopping me." She peered around. "I
wouldn't have thought you'd take us here."

"It was the nearest location that did not take us toward Zuu
or back toward Penacles! Had I had a moment more, I would
have chosen a better location. Away!" The last was directed
toward the increasingly inquisitive blades of grass.

"They don't mean any harm." Yssa lowered one hand

enough so that the grass could touch it. "They'd only harm a drake of clan Brown and there aren't many of those left."

"Nonetheless, I still do not like their inquisitiveness! Make them cease so that I can think!"

She whispered something to the plants, which immediately stilled. Yssa then smiled at the shadow steed, an action that did nothing to ease his tension. He was beginning to regret agreeing to take her on as his companion. If not for the fact that she knew Zuu so much better than he did . . .

"I only need a few minutes to create an illusion around us. We'll be a rider and mount from the southern horse ranches. All I have to do is weather myself a bit and make you look more like one of the browns they raise down there."

"I can easily form the proper disguise if you will but show me an image."

She nodded. "Good. The less spellcasting around us, the less chance of someone detecting it. The medallion's good, but it's got limits."

He twisted his head around to look at her. "Why are you doing this, Yssa? This need not concern you."

"But it does." That was all she would say, but a trace of anger in her tone hinted at something more. Her mood abruptly changed again. "Well, shall we begin?"

Yssa insisted on a quick journey to the south so that the shadow steed could study the horses raised there. Darkhorse needed only a few moments to inspect the creatures in order to make the adjustments to his form. His companion was delighted with his shifting abilities.

"Why do you always choose a horse, though?" she finally asked. "Why not some other form like that of a man? You could probably imitate one easily."

"I prefer this form. It has grace, beauty."

"But you could transform into something else . . ."

"With more difficulty than you imagine." That was not entirely true, but he saw no need for her to know all his capabilities. "I have adapted myself to the basic form of a horse, and having utilized that shape for so very long, minor transformations such as this are simple. It would require much

more effort to adapt to a completely new shape, such as that
of a man or a drake."

"A pity. It could've been handy."

The enchantress had also changed, although her transformation was simply an illusion. In order to avoid enshrouding
herself in too powerful a spell, Yssa had kept her alterations
minor, changing only enough to keep her from resembling
herself. She still looked like a native of Zuu, but one more
muscular and plain of features. Her outfit was simple and
functional, the type worn by those more accustomed to herd-
ing horses rather than city life. Her clothing was real, albeit
adjusted to conform with her illusionary appearance.

It was but a short leap to the vicinity of the city. Yssa chose
a location that would give them the privacy their sudden arrival required. After all, their disguises would not have mattered much if someone had noticed them materialize. Once it
was clear that they had arrived undetected, the pair immediately traveled to the main road, there joining others with business in Zuu.

"Less business than usual," the enchantress whispered. The
eternal could not reply, but he flicked his ears in a manner
they had decided would indicate his agreement. The southern
road to Zuu was indeed less congested than it should have
been. Horse trading was still important to the kingdom, which
meant that there should have been many travelers riding to
and from the city. A few merchants rode south, no doubt to
buy directly from the ranches, but their numbers were far less
than what would have been expected at this time of year. Not
all the horses bred in Zuu were used for Lanith's armies.
There should have still been a thriving business . . . except
that many of the kingdom's customers now faced the possibility that their former trading partner now eyed them as future vassals.

Not every inhabitant of Zuu had to be pleased by the king's
decision to expand his domain. Many of the merchants had to
be suffering greatly by now.

To their surprise, however, the gates were no more well
protected than during Darkhorse's previous visit with Cabe.
The shadow steed had expected more security, but while sev-

eral of the king's guard did patrol the gate, they asked no more questions than previous. Darkhorse received one or two admiring remarks, but otherwise the soldiers did nothing to slow the pair.

Before they were allowed to enter, though, the captain of the guard, a graying, hook-nosed woman taller and broader than the Gryphon, handed a token to Yssa. "You know the rules, right? Keep it with you at all times. You might be checked for it at any time by a member of the guard. Understand?"

"I do." The enchantress took the token and dropped it in a pouch tied at her side.

Darkhorse hoped that the medallion given to them by the Green Dragon functioned well. Between Yssa and him, the pair surely radiated much power. Even sorcerers as simpleminded as the bunch that worked for the king of Zuu could detect them given half the chance. Sorcerous shields were of no help, either. According to Yssa, someone among the horse king's hired mages, probably Saress, had devised the tokens so that the very shields that would have normally hidden the presence of the spellcasters actually betrayed them. That meant that neither Yssa nor the eternal dared add their own shield spells to that of the medallion.

No one confronted them as they journeyed through the city, yet Darkhorse could not shake his uneasiness. Everything seemed perfectly normal, but each moment he expected a legion of ragtag sorcerers to materialize from the shadows. He also still worried about the mysterious force King Lanith seemed to command. Even here in the city the shadow steed could detect no trace of its presence and yet he was certain that it lurked somewhere nearby.

Zuu itself presented nothing but the picture of calm and cleanliness. People still went about their daily business, arguing over prices in the marketplace or meeting with companions at the many taverns and inns around the city. Guards rode through the streets, but their manner was casual. Merchants from a few other kingdoms inspected horses for sale, a sign that business had not slacked off as much as Darkhorse had first supposed. Some folk, it seemed, were always willing to deal.

Despite all the horses, the streets and buildings of Zuu were among the whitest and newest-looking that the shadow steed had seen in quite some time. He noted men and women at work picking up after the horses. Others were scrubbing down a stable, one of many such structures located all over the city. The people of Zuu seemed to think nothing of the manual labor, however disgusting it might have seemed to some. Everything Darkhorse had heard about the horse people was true; they were bloodthirsty in battle, yet they also maintained a great belief in keeping their homes in order. The stench of hundreds of animals should have overpowered Zuu long ago, but one could barely smell them.

Yssa tugged lightly on the reins. Darkhorse slowed, then allowed her to guide him toward a stable.

As she dismounted, the enchantress took the opportunity to whisper, "My father has a man here. If anyone can give us some information about the palace, it'll be him."

He wanted to ask how a man who worked at a public stable would know much about the king's palace, but the coming of a groom prevented him from doing so.

"Good day to you," said the young blond man. "Can I help?"

"Is Trenlen here?"

The groom glanced back. "Trenlen's inside, but he's busy. Perhaps I could help you?"

"I'd rather wait. Trenlen's an old friend of my father's. He'll want to see me. You could see to my horse, though." She handed the reins to the groom, tossing him a coin at the same time. "Give him a good stall and some water. I'll take care of everything else as soon as I'm done with Trenlen."

"It would be no difficulty to rub him down—"

She smiled at him. Despite the plain features created by the illusion, she still had an effect on the young man, who blushed.

"I prefer to do that myself. He's special."

"All right." The groom stroked Darkhorse on the muzzle. "Come on, boy."

It frustrated the eternal to separate from his companion. What good would it do for him to wait in the stable? However, he had no choice. He would have to be patient while Yssa spoke with this Trenlen. He considered altering his appearance. Reshaping himself into a more humanoid form would gain him better access to things . . . but he was loath to abandon a shape that had served him so well.

He would be patient for the time being, but if the enchantress took too long, he would have to take charge of matters, whatever the cost. Each passing moment meant increased danger to Aurim. If not for the fact that he knew that Lanith wanted the younger Bedlam for his Magical Order, the shadow steed would have fretted more. Lanith would not want to harm Aurim; the lad had too much to offer the horse king if only the latter could bend the spellcaster to his will.

Be strong, Aurim. Be very strong.

Darkhorse's last glimpse of Yssa was of the sorceress entering the building next to the stable. Then his view became one of stall after stall, most of them inhabited. As he neared the first, the mare within grew anxious. The groom shushed her, but then the horse in the stall next to hers also grew jumpy.

They sensed the eternal's difference. Outside, the animals would have paid him little heed, but when trapped in close quarters with him, many horses were wont to grow nervous. Darkhorse wondered whether he would be able to stay here after all.

The groom evidently had similar thoughts, for he encouraged the shadow steed to a quicker pace. Soon they were past the other mounts and into an unoccupied part of the stable. Even then the young man with Darkhorse did not pause. The eternal began to suspect that he was going to end up back outside, but at the very last stall the groom finally halted.

"Can't go any farther, boy. I don't know why you make 'em so nervous, but they just have to be satisfied with you being all the way over here." The lad took a moment to stroke the eternal's muzzle. "Maybe they're just jealous because you look so good. I wonder if your mistress is trying to sell you to the master. Hope so. I'd get to ride you, then."

As much as Darkhorse appreciated the groom's good taste, he silently urged the boy to depart. While there was little the shadow steed could do from inside the stable, he could do nothing at all so long as his undesired admirer remained nearby.

Fortunately, the groom settled for watering him and then disappearing. By that time, the other mounts had settled down, although many turned a wary eye in his direction. Darkhorse ignored them, instead trying to decide what he dared risk.

Yssa had explained the range of her father's medallion and Darkhorse estimated that he was just barely within that safety margin. It was fortunate that the stable was not any longer; the shadow steed might have then risked the Order's notice.

Darkhorse was still debating his options when he heard someone approaching. It was Yssa, accompanied by a second, hulking figure with the look of a soldier upon him. The eternal tensed, suspicious that perhaps the Dragon King's talisman had not worked so well after all.

"I was beginning to think that you weren't in here at all," the enchantress whispered, her tone amused. "What did you do, scare all the other horses?"

"This is your partner?" asked her companion. Like many folk of Zuu, he wore his blond hair in a long ponytail. His round features were half-hidden by the thick, somewhat darker beard. "I admit he's a fine steed, but, my lady, that's all he—"

"You can speak to him, Darkhorse. This is Trenlen. He is one of my father's men."

"If you say so, then I am willing to risk speaking." The shadow steed chuckled as Trenlen's expression altered from disbelief to shock. "Greetings, Master Trenlen. You have a fine stable."

"I . . . thank you."

Yssa waited for the man to recover his wits, but when Trenlen continued to simply stare at Darkhorse, she finally snapped her fingers before him. "Pay attention, Trenlen. We can't remain here long."

"My . . . my apologies, my lady." Despite his best efforts to remain attentive, the man's eyes continued to drift to the cternal.

Sighing, the enchantress turned to Darkhorse. "We had a discussion concerning the palace and I think I've found out something of use to us. Lanith's sorcerers make their headquarters in what was once a part of the royal stables, but has long since been renovated. The king likes them near, but not too near."

"So Aurim is there?" Out of the corner of his vision, Darkhorse noticed Trenlen's eyes bulge. It seemed that each time the eternal did not behave like a real horse, the man was dumbstruck.

"No. I knew about the headquarters of the Order already and I didn't expect that your friend would be in there. Aurim Bedlam is too great a prize. Besides, he isn't one of Lanith's paid dogs. He's an unwilling recruit."

"So far you have told me nothing, then."

She frowned. "Just wait. Trenlen, tell him what you heard."

The stable owner recovered enough to explain, "Two of my daughters are in the palace guard. Brave warriors, brave lasses. They're loyal to my liege Green just as I am." His eyes narrowed in concern. "It's by their own choice they took such a position. They knew that it would help us keep an eye on Lanith. I've always been proud of them."

"I understand," returned the eternal, trying to maintain his patience. "They are to be commended. Yet, what news do you have?"

"Two things. One that I have known for a long time. That the king talks to himself at times, ignoring all others. Shadows seem to follow him, too. Maybe the work of his mistress, Saress. The other news I learned only two hours before you arrived. Saress arrived earlier with a young and—from my daughter's slightly biased description—handsome man who seemed to walk around as if half-asleep. He did whatever the enchantress told him to do."

So there was verification at last. The horse king did have Aurim Bedlam. "And is there more?"

"My eldest daughter was on duty when they brought the lad in. The king questioned him a little. Offered him a place in the

Order. The lad said he'd try to escape if he could. In fact, from what my daughter said, it looked like the boy was already fighting their control."

Aurim had been fighting back? Perhaps there was hope. Perhaps Aurim had even already escaped. Darkhorse pressed, "Then what happened, Master Trenlen?"

"I don't know. The king dismissed everyone, including Saress. The last my girl saw of your friend and King Lanith was His Majesty facing the lad as if he didn't have a care in the world."

"Very odd. Is Lanith also a spellcaster?"

Yssa snorted. "Him? There's been no trace of sorcery in Lanith's family for as far back as anyone can recall. Until his interest in gathering sorcerers, this was one of the parts of the continent where you were least likely to find a spellcaster of any competence. The past monarchs of Zuu relied on the people's prowess with arms and their riding skills."

The shadow steed dipped his head in agreement. The people of Zuu had always been proud of their heritage. It had been a surprise to many when Lanith had chosen to augment his armies with sorcery.

A pair of men entered the stables, the same young groom accompanying them. Trenlen immediately reached out and rubbed Darkhorse on the neck. "Are you sure you won't sell him for less than that? I'd like him, but I can't afford so high a price."

Taking up the conversation, Yssa shook her head. "Not for a coin less, Trenlen. Take it or leave it."

Darkhorse watched the newcomers talk with the lad, then retrieve a pair of dusky horses. A minute later all three had departed.

When they were alone again, Trenlen exhaled. "We can't talk for too much longer. There'll be more folks in and out of here. Always gets busier toward evening."

"I have still not heard much of great aid to us," insisted the shadowy stallion. He glanced beyond the stable owner to assure himself that no one, especially one of the grooms, might suddenly surprise them again. "Do you know where Aurim Bedlam is now or not?"

"If my daughter is correct, he is being kept in a chamber below the throne room. It's a place where the king goes when he desires to be alone . . . or, as some say, to talk to himself without staring eyes around."

Yssa removed a small piece of paper from a pouch. "Trenlen's given me this. A crude map showing where this chamber is located in regards to the palace grounds." She unfolded the map and showed it to the eternal. The detail was sparse, but sufficient to give him some idea of where they had to go. "Will this be enough, do you think, Darkhorse?"

He eyed the large man. "You are certain of the accuracy of this map?"

"On my life and that of my daughters."

"It will do, then, Yssa. We must not wait any longer. I fear for Aurim."

Trenlen eyed the pair. "What will you do? You can't just go charging into the palace!"

"Leave that to us, Trenlen," the sorceress replied. "But it would be good if perhaps you could watch the doorway for a few moments. Make sure that no one comes inside."

The man still looked uncertain, but at last he nodded. "Aye, I can do that. Good luck to you."

As Trenlen walked away, Yssa whispered to Darkhorse, "It's best that he doesn't know any more than he needs to. We've risked his position just by coming here."

"I agree." The eternal shifted position. "Mount. We will be in and out of the palace before Lanith knows what is happening."

"Are you certain you can do this?"

"I am Darkhorse! Of course I can!"

She smiled. "I love your confidence."

From the entrance came the sounds of argument. The loudest voice belonged to Trenlen. Darkhorse glanced at his companion. Trenlen had gotten to the entrance just in time, but judging by the others' insisting tones, there was no telling how successful he would be in keeping the newcomers out. By rights, the man could not keep customers from their mounts. He risked his business by doing so, not to mention raising questions better left unanswered.

An idea occurred to Darkhorse, one that would solve a small problem nagging him. "Yssa. I need a little more time for this. You had better help Trenlen delay them. Give me but two minutes, then hurry back. They must not enter, or they might see something they should not. I am going to have to create a very particular type of blink hole."

She looked uncertain, but finally agreed. "I'll do what I can."

"Then hurry." The shadow steed nudged her forward. Yssa ran toward the entrance, not looking back. Darkhorse watched her for a second, then backed into the most shadowy corner of the stable.

The woman was capable and had already helped him much, but what Darkhorse intended he had to do alone. He could not risk another's life nor could he risk his own concentration. The shadow steed had enough to concern him without also worrying about Yssa's safety. He had resigned himself to her presence, but secretly had hoped for some excuse to leave her behind for her own good. Now he had the opportunity.

The moment she was out of sight, Darkhorse acted. He did have to make a blink hole to enter the palace, but not one as complex as he had indicated to Yssa. Still, one part of his explanation to her had been true; no one else could be allowed into the stable while he was creating it. Blink holes ofttimes opened up with a bright flash that no one could have missed.

Darkhorse pictured the layout of the palace, combining what he knew of its exterior with what Trenlen's map revealed. It gave him a more than adequate path to create. Even if Aurim proved not to be in the chamber, Darkhorse expected to be able to sense the lad once he was so near. Cabe would have called him overly optimistic, but the shadow steed did not see it that way.

The hole opened up instantly, a glaring circle of light in the darkness of the stable. Several horses stirred, some of them kicking at their stalls or trying to pull free. Then, with one glance toward the entrance of the stable, Darkhorse sloughed off his disguise and darted inside. As he entered the blink hole, he thought he heard someone call out, but by then it was too late to stop him.

Darkhorse wasted no time trying to reach his destination. He wished that he could have used a quicker teleportation spell, but the shadow steed wanted *some* advance warning should there prove to be a defensive spell between himself and his destination.

A moment later, that proved to be a fortuitous decision, for Darkhorse nearly collided with a peculiar field enshrouding the entire palace. It was a complex warning spell, one that would have alerted everyone in the building had the shadow steed simply tried to transport himself inside. The field was an admirable effort on someone's part, probably that of Saress. None of the other spellcasters was likely this competent.

Despite its complexity, however, Darkhorse was not deterred. He had faced far more cunning spells. The knowledge gathered over centuries easily enabled him to cross through without causing even the slightest ripple.

He materialized in the chamber without difficulty, only to find that it was empty. Yet, Darkhorse still sensed the lingering presence of the young sorcerer. Aurim had been here not long before. It was very possible that he had missed Cabe's son by as little as an hour. Darkhorse, his sight completely adjusted to the gloom, glanced at his surroundings. The room was sparsely decorated. There were a few old tapestries on the walls, tapestries that were tattered and moldy, as if the chamber had been forgotten for several years. A single chair stood in the very center of the room, the only piece of furniture in sight. Dust covered everything but the chair and a path from the only door.

A slight tingle coursed through him. Something, some trace, reminded him of the past . . . but of what part of his past Darkhorse could not say. He searched with his power, but whatever it was was overwhelmed by Aurim's recent presence.

If the lad was not here, then where? The shadow steed reached out beyond the confines of the chamber, seeking the young sorcerer in every direction. Lanith would want to keep his prize nearby.

His probes met with no success, although once he thought he sensed Aurim. The trace vanished before Darkhorse could get a fix on it, though. He was forced to extend his search. As yet he had not sensed Saress or any of the other spellcasters, but the farther afield he had to search, the greater the risk that one of them might notice *him*.

Aurim, where are you? Darkhorse started to fear that Lanith had killed the young sorcerer, perhaps because Aurim would not agree to be his vassal. It was the only explanation that he had for not being able to locate the golden-haired spellcaster.

Darkhorse?

The mental plea was so tentative that at first the eternal did not realize what it was. Darkhorse sought out the source, but once more he was unsuccessful.

Darkhorse? Is that you?

Aurim? It felt like his friend, but still the shadow steed could not locate him. *Where are you?*

In a dungeon! Aurim sounded frightened yet relieved. *They've got a spell on me that won't allow me to use my powers to escape! Darkhorse, they tried to take control of my mind!*

Recalling how distraught Aurim had been when he had discovered that Duke Toma had once played with his memories, the eternal understood just how upset his young companion had to be now. Very few things frightened Aurim Bedlam as did the idea of another manipulating his thoughts. *Have they hurt you?*

No, but they'll be back to try again soon! Darkhorse, you wouldn't believe the power that Lanith controls! It—

You can tell me later, Aurim! The important thing now is to help me locate you so that we can depart this terrible place! You must concentrate! Concentrate as hard as you can so that I can find your position!

I'll try! The sorcerer ended the conversation, but did not sever the weak link. Instead, Darkhorse felt an increased sense of Aurim's presence. The younger Bedlam was powerful and even despite the handicaps his captors' spells had put on him, his will was great. In fact, it was more focused than Darkhorse could ever recall. If one thing good had come out of the kidnapping, it was Aurim's increased control over his will.

Slowly the eternal homed in on Aurim's location. Deeper down, as he had expected, but far more to the north. That placed Aurim near the vicinity of the Magical Order's living quarters.

Darkhorse had already risked discovery the moment he had abandoned Yssa and the protection of her medallion. By entering the palace he further increased the threat, yet he had no choice. *I must act the moment I know exactly where they keep him! We must be gone within seconds!*

He sent a subtle probe in the general direction of Aurim, trying to detect the nearby presence of Saress or any of the others. Darkhorse sensed nothing, but briefly he experienced a peculiar echo effect, as if his probe had turned around and detected his own presence. The effect was momentary and he shrugged it off. What was important was to rescue Aurim.

Darkhorse? Are you still there?

I am, Aurim. Prepare yourself. Are you chained?

Yes. They're iron chains. If I could use my powers, they wouldn't matter.

Any guards?

No. They didn't feel I needed one.

That was good. One less hurdle. Darkhorse readied himself. *Very well, Aurim. Here I come!*

The short distance was nothing in comparison to his earlier treks. Darkhorse vanished from the one chamber, almost instantly appearing at his destination. He felt a brief disorientation that caused his vision to blur, but the sensation passed.

"Darkhorse! Are you all right?"

"Aurim?" The shadow steed twisted around, finally locating the sorcerer. Aurim Bedlam was chained against the far wall of his cell. Torchlight shone weakly through the bars of the small window in the cell door, just enough illumination to reveal the haggard, pale features of the young spellcaster.

With a snort of disgust for his companion's captors, the eternal stepped closer and inspected the chains. They were, as Aurim had said, simple iron chains. Under normal conditions, the lad should have been able to remove them without any trouble, even considering his past lack of control.

A simple glance by Darkhorse caused both bracelets to quietly open. Aurim rubbed his wrists, smiling in gratitude.

"We must be away from here immediately, Aurim! Mount up and I will take us back to your parents!"

The sorcerer quickly obeyed, saying nothing. Darkhorse concentrated. No blink hole, this time. He needed the swiftest if least secure teleportation spell he knew.

The cell faded away. The vague outline of what Darkhorse knew to be the gardens of the Manor formed around the pair. They were nearly home.

That was when something pulled them back.

"Darkhorse!"

He could not reply to his friend, so caught up was he in trying to fight the forces acting against them. Whatever power Lanith had raised, it was stronger than he would have believed. It was also the most unusual force Darkhorse had ever fought, for it seemed to come from a number of sources even though it acted as if it came from only one.

Lanith's sorcerers working in concert? Darkhorse could not believe that the ragtag bunch could summon such strength even together. More important, he doubted that they could coordinate their efforts so effectively. This attack was being guided by a masterful force.

An intelligent force . . .

His struggles went for naught. Darkhorse and Aurim finally rematerialized, but their new location was neither the Manor nor the dungeon. The shadow steed and his companion now stood in the center of the very same dust-laden chamber that Darkhorse had first visited in his search.

This time, however, it was not uninhabited. A single torch posted in the wall by the door illuminated the room enough so that they could readily see King Lanith sitting in the lone chair. The horse king's eyes gleamed as he stared at the ebony stallion. It was a possessive stare, one that unsettled Darkhorse more than it should have.

"At last . . ." Lanith smiled wide. "Magnificent!"

Darkhorse attempted another spell. The same force that had brought him here crushed his attempt.

The horse king stood. "You're even more amazing than I could've believed! Truly you're worthy of being my mount!"

"Worthy of *what*?" Despite their predicament, Darkhorse could only laugh. "*I*? You think me your mount? You are more than mad, King Lanith!"

The monarch of Zuu paid his retort no mind, instead looking up past the shadow steed. "Aurim . . ."

A pair of hands, Aurim's hands, touched the eternal on the neck.

Darkhorse lost all control of his form. His legs stiffened as if frozen and he found he could not even move his neck. When he attempted to alter his shape, nothing happened.

"He is yours, Your Majesty." The voice was Aurim Bedlam's, but there was a coldness to it that the shadow steed had never heard before. Darkhorse felt him dismount as he added, "Just as planned."

"Very good. Very good."

Aurim! the shadow steed silently called. *Aurim!* His call went unheeded, though. Either the sorcerer did not sense it or he had no desire to respond.

The young man stepped before him, then performed a mock bow. "I'll leave you now, Darkhorse, so that an old friend can have a word with you."

Without waiting for permission from Lanith, Aurim Bedlam, smiling pleasantly, vanished.

"Well," the king of Zuu commented to the chamber walls. "You did it. You promised and you delivered."

A giggle echoed throughout the chamber, a giggle that grew stronger with each second. Shadows formed by the king, shadows that began to solidify into one form.

"I told you I would, great majesty, oh, yes, I did! Did you think I would fail you? Never, never . . ."

Had he been able to move at all, Darkhorse would have shivered. He knew the voice. Now the eternal even sensed the growing presence of its source, a thing that he had thought long, long trapped in a place from which it could not escape.

It cannot be . . . it cannot be him . . .

Yet as the shadows became a tiny, ebony puppet that floated at eye level, Darkhorse could no longer deny the truth.

Unbidden came the name that he had tried to forever eradicate from his memory.

Ice-blue eyes stared at ice-blue eyes. "And so the story continues . . ." The ebony being giggled despite having no mouth. "And what a part I have set aside for you, my brother, my *self*."

Yureel . . .

CHAPTER IX

Yssa sensed the spell even as she tried her best to aid Trenlen in stalling the two ranchers seeking to retrieve their mounts. Darkhorse had opened the way to the palace, which meant that she had to find some method by which to send the men away so that she could quickly return to him. The longer the hole remained open, the more chance there was of stirring the interest of the Order despite the talisman.

It was Trenlen who finally solved the problem. He put a companionable arm around each of the pair, saying, "Really, friends, it won't take long. The man's horse is skittish. He bought the thing in Gordag-Ai and you know what kind of horses they breed there." This brought some grudging nods from the men, both of whom, from what the enchantress understood, were members of a family controlling one of the largest breeding ranches of Zuu. "Why don't you come inside and we'll have a drink on me. I'd say that by the time we finish, the man and his horse'll be out of our hair. Isn't that right, darling?"

Yssa took his cue. "That's right. You take care of them, my love. I'll see to everything here. Gentlemen . . ."

The two men with Trenlen allowed themselves to be led away, the offer of a drink no doubt the deciding factor. Yssa watched them for a moment, then hurried back inside.

She caught sight of the eternal just as he stepped through a blink hole. The enchantress called out, but Darkhorse did not look back. The moment he was completely through, the hole vanished.

Damn him! What does he think he's doing? Yssa rushed to the empty stall seeking some trace of her companion, but the huge stallion had left no sign. She knew very well where he had gone and the knowledge made her shiver. Poor Miklo had entered the palace and he had never come out. The memory of the last seconds of their link still remained with her. A sense of falling and falling without end . . . then nothing.

Darkhorse was far more powerful than lost Miklo, but that did not mean the magical stallion was immune from danger. That had already been proven to her. More important, Dark-horse did not understand Zuu and its monarch the way Yssa, who had lived here for many years, did. Yssa was old enough to recall Prince Blane and the old king. Lanith was neither his brother nor his father. He had become a driven man, capable of anything if it furthered his goal, and now he appeared to have the power to back his obsessive nature.

I have to talk with Trenlen! He might have a suggestion! The enchantress rushed back to the entrance, wondering how she could interrupt him without raising the suspicions of the two men he had invited for a drink. With Darkhorse gone, Yssa supposed that she could tell them that their mounts were now accessible. If they were still in so great a hurry, perhaps they would forgo the rest of their drink . . .

Unfortunately, she had scarcely stepped outside when she sensed the nearby presence of at least two sorcerers. Not Saress, whom Yssa knew too well, but a pair of less competent ones. They had some power, though. The enchantress tensed. Ponteroy, perhaps. He was the only other senior member of the Magical Order that Yssa had any respect for. The man was an overdressed dandy, but he did have skill of a sort . . . and at this moment he was much too close for comfort.

Reaching into her pouch, Yssa checked for the medallion. Its presence did not do much to comfort her. She found it highly suspicious that the two sorcerers she sensed were closing on her general vicinity from opposite directions. Perhaps she had been wrong to think the medallion had been strong enough to shield both Darkhorse and herself.

Whatever the reason, she had to leave quickly. Yssa did not want to endanger Trenlen. Lanith dealt harshly with spies.

She contemplated transporting herself away, but decided that doing so would do more to reveal her presence. The medallion had its limits. Yssa looked around, studying the vicinity. Better to lose herself among the evening crowds. Her illusion still held, so even Ponteroy, who had seen her once in the past, would not recognize her.

A busy inn a short distance down the street seemed the perfect destination. Yssa walked casually toward it, trying not to look around any more than what would be normal. The two sorcerers were very nearby. Now she sensed that one was definitely Ponteroy, his presence ever tinged by a dark, almost oily aura. It was hard not to underestimate him because of his appearance.

The inn was as crowded as the enchantress had hoped it would be. The tone was slightly more subdued than she recalled from her years past here, but that was not surprising considering the current situation. Lanith might have his people stirred up for war, but that did not mean that they did not contemplate the possible results of that war on their own time. Yssa knew that the majority of Zuu's inhabitants preferred the peaceful life. They were always willing to defend themselves or a cause they believed in, but conquest was not a national goal. That was a part of their kingdom's nomadic past. Only Lanith dreamed of creating an empire, but then, Lanith was king and in Zuu that was enough for the people. He commanded and they obeyed.

Locating a seat deep in the common room, Yssa did her best to look like a weary traveler. A serving woman glanced her way but did not immediately come over, more concerned, it seemed, with the male customers. Yssa, who had plied such a trade for a time, grimaced briefly. Men and women in Zuu might be more or less equal, but personal prejudices were rampant. She would be lucky if any of the serving women came by soon.

Even among so many people, it was not difficult for her to sense the presence of the nearby sorcerers. They were not trying to shield themselves, which possibly meant that they were not actually after her. Yssa hoped that was the case, but their path continued to hint otherwise. Now they were both so near that she almost expected to see one of them walk through the inn door.

A huge woman carrying a tray stepped in front of her. "Do you want food or drink?"

Ignoring the serving woman's flippant tone, Yssa replied, "I want some ale." Her eyes darted back to the door. "Some bread, too."

"I'm not certain about the ale, darling, but they'll certainly serve you bread in the dungeons."

The enchantress stared into the eyes of the serving woman. "Hello, Yssa," smirked the tall, plain figure.

She felt an invisible web fall upon her, a web of sorcery Yssa immediately knew had been designed to sap her of her strength. It would have worked, too, but the ploy was so typical of her adversary that even without forethought Yssa was prepared for it. Before the web could completely settle, Yssa vanished.

She reappeared an eyeblink later in an alley not very far from the inn. The maneuver had been a risky one and only Yssa's comprehensive knowledge of Zuu had prevented her from possibly materializing in a wall. Such swift transportation spells were ever risky, especially those cast in the midst of danger . . . and there was no danger greater to Yssa than Saress.

I overestimated myself. She had evaded Saress for so very long that she had not sufficiently taken into account the other's skills. Yssa had told Darkhorse that the other sorceress might be a little stronger than she, but what she had failed to add was that Saress was also more practiced. Saress was at least a hundred years old, and it was said that at one time she had even convinced Azran Bedlam to reveal some of his secrets to her.

The alley was empty and Yssa sensed no sorcerers nearby, but she knew better than to believe that she was safe. The pair she had noted had possibly been decoys designed to keep her from noticing a shielded and disguised Saress. Now all three of them would be shielded. Worse, one of them *had* to be Ponteroy, who also could be quite devious. Saress would not waste her time working with the less competent spellcasters. She had been hunting for Yssa for far too long now to take such chances.

Hoping that the medallion would shield her to some extent, the disguised sorceress leaped to a new location. This time when she appeared, vertigo nearly overtook her. Yssa leaned against the wall of an elaborate house belonging to one of King Lanith's own generals, a veteran named Belfour who had been an admirer of hers when she had worked as a serving woman. Yssa often thought that it would have been better if Belfour had become king, he being remotely related to Lanith.

According to her sources, Belfour was supposed to be out in the field drilling His Majesty's armies, which was the reason she had chosen his estate for a momentary respite. Yssa doubted that Saress would expect her to use the home of so august a person as General Belfour. More likely the other sorceress would still be searching the vicinity of the inns and the grand marketplace.

It would have made sense to depart Zuu entirely and return to the safety of her father's domain, but Yssa was not quite ready to abandon Darkhorse despite his having left her. Of course, by this time the shadowy stallion should have rescued Aurim Bedlam and departed the kingdom for Penacles, but Yssa suspected that such was not the case. First, she was fairly certain that Darkhorse would have come back for her. Second, the confrontation with Saress had been too well executed to have been spur of the moment. Someone had been watching out for them.

The enchantress recalled her own words to Darkhorse. An intelligent force. She still recalled the first time she had sensed it. Never in her life had she felt such a peculiar, unsettling presence . . . although now that Yssa had spent some time around Darkhorse, she realized that there was something about the stallion that reminded her of Lanith's creature.

That was impossible, though. Everyone knew that there was nothing in the Dragonrealm like Darkhorse.

"So what do I do now?" she muttered. For years, Yssa had

depended only on herself. She had not had to worry about others. Now she feared for a companion not even human.

"You! What are you doing here?"

Startled, Yssa whirled around. Two soldiers, obviously members of the general's household guard, approached her with swords drawn. Yssa cursed herself for a mindless idiot. Of course they would be on duty even if their master was away. Being confronted by Saress so soon after Darkhorse's disappearance had left her much too befuddled for her own good.

She was not too worried, however. Swords might be a threat to most, but not to a skilled spellcaster. As the pair closed in on her, Yssa stared at their weapons.

The blades twisted, quickly intertwining with one another. Both men stumbled to a halt, tugging on their weapons. The enchantress concentrated, abandoning her latest location for the only one left that she believed to be safe. It frustrated her to keep running, but that was all that was left to her for now.

General Belfour's estate faded, to be replaced a moment later by thick forest. Yssa was back in the land of Dagora, her father's domain. She breathed a sigh of relief.

The sigh became a startled gasp as a hand took hold of her by the shoulder. She tried to vanish again, but nothing happened. Yssa tried one more time with the same results.

Her captor spun her around.

It had been quite some time since she had seen him, but Yssa could never forget Cabe Bedlam.

"I come here searching for my son and Darkhorse and find you instead. What are you doing here?" His expression indicated that he was not at all pleased to see her again.

The sorceress sought to regain her composure. She gave him the same smile that had enchanted so many without magic, but this time the results were not what she hoped. Cabe Bedlam was not at all moved by her beauty and her manner.

Belatedly, Yssa recalled that she still wore the illusion. He did not even know who she was, much less what she looked like. Seeing no reason to continue her masquerade, the enchantress dropped the illusion.

"You!" Bedlam's expression tightened further, as if he had suddenly found himself touching something rather foul. "Tori, isn't it?"

Rather disappointed in his lackluster reaction to her identity, Yssa did not immediately reply. The sorceress had changed since the last time she had met him, although admittedly their prior confrontation had been a short one. Perhaps this was simply a side that she had not noticed. Yssa was not certain that she cared for it.

"Darkhorse went looking for my son, who was supposed to be somewhere in Penacles. Darkhorse never came back with him and when I searched for both, I found no trace of their presence. It took some doing, but I tracked my shadowy friend to this general region . . . only instead of him, I sensed you."

"You *couldn't*. The medallion—"

Cabe's gaze cut off her protest. "I've the experience and knowledge of two lifetimes, although I can't expect you to understand what I mean. Sometimes it helps. Now, I'll ask you this once. What's happened to them? Some notions have been running through my imagination, but I'm hoping that you'll tell me I'm wrong, Tori."

Under his intense scrutiny, any thought of seduction faded. Only one thing interested Cabe Bedlam now. Yssa saw no reason to hold back. The master sorcerer was probably the only one who could really help her. "Lanith has your son . . . and I think he might also have Darkhorse."

"Tell me."

She did, trying her best not to leave anything out that might be of importance. The enchantress spoke of Sarcss and her masquerade, of Darkhorse's discovery and his determination to rescue Aurim as soon as possible, and of her own role in the situation. She ended with the shadow steed's disappearance and her narrow escape from the other spellcasters.

Yssa kept back only the truth about her origins. Knowing how Cabe Bedlam felt about her father, it made more sense than ever to avoid revealing the secret she had kept hidden so long.

As Yssa explained, Cabe Bedlam's expression grew so

grim that the enchantress feared that some of his frustration and anger would spill onto her. Yssa did not relish facing the might of the strongest sorcerer in the land. Fortunately, Cabe's gaze finally shifted from her to the west . . . where Zuu lay.

"Damn Lanith . . . what right does he have to my son? What right does he have to *conquest*? All I've ever wanted for the Dragonrealm is peace!"

Knowing he required no answer from her, Yssa took a step away from the robed sorcerer. Although Cabe Bedlam's voice was still quiet, she could sense the energy building around him, sorcerous energy that he would eventually have to unleash somehow. Yssa had a suspicion that it would not be long, either.

"You didn't see Aurim in Zuu, did you?"

"No. I only know what I told you. Trenlen's daughters saw him."

"Who's this Trenlen, anyway? Why did he help you?"

Answering those questions meant treading in dangerous territory, but Yssa did the best she could. "Someone I know from when I still lived there. He doesn't care for what the king is doing. Neither do his daughters."

Cabe clearly knew that she had not told him everything, but fortunately, he chose not to pursue the matter. "Do you remember where it was Aurim was supposed to be?"

"Yes." She described the location, but he seemed dissatisfied.

"Be silent for a moment. I'll try something." Cabe shut his eyes before the enchantress could reply. Energy continued to gather around him.

Yssa sensed a spell, probably a probe since she noted no changes around them. The sorcerer was seeking the mind of his son.

Moments later Cabe opened his eyes, frowning. "Hard to say, but I think I know where they are. Strange, though . . ."

"What?"

"Darkhorse . . . it was as if he were in two nearby but different locations . . ." The master mage waved off his own comment. "Zuu reeks with sorcery. It's even worse than we thought. Once I rescue them, we'll have to talk to the Gryphon. Lanith's gone too far."

"What are you going to do?" Yssa had a notion, but prayed that she was wrong.

Looking at her as if she should have understood immediately, Cabe replied, "I'm going in there, of course."

This was too much for her. Darkhorse she could understand charging into the fray, but Cabe Bedlam was supposed to have more sense. Had he not faced down the Ice Dragon, the Quel, Shade the warlock, and countless other foes? Surviving such adversaries required not only great skill and power, but also intelligence.

Yet . . . it *was* his son that the horse king had kidnapped. Even though her father and she had been estranged for several years, she knew that she would have tried to rescue him if he had been in the same predicament as the younger Bedlam.

"You don't know Zuu the way I do, though," she told him, feeling a sense of déjà vu. "You need me. I know the city."

Cabe eyed her with some skepticism, probably recalling their previous encounter. "This is something I'd best do alone. This time, I know what to expect."

Before she could say anything more, the sorcerer turned his gaze in the direction of Zuu. Yssa sensed power rising from within and around the master mage. Once again, Cabe Bedlam's incredible power astounded her. The enchantress briefly toyed with her old notion of seeking him as the perfect mate, but she doubted that even at her most seductive she would be able to turn his head. The sorcerer had that look that said he was very much married and enjoyed being so. Yssa had never seen the Lady Bedlam, but decided that the other sorceress had to be someone very special.

"I see the barriers," Cabe whispered. "Interesting. Grandfather would've liked their design."

Yssa had no idea what he meant by that, but the matter was moot. Cabe Bedlam blinked . . . and was gone.

"More stubborn than Darkhorse," she muttered. That was it, then. Cabe Bedlam had gone to retrieve his son and comrade from Zuu. If anyone could do it, he could. That left Yssa with the question of just what she should do next. Return to her father? Not yet. Perhaps she should journey back to the former Barren Lands. It was the one place Yssa was certain that Saress would not find her, not that the witch was probably looking for her anymore. Saress certainly had better things to do than go pursuing Yssa yet again. They had played this game often enough.

The grasslands, then. No matter how stirred up her emotions were, the enchanted field where she had brought Cabe and Darkhorse after their last encounter always soothed her. It still amused her how anxious the shadow steed had been to depart it. The grass would never have harmed him . . . it probably could not have done so even if it had tried.

Yssa felt for the medallion her father had given her. Considering how poorly it had worked so far, she was tempted to just leave it here, but her father would be upset with her if he found out. She decided that she would return it after she had spent some time recovering her calm.

Yes, a rest would do her nicely first . . .

What sounded like the crackle of thunder made her stiffen. A sudden, powerful gust of wind threatened to push her against the nearest tree. Yssa sensed sorcery, but from exactly what source or direction she could not say.

A man-sized projectile materialized out of the air, flying past at a remarkable rate of speed. Only as it dropped toward the earth did the sorceress see that it *was* a man. Cabe Bedlam, in fact.

Too startled to act, Yssa watched as the other spellcaster plummeted to what certainly had to be his death. He had materialized far too high up and flown at far too swift a speed to land safely. Belatedly she raised a hand, trying to concentrate enough to cast a spell.

At the very last moment, the sorcerer's progress slowed. A small blue aura formed around him. Cabe Bedlam struck the ground hard, but not nearly so hard as Yssa had feared. Probably he had been knocked unconscious.

She started toward him but then had to leap behind a tree as the air opened up again. This time, a half-dozen figures appeared. They stood together, surveying the area with varying looks of interest and trepidation.

In their lead was Ponteroy. In one hand he held a short staff topped by a crystal carved into the head of a horse. Yssa knew that the gaudily-clad sorcerer used the staff to better focus his own powers.

Of the other spellcasters, most, including the older woman, were vaguely familiar to her, but their identities were not so important as the fact that despite their obvious anxiousness, they began to search the area very methodically. This was not the collection of misfits that she recalled from several weeks back. They still had rough edges, but the Magical Order looked much more like a cohesive fighting unit than Miklo had indicated during their final meeting.

"Look over there," Ponteroy commanded a youth, the only one completely unknown to Yssa. She suspected that he was one of the students kidnapped from Penacles, but now he seemed an eager servant of Lanith.

They were searching for Cabe Bedlam, of course, but fortunately, Ponteroy had chosen to focus on the wrong area. That meant that she had a chance to get to the sorcerer first and spirit him away before the others noticed.

Crouching and hoping that the medallion would do her some good after all, Yssa moved slowly toward where Cabe lay unmoving. Fortunately for the master sorcerer, he had landed behind some trees. Yssa also noticed that she could barely detect the unconscious spellcaster, which meant that he had woven a fairly complex shield spell around himself. That would not hide him forever, though, which was why she had to reach him quickly.

The sorcerer's still unmoving form worried her immensely. The enchantress began to wonder whether he had been more severely injured than she had first thought, but since he lay on his stomach she could not see what his face might reveal. However, when Yssa tried to turn him over, an invisible barrier more than an inch thick prevented her. No matter how she tried to move him, the spell would not allow her to get any grip.

"Sometimes you can be too safe," she whispered to the unconscious figure. Yssa quickly glanced at the hunters, now distant, only partially visible forms. The longer they took, the better. She needed time to decide how to get around Cabe's protective spells.

Then a second crackle of thunder made her look around with renewed anxiety. She sensed that someone new and much more capable had joined the pursuing mages, someone with abilities far more impressive than those of either Saress or Ponteroy. An unfamiliar voice said something unintelligible, something that made Ponteroy reply angrily. The newcomer added one more comment, then an unnerving silence ensued.

Yssa redoubled her efforts to move Cabe. She tried to pick up his head, but only managed to cause him to shift a little. However, the movement evidently was enough to wake the sorcerer. Cabe Bedlam groaned, then slowly opened his eyes.

Yssa leaned close, whispering, "I can't touch you! Let me touch you so that we can get out of here before they find us!"

He closed his eyes, seeming to drift off again. However, the protective spells around him lessened, then vanished. Cabe opened his eyes again. "Do what . . . you can now. My concentration is still too . . . I can't focus enough . . . yet."

Yssa nodded, seizing hold of him.

A figure clad in brown sorcerer's robes suddenly materialized at her side. Yssa looked up into an ugly face whose most dominant feature was one of the longest, sharpest noses the enchantress had ever seen. The spellcaster was bald, not even having eyebrows. He reminded her of a vulture.

"Here he's lying," the vulture called out, "and he's got someone with—"

A heavy branch suddenly swung down and swatted the bald hunter in the face, cutting off his words. With a groan, he fell back, stunned.

Having momentarily disposed of one foe, Yssa found her mind now blank. She had to take Cabe away from here, but the question of where was too much for her muddled senses.

From all around her Yssa felt the use of sorcery. The other spellcasters were acting in *concert* now, creating some sort of prison . . . and yet she could still not focus her mind. Should she take Cabe to her father? That did not seem wise. Should she take him to the grasslands? He might react to them the same way Darkhorse had. Why of all times was it impossible for her to think?

As if sensing her dilemma, her companion whispered, "The Manor. Take us there. Let me show you."

With one hand, he touched her forehead. An image of a place formed, an image so lifelike, Yssa almost tried to reach out and touch it.

It was a house, an abode, but like none she had ever come across in her life. Massive stone walls merged with barriers formed from the very earth. Chiseled marble and cut wood had been used to build much of the structure, but the right side seemed to have been built into a huge and still living tree. Atop the roof and overlooking the front entrance was a metallic figure, a tall Seeker. The avian creature was so realistic he seemed ready to swoop down on unsuspecting newcomers.

The building was at least three stories tall and wider than some barons' castles that Yssa had seen. A small army could have dwelled within those walls.

"There. The Manor," the sorcerer concluded. "Now you know where to go."

She did and just in time, too, for several yards away, a second figure materialized. He was not one of the original hunters, but Yssa knew that he had to be one of their fellows. Although escape was what she should have been concentrating on, the enchantress could not help staring first. Before her stood a handsome, golden-haired man who resembled a hero from the epics spun in the taverns of Zuu. Her heart beat faster and Yssa had to remind herself that this man was an enemy.

"Who're you?" he demanded. The voice was the same one that she had heard giving commands to Ponteroy.

Yssa desperately thought about Cabe Bedlam's home, the mysterious and legendary Manor. She pictured it as he had shown it to her.

"Stop—" the other sorcerer began. A brief hesitant look crossed his features, then fury took over.

His darkening visage was the last thing the enchantress saw before the world around her faded.

For a moment she and Cabe hung suspended in the middle

of nothing, then, thankfully, a new scene unfolded. Gone was the forest, although in the distance Yssa could still see tall trees. Instead, the pair of them had ended up in a huge, well-manicured garden that stretched long into the distance. Some of the bushes had been trimmed into the shapes of animals. A marble walkway led toward what looked like a hedge maze. Here and there, benches dotted the area.

Someone cleared their throat. Yssa looked over her shoulder and saw a tall, scarlet-tressed woman dressed in a beautiful forest-green gown. Behind her was the back of a huge edifice one side of which was part of an immense tree.

"I would venture to say," the woman remarked in a very cold voice, "that you must be the one he called Tori. Now would you like to explain to me what you're doing with my husband?"

Knowing more than most about the legendary Lady of the Amber, Yssa involuntarily cringed.

"It's all right, Gwen," muttered Cabe. He untangled himself from Yssa and tried to rise. Halfway up, the sorcerer seized his head in both hands. "Except for every bone and muscle aching and an incredible throbbing in my head, that is. If anything . . . if anything, Yssa probably saved me from capture."

"Yssa? I thought her name was Tori . . . and what's this about capture? You went to find our son." Lady Bedlam's tone grew anxious. "What's happened to him, Cabe? Where is he?"

"He's a prisoner of Zuu. The young woman he met in Penacles was evidently a sorceress working for the horse king. Saress was her true name, I believe."

"A . . . prisoner." Cabe Bedlam's wife grew furious again, but at least this time her fury was not focused on Yssa. "How *dare* that barbaric horse trainer hold my son! We have to get him back immediately!"

"That may not be so simple—" Yssa began, clamping her mouth shut the moment the other sorceress looked at her. She had made a mistake reminding Gwendolyn Bedlam of her presence.

"What she means," Cabe quickly interjected, "is that Zuu is

better protected than I could ever imagine. I can't even get inside the city walls. In fact, when I tried, I was thrown back so hard it stunned me for several minutes. If not for Yssa, Lanith's spellcasters would've captured me." He shook his head, then grimaced in evident pain. "They acted in unison, nearly perfect unison. I felt it even as they hammered me. I don't think I've ever heard of spellcasters working so well together, not even the Dragon Masters."

He suddenly turned his face away from his wife, but Yssa, who now had a clear look at it, saw the anxiety and pain. Her suspicions about what she had seen just before they had escaped were now verified by his obvious pain. He knew the golden-haired sorcerer who had nearly captured them.

If she could not see his expression, Gwendolyn Bedlam could certainly read his turbulent emotions in his actions. The enchantress put a comforting hand on her husband's arm. "Cabe, what is it?"

Swallowing, Cabe looked at her. "Gwen, one of the attackers was . . . it was *Aurim!*"

"That's impossible!" She jerked her hand away. "He wouldn't—"

"And I don't think he did." The robed figure stared at Yssa. "Did you sense it? Did you get a chance to probe him?"

It had not occurred to Yssa to do any such thing. All that had concerned her was to escape, taking her stunned companion with her. "I didn't . . . I don't understand . . ."

"No, you wouldn't. I probably sensed him just before you did, I suppose. I reacted without really thinking. I could feel the presence of my son, but when I tried to speak to him through his mind in order to avoid alerting the others, I ran across—" He stopped, clearly unable to believe what he was saying. "There was another mind overlapping his own. I couldn't even reach Aurim's!"

"Possession?" Lady Bedlam snapped. "Not possession! Not after what Toma did to him!"

An intelligent force . . . Yssa recalled Miklo's last moments again. "The thing in the palace! The thing that Lanith controls!"

Oddly, Cabe Bedlam shook his head. "I would've thought

so, but it can't be. That can't be what I sensed . . . and yet, what I sensed could not be the truth, either." He looked at both of them. "What I sensed . . . was *Darkhorse*."

"What?" both women cried. Yssa wondered if Cabe still suffered from a concussion. He had to be mistaken.

"It was Darkhorse," he insisted. "I know Darkhorse's magical trace. There's nothing like it in all the Dragonrealm. *He's* seized Aurim's mind . . . and now it seems he's forcing our son to serve the king of Zuu, even if it means fighting us!"

CHAPTER X

Yureel.

If there was a thing in all of creation that Darkhorse feared, it was Yureel. He had believed he had seen the last of the monster, but here Yureel was, once more turning living beings into puppets to be wasted in horrific tableaus of violence all for the sake of the mad creature's personal entertainment. That was all any other being was to Yureel, a thing to be utilized for his enjoyment, then discarded when of no further value.

The shadow steed still could not move. The spell that Aurim had cast was a thorough one thanks to the guidance of the macabre little figure. Aurim Bedlam had probably been the thrall of Yureel since soon after his capture, a thrall now eager to do whatever his master desired. Somewhere deep inside, the young sorcerer's mind might still be active, but it hardly mattered. Darkhorse had seen few who could escape the control of the shadow man.

He himself had been one of those few, but now Yureel had him again.

Through Aurim's sorcery they had moved him to a stone structure that had, until recently, served as part of the royal stable. That was all he had been told by the king of Zuu, who, whenever he visited, stared at the shadow steed with a greedy eye. Darkhorse had been here for two days now, unable to move or even use his power to send a mental summons to Cabe or the Gryphon. It was clear that Yureel had spent much time plotting Darkhorse's capture.

Why this, Yureel? Why not simply do what I know you desire? Why not finish me? The sinister little demon had some wicked torture in mind. That had to be it. Yureel wanted him to suffer great mental anguish, vengeance for the ebony puppet's long imprisonment in the empty realm known only as the Void.

Perhaps that was why Darkhorse was here. Perhaps Yureel planned on keeping him here for a few centuries . . . but, no, that was ridiculous. Besides, King Lanith seemed expectant about something. *If the madman thinks—*

A dread rolled over him. Darkhorse sensed another presence, one so much like himself that only he could have noticed the difference.

The insane giggle floated about the chamber. A tiny speck of darkness in one far corner suddenly expanded until it formed a nearly human figure only a foot tall. Once fully shaped, Yureel floated serenely toward his prisoner.

"I do hope you've been enjoying the accommodations, brother dear!" The miniature phantom drifted to eye level. "I wanted you to feel at home since you enjoy that absurd form so much!" Yureel cocked his head. "Oh, dear. I forgot that you're speechless for now, aren't you? That'll teach you to be impolite to our gracious host."

Briefly granted speech in the room where he had been captured, Darkhorse had used it to tell King Lanith what he thought of his part in this. The would-be conqueror had not been amused, although Yureel had been. Nonetheless, the shadow puppet had ordered Aurim to silence the prisoner and Cabe's son had obeyed without hesitation.

"We had quite an interesting time shortly after you were captured, Darkhorse. A little side note to my growing epic. It seems a loyal friend of yours wanted to visit. He tried to enter without great Lanith's permission." Yureel giggled. "I'm afraid that we had to destroy him. I hope Aurim won't miss his father *too* much!"

Cabe? Cabe had already tried to rescue him? What was Yureel trying to say . . . that Darkhorse's dearest companion had been killed in the process? *Impossible!* he wanted to roar. *You are as bald a liar as ever, Yureel!*

"You have a twinkle in your eye! Are you trying to tell me something?" He giggled again.

Darkhorse felt the tingle of sorcery. An instant later Aurim Bedlam joined the pair. He bowed to Yureel, completely ignoring his friend.

"I've done as you requested."

The tiny figure turned. "Really? So soon? I'm so proud of you! Show me, quickly!"

Aurim stretched forth his arms. Something made of leather and metal appeared on the floor before him. It took Darkhorse a few seconds to identify the creation as a bridle and bit.

"Is that all right?"

"Lovely, lovely, indeed! And the best of all?"

The sorcerer actually smiled. It was a smile that made the shadow steed want to cringe, so much did it seem more the expression that Yureel would have worn . . . had the latter actually had a mouth.

"Here." Aurim pointed next to the bridle. A glittering, golden saddle materialized. A strip of silver lined the edge of the saddle and the horn vaguely resembled an equine head. To Darkhorse the object was gaudy, which meant that it likely had been designed by his counterpart, not the sorcerer. "Is that the way you wanted it?"

Yureel clapped his tiny hands together. "Perfection! Simply perfection!" He turned to Darkhorse. "You should be extremely proud of him, brother! He's overcome all of his inadequacies quite quickly, hasn't he?"

"He can't talk," Aurim commented.

"Let him . . . for the moment."

"Release me, Yureel!" cried the ebony stallion the moment he realized that the spell of silence no longer held. "End this folly before it comes crashing down on you!"

"You do like to pontificate . . ." His tone switched, shifting from taunting to bitter. "Perhaps I should throw you into the Void so that *you* can try listening to yourself as you float trapped without hope! Trapped!"

"You were responsible for your own imprisonment, Yureel!

You tried to turn a land into chaos and disaster! You caused death and destruction on a grand scale and felt nothing for the mortal lives you wasted! The sorcerers who finally discovered you and found a way to bind you could have destroyed you instead!"

The shadow puppet's icy eyes narrowed. "But they couldn't, Darkhorse! They couldn't! For a long, long time, I wished that they had . . . for having tasted so much life, realizing that there were so many epics to create, I wanted more!" He giggled again. "And now, I shall create my greatest!"

He is more insane than ever! "Again with the stories, Yureel? What is it with you and your pathetic yearning to create these so-called epics? Is it because you so little understand the lives of the creatures you torment that you think you can learn something by manipulating them in scene after scene of devastation?"

Without removing his gaze from that of Darkhorse, Yureel snapped, "Replace the spell!"

Darkhorse found himself silenced again. He had apparently touched upon a tender point. Yureel looked ready to say something else, but was interrupted by another newcomer.

It was Lanith. The horse king was alone, probably because he wanted no one else to see his phantom servant . . . if the shadow man could be called *anyone's* servant. From what Darkhorse knew of Yureel, it was the horse king who was the puppet.

"How much longer, imp? I've been more than patient! When will he be ready?"

"Your timing is impeccable, O great emperor!" Both Yureel and Aurim performed bows before the king of Zuu, although the former's was decidedly perfunctory. Lanith, however, did not seem to notice the lapse. "Only this moment has your young but so capable master sorcerer completed the tasks I set before him!"

Aurim indicated the bridle and saddle. The horse king, unable to sense the incredible amount of power imbued into the items, seemed somewhat disappointed.

"This will do it? I've a hundred saddles better-looking than this, all made carefully by the best craftsmen in the kingdom.

This hardly looks like a suitable saddle for a king, much less an item that'll make *him* behave as he should."

"You don't like the design?" asked Yureel with what sounded like actual disappointment. The floating figure indicated Darkhorse. "Well, you'll like what it does, I promise you that! Aurim?"

Retrieving the saddle and bridle, the young sorcerer turned to Darkhorse and stared.

The shadow steed felt the bit in his mouth and the strap of the saddle around his torso. Try as he might, Darkhorse could not free himself of the magical items his ensorcelled friend had constructed. Aurim's spell still held sway.

"Now release him."

"Yes, Yureel."

Darkhorse felt a great weight lift off of him, but it was immediately replaced by another, more subtle spell that he quickly realized emanated from the bridle and saddle. He could move his head a little, but that was all. The shadow steed still had no control over his general form.

"He's ready, Your Majesty," the sorcerer announced.

Yureel laughed, then floated to the stallion's head. Darkhorse could just barely see him in his peripheral vision. "As promised, great majesty, the only mount *fit* to be yours! A steed perfect for the conqueror of the Dragonrealm, the future emperor of all!"

"Magnificent!" Lanith strode to Darkhorse, who wanted to rise up and kick the king away but could not. The tall human stroked his neck, whispering what the eternal considered inane comforting noises that might have worked on a true animal but only served to annoy him further.

Lanith mounted, the action marred only by a brief giggle from Yureel. The warrior king adjusted his seating slightly, then said, "I want to take him out and run him around the yard."

"You have only to guide him as you would any other horse," Aurim replied. "He'll show only as much spirit as you desire, Your Majesty. The saddle and bridle ensure that."

"Seems a bit of a pity. I normally like to break in my own mounts."

Flittering around so that Darkhorse could see him, Yureel chuckled. "You will still have that pleasure, my wondrous majesty! The longer you ride him, the more he will see that he now only lives to serve you! There is plenty of spirit there to be broken and with a little guidance from me, he will soon be yours in mind as well as body!"

More lies, Yureel! Darkhorse tried to shout. *I will not break! Never! And if I know you, you do not expect me to. You have something else in mind eventually, don't you?* This was merely the shadow puppet's way of weakening Darkhorse. The ebony stallion already knew what fate awaited him. Yureel would not be satisfied until there remained but one of them.

"Open the gates."

"As you've got things well in hand, my glorious monarch, I'll not bother you with my unworthy presence. In my place I shall leave our most loyal Aurim."

Darkhorse could clearly hear the sarcasm in every word, but King Lanith noticed nothing. For the first time, the eternal began to realize how great were the strings with which Yureel manipulated his human "master."

"You're dismissed, imp. Aurim! Open the way to the yard! I want to see what he can do."

"Yes, Your Majesty."

As the sorcerer obeyed, Darkhorse caught one last glimpse of Yureel. The shadow puppet stared back at him, icy eyes glimmering with glee, as he faded back into the shadows.

"Come on, you."

It took Darkhorse a moment to realize that Lanith meant *him*. At first he thought how absurd it was that the king of Zuu would assume that he would quietly obey his dictates. Then, when his body began to move of its own accord despite his best efforts otherwise, Darkhorse realized just how powerful the bridle and saddle were.

Aurim stood by the open entrance of the stable, beaming with pride as the king and Darkhorse moved by. The shadow steed found he could move his head, though not turn it around. His body seemed to have the normal limitations of a true equine. Darkhorse looked at his young friend, but the golden-haired spellcaster merely smiled smugly at him, then looked up at the king.

Lanith urged Darkhorse out into the yard, where he forced the shadow steed to trot. The saddle and bridle functioned as if linked to the monarch's mind; they made Darkhorse do whatever his rider desired. The eternal watched in frustration as his ensorcelled body performed like a trained animal for the horse king.

Feminine laughter accompanied by clapping caused Lanith to finally rein him to a halt. Standing near one wall of the yard was Saress. The enchantress was clad in a very low-cut leather riding outfit. "May I ride him when you're done, my darling?"

Lanith patted Darkhorse on the neck in an obviously possessive manner. "Not just yet, Saress. Perhaps after I've grown more accustomed to him myself." The king stroked the eternal's mane. "Perhaps."

The enchantress pouted theatrically, then pretended to notice Aurim. "There you are!" She crossed the yard slowly, each step designed to attract the attention of both men. "Did you make the saddle? I can sense the spells on it, but they're tied together so intricately I'm amazed that anyone could do it!"

The king had guided Darkhorse around just enough that the eternal could see both spellcasters. Aurim did not seem to take Saress's compliments in the manner that she no doubt hoped he would. In fact, the young sorcerer looked very uncomfortable. Small wonder as the woman practically wrapped herself around him the moment she was near enough.

If she sought to make Lanith jealous, it was a losing cause. Saress's devotion to her king was so clear that Lanith had to know that all he had to do was snap his fingers to summon her to his side. The enchantress might find other males of momentary fascination, but her soul belonged to her master. In some ways, it was ironic justice, considering what she had done to Aurim and others.

"I made them, yes," Aurim answered somewhat hesitantly. No mention was made of Yureel, which confirmed to Darkhorse that Lanith did not share all of his secrets with Saress.

The shadow steed wondered what she thought of Aurim's sudden loyalty to the king or if she even thought of it at all. The enchantress was not a thrall like the younger Bedlam; she was a willing servant. Surely Saress noticed some trace of Yureel's foul presence.

"Come." Lanith, sounding bored with the shift in conversation, turned Darkhorse away from the pair. He made the shadow steed trot once around the yard, then forced him to pick up the pace. Darkhorse tried to reject each command, but the saddle and bridle continued to override his will. Yureel had planned his revenge very well.

Around and around the yard Darkhorse raced, Lanith putting him through a variety of maneuvers that would have pushed even the strongest of mounts to their limits. The eternal performed all of them with ease, which only served to encourage the horse king to try yet more difficult stunts.

He could neither see nor sense his counterpart, but the shadow steed knew that Yureel watched him from somewhere, no doubt giggling merrily all the while. A startling thought occurred to him. *Was this part of Yureel's plan all along? Did he somehow manipulate matters so that I would be the one to come rescue Aurim?*

The macabre little figure had probably not planned things quite so perfectly, but if he had been in the Dragonrealm even for a short period, then he would have had time to study his adversary. He would have known enough about Darkhorse and his relationship with the Bedlams to know that sooner or later the shadow steed would involve himself if one of his mortal friends was kidnapped. That would explain the number of spell traps that Yssa had located around the barony of Adderly. Yureel could not predict *exactly* where Darkhorse would show up, but he could make a fairly good guess . . . and had.

"He handles magnificently!" Lanith called to the others, reining Darkhorse up in front of them. "Never has any king had a finer mount!"

"You look perfect, darling!" The enchantress abandoned Aurim, who looked quite relieved, and put a caressing hand on the king's leg. "Like a warrior god!"

"I do look good, don't I?" Lanith reached down and cupped Saress's chin for a moment, then looked up again and said, "Aurim, you've served me well. He obeys my every command perfectly. Every movement is flawless. He'll serve me well in battle. He'll put the fear into my enemies . . ."

Put fear into his enemies . . . Darkhorse had tried to keep from thinking about what Lanith might desire from him. He had hoped that the horse king might simply keep him in Zuu, but it was clear now that Lanith wanted to take full advantage of the eternal's abilities. The shadow steed was to be the king's warhorse.

He wanted Darkhorse to attack the very people the eternal had always fought to protect. Yureel's vengeance was to be even more terrible than Darkhorse had supposed; the shadow man wanted his counterpart to watch as his own substantial powers were turned on his friends.

King Lanith dismounted with a flourish. His face was flushed from excitement. "Saress! Summon Belfour and the others for me! Why wait any longer? Everything I need is mine!"

"Surely you're not—"

"And why not? There's no power strong enough to stop me! I've got an armed force like none other in the realm. My Magical Order's proven itself against the greatest sorcerer of the realm, Cabe Bedlam himself! Better still, the legendary demon Darkhorse is mine to control, mine to ride! I can't lose now! I will triumph against all foes! I'll be Emperor Lanith, ruler of the Dragonrealm!"

Aurim smiled obediently and Saress, after some initial expressions of concern and confusion, laughed and clapped her hands. They were the perfect puppets, Darkhorse decided, for the puppet king.

He wished that he could speak. Surely Lanith did not think that even with magic and arms behind him he could conquer the entire continent. The Aramites had managed to do that on the other continent, but they had only done so with a power rumored to be greater than Yureel and Darkhorse combined. Even so, their empire had crumbled, unable to stave off numerous rebellions that had risen nearly simultaneously under the Gryphon's guidance.

The monarch of Zuu tossed the reins to Aurim. "See to him. Make sure that he's ready when I need him. I want to ride him slowly through Zuu at the head of my personal guard, to show the people that our destiny is assured." To Saress he added, "Tell Belfour and the others I'll meet them in the throne room. They're to be gathered there in half an hour, no more."

"Yes, darling."

Aurim pulled on the reins. "Come."

Unable to resist, Darkhorse was led back into the stable even as the king gave Saress some last commands. The eternal heard something concerning "that witch," which either referred to Gwendolyn Bedlam or, more likely, the still missing Yssa.

With a gesture, Aurim sealed the entrance behind them, then led Darkhorse back to his stabling. Only then did the human look Darkhorse in the eye. "You won't be able to move now, so don't strain yourself trying." Perhaps he saw something in the shadow steed's stare, for Aurim abruptly removed the spell of silence. "You want to say something?"

Darkhorse forced himself to remain calm. This might be his only opportunity to break the lad free of Yureel's insidious spell. "Aurim, you must listen to me. This is not you. You would never serve a monster such as Yureel or this pathetic, would-be conqueror. You would never attack your own family or use your abilities to rain down destruction on people simply trying to defend themselves."

"If the king commands me to use my powers to aid his efforts, I'm bound to obey."

"You are *not*! It is a spell that binds you, not loyalty. Think! This is Yureel's foul doing! He has seized your mind, twisted your very thoughts. This is not *you*."

The sorcerer's face went blank, then slowly his expression twisted, as if he fought with some inner demon. "No . . . I'm simply loyal to the king . . . but . . . Saress . . . she fooled me . . ."

Darkhorse's eyes flashed. "Fight it, Aurim! You are stronger! You are not Yureel's pawn!"

"*Darkhorse . . .*" The young human looked ready to scream. "I can't—"

"You must!"

"I can't . . . really believe you'd think my hold on him was that weak, brother!" Aurim flashed a smile and giggled, sounding much too much like someone other than himself.

The eternal tried to probe the chamber, but the spell that bound him did not allow him that much power. Still, there was no doubting that Yureel was present nearby. "So, only a game again, eh?"

"A game, a chapter in our epic, call it what you will." The golden-haired man froze, his expression growing slack. "Just as you once told me, I'll tell you now. There is no escape for you and your friend, Darkhorse, not now . . . not ever."

"Yureel—"

Aurim giggled once more, then blinked as if waking. He studied the captive for almost a minute. Darkhorse felt the spell of silence envelop him again. "You'd better behave now. I've got to go."

The human seemed to have no recollection of what had just occurred. Darkhorse did not try to stop him from leaving, not that there was much he could have done. He could only watch as Aurim abandoned him to the silence and darkness of the stable.

The shadows only served to remind him of Yureel, who had proven as masterful as he was cruel. Yureel thoroughly controlled his puppets, utilizing their abilities proficiently so as to preserve his own strength for when it was truly needed. Now he had control of one of the potentially greatest sorcerers alive; there was no telling to what limits the sinister little demon planned to push the younger Bedlam.

He will surely use the lad against his parents just as he plans to use me against them. If Yureel follows true to form, he will probably do his best to see that Aurim injures or perhaps even kills Cabe and Gwen . . .

The very thought would have made him shudder had he still had the ability to move that much. Yureel's mad epic promised blood, destruction, and betrayal. The shadow puppet obviously understood human emotions to such a point that he knew that Aurim's family would find it difficult to unleash their full might against their son. Hesitation would be their fatal flaw, the key to eliminating the only opposition possibly able to put an end to the mad crusade before it spread too far from the borders of Zuu.

He will do it. He will make Aurim attempt to slay his parents . . . and if I am any judge of ability, the lad has the power to succeed.

Aurim had no control over his body. The monstrous thing in his head danced him around like a marionette, making him do this and that for a man the creature obviously disdained. And Darkhorse probably thought Aurim had betrayed him. Thanks to the younger Bedlam's work, the shadow steed was now also a helpless captive. Even if Darkhorse did not believe his friend had turned on him, Aurim felt as if he had.

As he marched obediently through the palace halls toward the throne room, Aurim struggled to regroup his thoughts. He had never felt so frightened in his life, not even when Toma had seized hold of his thoughts for a time. The drake had merely blocked some of his memories; he had never actually possessed Aurim. That had been unsettling enough, but his predicament now was . . . hideous.

Everyone in the palace assumed that he was now the loyal servant of King Lanith. Inwardly, that could not have been further from the truth. The link that the demon Yureel maintained with Aurim made him do whatever the graying warrior demanded, but only because Yureel desired it as well. Lanith was almost as much a puppet as he was. However, the dark imp dared not completely seize control of his so-called ally because others would have eventually realized that the king of Zuu was not quite himself. Besides, Yureel did have limitations of his own.

That was the only thing that gave him some hope. His captor did not have complete access to his thoughts, not if Aurim exercised some of the concentration tricks his parents had taught him. To be truthful, Yureel probably did not even care that Aurim still sought out ways to free himself. If there was one trait that both Darkhorse and the imp shared, it was a sense of overconfidence. Yureel believed that he now owned the sorcerer body and soul. Aurim hoped to prove him wrong, although he did not know how. All he knew was that he dared not lose hope. He had to escape, if only because he knew some of what his captor had planned for him. Aurim was to lead the sorcerers of the Magical Order in battle. He was to create a link between them even stronger than the one that existed now. Through him, Yureel would combine the Order's abilities to unleash such powerful sorcery as had not been seen since at least the Turning War, when human and drake power had clashed time and time again.

There has to be a way to free myself! There has to be! Already he had been responsible for injuring his own father. Only a brief moment of brittle control had allowed him to soften the spell he and several of Lanith's pet sorcerers had hurtled at the elder Bedlam. Aurim's rising hopes of rescue, dashed once already by his part in the capture of Darkhorse, had sunk swiftly again the moment Yureel's link forced him to attack his father. The thought had so repelled him, however, that he had been able to slow his movement just a fraction enough to decrease the intensity of the assault. Even then he had feared that he had killed his parent.

It had been even more chilling to join in the hunt to track his father down, especially with the increasingly bitter Ponteroy around. The other sorcerer had been told only a short time before that he was now third in rank behind Saress and Aurim and that news still stuck hard in the northerner's throat. The king himself had suggested that if the elder Bedlam could be captured, he would be a valuable addition to the ranks once he was "convinced" of the righteousness of Lanith's cause. However, Aurim believed that given the opportunity and the necessary seclusion, Ponteroy would have very likely *killed* Cabe Bedlam for fear that here would be another who would become his superior in the Magical Order.

Fortunately, it had been one of the less proficient mages who had found the injured sorcerer. And what had happened next had both startled and gratified the helpless Aurim. He had both heard and sensed the attack on his fellow hunter and had immediately transported himself to the spot. Instead of

finding his father alone, however, there had been a woman—
one of the most beautiful women Aurim could frankly recall
ever seeing—protecting his father. Her presence had so startled him that even had he been willingly working for the king
of Zuu, he would have hesitated that important fraction of a
second.

When she and his father had vanished a moment later,
Aurim had wanted to breathe a sigh of relief. He was certain
that the woman had taken his father to safety. That meant that
word concerning his plight would eventually reach the Manor
and Penacles. They would realize that he could not possibly
be voluntarily working for Lanith. Someone would come for
both him and Darkhorse.

Which meant that he would probably do his best to capture
or even . . . kill . . . his rescuers, be they his parents, the
Gryphon, or even his young sister.

*I can't let that happen! I've got to free myself from that
monster before they come!* How he could do that, though,
Aurim did not know. True, he had had some minor success,
but hardly enough to indicate that Yureel's control was slipping. Yureel was certainly not Saress, whose abilities were far
more limited. The shadow creature was as powerful as Darkhorse, maybe even more so.

He nearly collided with another figure coming from a side
corridor. Aurim at first thought it was a guard, but then he
noted the garish, aristocratic clothing.

Ponteroy. The renegade sorcerer from Gordag-Ai sneered
at him. "And good day to you, Master Bedlam. Shouldn't you
be in the throne room? I've heard that the king wants all important members of his staff there. Of course, that no longer
includes me, but I know it does you."

"I'm on my way there now," Aurim heard himself say. It
amazed him the way Yureel had made him two people in one.
The puppet half of him acted and responded as if everything
he did was normal. Only occasionally did the true Aurim
show through, mostly when Saress got too close, but also on
occasion when dealing with jealous Ponteroy.

He started past the other spellcaster, but Ponteroy thrust an
arm in front of him. The horse-headed staff gleamed in the

dimly lit corridor, a sign that Ponteroy was ready to utilize his power. "Consider yourself fortunate, boy. It was your fault that those two escaped, but for some reason His Majesty has chosen to be benevolent to you, his new champion. He won't be so kind next time you make such a mistake. I know, trust me. Don't become too comfortable in your position. That could be disastrous for you."

"Is something the matter, Ponteroy?" Saress walked lithely toward them from the direction of the throne room.

The bitter sorcerer immediately pulled his arm back. "No, nothing at all, Saress. I was merely discussing a few minor matters with our new comrade here."

"You've some things to attend to, Ponteroy. See to them."

Summarily dismissed, the sorcerer from Gordag-Ai managed one final glare at his replacement, then stalked away. Saress watched him depart, amused by his anger and frustration. "Poor little Ponteroy! This demotion was just such a blow to his oily little ego. I don't know why he's so distraught; he's still being paid his gold."

"I've got to go," the puppet part of Aurim stated. He tried to work his way past Saress, but the enchantress would not allow him.

"There's nothing to worry about. We still have time. I'm supposed to be there, too, silly." She folded her arm around his, leaning close. "We'll walk together."

She was using him again. It had not taken Aurim long to realize that while Saress might find him desirable, he was in the end only a tool in her constant quest to maintain the attention of her king and lover. The enchantress was obsessed, and Aurim finally believed he knew what she wanted. Lanith was not married and had no heir. Saress wanted to be his queen.

Aurim doubted that Lanith would ever go that far. It was one thing to make Saress his mistress, but making her queen was an entirely different matter. Few humans anywhere would be comfortable with a spellcaster on the throne. In Penacles, the Gryphon had replaced the tyrannical drake lord. In Talak, Queen Erini kept her use of her powers to such minimal tasks that many of her subjects had forgotten she wielded them in the first place. These were the exceptions, however, not the accepted. Saress would never be queen, no matter how great her attempts to stir her master's jealousy.

Perhaps deep down the sorceress knew, too, for her attempts to seduce Aurim grew stronger each time they were alone. She might be devoted to Lanith, but Saress did not seem to mind the thought of a temporary lover.

Aurim shuddered, his own reaction this time.

"Even here in the southwest the halls are chilly, aren't they? We'll just have to stay closer together, I suppose." She led him slowly along the corridor.

Fortunately, the journey was short. He and Saress entered just as King Lanith, standing over a table where a large map had been placed, finished giving orders to an older officer Aurim knew to be General Belfour, the monarch's chief commander. Belfour looked none too pleased by the instructions his liege had relayed to him, but he nodded.

The horse king looked up as the two entered. "Saress! Aurim! Where by Haron's Mare did you get to? I've got plenty of things in store for the Order and I don't intend on saying them twice!"

"I was only retrieving our wayward friend, Your Majesty. Poor Aurim seemed lost in the halls and I was afraid he might not make it here in time."

Lanith grunted. "All right, then! The two of you had better listen close, because there's going to be a few changes in the intended plan."

"Your Majesty," Belfour interrupted. "I really think that we should reconsider these changes. The terrain alone makes victory uncertain. Our riders will have a hard going with it—"

Lanith's darkening countenance was enough to silence the general. "Your protest's noted, Belfour . . . now put an end to it. The decision's been made." The would-be conqueror turned an evil grin on the two spellcasters. "Besides, terrain won't be so terrible a problem with the Order now working so well together, will it, Aurim?"

It was a curious Saress who responded before Aurim would have been forced to. "Exactly what do you have in mind, Lanith? Are we ready to trample Gordag-Ai?"

It had to be that, Aurim realized. King Lanith's reaction

after riding Darkhorse made more sense now. With Aurim and Darkhorse now his to command, Lanith probably felt his forces were ready to attack the northern kingdom. Yureel had turned Aurim into the perfect link for the Magical Order, a link that would enable them to focus their combined might. With Darkhorse also ready to fight for him, the king had no more reason to wait. Gordag-Ai had no defenses strong enough to deflect the magical and physical forces of Zuu.

"We ride, Saress, but not to Gordag-Ai. I've changed my mind. A more important foe must be dealt with first, a foe whose defeat will mean more to the people than even conquering the northerners would've." He slammed one fist on the map, all but obscuring the name of the massive green land underneath. "Here."

Saress leaned forward, trying to read the map, but Aurim did not need to see the name to recognize the horse king's intended target.

It was Dagora, the vast forest domain east and north of Zuu. Dagora, land of the Green Dragon.

CHAPTER XI

The eyes of the Green Dragon came in many forms, some natural, some not. Among the more prevalent servants who patrolled his land were the elves. They were no longer his subjects, but it behooved any elf who chose to live in the immense Dagora Forest to assist in its defense and so a pact still existed. The Dragon King aided the settlements and in return the elves aided him in watching for and ousting any unwelcome newcomers.

Of late, the patrols had come to watch the west with great interest. Everyone knew that the human king of Zuu would sooner or later lead his warriors northward to attack the other human kingdom of Gordag-Ai and there was always the chance that a few stragglers might intrude in the forest. Besides, the drake lord had requested any news of the horde's progress so that he could relay it to his sorcerer associates in Penacles. They were taking this new conqueror seriously, even if the elves on patrol were less inclined to worry. Humans and drakes were always warring.

Sean Blackwillow led a patrol of four elves presently watching the eastern edge of Adderly. The horsemen had for the most part abandoned their bloody conquest almost immediately after taking it, but some activity still took place there. Sean was of the opinion that he and his friends were wasting their efforts, but it was his turn to lead a patrol and he always obeyed the dictates of the elders.

"We get to go home tomorrow, don't we?" whispered a thinner, younger elf. This was his first patrol and he was proving the most irritating of companions. In Sean's erstwhile opinion, the coming generation of elves seemed to have no patience. Of course, the elders spoke the same way of him, but they were slow, cranky grandfathers . . .

"Yes, Dyyn," he finally replied. "Tomorrow."

The four of them hid among the trees just a few yards into the thicker part of the forest. From their vantage point, they could see the easternmost hills of Adderly and, because of their exceptional eyesight, even the vague outline of the castle. Things remained unchanged, just as they had for the past four days.

Only—Sean squinted—suddenly there seemed to be a fairly wide shadow spreading along the western horizon. He stiffened, then moved a few feet forward, trying to see better.

"What is it, Sean? Another sheep?"

"Not unless sheep are swift and carry riders . . ." The lead elf blinked, hoping that what he saw was a trick of the still dim western sky. Unfortunately, the massive shadow continued toward them, coalescing slowly into identifiable human forms on horses. There were hundreds and hundreds in sight with more following with each passing second.

"What are they doing here?" asked Dyyn. "I thought that they already stole everything of value in Adderly. Why bother coming back?"

"Be silent, Dyyn." Sean's stomach turned. This was not right. The horsemen of Zuu were supposed to head north toward Gordag-Ai, not east. Not toward Dagora.

Yet, here came the golden horde, their impressive mounts quickly racing toward the edge of the forest. At the rate they were coming, they would reach the trees in no more than a quarter hour.

"Bracha, get the mounts." An older, stockier elf hurried off. To the remaining pair, Sean commanded, "You two spread out a little—"

A huge tree only a few yards in front of them burst out of the ground and flew high into the sky. Awestruck, the elves watched it go higher and higher. Only when a second tore itself free and followed after the first did they finally awaken to their danger.

"Bracha!" Sean cried. "Where are those mounts?"

A third and fourth tree shot from the earth, these so near that the three elves were pelted by a shower of dirt and rock. Sean signaled retreat. If Bracha would not bring the mounts to them, then they would go to him.

"What's happening?" Dyyn cried.

No one answered him, the answer so obvious even the young elf would soon figure it out for himself. Sorcery. Powerful sorcery. Sean knew that the human king had spellcasters working for him, but all reports had indicated that most of them were little more than sleight-of-hand artists. This attack . . . this attack was by someone much more skilled.

A tremendous crash threw Sean off his feet. He yelped as something jabbed him in the cheek. Blood trickled down the side of his face.

"Sean!" Bracha's strong hands took hold of him, dragging the injured elf to his feet. "Are you hurt bad?"

"What . . . what . . . ?"

"A *tree* just fell from the sky! A tree! I think . . . I think Dyyn's dead."

The patrol leader looked around. It looked as if about a dozen trees had rained down on them. An entire area to one side had been cleared, the trees lying in a jumbled pile. Sean did not see Dyyn, but he recalled the younger elf moving into the zone of destruction.

He put a hand to his cheek, wincing in pain when he touched the bloody area. Something hard and sharp still protruded from the wound. Bracha carefully removed it for him. It was a splinter of wood nearly four inches long. Sean considered himself fortunate that he had been so lightly injured. He looked around for the fourth member of the party. "Where's Iryn?"

"Over there." Bracha pointed behind himself. Sean could just make out the other elf and the mounts. "When I saw you go down, I yelled for Iryn to take hold of the animals for me while I got you."

"Thank you." A loud, lingering crash in the distance warned

Sean that not all the other trees tossed high into the air had landed. They had to leave now. The Green Dragon likely knew that something was going on at the edge of his domain, but the patrol had to report specifics not only to him, but to their own people.

Bracha helped him back to the mounts. Sean ignored his wound as best he could. It was inconsequential compared to the threat from the west.

"Bracha. I want you and Iryn to hurry back to our people. I'll carry the news to the drake lord."

"All right, Sean, but I do not see—"

A searing gust of wind nearly bowled them over. The animals grew frantic, fighting their riders for control. Behind Sean, a brilliant burst of light suddenly illuminated the entire area. A heat wave of incredible magnitude swept over the elves. Without even seeing it, the elf knew what had happened.

"Ride!" Bracha cried out, his eyes round with fright as he stared at what was occurring behind Sean.

The mounts needed no urging. They moved off at as fast a gallop as they could. Being elfin-raised, the animals could maneuver around forest paths that other horses would have found most difficult, sometimes impossible. Unfortunately, Sean knew that the thing now pursuing them would not be slowed by treacherously winding paths or wide trees. It would eat through such obstacles as if they were nothing.

He looked behind them and saw the wall of fire. It rose taller than the trees and the slight green tinge he noted was all the verification Sean needed to know that the fiery wall was yet another product of sorcery.

They will burn down the entire forest if they keep that thing alive for very long! Are they mad? What will they gain by reducing this land to ash?

The questions quickly became moot, for the wall moved with such swiftness that the heat washing over him became unbearable. Now only one thing concerned the elf as he and his companions fled and that was whether or not *they* would be able to outrace the wall of death.

Sean had his doubts.

The western edge of the forest was a blazing inferno and there was nothing Darkhorse could do to stop it. The coordinated power of the Order was so tremendous that it was very possible they would burn down all of Dagora if someone did not stop them. Unfortunately, at this point the only one capable of putting a halt to the wholesale destruction was King Lanith and he did not seem inclined.

The captive eternal suspected Yureel's hand in the matter. It served no real purpose for Lanith to destroy what he sought to conquer. This horrific assault on the forest was more to the tastes of Darkhorse's counterpart.

General Belfour, riding next to the king, asked, "Your Majesty, shouldn't they put an end to that fire now? We can't send the men in until things cool down a little and that will take time."

"A bit longer, Belfour. I want the drake to know what we can do to him." The king smiled triumphantly. "Don't worry, General. I don't plan on burning down the entire Dagora Forest. Just enough."

Darkhorse seemed to be the only one who noticed a shadowy presence around the king and himself, a presence he knew to be Yureel. Yureel had not spoken to him since Lanith and his warriors had departed Zuu, but had made no attempt to hide the fact that he was there and obviously in contact with the horse king.

Curse you, Yureel! Cease this terror! If you will have a war, then have a war, not this wholesale destruction!

Whether it was his demand or, more likely, pure coincidence, Lanith raised his hand but a minute later. A soldier raised a horn to his lips and blew a long, low signal.

In the distance the towering wall of fire ceased. For some distance all that could be seen were the charred remnants of once magnificent trees. Darkhorse estimated that in the space of less than an hour, the king's sorcerers had burned away several hundred acres of ancient forest.

"Give the second signal."

The soldier raised the horn to his lips again and blew out a short series of higher notes. Darkhorse felt the sorcerers at work again.

"The path is cooled," the horse king announced. "Our warriors may progress. Everyone should be ready for battle the moment we finish crossing the charred region."

Everyone, including the shadow steed, knew very well that resistance would begin the moment they entered the forest. The Green Dragon surely had been notified of their presence the moment the sorcerers had first struck. The warriors of Zuu would face hidden archers in the trees, covered pits, surprise attacks on stragglers, and, of course, sorcery both human and draconian. Somewhere in the forest they would find another army, its warriors bitter and furious, awaiting them.

I must escape! I cannot allow this to continue any longer! Once more, Darkhorse tried to overcome the slave spell of the bridle and saddle, but all he succeeded in doing was weakening himself. Aurim had followed Yureel's orders to the letter.

Lanith noticed his momentary loss of strength. "I'll brook no hesitation from you, demon steed. Move."

A sharp pain coursed through Darkhorse as Lanith pulled on the reins, a new addition to his torture that had no doubt been whispered in the king's ear by Yureel. The saddle and bridle seized complete control again, forcing him forward at a quickening pace.

Scents mingled as Darkhorse stepped into the burnt portion of the forest. Smoke still lingered in some places. The shadow steed marked most of the scents as originating from charred trees and foliage, but his sharp senses also detected some sickly odors that he hoped were not what he suspected.

The warriors of Zuu spread out as they moved. Lanith did not rely on cavalry alone; he had foot soldiers as well. Even in heavily wooded regions such as Dagora the warriors of Zuu were not slowed much. Darkhorse had the least difficulty, but he began to have a grudging respect for the abilities of his mortal counterparts. The horses of Zuu were indeed remarkable.

They left behind the burnt ruins of the forest's edge none too soon as far as the shadow steed was concerned. If the eternal could still trust his senses, at least one blackened form that he had passed had been some unfortunate being, likely one of the elves who inhabited the domain of the Green Dragon.

Darkhorse hoped there would be no more, but sooner or later Lanith's warriors *would* encounter resistance and then the shadow steed would be forced to battle those who should have been his allies.

There must be some way to stop this! I will not fight for your pleasure, Yureel! Yet, he still had no idea how to keep from doing so.

All around them, the air was suddenly filled with hissing. One of the lead riders grunted in surprise, then slipped from his horse, a long bolt through his throat. Three other warriors within Darkhorse's view joined the first.

The bolts were not elven. In fact, from the brief glimpse Darkhorse got of one, they more resembled massive thorns from some plant. Lanith and Yureel had just gotten their first taste of the magical defenses of the Dagora Forest.

"Shields!" roared Belfour.

Above Darkhorse, the king stiffened. The shadow steed felt the growing presence of his counterpart. It was as if Yureel and not Lanith now sat upon his back. "Command the men to hold back, General Belfour. The Order will deal with this prickly situation."

Only Darkhorse heard the brief giggle that escaped King Lanith.

Belfour signaled a halt to the advance. Silence fell over the forest. The general glanced at his liege, but Darkhorse could not see what expression now graced the features of the warlord.

Someone gasped. Ahead of them, a dusting of white fell upon the trees. Wherever the dust fell, limbs and leaves crystallized and began to shudder. The sunlight that managed to shine through created a glare that forced more than one warrior to squint. The storm was short but heavy, lasting all of perhaps five minutes but covering everything in sight ahead of them.

"Give the order to move on again, General."

The senior officer nodded. At first, movement was slow and hesitant, but when no new rain of death fell upon the foremost soldiers, the pace of the advance increased.

When they reached the whitened area, the advance faltered

again, but this time it was because of fascination, not fear. The trees and plants in this region not only looked crystalline, they were. One rider broke off a gleaming branch and brandished it briefly before being reprimanded by an officer.

In the center of the crystalline region, they came upon several barrel-shaped plants with hundreds of long, pointed spikes growing out of the sides. Each plant, though, had areas upon it where it appeared the spikes had been removed. No one had to ask if these were the sources of the hail of bolts. Like the other plants, though, these were also dead.

At sight of this, the morale of the warriors grew yet stronger, so much so that Darkhorse actually began to have hope. Yureel was allowing his human puppets to become too overconfident in their safety. However, the spines had been only the first line of defense. More was surely to come.

Lanith reined him to a slower pace. Belfour and the king's other senior officers followed suit, but the rest of the invading horde pressed forward, soon leaving their leaders far in the rear.

"Is something amiss, Your Majesty?" Belfour himself seemed uneasy, as if he shared the shadow steed's opinion concerning the increasing danger.

"No. Nothing's wrong." Although he spoke in the voice of the horse king, it was Yureel who yet held the reins. "Nothing at all."

What do you plan, Yureel? What is going on? Surely you of all here would best know what danger lies—

Darkhorse paused in midthought, unable to believe what Yureel might be considering. It was wasteful, horrible . . . and so like his counterpart. He wanted to warn General Belfour at least, the elder warrior seemed to be more a man of honor than his liege had probably ever been, but the slave spell prevented even that.

Again, a brief giggle escaped the king. This time, one of Lanith's officers glanced his way, but only for a second or two.

The possessed king did a peculiar thing next. He reached down and patted Darkhorse on the head. The ebony stallion tried to shy away from the touch.

Far ahead, the forest ground shook without warning.

Despite his superior vision, Darkhorse caught only momentary glimpses of what was happening, but it was more than enough. As if churned up by a legion of huge, burrowing Quel, the earth first shook, then crumbled. Huge gaps opened up in the soil, gaps in which startled horses planted hooves or unsuspecting infantry their feet. Warriors and horses cried out as they stumbled and fell, only to find themselves being pulled beneath the moving earth.

The possessed king urged Darkhorse forward, reining him to a halt only when they were near enough to the terrible sight to see everything. Around Darkhorse and Lanith pandemonium threatened to destroy what remained of the invaders' organization, but the horse king seemed unbothered. Lanith— or, rather, Yureel—was far more interested in the disaster ahead than in what was happening to the rest of the huge force. Yet, despite his interest in what was happening to the unfortunates caught in the trap, the possessed monarch made no move to save them, instead perhaps actually *enjoying* the tragic spectacle.

Men, women, and horses were sucked under. Some souls attempted to find safety in the trees, but when they sought to take hold of a branch or trunk, their hands slipped away and they fell back into the earthen maelstrom, vanishing moments later with shrieks of despair. Some of their comrades tried to rescue them by throwing in ropes. This actually saved two or three, but at least one rescuer tumbled in before anyone could seize her. She disappeared beneath the surface before she could finish screaming.

Although they were the servants of his captors, Darkhorse agonized over each death. None of them needed to have perished. This entire war was the notion of Lanith and Yureel, possibly even only Yureel, although Darkhorse doubted that the king was an innocent in this matter.

Someone sounded a retreat, not that it was really necessary to do so at this point. With the exceptions of those attempting to aid the last few victims of the Green Dragon's latest defense, most of the warriors had already retreated some distance back.

"Who gave that command?" shouted Lanith with a snarl.

Belfour rode up. "My liege, it was me. I apologize, but there was no other choice! If someone hadn't given some signal, some indication that command still functioned, instead of a retreat we might've had a complete rout!"

Lanith's body quivered with barely contained rage. Belfour had interrupted Yureel's pleasure. The general could not have possibly realized how tenuous his situation, his very life, had just become.

Surprisingly, the possessed king calmed. "Very good, Belfour. You're to be commended, yes, indeed." Yureel's presence retreated into the background. More and more, Lanith sounded and reacted like himself. "Get them reorganized and have them pull back a hundred paces . . . for now."

"What kind of war is this?" muttered Belfour, still unaware just how near to death he had likely come. "Where are the warriors? Where are those we can bury good steel in? We can't keep fighting sorcery!"

"Sorcery's the drake lord's first defense, General," Lanith replied. "It's also his main defense. Cut through what he's got set up and he'll have to rely on his own warriors. Fierce but few compared to my proud, vast legions."

"I hope we *can* cut through these devil defenses!"

"Have you so little faith yet in my Magical Order?" The king snapped his fingers. Yureel might have receded into the background, but his influence was still strong. Darkhorse sensed that Lanith still listened to him. The horse king probably did not even realize that he had been momentarily possessed.

"You summoned me, Your Majesty?"

Aurim's arrival was so abrupt that even Darkhorse was startled by it. Only Lanith reacted as if fully expecting the young sorcerer to appear.

"I did. You see what lies before us . . ."

"Yes, Your Majesty."

"Deal with it."

"We'll do our best." Aurim made to leave.

The king turned Darkhorse toward the sorcerer. "You'll do

more than that. I gave a royal command. I expect nothing but success!"

"Your Majesty, at least two of our number are hard-pressed to continue. It would be best if we could have an hour of rest. There are limitations."

"You'll rest when I give you the command and no sooner!" The king urged the shadow steed forward, then drew his blade and touched the sharp tip against Aurim's chest. "Deal with the trap. Clear the way. I want results! Men've died and there're those who must pay! They must pay!"

This last the king cried out so that all within earshot could hear him. Many of the nearest warriors nodded or muttered their agreement with his sentiments. More than a few clutched their blades, even brandishing them in a sort of salute to their monarch's demand for retribution.

And what would they think, Darkhorse wondered, *if they had seen their glorious king not more than a minute before enjoying the tragic deaths of their comrades?*

As Lanith withdrew the blade, Aurim Bedlam nodded. The shadow steed noted that the young sorcerer's eyes had a hollow look, as if Aurim was exhausted. Not surprising, considering the fact that he not only contributed greatly to each spell, but acted as the focus for all the others.

"It shall be done." With those words, the sorcerer vanished.

The horse king turned to his officers, his voice still loud enough for all around to hear. Darkhorse sensed the work of Yureel; no human's voice could have carried so well. "Cowards that they are, I say that they *will* pay! Afraid to face us with steel and bow, that's what they are! Well, if that's what they want, we'll answer them in kind and in blood until they have no choice *but* to meet us with arms!" The warrior king straightened in the saddle and even Darkhorse, his head twisted around as much as the bridle would allow, could see how the human wielded his sword against the distant, unseen foe to the east. "And when that time comes, we shall show them the same mercy that they showed our friends and kin here! Ten lives for every one of ours lost!" The horse king's eyes shifted to his officers as he cried out again. "Ten lives for one!"

Taking the cue, Belfour raised his own blade. "Ten lives for one!"

"Ten lives for one!" called out the rest of the officers obediently, each raising a weapon.

The cry was picked up by other warriors, until it became a chant. Lanith swung his blade around once, then again pointed it toward the east.

Perfectly timed, a green cloud formed over the heaving land. Yureel had coordinated the sorcerers' efforts with the king's words. Not so difficult a task when both Aurim and Lanith were under his sinister guidance, but the results were nonetheless spectacular. The cloud drifted down upon the earth and as it did, the convulsions slowed until finally they ceased altogether. The ground quickly reshaped itself, becoming flat and hard, perfect for men and mounts to travel across.

The warriors of Zuu continued to chant. Lanith paused to whisper something to Belfour, who caught the attention of the horn bearers. As soon as the land before them appeared stable enough, the general nodded. The blare of horns echoed throughout the area, even cutting through the chant. Slowly but with building determination, the horde moved forward again.

King Lanith sheathed his blade, then, after most of his forces had already passed by, he urged Darkhorse on. The shadow steed contemplated throwing his rider, but regrettably, all he could do *was* contemplate his revenge. He was still as helpless as Aurim.

To everyone's surprise, they encountered no more resistance that day, although the terrain did become more and more difficult to traverse. By the time the sun neared setting, the invaders were exhausted from having to pick their way through thick brush and rising and falling landscape. Lanith grew furious at the slowing pace, but did not order the sorcerers to clear the forest for him as they had done in the beginning. After Belfour's fourth request, the king finally granted him permission to give the command to make camp.

The invaders might have had some knowledge of the Dagora Forest, but they could not know it as well as Darkhorse, who had crossed it time and time again over the centuries. However, the immortal could not recall so troublesome a trek in this region. He was of the suspicion that perhaps the Green Dragon had decided to be more subtle, that instead of outright assaults, the drake lord now utilized delaying actions such as small but significant alterations in the land. Not only would it frustrate the invaders, possibly make them more prone to making mistakes, but it bought the master of Dagora time to prepare for the massive force that had suddenly decided to invade his land.

Thirty, possibly even twenty years ago, it would not have been so possible for Lanith, even with his sorcerers and Yureel, to conquer his former master. However, with the coming of Cabe Bedlam and the death of the Dragon Emperor, the centuries-long rule of the drakes had begun to collapse. Humans saw that their draconian masters were no longer invincible. More important, the Dragon Kings, ever untrusting of their own brethren, finally began to turn on each other. The clans of Iron and Bronze tried to seize power from their emperor, only to be crushed. Treachery abounded. Green allied himself with humans, which enabled his kingdom to survive relatively intact, but his control over many of his human vassals dwindled, especially over distant Zuu.

The Dragon King was hardly defenseless, however, as had proven so far. Darkhorse had no idea what the drake's next move would be, but he suspected that the night would not be a calm one.

Making camp in the thick forest was not the most pleasant activity for Lanith's warriors, but they tried to make do as best they could. Because of the thickness of the foliage, Belfour tripled the normal number of sentries. In addition, members of the Order were divided into groups of three, with each group using their combined abilities to monitor the region around the massive encampment.

Aurim was exempted from this. Lanith wanted his prize sorcerer to sleep through the night, although if any of the spellcasters on sentry duty sensed anything amiss, they were to alert the younger Bedlam immediately.

Darkhorse found himself handed off to an aide, who

seemed at a loss what to do with the eternal. The man first tried to deal with the shadow steed just as he would have with any normal mount, but when he found that Darkhorse neither needed nor desired anything, the aide threw his arms up in frustration and simply left his charge tied up to a tree next to the tent that doubled both as the king's personal quarters and his strategic headquarters.

The shadow steed had hoped that his caretaker would make the mistake of removing the saddle and bridle, but evidently the human had been warned against doing so.

Unlike his imprisonment in the palace, Darkhorse discovered that he could move, although if he tried to do much more than turn his head or take a step forward or back, he froze up for more than a minute. The eternal still could not use his power, not even to probe for any possible sorcerous activity in the forest around him. He had no idea whether the Dragon King even knew that he and Aurim were part of this sinister force. Darkhorse did not worry about himself so much as what might happen to Cabe's son if the Green Dragon tried to eliminate Lanith's most powerful tool, the Order.

Although he was fairly near to the king's quarters, Darkhorse could not hear what was going on inside save that Lanith appeared to be berating one of his staff. Not surprising, especially if the one being berated was General Belfour. Belfour was still the most outspoken officer, although he had so far never actually defied his liege. If Darkhorse was any judge, the general would have opted for continued peace rather than this war King Lanith so desired.

Be careful, General, lest Zuu lose its only voice of reason.

The eternal's ears twitched as a crackling sound rose without warning from the encampment's edge. At first he thought it was a new attack, but nothing more happened. The crackling continued to rise in intensity, causing some consternation among the warriors, who had just started to settle down for the night. Just as it seemed panic might arise, though, someone made an announcement that caused calm to resume. Darkhorse could not hear what was said, but gathered from the renewed quiet that the spell causing the noise was the work of the Order.

Time passed slowly for the captive. Belfour and the other senior officers departed the king's tent, vanishing into the encampment. Lanith made no attempt to check on his reluctant mount, instead evidently retiring the moment his subordinates departed. Darkhorse marveled at the horse king's attitude; the human treated the eternal as he would have any mortal steed. Away from combat, it seemed not to impress him that Darkhorse was so much more. The eternal resembled a horse and so Lanith treated him like one. It was almost insulting.

Yureel, too, was oddly absent, something that bothered the stallion. Neither of the pair required sleep and only needed rest if worn from battle or extensive uses of power. That Yureel had not come to taunt him meant that the shadow puppet had other things to occupy his time. Darkhorse wondered what the sinister imp found so diverting.

Time passed. Since the aide had departed, no one else had come to check on him. How long he stood facing the tree around which his reins were tied, Darkhorse did not care to know. On occasion, the distant, faint sounds of a sentry moving about or some warrior grumbling in his sleep disturbed the silence, but in general the night was quiet save for the calls of a few nocturnal creatures. After several futile attempts to do something more about his captivity, Darkhorse finally gave up.

He had nearly drifted off into a state similar to dozing when he sensed an approaching figure. His first thought was that it might be Aurim, but as he carefully studied the newcomer, Darkhorse realized that it was a warrior and a woman at that.

She approached him tentatively, as if not quite certain what to make of his imposing figure. The woman was typical of an inhabitant of Zuu, blond, tall, and muscular. She was no one that Darkhorse could recall, but the traditional outfit she wore reminded him of the king's Guard.

With a quick glance around her, the female stepped close enough to whisper. "My name—Herion's Mane, I feel like a fool to be doing this—my name's Rebatha. I was told you might be a creature called—gods!—called Darkhorse. Is that true?"

Unable to do anything else, the shadow steed nodded.

Rebatha looked uncertain. "Did you nod your head in reply? Maybe . . . if you really can understand me . . . stamp the ground lightly three times with your left front hoof."

Darkhorse obeyed, moving slowly so as not to frighten away his anxious visitor. Rebatha was clearly not supposed to be here. He now had a notion as to just who she was.

She watched him perform exactly as she had asked, shaking her head afterward in disbelief. "I didn't believe my sister or my father, but it must be true. You are Darkhorse, I guess. My father's Trenlen. He told me that you disappeared after trying to rescue your friend the sorcerer. When I heard King Lanith had a new mount, a horse like none anyone had ever seen, I had to find out if it was you. This was my first chance, though."

While he appreciated her efforts, Darkhorse wished that he could tell Rebatha to hurry and remove the saddle and bridle. Unfortunately, the spell of silence prevented that and it appeared that the woman did not realize that it was the equipment that prevented the eternal from escaping.

"I'm going to untie the rope and lead you away. Is there anything you can do, then?"

The saddle! The bridle! Can you not see that they are the reason I can do nothing? He twisted his head, trying to indicate the items, but Rebatha still did not understand what he wanted. As the woman turned to undo the reins from the tree, Darkhorse gave up his attempt to communicate. If he could at least escape into the forest, then it might be possible to find someone who would remove the magical bonds from him.

"I don't know what else to do," she whispered, tossing the reins over his back. "I'd better leave before they notice me missing. Can you escape on your own?"

At last something to which he could reply. Darkhorse nodded vigorously. Rebatha blinked, then began to back away.

"Good luck . . . I guess. I'd better leave before anyone notices."

The warrior vanished back into the camp, her departure as silent as her arrival. Darkhorse watched her until he was certain that she was safely away, thinking all the while of the bravery of Trenlen and his daughters. They had already risked much for him, a creature who they did not even really know. It now behooved him to make those risks pay off.

He moved slowly from his position, both because he feared disturbing Lanith and because of the possible danger of snagging the loose reins on a limb. No sentries were in sight, but they had to be nearby. However, the sentries were not as great a concern to him as the sorcerers were. Depending on what spells they had cast, they might take notice of him disappearing into the forest. If so, he hoped that they would simply think him some warrior's mount that had accidentally wandered off and assume that his master would soon retrieve him. By the time they realized otherwise, Darkhorse hoped to be far away and free of his bonds.

It does not matter whether they notice me or not, though, does it? I have no real choice, do I? This is my only opportunity to escape! With careful steps, he wended his way to the nearest path wide enough to enable him to enter the forest, then plunged in. He felt nothing as he passed through the area of the spell, but that did not mean that he had left the camp unnoticed by the sorcerers. Darkhorse chose not to worry about them, his path to freedom more important. The saddle and bridle prevented him from squeezing through extremely narrow gaps, which meant he had to constantly shift direction every time he was confronted by a breach too small. This slowed his flight, but at the same time meant that any pursuit would in turn be slowed.

That his opportunity had come so quickly had been surprising at first, but in retrospect could have possibly been predicted. Lanith could not help thinking of him as a horse even though he should have known better. Yureel clearly had many other deeds of evil to attend to, so he also had left the seemingly helpless shadow steed alone, probably on the assumption that the king would pay more attention to the guarding of his new prize. Aurim, the only other one who might have been concerned with Darkhorse, was trying to recover from the heavy stress caused by his monumental part in the Order's tasks. As for Lanith's warriors, their only concern was the as-of-yet unseen enemy.

The path continued to be treacherous and was made worse

by the fact that the saddle and bridle forced Darkhorse to remain solid. That meant that each step, each movement, caused branches and foliage to rustle or crunch. To Darkhorse, each noise echoed through the forest with the reverberation of a thunderclap. How did mortal creatures survive such racket?

Adding to his misery were the reins, which had long slipped off his back and since then had been catching on every other tree limb or bush he passed. It was a wonder he was making any progress at all, but fortunately, pursuit had yet to materialize.

Perhaps no one will discover my absence until the morning. He hoped so, but dared not slow down. The farther, the better—

The reins grew taut again. Darkhorse pulled up short. He was beginning to despise the disorder of the forest. The shadow steed backed up, trying to see what limb had snared him this time.

Instead of a tree, however, he discovered the reins in the hands of a being startling even to him, a being more at home in the forest than an elf.

"Little horse, little horse, where is your rider?" The figure, no more than five feet tall, resembled a tree herself. With his superior vision, one of the few attributes left to him, Darkhorse noted the barklike skin and leafy hair. She was nearly the same shade as the tree next to her. Her features were somewhat human, somewhat elfin, and very youthful. Some males of either species would have probably found her very exotic, although based on what little knowledge he had of tree sprites, any relationship between her and a male of another race would have been short and deadly. Tree sprites were born from shoots broken off and nurtured by their mother sprite; males of any sort were considered little more than sport and, when the woodland creatures were done with them, excellent planting soil. Only their fear of the Green Dragon kept them from mischief, that and their rarity. Few shoots took root and fewer still survived to maturity.

Whether she now acted as a sentinel for the drake lord or simply dwelled nearby, Darkhorse saw in her the possibility of either freeing himself or, at the very least, being led to the

Green Dragon. The tree sprite would have no need for him and certainly a being as magical as she could see that he was no normal steed.

Darkhorse tried to indicate his predicament, but she pulled hard on the reins. "Little horse, come with me."

With strength far greater than that of a dozen men twice her size, the sprite pulled Darkhorse toward her. To his surprise, the eternal discovered that he had to obey; the same spell that gave Lanith control over him now worked for her. So long as she held the reins, the sprite was in command. Aurim had been very thorough with his spell.

If she takes me to the drake none of this will matter. That must be where she goes. What else would she plan?

"Come, come!" The sprite led him along a path that looked impenetrable at first, but seemed to open up just before them as they proceeded. However, while it was somewhat difficult to see the night sky from within the forest, Darkhorse quickly realized that he and his companion were heading southeast, not northeast, which would have brought him toward the caverns of the Green Dragon.

What is she up to?

It did not take long to discover the answer to that. The sprite led him to a secluded location where what first appeared to be a young sapling about two feet tall grew. However, the sapling twisted toward the sprite as they neared. Darkhorse's companion had led him to her offspring.

"Little one, do you see what I brought you? You will grow big and strong with this."

The sprite was not a guardian posted by the Dragon King; she was a mother seeking sustenance for her child. He noted the remnants of a pair of small animals nearby and a much larger mound that indicated that something roughly the size of a man had been buried there quite some time before. The sprite intended to slaughter Darkhorse and add his body to the sapling's larder. With such sustenance to support it, the sapling would grow into a more mobile sprite in only a few weeks.

The immature creature continued to lean toward them, reminding Darkhorse of the grass in the Barren Lands. The grass might have been harmless, but this creature certainly was not. Nor was her progenitor.

"Good little horse . . ." The delicate-seeming hands of the sprite had altered into long, wicked claws. She meant to tear open his throat.

Darkhorse could not move, but he was hardly fearful. A captive of the bridle and saddle he might be, but the eternal was still no creature of flesh and blood.

The sprite raised one hand, then slashed at his neck . . . only to have her claws glance off. She hissed, trying again. This time, the forest creature nearly broke one of her claws. Her second failure left her livid. Her other hand became entangled in the reins, causing her to try to tear it off. When that failed, the sprite moved closer and inspected the bridle.

"Sorcery?" Her interest piqued, she ran her hands over the saddle. Her tone grew merry. "Little horse, you have a pretty, pretty saddle . . . a pretty saddle that makes you so tough-skinned, yes? Must not get it bloody. Must take it off."

Still convinced that she could slaughter Darkhorse for food, the sprite worked at the fastenings of the saddle. Darkhorse stood as still as possible, not wanting to disturb the sprite's precarious attention span. Once he was free, she would see what it meant to threaten lives.

"Here," she whispered. "Here." The sprite tugged at the fastenings. They did not seem to want to open at first, but gradually Darkhorse felt her loosen the buckle.

"Please don't do that."

No, it cannot happen now! Not when I am so close! Darkhorse glanced to his side, already knowing who it was who had discovered them. Aurim. The sorcerer looked and sounded almost sad as he studied the eternal.

"I'm almost sorry you didn't make it." The young sorcerer reached out, as if trying to seize the reins from where he stood despite the fact that they were well out of his reach. "But now I'm going to have to take you back, Darkhorse."

CHAPTER XII

With one last tug on the partially loosened saddle, the tree sprite looked around Darkhorse at Aurim. The shadow steed stared bitterly at his friend, frustrated that he had come so close to freedom, only to have it torn away from him.

The sprite's demeanor shifted the moment she realized what stood before her. All savagery vanished. She was now a delicate, vulnerable creature . . . and very much female. It was this she emphasized most as she moved closer to the sorcerer. Her movements were more natural than those of Saress, but still of the same school of seduction.

"Pretty, *pretty* man. Is this your horse? He's very pretty, too. Do you think I am pretty?" She was nearly close enough to put her arms around him. Whether the nymph hoped to seduce Aurim first or simply crush him with her incredible strength was a question Darkhorse would never know the answer to, for Aurim suddenly raised his hands to eye level, then brought them down toward the tree sprite.

He barely touched her, but the sprite transformed. She hardly had time to gasp as her arms stiffened and lengthened and her legs melded into one. Her feet sank into the soil, growing roots as they did. The sprite's face all but vanished as her neck thickened and her hair became a leafy canopy.

A few seconds later, where once she had stood, there was now a miniature yet adult tree.

"I'm sorry," murmured Aurim. His interest in the sprite

faded. "You should've known someone would notice you pass through the detection spell we placed around the encampment, Darkhorse. You only got this far because the sorcerers on duty didn't make anything of it at first, but out of fear of the king's wrath and probably Saress's as well, they finally woke me."

Darkhorse twisted around to better face his friend. Aurim's brief moment of regret for the eternal had clearly passed and once more Yureel's spell held sway. Fortunately, it appeared that Yureel himself was not present. That meant that the shadow steed had only Aurim's affected mind to deal with.

What could he do against the sorcerer, though? So long as the bridle and saddle were attached, Darkhorse was little more than an obedient animal.

"Why don't you come to me, Darkhorse?" Aurim asked hesitantly. "You know I don't want to hurt you, but I've got to if you don't come willingly."

He sounded too sincere to be simply mouthing the words of Yureel. Aurim's will was stronger than even the shadow steed would have believed. *Perhaps with a little more time, he can free himself!*

What might happen in the future did not matter now, though. Aurim might be fighting against the spell that controlled him, but for now he was still a thrall to Yureel. Darkhorse wanted to go to his young friend and help him, but he could not do that until he himself was free and that was hardly what Aurim had in mind at the moment.

He backed away. So long as the sorcerer did not touch the reins, Aurim could not command Darkhorse to do anything. The reins seemed to be the key to controlling the eternal's actions.

"Please don't do this, Darkhorse. He'll make me hurt you. I won't be able to stop myself. It's taken me this much just to keep from attacking already. I—I don't think I'm strong enough to free myself from his will."

But you can! the shadow steed tried to roar. However, no sound, not even a whinny, escaped him. The spell of silence still held. Darkhorse's frustration grew tenfold. He *had* to be able to talk, he had to be able to tell Aurim—

"You are not completely his!"

The words startled both of them. Darkhorse blinked, then laughed. Aurim took a step back, hands raised. He seemed caught between attacking and retreating.

Darkhorse reared, kicking out with his hooves. The shadow steed had no intention of striking Aurim, but he wanted to keep the sorcerer off-guard for the moment. His unexpected success against the spell of silence encouraged him, but he could still sense that complete freedom was not his. The sprite had loosened the saddle, but while Darkhorse could feel it shifting back and forth, it was still attached to him. So was the bridle. He had regained some of his abilities, but not nearly enough.

Aurim, however, did not yet realize Darkhorse's dilemma. The stallion had to use that to his advantage. "I do not want to hurt you, either, Aurim, so I tell you now to stay back! You are not responsible for yourself! It is Yureel and Lanith who are the true enemies! You know that! Fight their control!"

"I—" The human shook his head. "You have to—"

His demeanor shifted, going from confusion to mockery. Darkhorse vaguely sensed a new presence. It was not exactly here, but its attention was.

Yureel! The shadow puppet had evidently discovered Darkhorse's escape and had linked to the sorcerer in order to recapture the stallion. The transference of control was slower this time, however, possibly a sign that Aurim had indeed shaken off part of the spell. Unfortunately, Darkhorse knew that Cabe's son was not yet strong enough to do more than delay the inevitable.

"Darkhorse . . ." The true Aurim momentarily broke through. Tears coursed down his face. "I can't—"

He suddenly seized his head and screamed. Darkhorse fell back, not at all certain what to make of the human's mad struggle. He wanted to help Aurim, but did not know exactly how. A part of him suggested running since nothing would be gained by both of them being captured. Only by regaining his own complete freedom could the shadow steed hope to help his companion recover his own.

Yet he made no move to depart. Aurim's struggle was so

desperate, Darkhorse feared that the lad might be injured or worse. That he could do nothing to help made the matter that much more terrible.

Aurim screamed again. Darkhorse took a tentative step toward him.

The sorcerer gasped, then collapsed.

"Aurim!" Heedless of the possibility of a trap, Darkhorse trotted over to the still figure and inspected him. Aurim Bedlam was definitely unconscious. His breathing was slightly ragged, but steady. Even in the shadows of the night, the ebony stallion could see how pale and drawn the human was.

When the sorcerer still did not move, Darkhorse gently nudged Aurim's side with his muzzle. The human might have been dead, so limp had he become. Only his regular breathing kept the eternal from fearing the worst. Still, Aurim could not be all that well, not after such a titanic struggle. Darkhorse was amazed at the young man's incredible will. To have battled Yureel to this point . . .

I have to do something! I cannot simply leave him here. Now there is the chance to completely rid him of Yureel's foul touch. One major problem faced the eternal, though. How was he to move Aurim anywhere? The saddle and bridle still kept him trapped in a solid equine form, useless for lifting objects as large as the sorcerer's body, much less tossing them up onto his back.

He had only one slim hope. If his power was great enough to remove the fairly simplistic spell of silence, then perhaps, just perhaps, Darkhorse had enough ability to levitate the sorcerer. It was worth a try; he had no other ideas.

Thanks to the saddle and bridle, the shadow steed could not even estimate how much of his power he now controlled. He could only concentrate and hope that he did not fail. Levitating a heavy, still body was in some ways a much more complicated task than removing a minor spell such as the one that had kept him silent. Removing the simple silence spell had required only momentary effort; levitation demanded constant concentration and a steady flow of energy throughout the entire process.

Darkhorse focused on Aurim and imagined him slowly rising into the air. At first he grew optimistic; Aurim's arm rose, followed gradually by the rest of his form. However, Darkhorse managed to raise the sorcerer only a few inches high before he lost control and Aurim dropped back to the earth.

I will not be denied! Darkhorse readied himself and tried again, throwing his will into the task as he had not done in centuries. He was hardly used to such a relatively minor feat being so straining. He was Darkhorse, after all. No spell so simple should have defied him so.

Perhaps fueled by his growing ire, his second effort met with better success. Aurim's body shot up more than six feet into the air and would have risen even farther if not for the eternal's quick thinking. He regained control of the floating form, then immediately summoned the sorcerer toward him, keeping his concentration steady.

Darkhorse's most unsettling moment came at the very end, just after he had grown confident enough to believe success a certainty. He lowered Aurim to his back, but just as he was about to release his hold on the unconscious human, the loose saddle shifted somewhat. Aurim nearly slipped head first from the shadow steed's back. It was only through quick concentration that Darkhorse saved his young friend.

More cautious, Darkhorse repositioned Aurim so that this time he would be secure. Even so, Darkhorse knew that he would not be able to move very swiftly through the forest. The saddle would continue to shift around as he moved, upsetting Aurim's balance again. Carrying the sorcerer across his back also meant that the shadow steed now needed an even wider path. In a forest as thick as Dagora, that was bound to cause trouble at more than one point during their flight.

By now, Yureel had to know that he had lost his hold on his puppet sorcerer. The other members of the Order would also realize that one of their own was missing. Some sort of pursuit could certainly not be far behind. Darkhorse had to move on.

He passed the tree that had once been a thinking being. There was nothing Darkhorse could do for the sprite, but he did vow that he would alert the Green Dragon to what had happened. Despite his distaste for the creatures, her fate was a matter for her master to decide. If the drake chose to free her, so be it.

Handicapped as he was, reaching the Dragon King was still his best option. The drake lord had eyes throughout the forest; someone or something would take note of the huge black stallion and his unconscious charge. Hopefully, this time it would be a creature actually serving the Dragon King.

As the shadow steed traversed the thick forest, he continued to keep a wary eye out for Saress or any of the other spellcasters. For some reason the enchantress had not been part of the invasion force. Darkhorse supposed that her present duties now included monitoring Zuu while the king was away, although certainly Lanith could contact her through one of the other members of the Order if necessary. Still, it would have been nice to know where the treacherous woman was.

The night quickly aged. The shadow steed paused momentarily to assess two possible paths ahead. More than two hours had now passed since Darkhorse had left the region of the sprite and still he had come across no one who could help him. At this rate, dawn would soon arrive. *Where are your spies, drake?* Surely some creature other than the sprite dwelled or hid in this part of the forest. So far, the only signs of life other than the trees themselves had been the occasional cry of a night bird and the constant rustle of leaves as the wind blew—

It suddenly dawned on Darkhorse that although the leaves rustled even now, this time there was no wind. Something else was causing the branches to shift, something very large.

What dropped from the high, night-shrouded treetops was no bird . . . or, rather, *was* a bird, but also much more. It stood approximately the height of a human, but other than also having the general shape of one, the creature was avian. In many ways, it resembled the Gryphon with its predatory beak and its intelligent, searching eyes. However, where the king of Penacles often showed compassion, an aura of arrogance surrounded the newcomer.

Wide wings now folded, the avian pointed a taloned hand at Darkhorse's cargo.

"Stand aside, Seeker, I have no time for you!" The eternal kept glancing about the area. Where one Seeker lurked, there was generally a full flock nearby. Prior to the Dragon Kings, the avians had ruled this land, but their own audacity coupled with their continual war with the earth-burrowing Quel had led to their downfall. Rookeries still existed, though, and many Seekers still believed that they were masters of the Dragonrealm.

The avian, a male judging by his height, opened his other hand, revealing a medallion. The Seekers were renowned for the magical medallions they had created and many humans, elves, and drakes had hunted ruined rookeries looking for such prizes. Darkhorse, who knew how devious the devices could be, took several steps back until he heard fluttering behind him.

A second Seeker just a little smaller than the first and therefore likely a female blocked his path of retreat. Darkhorse wondered if they were aware that his power was hindered by his trappings. Certainly they wondered why he took such a slow, methodical route to bring Aurim Bedlam home. The avians were very familiar with the Bedlams, especially Cabe and his mad father Azran. Darkhorse suspected that the Seekers respected Cabe for his past dealings with them, but that did not mean that such respect transmitted into concern and respect for either the master sorcerer's friend or his son.

Seeming somewhat irritated, the first Seeker squawked quietly, then held the medallion up. The shadow steed readied himself for whatever assault the birdman planned.

Images flooded his head, images Darkhorse immediately recognized as originating from the mind of the Seeker. The avians could communicate with those of other races by either using their talismans or, better yet, touching their clawed hands to the forehead of the one with whom they desired to converse. Communication always occurred in the form of a series of images, not all of them necessarily based in reality. This Seeker had chosen the medallion, likely well aware what it might mean to touch the legendary demon steed.

In his mind, Darkhorse saw the Green Dragon, now seated on his throne, making a demand of a pair of elder Seekers.

The image was followed by one of the armies of Lanith poised at the edge of the Dagora Forest. That picture, in turn, was followed by the vision of a blazing forest. Next came a series of swift scenes, all of them of flocks of Seekers rising swiftly into the night sky.

"So your flocks serve the drake lord of this forest, do they?" An interesting alliance. Seekers despised drakes even more than they did humans.

The vision shifted without warning, showing avian against drake in combat. The alliance was only temporary, foes joining together to combat a common enemy. Lanith's horde lay destroyed, their pitiful weapons no match for the combined might of the Seekers and the Dragon King.

"And what about his sorcerers? Your victory will not be an easy one, bird!" Pride was still one of the Seekers' greatest weaknesses. Too often they dove into conflicts, assuming that they were destined to be the victors.

The winged figure ignored his question, instead indicating the prone form atop the back of the shadow steed. An image of Cabe Bedlam materialized in Darkhorse's thoughts. The avian had made the link between Darkhorse's unconscious charge and the master sorcerer. How he had made that link became a little clearer a breath later when a vision of Yssa formed. Evidently the Seekers held her in as much respect as they did Cabe. For some reason, the eternal was not at all surprised. The drake's half-human daughter seemed to have a way with some creatures.

Pulling the medallion to his chest, the birdman indicated that Darkhorse should follow him. While the eternal would not normally have trusted the creature enough to obey, he decided that it was best to risk it at this time. After all, the Seekers only had to seize the reins to put him under their complete control, something he did not want them to discover. If he cooperated, they would not be tempted to forcibly lead him along.

One benefit of the avians' unexpected appearance was that any pursuer would think twice before attacking while the Seekers were nearby. Even the Order would pause. Seeker magic was a force to be reckoned with.

While it was clear the pair with him would have preferred to return to the sky, they remained earthbound for the trek, flittering through the woods like graceful yet deadly dancers. However, Darkhorse did not doubt that at least half a dozen more just like them lurked above, flying from tree to tree and keeping a silent vigil on the surrounding area with both their eyes and their medallions.

The Seeker behind Darkhorse suddenly bumped into him. He glanced as best he could at the smaller of the bird people, discovering her all too interested in Aurim. While reading the shadowed, inhuman features was ofttimes difficult, the stallion thought he saw suspicion and uncertainty in her eyes. She started to reach for the sorcerer's dangling arm, but Darkhorse took a quick step forward. She glared at him but could not match his icy gaze for very long. The Seeker retreated a few steps and did not try to touch Aurim again.

As pleased as he was to be making apparent progress, Darkhorse again grew impatient with the length of the journey. Surely the Green Dragon had to know where he was by now. Why did the drake not simply use his vast power to transport the eternal and his companion to his caverns? Why trust to the untrusting Seekers?

The lead creature paused without warning. Darkhorse looked around, but saw nothing significant about the location. The Seeker, ignoring his impatience, went down on one knee, lowering his head at the same time.

With the other Seeker keeping watch, the first avian raised his hands upward. Darkhorse could not sense any use of sorcery, but he suspected that his guide was trying to summon someone very far away.

When enough time had passed and still nothing had happened, the shorter Seeker squawked angrily. The male looked up at her and squawked back, his annoyance seeming to be focused more on his companion than the one he was trying to summon. When it was clear that there would be no more interruptions from the impatient female, the taller Seeker renewed his summoning.

As if in response, a figure formed in the darkness just before the male.

At last! the shadow steed thought, his exasperation having grown nearly beyond his control. *I will have some very choice words for you, drake lord, for making me journey this long when the situation is so dire!*

However, the newcomer was not the Dragon King, but a shorter, more familiar person.

Yssa.

"I'm here, J'K'i'RU—" The enchantress paused when she saw the steed and his cargo. "Darkhorse! You escaped! Is that . . . is that Aurim?"

"It is, Yssa, and while I am indeed happy to see you, perhaps you can explain to me how you come to be associated with these . . ."

"That can wait." She folded her arms tight. "I don't think that I want to let Lady Bedlam wait any longer than I have to. Not after our first encounter. She doesn't even know why I left so suddenly." Yssa turned to the male Seeker, reaching out a hand at the same time. Surprisingly, the avian, now standing, took her hand and held it. He squawked something, to which Yssa replied with a nod. "Thank you again, J'K'i'RU. I know it wasn't easy to convince your flock to do this, even for me."

"Do you actually understand that noise? What is this Jkiroo you've said twice already?"

"J'K'i'RU. That's the shortened version of his name. Don't ask me to repeat the full version; I don't think my mouth and lungs could take it. Yes, of course I understand him, just as I understood the grass."

She said it in such a matter-of-fact tone. Darkhorse doubted that anyone save perhaps Azran Bedlam had ever been able to understand the natural language of the Seekers. Most had to rely on either the medallions or being touched by the avians. Truly there was more to Yssa than anyone realized.

However, she was correct about one thing. Now he, who had been so impatient to end his journey, was delaying it further. Aurim needed to be attended to and the sooner the better.

Behind him, the female said something. The male shook

his head, but she insisted. Finally, he squawked at Yssa, who nodded her head. "I'll tell him that."

"Tell who what?"

"A message for Cabe Bedlam. A personal one. This flock holds him in especially high regard because of something concerning his father . . ." The enchantress sounded somewhat puzzled.

"He can explain in more detail, but I will tell you that it is because of Cabe that many Seekers were freed from their servitude to Azran, his father. Azran was nothing like his son."

"So I've heard." She approached the eternal. "The saddle. It feels . . . evil. The rest of the equipment does—"

"Lady Bedlam is no doubt very upset, Yssa. We should go to her as soon as possible." He dared not let her continue speaking about the saddle and bridle until they had been removed. If the Seekers did not realize just how handicapped he was at the moment, he had no intention of illuminating them in that regard. Darkhorse did not trust them enough to not think that they might turn on Yssa, even if she was respected by them.

"You're right, of course." The blond enchantress held both hands out, thumbs together and fingers fanned out. The Seekers returned the gesture, the male actually touching palms with Yssa. Darkhorse, studying the hands, wondered if the gesture was supposed to represent a flock coming together in harmony. When there was time, he intended on discussing much with the young woman.

The Seekers suddenly darted up into the air, vanishing into the darkened treetops. Yssa watched them disappear, then turned her attention back to the ebony stallion and his unconscious passenger. "You can't transport the pair of you back to the Manor, can you?"

"No, I cannot . . . can you?"

"I think I can do it, but we might have to appear just outside the magical barrier that surrounds their domain. I don't think Lady Bedlam trusts me quite enough yet to let me immediately enter. I only made it last time, I think, because I was with Cabe. She's very protective of him."

"Like me, Yssa, she is very protective of all of those close to her." The shadow steed studied the darkened forest. "I am very distrustful of the lack of attention Lanith has given our escape so far. You had best send us on our way before that changes."

"I agree." She closed her eyes, concentrating.

The blink hole illuminated the entire area. The moment Yssa indicated everything was ready, Darkhorse wasted no time in entering.

Nothing hindered them as they crossed from one end of the hole to the other. Yssa and Darkhorse stepped out of the other end, only to find that what she had feared was true. They had not materialized on the Manor grounds, but rather in the surrounding forest. Darkhorse recognized the region and knew that another two or three steps would take him up to the barrier that prevented those without permission from entering.

"There's something I should warn you about first, Darkhorse. I nearly forgot. The Bedlams think—"

"Darkhorse." The voice that interrupted was that of Gwendolyn Bedlam, but the tone was hardly one of relief or greeting. Instead, it almost sounded accusatory. "What have you done to my son?"

"My lady?" He turned, nearly jostling Aurim loose, and found the legendary sorceress standing behind Yssa. An aura surrounded Gwendolyn Bedlam, a crimson aura that mirrored the outrage in her expression.

"Careful, Gwen," called Cabe from yet another direction. He, too, faced his old friend as if confronting a possible foe, but his expression was more a combination of curiosity and sorrow. "Let's hear him out."

"Our son lies on his back like some gutted stag. I want to know if he's all right before anything else happens, Cabe."

"He is not all right, Lady Bedlam. He has been through far too much. The sooner you are able to care for him, the better his chances of full recovery are!" The shadow steed sidled close to them so that the Bedlams could retrieve their eldest offspring.

The emerald-clad enchantress seemed to relax a little. Darkhorse, neck twisted to the limits the bridle allowed him, saw that the aura had faded somewhat. She was still furious with him for some reason, but parental concern had taken the forefront.

Aurim's still form rose from his back, the young sorcerer's flight guided by his father. Cabe Bedlam brought his son up to eye level, then floated him toward his mother, who immediately began to inspect him.

"He seems all right on the surface, but something's been done to his mind." She glared at Darkhorse. "What did you do to his mind?"

"I did nothing!" the eternal instantly protested. He slowly began to understand what was happening. As impossible as it was to imagine, they believed that he was somehow responsible for Aurim's condition.

Stepping forward, Cabe interjected, "Darkhorse, I felt your presence when Aurim and the other sorcerers attacked me. I also sense your touch in his mind. Everything points to you being responsible for possessing and possibly injuring our son. Can you explain that?"

"I can, but it would be better if we did so in the safety of the Manor. You must understand—"

"You're forbidden entrance for now, Darkhorse. I'm sorry. Gwen and I can't take that chance."

"Cabe! You cannot possibly believe that I would ever harm either you or yours! I am your friend! I was your grandfather's friend! I have stood by your line more times than even I can count! I have fought beside you against drakes and more! How could you, how could even your lady, believe that I would harm your son?"

Even Gwen was moved by his words. "I don't want to believe that of you, either, Darkhorse, but something did happen to my son and your trace is on him."

"Not *my* trace, my lady, although I can clearly see why you would think so. No, to my shame, that which you sensed earlier, Cabe, was not me . . . and yet I must also say that it was. The villain you seek is an abomination, a travesty of everything that I have sought to be, whose foul name is *Yureel*."

"Yureel?" The Bedlams and Yssa stared blankly at him. He had hoped that at least the young enchantress would make the link between Lanith's mysterious intelligent force and what he had just revealed, but such was not to be the case.

"Yureel," Darkhorse repeated. "A creature whose trace is so very much like mine because ... because once, before there were two of us, there was only one. Him." He shook his head. "I will say no more out here. We risk his presence by doing so. Besides, Aurim needs aid."

Cabe walked over to him, reaching out to touch his muzzle. The eternal felt a sorcerous probe enter his mind. He did nothing to deflect it, knowing that the spellcaster sought the proof of his words.

Stepping away a minute later, the sorcerer said, "I believe him." When he saw that his wife was about to protest, Cabe Bedlam added, "And yes, I also believe it's him, Gwen. I thought of that, too." The human did not bother to explain to Darkhorse what he meant by the last, but he did apologize. "I'm sorry, my old friend, but we've been on edge for the past several days. We know all about the armies devastating the western edge of the Dagora Forest and we're painfully aware that our son seems to be a part of the horse king's Magical Order, the ones most responsible for what was happening."

"The Gryphon's been speaking to the Green Dragon, although if they've accomplished anything yet, we haven't heard," Gwen added. "We wanted to go and confront Aurim ourselves, but the Gryphon convinced us that it was more likely we would fall prey to the same power that had taken him. Worse, it was even more likely we'd have to fight our son."

"Well that risk is past now." Cabe raised an arm high. "And I think we can take this conversation into the Manor now ... unless there's still some objection?" He looked at his wife.

Lady Bedlam's gaze did not fall on Darkhorse, but rather Yssa. "I suppose not."

"Good." Even as the sorcerer spoke, their surroundings transformed. Now they stood in a hall that on one side was made of marble and on the other was carved from living wood. Newcomers always stared at the point where stone and plant melded with no discernible seam. The marble became the wood or perhaps the wood became the marble.

Yssa looked around in awe even though Darkhorse was certain that she had been here at least once since they had separated. It took quite some time to become even somewhat used to the Manor. Although the marble was bright white, almost as if it had been quarried only yesterday, the sense of great age was so evident that even the most jaded person had to stop and stare.

"Aurim needs to be put to bed," Gwen declared. "I'll get Valea to help me with him as soon as I have him settled."

"Please," interrupted Yssa. "May I . . . may I help you, too? I might know a few . . . unusual . . . methods that might work to heal him."

From her expression, Lady Bedlam was anything but pleased by this offer of assistance, but after glancing at her son, she finally acquiesced. "Thank you. Any assistance would be appreciated."

The two sorceresses and their patient vanished, leaving Darkhorse to deal with Cabe. This was not going to be a conversation that the eternal looked forward to, but he had no choice. It was time that someone knew about Yureel.

"She seems harmless," Cabe Bedlam remarked. "And more able than I would've expected after our first encounter, but Tori—or rather Yssa—isn't telling us everything, Darkhorse. Do you know anything about where she comes from? She's scarcely older than Aurim by sorcerer standards. She was born a decade before the death of the Dragon Emperor; that much I've figured out, but just where is still a question. Actually, I've several questions concerning her. How did she escape the drakes' notice? What's her heritage? Yssa looks like a native of Zuu, but for some reason I think that there's more to it than that . . ."

Although he could have answered most of the questions rather easily, Darkhorse chose to remain silent on the subject. Those answers were best left to the young enchantress and her father. Knowing the truth would not help the present crisis and, in fact, might only serve to complicate things further. "I cannot say, Cabe, but that is an issue to be dealt with later, would you not say? We must speak of Yureel and quickly."

The sorcerer's mood shifted. "Yes. Yureel. I've never heard

such a name... and you said... I still can't believe I heard it... you said that he's just like you? How can that be possible, Darkhorse? I don't think I've ever come across any mention in any of the journals and spell books I've collected of another creature like you!"

"Yureel is far more than simply a 'creature like me,' Cabe. Yureel is more me than I am, I regret to say. Did you not listen closely to my words when we were outside? Yureel and I share an origin. It is because of *him* that I exist at all!"

His last words seemed to reverberate about the hall. Cabe Bedlam stared wide-eyed at his friend, perhaps, Darkhorse pondered, seeing the eternal truly for the first time. Darkhorse had struggled for so very long for so many centuries to prove, mostly to himself, that he was a unique being. Now, Yureel's return had reminded him of the truth; he was nothing but the foul monster's creation.

"I think... I need to sit down for this," the sorcerer finally blurted.

"Allow me—" Darkhorse paused, recalling that he still wore the bridle and saddle. The shadow steed had been so unnerved by the coming conversation that he had completely forgotten about his impediments. "Before we do anything, Cabe, may I ask you to please remove these wicked trappings from me? They hinder my powers."

"Oh, gods, I'm sorry! Let me take care of your concerns and mine at the same time." The human waved his hand.

Their surroundings shifted yet again, this time becoming one of the more private regions of the vast garden. Cabe now sat on a stone bench. High, trimmed bushes shielded them on all sides from the world. It was a perfect place for what would be an unsettling conversation.

Darkhorse barely noted the change in scenery, though, for Cabe had, true to his word, at the same time removed the bridle and saddle. The sensations caused by their vanishing made all else insignificant. To Darkhorse it was as if he had been born a second time. He felt energy flow through him like a river filling an empty basin. The eternal wanted to caper about, fly up into the heavens, or simply shout his joy, but he immediately reminded himself that his freedom was insignificant compared to what he had to tell his friend. "My thanks, Cabe! You have been there to help me as few others have through the centuries. I have ever been in your—"

"Darkhorse . . ."

Cabe knew he was stalling now. The eternal steadied himself. Only Yureel could turn Darkhorse from proud and confident to uncertain and anxious. "I will make this as short and concise as I can then, for even simply talking about it unnerves me greatly." He stared at his long-time friend. "You know about the Void, the empty place from which I was spawned."

"I remember that when I was there I not only wanted desperately to get back here, but I wondered how you could've existed there so long without going mad."

"An astute question and one that I have asked myself since I first arrived in the Dragonrealm. Perhaps because I knew little else when first I came into being, it was easier to suffer my fate . . . but I digress." The stallion shook his head, sending his mane flying. "Let me start again and, please, this time I must get through this."

"Go ahead."

Darkhorse drew upon his renewed strength. He would need much of it in order to finish his tale. "Now there are two of us. Yureel and myself. Once though, there was only one." Darkhorse briefly glanced away, not wanting to witness Cabe's reaction to what he was about to reveal. "It was not *me*. That one was Yureel . . . my creator . . ."

CHAPTER XIII

Yssa helped Gwendolyn Bedlam guide her son to his bed. The young man was still unconscious, not a good sign in Yssa's mind. She found herself more anxious about his health than she would have expected, considering that their only encounter had been a momentary one. The young enchantress decided that it was probably because her time at the Manor had allowed her to know his family just well enough to understand what he must be like. What she had heard of him sounded amazing and quite appealing.

Control yourself, Yssa! she silently chided. *He'd have no more to do with you than his father did!* Besides, Lady Bedlam would probably turn her into something grotesque if she discovered the younger woman eyeing her son with anything other than a clinical attitude.

He *was* handsome, though . . .

"How is he?" asked a voice from the doorway. Yssa turned to see Valea Bedlam, her complexion pale, walk toward the bed. To look at the daughter was to see a memory of the mother as she had been at that age. Once they reached adulthood, most spellcasters, especially those with better-than-average ability, did not age much over the rest of the three hundred or so years of their life span unless they chose to do so. Even then, with effort they could reverse the process for a time. Only when they had reached the end of their third century did it become impossible for even the best sorcerers to hold back the ravages of time any longer. At that point, they began to age normally, turning old and gray over the next decade, two, if fortunate. Few were the cases of a spellcaster completing a fourth century.

As for those with only a trace of ability, age generally came to them as it did any other mortal. Power was indeed life.

It was not then surprising to find that time affected the Bedlams little. Mother and daughter looked more like twins born a few years apart. Lady Bedlam was slightly taller and Valea's eyes were more like those of her father, but other than that, the differences were negligible. Both had a fondness for the color green, although where the elder Bedlam wore an elegant gown befitting a master sorceress, the younger was clad in a trousered hunting outfit that still somehow managed to be quite feminine.

They had spoken with one another only briefly during Yssa's initial visit to the Manor, but in Valea Yssa believed she had found an ally, perhaps even a friend. "He's still unconscious," she said now. "We only just lowered him onto the bed."

"He seems all right physically," commented Lady Bedlam as she ran her hand over her son's forehead. Her brow furrowed. She repeated the gesture, moving slower this time. "Odd. I don't sense Darkhorse's influence . . . or rather the influence of that thing that seems like him. Now it seems like he's just sleeping."

Yssa joined her. "May I?"

When Lady Bedlam indicated she had no objections, Yssa reached forward, touching her fingertips to the center of the unconscious sorcerer's forehead. She probed deep, trying to make certain that Aurim Bedlam was indeed free of the spell that had bound him. Her initial search verified what Lady Bedlam had said, but Yssa probed deeper yet. They had to be certain that he was cleansed of any influence.

Layer after layer of his subconscious gave way to her. Although Yssa did not try to read his mind, she did pick up general emotions, enough to know she had been correct about the sort of man he was. Very admirable. Much like his father was said to be. The enchantress was tempted to linger, but knew better than to do so with Aurim's mother next to her. Besides, nothing she had noted contradicted Lady Bedlam's conclusion.

And yet . . .

Exactly what it was she sensed, Yssa could not say. When she searched for it again, the enchantress found nothing.

"Well?" asked Gwendolyn Bedlam, her tone one of growing impatience.

The interruption broke her concentration. Whatever she believed that she had sensed had to have been the product of her own overwrought mind. "I can't find anything. He just doesn't seem to want to wake up."

Cabe's wife nodded. "From what Darkhorse said, this was more traumatic than when Toma seized control of Aurim's mind. Lanith made my son do things that he would've never willingly agreed to do, things that must have *revolted* him." Her hands tightened into fists. "We stayed out of this for as long as we could, first because Zuu had once been a great ally to us and we didn't wish to make the political situation worse, then because Aurim was a prisoner. It's terrible . . . generally I'm the voice of peace, but this time Lanith's gone too far! He has to be *stopped*, Magical Order or *not*."

"I'll help in any way I can, Lady Bedlam."

Gwen eyed Yssa, possibly trying to find a kind way to turn down her offer. However, before the master sorceress could reply, her daughter interjected, "Anything you can do would certainly be appreciated, Yssa. I know I speak for my entire family, including my brother. I know he'd welcome your presence."

The last made Lady Bedlam's eyes widen briefly, but gradually she nodded. "Yes, we can certainly use your aid, not to mention your knowledge. You know Zuu better than any of us. Were you born there?"

From the tone of her voice and the slight shift of her eyes, Gwendolyn Bedlam was clearly still suspicious about Yssa's origins. So far, none of the Bedlams had *demanded* the truth, but Cabe's wife was not going to be patient with her much longer. Yssa recalled that her father had once acted as secret patron of the sorceress, but that had been long, long ago, before Nathan Bedlam, the Turning War, and the lady's own imprisonment by Azran Bedlam. If anyone might recognize her for the half-breed she was, it would be the woman before her.

"No, my lady. My grandparents were from there and I lived there for some time after I grew up, but I was born and raised in a small village to the north."

"I see." That seemed to settle matters for now. Lady Bedlam leaned over her son. "I wish I knew why he slept like this." She pushed a lock of hair back from his face. "I don't dare take a chance, not after last time."

"Do you think there's a risk of that, Mother?"

Yssa could not follow the sudden shift in the conversation. She looked at Valea. "What risk? Of what?"

It was the elder woman who responded. "Aurim wasn't the only one Toma seized control of. I nearly killed my husband. It was a spell, actually, not really possession, but it might as well have been. We can't risk that Aurim might not still be under some subtle spell." Gwen spread her hands, then again gazed down at her son. A pink aura formed around him. "That should hold him."

"Is that necessary?" Yssa hated the thought of him being bound. It did not seem fair after all Aurim Bedlam had already been through.

"I think so, yes." Lady Bedlam stepped away from the bed. "Now I can concentrate on what ails him without fear that he might attack us while under some carefully hidden spell."

Her words made Yssa think again about the momentary sensation she had felt while probing the sorcerer's mind. Perhaps she should not have so readily dismissed it as nothing. "My lady, I might've made a mistake. You might want to probe his mind again. For a brief moment I thought I sensed something, but it wasn't there when I looked again. Maybe you'd have more luck."

Lady Bedlam extended her hands over her son again. She closed her eyes, but opened them only a breath or two later. "I still sense nothing. I went very deep, too, just in case you might be wondering, Yssa."

While it was a relief to know that her fears had been nothing but empty air, Yssa could not help but be affected by the rebuke she sensed in Gwendolyn Bedlam's words. She began to wonder if Aurim's mother would ever trust her. Perhaps she thought that the young enchantress sought to bedazzle the son since the father had turned down her offer.

It was a reasonable thing to assume. Yssa had always wanted to find someone capable of understanding her and coping with her past. It would have to be a spellcaster; she had learned long ago that most normal humans either feared or sought to make use of her abilities. The drakes were no better. Cabe Bedlam, whose reputation for understanding was legend, had been the perfect choice—so she had thought at the time. Had he left his wife for her, though, Yssa suspected he would have quickly lost favor in her eyes. That was not the kind of mate she desired. The sorceress wanted someone she could trust enough to love and someone she could also trust to love the mixed-blood offspring that would come.

She had reminded both Cabe Bedlam and Miklo of the power her children would wield thanks to both their parents, but had done so only in the hopes it would be an added enticement. Yssa knew now that with Miklo that had not really mattered; he would have accepted her even if she had had nothing to offer him, even children. That she had not loved him in return would not have mattered. Poor Miklo would have accepted her and that would have been enough.

With Aurim Bedlam, however, it was different. Something stirred in her when she looked at him, something that had blossomed quickly since their first brief encounter. It was true that Aurim's power did impress Yssa, but her emotions went much deeper than that. Having touched his mind, she had discovered that the man behind that power was also worth knowing. The blond woman only hoped that she would have the opportunity.

"What do we do now?" Valea asked, gazing down at her brother.

"It looks to me like this will require some private study of my own, dear. Why don't you take Yssa and show her around a little more, darling? If I need either of you, I'll let you know."

Yssa found herself greatly disappointed by Lady Bedlam's

dismissal. She said nothing, though, knowing it would only upset the woman. Lady Bedlam did not need more aggravation; her son's recovery was of the utmost importance and if anyone could bring him out of his slumber, it was probably her.

"Yssa?" Valea gently touched her arm. Lady Bedlam had already forgotten them, her attention completely fixed on the still figure. "Let me show you the main library. You didn't get a chance to see that before, did you?"

She actually had gotten a glimpse of it, but Yssa understood that the younger woman was trying her best to keep the peace. Or perhaps Valea feared that Yssa would say something regrettable in response to the rebuke. Yssa gave her a comforting smile. "No, I haven't really seen it. Is it far?"

"Not too far . . ." With one last worried glance at her mother and brother, Valea Bedlam led Yssa from the room. They did not talk at first, Yssa's companion seeming more concerned with getting as far away from her brother's chambers as quickly as they could. Only when they reached a staircase at the end of the hall did she start to calm down. "There's so much to see in the Manor. Every now and them I find some little thing I don't recall ever seeing and I've lived here all my life!"

"I know your mother is worried, Valea. I didn't take any offense from her attitude. She's also got a right to be a little leery of me. I did try once to seduce your father. To be honest, I'm rather surprised that you aren't my enemy."

"If you had tried to seduce my father *again*," Valea replied, her voice suddenly so very like Lady Bedlam's, "my mother would have been the least of your worries." Intense levels of power abruptly radiated from the young woman. Yssa now saw that the incredible abilities Aurim had inherited had also been passed on to the Bedlams' daughter. Whether she was as powerful as her brother, Yssa could not tell, but Valea Bedlam was clearly not someone with whom to trifle.

"I understand perfectly."

The summoned power immediately dwindled away. Yssa's companion smiled apologetically. "Good. I like you. I think my brother would like you, too."

Yssa felt her face redden: a rare occurrence. Valea's simple statement had embarrassed her as little else had during her colorful life. "Well, if he's as nice to others as you are, I'm sure that I'll like him."

"Good!"

Trying not to smile at Valea's enthusiastic response, Yssa focused on the path ahead. The staircase wound several times as it descended but the bottom was visible from where she stood. The Manor was a wonder in design. The enchantress pondered its creators, who, according to what Valea had told her the last time they had met, still remained a mystery to the Bedlams even after all these years. They had suspicions, but nothing verifiable.

"Is something wrong, Yssa?"

Realizing she had been standing and staring, Yssa shook her head and started down. However, a few steps later she happened to glance at the bottom and what the enchantress saw then made her stop. There was a figure at the bottom of the stairs, a figure that should not have been there.

It was Darkhorse, but not Darkhorse as she knew him. The huge ebony stallion looked distorted, as if he had forgotten how to form his equine shape. His legs were twisted, the body looked bloated, and the head was only in part formed. Worse, other appendages of varying design sprouted from his body.

"Rheena!" her companion gasped.

The shadow steed did not move. Yssa slowly descended, her eyes fixed on the bizarre tableau. What had happened to Darkhorse? Why was he frozen in place like some statue?

"Yssa, wait!" Valea darted down the steps to her side. "I think that it's just—"

"Look!" Before the blond enchantress's eyes, Darkhorse faded away. It was as if someone had erased the stallion. "We've got to find out what—"

Valea seized her arm. Aurim's sister was a surprisingly strong woman for her size. "Wait! Listen to me. It startled me, too, at first, but only because I've never seen that one! Don't worry, Yssa, I know what it was now."

"What are you talking about? That was Darkhorse! He's in danger!" How could Valea be so calm?

Looking Yssa straight in the eye, the other woman quietly said, "It was a ghost. One of the Manor's ghosts. They're images from the past, usually, images that for some reason remain behind. Some of them move, some of them even talk."

"I've never heard of that!" Tales about ghosts and the like abounded throughout the realm, but Yssa had never confronted any such spirit herself. She knew something of the Manor thanks to her father, but he had failed to mention this interesting tidbit of information.

"It doesn't happen very often. Generally it's either Father or Aurim who sees them. I don't know why. I've seen my own share, though. You should witness the wedding scene; it's beautiful if a little sad when you think about the fact that the bride and groom are long dead."

"So the image we saw . . . that happened in the past?"

Here Valea hesitated. "I don't remember ever hearing about this one, but there's one way to be certain. We can ask Father. After all, he's with Darkhorse now."

That was exactly what Yssa wanted to do. The ghost had been too real, too immediate an image. The memory of its appearance still made her shiver a little.

"They're out in the garden maze," the younger sorceress announced, evidently having searched for them with her mind. "They seem to be all right. I didn't probe hard enough to disturb them. Darkhorse is telling him about something."

Yssa had forgotten that. Something about a creature like him. That in itself sounded fascinating, although also frightening if there was any truth to it. She hoped to ask the shadow steed some questions herself when she had the opportunity.

"I don't think I want to disturb them just yet, Yssa. There's another way to check, though. My father keeps a journal of sightings in his private library. He won't mind if I look there. He asked us all to record sightings whenever possible. It's a hobby of his, I suppose."

Yssa still wanted to interrupt Cabe and Darkhorse, but she was a guest, a somewhat undesired guest at that, and so it behooved her to follow the suggestions of her host. Fortunately, Cabe Bedlam's private library was nearby. The room was small but neat and consisted mainly of a desk and some shelves filled with journals, scrolls, and the like.

Valea reached unerringly for one of the journals. She opened the volume, then placed it on the desktop so that both of them could read its contents at the same time. To her surprise, Yssa saw that over the years, Cabe Bedlam and his family had listed hundreds of sightings. Fortunately, Valea evidently knew most of the listings by heart, for she ran through the list so fast that the other sorceress barely had time to read some of the entries. Those that she did read surprised her. Besides the wedding, which she spotted just before Valea turned the page, there were sightings of Seekers, sword fights, even a Quel. Oddly, many of the visions were mundane ones. Yssa even noted more than one listing concerning a woman cooking in the kitchen. There seemed to be neither rhyme nor reason to which images appeared.

Two toward the end of the listing interested her. One, recorded by Aurim, noted that Cabe Bedlam himself had materialized as an image. The other, recorded in turn by Cabe, concerned the drake Toma, with whom Yssa had long been familiar thanks to her father. Although he was now dead, simply seeing the renegade's name made her uneasy. To think that Toma had come so close to seizing control of both the Manor and the young successor to the Dragon Emperor's throne . . .

The listing was a particularly long one, but before Yssa could read more than a line, Valea interrupted her by pushing aside the journal. "Nothing! I didn't see one mention of Darkhorse in here. Now I'll have to interrupt them." The young woman sighed. "But first I guess that I'd better record this one, otherwise Father will probably scold me later on. He takes this so seriously."

While Valea wrote, Yssa took the opportunity to read the rest of the entry concerning Toma. The sighting had taken place not long before Emperor Kyl's ascension and had evidently been a shocking sight to the one confronted by it, namely Cabe Bedlam. He had noted that there had been several unusual factors concerning the vision, including the fact that it had been of a very recent event. The vast majority of the other sightings had been of things and events from the far past. More important, Cabe had noted that the image had probably been some sort of *warning*, the Manor's way of trying to alert its inhabitants to the drake's intrusion. Toma had actually entered the Manor, having stolen the identity of a trusted human scholar named Benjin Traske.

The entry was interesting, but Yssa could make no link between it and the image of Darkhorse they had witnessed. She leaned back, pondering the matter while her companion finished the new entry.

"Do you want to add anything, Yssa?"

Relegating the other entry to the back of her mind, the enchantress read what Valea had written. "No, I don't think I could add anything. You were very thorough."

"I have to be. Father generally questions us about the sightings later on. The more I write down, the less I have to try to recall later on. It's self-preservation."

"Then he'll want to know about this as soon as possible." Yssa straightened. "Is it far to where he's located? Your lands are vaster than some baronies. The garden seems to go on forever."

Valea giggled. "I know, believe me. It won't take us long to walk there, though. There's no reason to use a spell for something as minor as this probably is. My parents don't like us to waste our strength popping from place to place." She turned toward the doorway and her amusement vanished. "That's odd. I don't remember the door being closed."

Neither did Yssa. "One of us probably did it when we came in and we just forgot."

"You're probably right." Valea tried to open the door, but it remained shut. She tugged again with no better success. "I don't understand. It's not locked."

"Let me try." Yssa tugged, but also failed. Lacking the patience of her companion, she did not try a second time, but rather concentrated her power on the defiant door.

It still would not budge.

Valea looked at her. "Something's terribly wrong. You just tried to open the door with sorcery, didn't you?"

"I did. It should've opened easily."

"Maybe if we both try."

The pair stared. The door glowed bright green and quivered, but it remained sealed.

"Take my hand," Yssa commanded. They had one option of escape left, but she suspected that they had to act fast or not at all. "Don't lose your hold, whatever you do."

Once Valea obeyed, Yssa completely focused her attention on her spell. She had always been good at travel spells, be they blink holes or otherwise. What she planned should be simple.

At first, it seemed it would be. A circle of light formed before them. Yssa's hopes rose. The blink hole was forming perfectly . . .

Before the enchantress could open it, the hole suddenly dissipated. A slight backlash of power sent Yssa to the desk, where Valea barely kept her from falling onto it. Both women stared at the sealed entrance.

"That should've worked!" Yssa nearly hissed, but managed at the last moment to smother the sound. Hissing was a habit she had acquired as a child, but one she purposely worked to suppress for fear that others might discover her origin.

"Maybe I can contact my father . . ." Valea stared toward the ceiling.

A giggle echoed through the room, a malevolent, taunting giggle that did not sound human.

No! Yssa whirled around, but could neither see nor sense the source of the foul laughter. Valea shook her head as if trying to clear it. She had failed to reach her father, of that the half-breed enchantress had no doubt.

"What was that, Yssa? Where did it come from?"

Zuu. Zuu is where it's come from . . . A sense of dread rose within her. A short time past, the Manor had warned the Bedlams about the drake renegade in their midst. She wondered now if perhaps it had been trying to warn them again. Darkhorse had said that the thing that served Lanith was like him, so much so that even Cabe could not tell the magical signatures apart. The mad image of Darkhorse, his form twisted into something perverse, might have been the Manor's unique way of trying to tell someone that the evil had gained access to what should have been the safest domain in all the Dragonrealm.

Worse, if what she believed was true, it was now moving against them . . . and Yssa wondered if *anyone* would realize the danger before it was too late.

Cabe Bedlam was his dearest friend and yet telling him of Yureel was a task Darkhorse found daunting. He forced himself to proceed, though, knowing that it was necessary. If anyone might be able to help him, it would be Cabe.

"I neither know when nor where Yureel first came into being or whether, like the Void, he was simply there when the multiverse blossomed. If age matters at all in that empty realm, Yureel is far, far more ancient than I. He existed there, floating about and, on occasion, inspecting the few bits of matter that slipped into the Void, but never finding their place of origin. I do not even know if at that time he cared where such bits came from. It is my suspicion that for as long as Yureel has existed, he has mostly concerned himself with his own amusement. Other matters, other creatures, existed only to entertain him."

"You say he was first," Cabe interrupted. "If so . . . how did you come to be?"

The stallion shuddered. "The notion was evidently one long in the forming. Its origin, I believe, was due to an encounter like none he had ever experienced before. Yureel himself told me of the encounter time and time again. He seemed to take particular pleasure in repeating it to me whenever I did not care to join in his foul games, which was often." Darkhorse faltered, recalling the ruthlessness of those games. It was fortunate that Yureel's opportunities for such sport had been rare. "A being of intelligence—Yureel described it only by saying that it talked and had six limbs—had the misfortune to be cast into the Void. Yureel, who had no name at the time and did not even understand the meaning of 'self,' found the hapless one. He was fascinated. Never had he come across such a thing. Yureel decided that he needed to completely understand what this new and unusual toy was like."

"What . . . what did he do?"

Darkhorse gouged the earth with one hoof. "He did as he had always done with the objects he found. He *absorbed* him, Cabe. Swallowed him as a pit of tar would a helpless riding drake. You have seen me open myself when touched by a foe and you have seen that foe vanish within as if falling forever. It is not a fate any would desire, but some might find it more suitable than what Yureel did to this one. He took in the lost one, took in his essence, his very being . . . and made it his own. Where there had been two, there was now only one, but one who now held much of the knowledge, the experience, and the power of the one taken."

The sorcerer shifted uneasily. "Darkhorse, are you saying that you can do this? You can . . . swallow . . . someone and make what they knew, what they *were*, yours?"

For quite some time, the eternal could not look at his friend, much less respond to the question. Finally, with a slow, regretful dip of his head, Darkhorse answered, "Yes . . . I can, Cabe. If I were wont to, I could seize a full-grown human, take him inside, and make mine all that he is." His icy eyes widened. "But I would *never* do such a thing! Never, Cabe!"

"I know you wouldn't, Darkhorse. I know."

What he could never tell the sorcerer was that he *had* done so, far in the past. In the Void, he had not understood what he was doing, only that this was what Yureel always did. In the Dragonrealm . . . there had been a couple of times when the only way to save others had been to take lives in such a manner. The ones he had taken had deserved no mercy, but he could not help feeling sorry for them nevertheless.

The story. He had to keep his mind on the story. "Now Yureel saw things as he had never seen them before. He knew that there were other places beyond his reach, places full of things, full of life. It frustrated him that he could not find these places, although I know he did try. The frustration grew worse the longer he dwelled upon it. When next he confronted a hapless visitor to the Void, he seized that one faster than the first, thinking it would help alleviate his frustration. It did not. It only added new dimensions to it. Now Yureel realized that the places he could not reach had to number into infinity. So many creatures, so many *playthings*, kept from him . . ."

The shadow steed paused, momentarily distracted. For a moment Darkhorse thought he sensed someone using sorcery to contact him, but when he tried to verify it, the eternal felt nothing.

"You don't have to go on if you don't want to," Cabe commented, taking his latest pause for reluctance.

"I need to." It had only been his distraught mind. That was it. Nothing more. "This has to be told." He shook his head, trying again to clear his thoughts. "As I have indicated, to Yureel, the unfortunates were nothing but entertainment. Those that he did not take immediately he generally killed soon afterward for one reason or another. However, it was not until he happened upon a pair of identical beings, creatures who spoke and acted together at all times, that a fantastic notion occurred to him. In his mind, they were the same being but in different shells. They had one another to ever work with . . ." The shadow steed thought over the last statement and corrected himself. "They were never *alone* . . ."

Yureel had taken them as he had taken the others, but this time he studied them closely first. If they could have each other, then why could *he* not have another "self" with whom to play, with whom to share his pastimes . . .

Never had Yureel found any being akin to himself, so he decided that he would create one. The concept of creating something was one he had learned from some of his toys, but until that moment it had made no sense. He pondered it long, testing out one process after another. Nothing seemed to work.

"Then he hit upon the answer, Cabe. If he could absorb other things, make them part of him, why could he not reverse the process and separate a piece of his being, give it strength, and make it grow into another version of himself? There had been incidents when he had misjudged some of the playthings he had found and they had injured him, separating one bit of his essence from the whole. Being a creature much like . . . shall we say a cloud or puddle, for lack of a better earthly description . . . he was generally unhurt by these attacks and always afterward reabsorbed the fragments. It had never occurred to him to do anything otherwise."

"Didn't he ever miss a . . . a piece . . . before?"

Darkhorse understood. "Small fragments, yes, Cabe, but the small ones did not last. That, in fact, was something Yureel discovered for himself during his initial experiments. His first attempt was a tiny blob that he could manipulate but that had no intelligence of its own. He tried yet a larger one, but ended with the same results. It came to the point where Yureel understood that he would have to divide more or less into two *equal* parts to achieve his goal. Unfortunately, he had also learned that the constant attempts to divide *had* weakened him already. He needed to absorb more substance to make further attempts but in the Void there was little to find. His patience, though, had reached its limits and so Yureel dared to try one more time even despite his weakness."

Like a mass of wet clay pulled apart by an artisan, Yureel had stretched in two opposing directions. At first the creature had felt no change, but the more tenuous the physical connection between the two parts became, the more separate the controlling forces of each half also grew. The process also began to speed up, perhaps because the second portion now had some desire for existence of its own.

When had Darkhorse first experienced consciousness? Even the shadow steed could not really say. He thought he recalled some part of the separation, but if so, the memory was a faint one. More distinct were the first memories after the process had finally come to an end, when both shapeless forms had floated weak and unmoving in the vast emptiness. That weakness had threatened both and at one point the new "self" had been forced to retreat from the other, for in hunger the elder had tried to reabsorb his offspring. That was a memory that always haunted Darkhorse. Yureel had thought nothing of the separate personality he had created; he had been just as willing to reabsorb his new counterpart as he had his many ill-fated playthings.

Yureel was a name that would come later. At this point, the two identified themselves by such concepts as "self" and "other self." In appearance, they were identical, but even from the start, subtle differences in personality became evident.

"It was when I first encountered a creature other than either myself or Yureel that I learned just how different we were, Cabe. The one who I found was nearly dead, but he struggled to live. I was curious, for I did not retain much memory of Yureel's encounters. The newcomer seemed weak, so I, who had regained strength by then, gave him enough to heal him. I wanted to know what he was and why he looked different. Naturally, my newfound toy was frightened, but he overcame that."

"How were you able to talk to him?"

The stallion considered this long before answering. "I cannot say for certain, Cabe. In the Void, it seemed much easier to touch the minds of others, especially those unshielded. I have not always found it so in the Dragonrealm. Regardless, we eventually did communicate and I found him so fascinating that I just wanted to listen and learn."

Something in his tone evidently made the sorcerer extremely uneasy. "What happened to him, Darkhorse? I can tell that something did." The human's eyes narrowed. "Yureel . . . he didn't really—"

"Yes, my friend, he did." Darkhorse kicked at the earth again. "He found me, not so difficult a task then, and was delighted with the new toy. Yureel seized him, wanting to play, and when I protested . . . he grew angry and *absorbed* him."

"God!"

"I did not at first understand how terrible that was, but I did not think his actions right. You must understand; Yureel was not kind with his captives before he absorbed them . . . not kind at all. That was what drove me away more than anything."

Darkhorse paused to think, not wanting to say anything more that might hint at how *he* had been little better than Yureel. Best to move on to the end. The final fear that had sent him fleeing from his counterpart. "I will not bore you with the tale any longer. I will only say that there came a time when because of his cruel actions to the creatures he found, I did not want to remain near Yureel any longer. I started to drift farther and farther from him, but he caught up to me and demanded to know why I had left him behind. I told him that I wanted to be by myself, that I did not like his games." The shadow steed shuddered. "He said that I did not have to leave. He would simply reabsorb me and create a new playmate, a better one. Before I realized what was happening, Yureel was trying to envelop me!"

The sorcerer shifted uneasily on the bench. His face had grown pale with each successive revelation. "You don't have to go on, Darkhorse! Not if you—"

"I felt my mind, my *self*, dissipating!" the eternal cried, almost talking to himself now. "He tried to do with me what he had done with the others! I am sorry to say that at the time the realization of what they had suffered did not strike me; I only knew my own personal terror, that I was about to cease to be!" Darkhorse stomped the ground in an attempt to relieve himself of the remembered fear. "Yureel did not expect me to be able to resist. *Nothing* had ever been able to resist him! I left him stunned, no doubt also shocked, and fled through the Void until long past the time when I could sense his presence, much less see him in that empty place! I do not know how long I journeyed, for you yourself know how meaningless time can be in the Void, but ever I kept careful watch in case he had tracked me down. I feared him then, Cabe, just as I admit to fearing him now! After the Dragonrealm was revealed to me by a lost sorcerer, I believed that at last I was free of Yureel, but that assumption proved false. He had never ceased following me, so I later discovered. Once before he found his way into this world and only through luck did others succeed in banishing him, again, supposedly *forever*." The stallion shook his head. "But forever is a long time. He has finally returned . . . and although I fear for the Dragonrealm, I fear more for myself."

Cabe Bedlam rose from the bench. "Why didn't you ever tell me this before?"

"The spell the other sorcerers used to bind Yureel in the Void seemed perfect. I thought him gone forever, unable to harm even those unfortunates who drifted into his realm. I thought myself rid of him."

"How long ago did this happen?"

Darkhorse hung his head low. "Your grandfather's grandfather had not yet been born. I know that because I knew the man. Zerik Bedlam, by the way. Among the spellcasters who forced Yureel back to the empty realm was the woman who would be his mother. I only remember her as Lamaria of the Hidden Grove."

"Someday, you and I will have a long talk about just exactly how many of my ancestors you've met." The human reached out, putting a calming hand on the shadow steed's muzzle.

Although Darkhorse was no true equine, he appreciated his friend's gesture. Telling the story had filled him with shame, not only for his own weaknesses, but the excesses of his brother, his other self. Yureel was a monster in every sense of the word, the demon that mortals had always mistaken Darkhorse for. Some of the sinister legends that had made the ebony stallion so feared had their roots in the battles against Yureel.

"He must be destroyed, Cabe. Somehow, we must destroy Yureel. He will not listen to reason, and no earthly prison is secure enough. There can be no safety from him. Somewhere in the past, he developed a fondness for epics. I think more than one mortal tried to placate him with such stories. Yureel now sees worlds such as the Dragonrealm as the setting for his own tales, and those tales always revolve around destruction on a massive scale. I believe that it was he who saw the taste for conquest in Lanith's mind and then seduced the horse king with grand promises of an empire spanning the continent."

"But I can't imagine how Lanith thinks he'll win even with Yureel and the Order. All he'll do is maybe succeed in destroying the last vestiges of peace. The entire Dragonrealm could erupt as some kingdoms fight him while others try to take advantage of the chaos!" Cabe mentioned no names, but they both knew that two Dragon Kings, Storm and Black, were among those who would take such an advantage.

"Yureel does not care if Lanith is victorious! He wants only for the armies of Zuu to create such havoc that it takes years for peace to prevail! Yureel is anarchy, Cabe! That is all he strives for!"

The sorcerer looked shaken. "I can't believe that he's so terrible a monster. The way you talk about him . . . Darkhorse . . . is he that much more powerful than you? I'd think the two of you would be equals, yet . . . you really fear him . . ."

"I do. Cabe, I have never been Yureel's equal. To be his equal, I would have to do as he does. That would give me but two choices. I could *absorb* power wholesale as he has always done . . . and spellcasters, of course, provide the greatest source of power . . ." Darkhorse gave thanks that Aurim had escaped the fate of so many others in the past. From Cabe's shifting expression, it was clear the elder Bedlam's thoughts ran a similar course.

"And . . . the other method?" the human finally managed.

"Yureel is a parasite in every sense of the *word*, Cabe! What he does not swallow whole, he often slowly sucks dry. I cannot be certain, but I suspect that he has been drawing strength from the sorcerers of Lanith's Magical Order . . . and was doing so from your son as well."

"He wouldn't!"

Darkhorse shook his head. "There is nothing Yureel would not do, friend! Nothing! If we do *not* destroy him, my foul twin will certainly destroy *us* . . . but only after we are nothing but empty *husks*. We must—"

His warning was interrupted by the sudden materialization of Lady Bedlam. The scarlet-tressed sorceress's expression was dark. The shadow steed found himself somewhat relieved to see her; her intrusion put a welcome end to his painful conversation. Rather would he deal with trying to free Aurim of the spell that bound him than speak more about the past he shared with Yureel.

"Darling, have you seen Valea and that woman?"

"I've not seen *Yssa* since the two of you took Aurim to his room. I expected Valea to join you there."

Gwendolyn Bedlam looked uncomfortable. "I found I didn't need help from either of them and so I asked Valea if she wouldn't mind showing that woman more of the Manor. Now I'm beginning to regret that decision."

The sorcerer shared a worried glance with Darkhorse. "Why?"

"Because I can't sense them anywhere. I wanted to ask Valea to look up something for me in the main library, but I couldn't locate her. I tried a stronger, more direct probe, but for all practical purposes, both she and that wood witch are missing."

"Valea wouldn't leave the Manor without telling us, dear, and you've got nothing to fear from Yssa. She's not a threat."

"Isn't she?" Lady Bedlam's eyes burned into those of the shadow steed. "What do you say, Darkhorse? Considering what she is, or at least is in *part*, wouldn't you say she might be a threat? I was a fool to let my daughter be alone with that creature . . . that abomination!"

She knows! It should not have surprised Darkhorse that Lady Bedlam had discerned Yssa's heritage. At one point in her young life, the Green Dragon had been Gwendolyn Bedlam's patron, a tutor of sorts. She had lived among drakes and possibly had even come across half-breeds such as Yssa. Still, Darkhorse guessed that Gwen only knew that Yssa was part drake. "She is no threat, Gwendolyn Bedlam. I will swear on that. Yssa, whatever her heritage, has worked only to aid us against the horse king!"

"What are the two of you talking about?" Cabe demanded.

Neither answered him, Lady Bedlam staring long and hard into the eternal's inhuman visage. At last, the sorceress tore her gaze away, instead focusing on the Manor. "Cabe, can you detect our daughter anywhere? Either her or . . . or Yssa?"

The sorcerer shut his eyes, but opened them a second later. His expression now matched that of his wife. "I can't find either of them . . . but . . . but I'm sensing Darkhorse."

"He's here with us! Of course you'll—"

"Not here, but in the Manor!"

Now she looked confused. "You must be mistaken, Cabe. How could he be in there, too?"

"Because it is *not* me, Lady Bedlam! Not me!" A horrible

realization crossed Darkhorse's mind. The eternal immedi ately sent a probe of his own toward the ancient edifice.

The search was no search at all. The building, nay, the entire domain of the Bedlams reeked with the magical trace that only to Darkhorse differed at all from his own. How, though, could the unthinkable have happened? The barrier should have noticed, should have prevented access—

No! Cabe had the right of it more than he realized! The barrier could not tell the difference! When Cabe allowed me access, Yureel, shielded by either his own sorcery or more likely that of Aurim, entered at the same time!

Yureel had succeeded in invading the protected domain of the Manor . . . and it was Darkhorse who had unwittingly provided him the *key*.

CHAPTER XIV

Yureel had invaded the Manor while their attention had been focused elsewhere. Darkhorse's counterpart had planned well. Too well. Where, though, was the monster now? He would not have fled already.

"Aurim!" Darkhorse looked at his friends. "We must see to Aurim!"

Lady Bedlam took control, gathering the trio together and immediately sending them to the young sorcerer's chamber. However, they discovered only an empty bed. Cabe did a quick check of the area, but could not locate either his son or the two other women.

"What a fool I was!" the eternal roared. "Each way I turn, Yureel has already planned ahead! He no doubt saw a rich opportunity when Aurim confronted me and made it *appear* the boy had broken free of his hold just so I would help him gain access to the Manor! I never would have believed that Yureel would risk himself so! Your home is the one place of which he should have been wary."

"Never mind that," Cabe interrupted. "What we need to do now is find the children and Yssa." He blinked. "I think . . . I think that I sense the women downstairs . . . in my library."

Lady Bedlam looked confused. "But we both tried to locate them earlier! How could you be able to do it now?"

"There presence is faint, but I'm certain it's them, not a false trail."

That was enough. In the blink of an eye, they were downstairs. Instead of Cabe's library, though, they stood in the hall just beyond it. The door before them was shut and Darkhorse and the others knew immediately that it had not been shut by a human hand. The moment Gwendolyn Bedlam tried to touch it, the door glowed a bright green around the edges.

Darkhorse stepped up to the bespelled entrance. "Leave this to me! Yureel might have incorporated a few more surprises!"

He reared up and kicked, but the door was not his target. Instead, the shadow steed first struck the left side of the doorway, then the right. Each strike was accompanied by a flash of crimson and after the second assault, little remained of the green band. Darkhorse moved closer and nudged the door with his muzzle.

It swung open to reveal two anxious women, their backs pressed to the side wall and their gaze riveted to the eternal's huge form.

Valea was the first to move. She ran to her parents, hugging them both.

Yssa paused at the doorway. "Thank you, Darkhorse."

"Yes, thank you," added Valea, coming over to hug him around the neck. "I didn't mean to pass you by."

"That is all right."

"We were sealed in," Yssa began. "We saw . . . we saw a distorted vision of Darkhorse . . ." She described what had happened.

"Yureel, yes . . ." Darkhorse snorted. "He is still near, too, I am certain of it!"

Cabe Bedlam's fists clenched. "He has Aurim. He has to have him. Valea, Gwen. Give me your hands."

Separating from the others, the Bedlams joined hands. Gwen and her daughter shut their eyes while Cabe stared toward the ceiling. Energy circulated between the three of them, so much that even the eternal was greatly impressed.

"He's at the western edge of the barrier," the sorcerer announced. "I see only Aurim, but I feel something else nearby. Aurim is trying to open the barrier . . ." Cabe pulled his hands away from his family, breaking the link. "I've strengthened the barrier. They can't possibly exit now."

"Do not be so certain of that—" Darkhorse began, but Cabe paid him no mind. The sorcerer vanished, leaving the rest of the party stunned by his sudden action.

"Damn him!" Lady Bedlam gathered her power. "Always willing to sacrifice himself! Stay here, Valea!"

She, too, disappeared. Darkhorse did not wait to see what the two younger women would do. He followed Gwen's lead. They would need his aid against Yureel.

A disturbing sight greeted him. The elder spellcasters faced their son, whose expression was answer enough as to the depths of Yureel's control. Aurim looked ready to attack his parents. Worse, it looked like he might even be willing to *kill* them.

Aurim looked his way. "Darkhorse! You'd better stay back! I don't want to hurt you, but I will if I have to!"

He still sounded so much like the true Aurim that it was even difficult for the shadowy stallion to believe otherwise. Only the fact that he could detect Yureel's foul presence in the area kept Darkhorse from wondering.

Trotting forward despite the warning, Darkhorse looked not at the young sorcerer but the slight shadow he could barely detect above the human. "Ever playing with puppets, Yureel! Are you so fearful, so untrusting of your power that you cannot face your foes directly? Are you so great a coward, brother?"

Cabe Bedlam stepped toward the shadow steed. "Darkhorse! What're you doing?"

He knew that the human feared for his ensorcelled son, but Darkhorse believed that what he was doing was their only hope. If he could goad Yureel into forming, then they had a better chance of defeating their foe.

The now-familiar giggle floated toward them. Over Aurim, darkness coalesced into the tiny ebony form that had taunted Darkhorse in Zuu. Ice-blue eyes identical to his own stared down in mockery at the eternal and his allies. Darkhorse heard more than one gasp from the spellcasters. It was one thing to be told that there was indeed another creature like Darkhorse, but another to actually be confronted by him.

"The tale spins itself rather well," remarked the foot-high puppet, "and the actors play their roles to the hilt! Oh, I am indeed appreciative of your efforts, my brother, my self! You have added elements without which surely my epic would have seemed hollow!" Yureel giggled again.

"Epics, stories, tales . . ." Darkhorse chuckled, mocking Yureel's mockery. "Never a truly original thought in your mind, though! You cannot even fight your own battles; you must use deceit! Well here is your opportunity to create an epic of your own, *brother*." The stallion reared. "You and I have something to finish! Come to me! Let us at last end what should have ended long ago in the Void!"

The shadow puppet started to float forward, but halted before moving more than a couple feet from Aurim. "It was a brilliant notion to make you the mortal's steed, Darkhorse! He already desired you for that purpose! The thought of such humiliation and regret was delicious! A mortal would have commanded you and under his control, you would have destroyed these insignificant specks you claim to care for and wreaked havoc upon your beloved world!"

"Yet another of your plots that shall never come to fruition, Yureel! Yet another failure!"

"A failure? Oh, no! Hardly a failure! Short but so very enjoyable! Besides, I have many, many other chapters to add to my epic! If not as Lanith's ignoble steed, then I shall find another place for you, my brother, my self!" He giggled again. "Your friends, however, will have to live with minor roles . . . while they live. Are they the patient kind, Darkhorse?"

"What does he mean?" whispered Valea.

Yureel bowed. "We must depart."

"You shall not!" Darkhorse unleashed his power, aiming not at the torso of the small, shadowy figure, but rather between the pupilless eyes. Unfortunately, a gleaming, transparent shield rose up between the eternal's attack and his adversary. The spell dissipated as it struck.

Aurim smiled. Had Yureel formed himself a mouth, the smile he would have worn would have been identical. The younger Bedlam was proving all too well just how proficient he now was in the use of his abilities.

"It might have been extremely interesting to see what he could do against all of you," Yureel commented blithely, "but I have far, far more interesting games to play and, thanks to you, Darkhorse, the one point of concern has now been dealt with!"

They waited for Yureel to say more, but the puppet suddenly vanished . . . no, vanished was not quite right, because Darkhorse, at least, could still slightly sense his presence. Yureel was a master at hiding himself.

Aurim turned from them, moving as if he no longer even knew that they were there. There was no time for the others to react. The golden-haired sorcerer crossed through the invisible barrier surrounding the Manor grounds.

"That's impossible!" Cabe cried, looking at his wife. "Even Aurim shouldn't have been able to cross without my permission!"

Darkhorse was not so concerned about what Aurim should or should not have been able to do as he was about what Yureel had done at the same time. The shadow puppet had drifted through the shield in perfect unison with the human. Worse, Darkhorse sensed a subtle shift in the barrier spell. A sudden thought filled him with dread.

"Cabe! You must cancel the spell that protects your domain! Do it immediately!"

It was a sign of the master sorcerer's faith in his friend that Cabe Bedlam obeyed immediately. Darkhorse, however, did not wait to see the results of his companion's work, but rather leaped toward the barrier. It was a risky chance he took, considering the many things Yureel might have done to the protective spell, but the shadow steed knew that he had the most hope of catching the escaping pair.

The speed at which he reached the barrier was enough that if he was wrong, the backlash would possibly do him great damage. Darkhorse did not care. He was his friends' only hope to rescue the lad.

To his surprise, whatever Yureel had done did *not* affect the shadow steed. Darkhorse flew through the spell, only slightly slowed by it. He landed on the grass beyond and looked around. Aurim could no longer be seen, but his magical trace was still evident. The shadow puppet had not bothered to hide the trail, which was disturbing. However, Darkhorse had no intention of stopping the chase simply because of the possibility of a trap. He dared not.

"Darkhorse! Wait!"

Yssa had materialized before him. The eternal came within a hair's breadth of overrunning the enchantress, but turned at the last moment. Despite the danger of losing track of Aurim, Darkhorse paused to glare at the woman. "Do you realize just how close you came to possible disaster, mortal? Do you realize that a collision between us would have been more than simply two bodies striking one another? I am *exactly* like Yureel! A simple touch could have meant your death if I had been caught off-guard!"

"It was the only way to get you to stop!" she countered. "I couldn't let you go running off and getting recaptured, especially with the others being prisoners!"

"The others—?" Darkhorse blinked. "You stand before me as free as a bird!" He twisted his head around in the direction of the Manor. "I would assume that the others were—"

His voice died abruptly. A massive silver dome covered the Manor grounds for as far as he could see. Judging by the way it extended beyond the trees, it covered not only the Manor and the garden area, but also the homes of the many humans and drakes who lived under the protection of the Bedlams. Yureel had turned the barrier spell into a glittering, reflective prison. Darkhorse could not see Cabe and his family even though they surely had to be where he had just left them.

"I followed after you," the enchantress explained. "I didn't even think about what you'd said to Cabe Bedlam about trying to cancel the barrier spell until I reached it." She shivered. "It felt like forcing my way through hardening clay even *with* the aid of my powers. There was even a moment when I thought that I might become trapped halfway through."

"What about the others?"

"I don't know. I just know that when I turned around, no

one had followed and *this* was in place. I think it's the barrier spell . . . but different."

"It is!" Despite the need to track Aurim, Darkhorse trotted back to the opaque shield. Even up close, he could not sense the spellcasters within. A mental probe proved futile; the barrier was impervious to his sorcery. Out of mounting frustration, the shadow steed rose up and struck it with his hooves. Bright sparks flew, but otherwise the silver shell was unaffected.

Yssa put a hand on the shield. "I can't sense anything. It deflects every attempt I make to contact them."

"Aurim had a hand in the making of this, albeit an unwilling one. The lad is possibly the most powerful spellcaster I have come across since . . . since perhaps even the warlock Shade! When he and Yureel departed, I feared that this might be what my foul brother intended."

"Is there nothing we can do for them?" The enchantress was pale, in part because she was still recovering from her effort, but also because she, like the eternal, knew what it meant if the Bedlams remained imprisoned. Cabe and his family represented the greatest threat to Yureel's plots. Even against Aurim, the Order, and Lanith's legions, the Bedlams were powerful enough to counter the shadow puppet's dreams of mayhem. Yureel had his limits; he could not control all of his foes. Probably he had not dared an attempt on their lives for fear that it would be enough to destroy his hold over Aurim. At least, Darkhorse hoped that was the reason. Whatever the reason, sealing the others inside this prison had been Yureel's best opportunity to be rid of them without endangering himself.

Once more I have been too slow to realize! Once more he has made me a fool! To Yssa, he said, "There is nothing I can do. Aurim is the one best suited to return the spell to its original form."

"But he's—" Yssa hesitated, frowning. "I'm . . . I think I'm hearing something . . . it's *Cabe Bedlam*."

"I hear nothing!"

She quickly quieted him. "I hear him, but he's very faint! I think—" Her voice suddenly shifted, growing deeper, masculine. It was, in fact, Cabe Bedlam's voice. ". . . *do any-thing now. Tell Darkhorse that he needs to alert the Gryphon! He's our best hope now. We're all right here and the air seems unimpeded. I'm pretty certain that given time and the resources of the Manor library, we'll be able to es-cape. If the Gryphon can organize some alliance between drakes and humans in the east, they can keep Lanith and Yureel from pushing forward!*" Yssa paused, then in Cabe's voice, added, "*Don't go after them, Darkhorse! Please! Contact the Gryphon . . . Kyl . . . and the Green Dragon! Don't go charging off!*"

"Cabe! Can *you* hear me? I—"

The enchantress let out a gasp. "He broke the connection! Thank Rheena! I don't think I could've kept that up much longer!"

Darkhorse was hardly so relieved. He turned to the opaque wall. "Cabe!"

"He can't hear you. It took a lot to get through. I don't think it would've even worked . . . except that I'm more receptive than many spellcasters."

"So it would appear!" The ebony stallion kicked at the earth. "There is still hope of catching up to Aurim before Yureel can get him back to Lanith's armies. The spellwork will have weakened him enough to force him to travel by short leaps, not one long, direct jump! I cannot pass that chance up! The boy is our best bet to quickly freeing his fam-ily, not to mention severely weakening the horse king's Mag-ical Order!"

"But what your friend said is true; we really need to speak to the Gryphon! I've heard much about him, Darkhorse. That's why I sent the messages to him, so that both he and Cabe Bedlam would be informed about what was going on. If anyone can help us, it's the Gryphon." Yssa bit her lip. "Cabe Bedlam mentioned my father. I should've returned to him by now. Maybe I can convince *him* to talk to the king of Pena-cles."

As much as it pained him, Darkhorse finally gave in to Cabe's suggestions. Chasing after Aurim and Yureel *was* in-deed folly, no matter how much the shadow steed wanted to rescue the young sorcerer. Darkhorse still felt guilty about Aurim's kidnapping; he should have kept a more careful eye on the lad.

The Gryphon. He was the best chance. With the magical libraries his to use, the lord of Penacles might be able to solve the problem of the altered barrier spell in short order. Cabe might have confidence in his eventual success, but Darkhorse had his doubts that such success would come soon enough. Yureel would have Lanith moving swiftly now that the Bedlams were not a concern, and it would take some doing to get Black and Storm to agree to aid their rival Dragon King. Blue might be willing, but his might was concentrated on the eastern coast of the continent, which meant that by the time his forces reached Dagora, the armies of Zuu might have already overrun it.

"Very well!" The eternal tried to sound as confident as possible. He was all too aware of his missteps. "A suggestion, though. I would rather *you* speak with the Gryphon while I confront your sire. You have much knowledge concerning Zuu and its situation that would be valuable to him. You would also be more likely to convince him of working not only with your sire, but also the other drakes."

His companion did not sound at all convinced. "And what will you talk about with my father?"

"Matters which are too lengthy to discuss now. Cabe has done right to set our course." Darkhorse subtly summoned power. He had to do this carefully and quickly before Yssa could react. "If there is anyone who can help me deal with Yureel, it is one who has made a study of the techniques of sorcery utilized by past races. I have some questions to which he might have answers."

It was clear that she still was not convinced about his choices. "I think it would be better—"

Now. The eternal's eyes narrowed ever so slightly.

The protesting enchantress vanished in midsentence.

The Gryphon would understand her sudden appearance. It was not the first time guests had literally dropped in at the palace. Besides, Darkhorse had also taken the precaution of sending a magical missive to the inhuman king.

Now that Yssa was on her way, Darkhorse turned toward the west. Although he had spoken with the Green Dragon but recently, the shadow steed was not at all certain what greeting he would receive. Helping the drake lord's daughter trick her father was reason enough for the Green Dragon to shun him. With the war raging to the west, it was possible that Darkhorse would not even be able to get within more than a few miles of the drake's sanctum.

But I will because I have to! Readying himself, the eternal concentrated on the region of the Dagora Forest where he knew one of the entrances to the Green Dragon's caverns was hidden.

To his amazement, Darkhorse was not hindered by any defensive spell. With the forces of Zuu already so near, he would have expected the drake to have installed stronger measures to protect his domain. Was the situation already that desperate? Did Yureel and his puppet king already have the master of the Dagora Forest trapped against a wall?

Carefully, he trotted in the direction of the entrance. Hidden by both camouflage and sorcery, it was impossible for any except the most accomplished spellcasters to locate. Darkhorse, though, had made use of it once or twice in the past. He and the Dragon King might not get along that well, but circumstances occasionally demanded they meet. It would have been simpler to materialize in the caverns, but that method was surely now not open to him.

When Darkhorse did locate the entrance, he was somewhat disturbed. It was still hidden by camouflage, but there was no trace of any spell protecting it. Darkhorse paused before entering. The drake lord had never been a careless sort. This should not have happened.

Even knowing that something was definitely wrong, he finally entered. The cavern entrance was large enough to admit him; not surprising since it had originally been created with dragons in mind. Darkhorse picked up his pace as he descended, his eyes adjusting to the increasing darkness at the same time. Some natural illumination kept the tunnel from growing completely dark, but any human would have been hard-pressed to see more than a few yards at a time. The eternal could see ten times that distance.

No one barred his path, demanding the reason for his coming. Nor did Darkhorse sense any more spells, although in the past the caverns had been riddled with defensive measures. Now he was glad that he had chosen to come here himself instead of allowing Yssa to do as she had planned.

At last he entered the first chamber of the cavern. It was huge, wide, and entirely devoid of any trace of the drake or his clan. Darkhorse turned in a circle, trying to find some sign of life, some clue as to where everyone had gone.

Where are you, drake? Where are your people? The stallion moved in silence as he tried to sense the presence of anyone other than himself. The first chamber appeared to have been systematically emptied of all contents. He had the growing suspicion that it would not be the only chamber he would find so.

The next chamber he reached was as devoid of evidence as the first had been. A pair of vine plants grew together like a wreath over the entrance to the next major chamber, the only things that the Dragon King had been unable to move.

At last he found the throne room. The dais and the chair remained, but their trappings had been stripped away. Darkhorse sent a probe toward the chair and sensed a slight trace of energy, but nothing significant enough to investigate further.

He had seen more than enough to convince him that the caverns of the Green Dragon were utterly empty. The entire clan plus those members of other races who served the drake had abandoned the ancient lair.

Why? Why abandon this place? Things could not have grown so dire in so short a time! What has happened here?

No longer worried about disturbing someone, the shadow steed transported himself to some of the deeper chambers. He soon verified that the birthing areas, the clan sleeping chambers, and even the private chambers of the Green Dragon himself had been emptied. That the last rooms had been stripped clean particularly surprised him considering the vastness of the drake's collection of sorcerous antiquities.

The Green Dragon would not abandon his homeland. He would never do that. What does he plan? The abandoned caverns revealed no answers, however, and before long, Darkhorse finally decided that he had had enough of the place. With one last, brief inspection of the drake lord's chambers, the shadow steed summoned power for a return to the surface.

Instead, he found himself in another of the countless chambers that made up the huge underground labyrinth. Darkhorse glanced around, not recognizing the place. It was not among those he had inspected earlier.

"Now what?" he muttered. His concentration had not been at its best. Yureel could twist his thoughts around so easily it was a wonder that Darkhorse had not ended up transporting himself to the icy Northern Wastes.

Once more the eternal summoned his strength, this time his mind focused on his destination.

The new chamber in which he found himself was virtually identical to the previous. Judging by the odor, riding drakes had clearly made much use of this location. However, the habits of the animalistic lesser drakes did not concern him nearly as much as the fact that twice now he had failed to reach his intended destination. Darkhorse searched the caverns as best he could with probes, seeking some trace of a spell, something that would explain how he could twice err so terribly.

Still nothing. This made no sense, no sense at all. He had to be missing something.

A third attempt landed him in a sulfur-ridden, steamy cave where the temperature was enough to make most nondraconians collapse from heat exhaustion. Another birthing chamber. Other than a few pieces of shell, there was no sign that drakes had ever been here. Someone had very carefully removed every unhatched egg.

Each time he tried to transport himself to the surface, he landed in yet a different part of the cavern complex. Sorcery was at work, that was obvious, but it was of a sort so subtle that even Darkhorse could not readily detect it. *Trust the lord of the Dagora Forest to devise something so devious!*

In order to test the limits of the trap, Darkhorse trotted to

the exit of the birthing chamber. Traveling by spellwork had
failed; perhaps a physical trek was called for. He stepped into
the tunnel beyond, fully expecting to be shifted to another location, but to his surprise, nothing impeded his progress. Perplexed but pleased, the shadow steed trotted swiftly in the
direction that he assumed led to the surface.

Darkhorse moved from passage to passage without any
delay. He was glad that nothing more had happened, but not
at all lulled by the fact. Escape could not be this simple, not
if the Green Dragon had gone through all this trouble. Each
corner he turned, he expected some new trick to be sprung.

It was not until he passed yet another birthing chamber that
he began to see the cunning with which the drake lord had set
his snare. There should have been no birthing chamber this
close to the surface. They were generally buried deep in the
cavern complex where they might best make use of the
world's inner heat. By this time, Darkhorse should have been
near the entrance through which he had entered, a region far
too cool for the sensitive dragon eggs.

Thinking of eggs made him think of Yssa, whose birth
would certainly have been unique among the drakes. From
what the Dragon King and his daughter had told Darkhorse,
Yssa had been born like a human even though part draconian.
He wondered what the event had been like.

He dropped the interesting but useless line of thought and
pondered again his quandary. Spells sent him from chamber
to chamber at random, while journeying physically meant an
endless trek through the same tunnels over and over in some
insidious loop. Either one by itself would have been insidious
enough a trick on invaders, but both guaranteed that even
Lanith's mages would have been left baffled and frustrated . . .
at least for a time.

*A wonderful ploy, Dragon King, but I wish you had con-
sidered the possible arrival of one of your allies!* Had this intricate spellwork already been prepared when last he had been
here? If so, it would have behooved the drake lord to warn
him.

"Very well, then! If I cannot escape like that, perhaps a little random destruction will do the trick!" He did not like the

thought of damaging the caverns of the Green Dragon, but the latter had left him no choice. Darkhorse summoned up as much strength as he could muster. No half measures now, not when so much depended on his escape.

Energy flared from him, crackling blue bolts that darted in every direction. Darkhorse left no part of his immediate surroundings untouched. If there was a point of weakness, he would find it.

The cavern passage was afire, the blue, flickering light blinding. Even Darkhorse had to readjust his vision. He did not lessen his assault, though. There was a way out of this trap, just as there had been a way out of so many others in the past.

Of course, he *had* required the aid of others to escape some of those traps . . .

A sense of displacement made him falter. His surroundings took on a surreal look, the walls shifting and the floor rising and curling. The disorientation grew worse, so much so that Darkhorse had difficulty even retaining his footing. His concentration faltered and with it his attack. The lightning storm dwindled, then faded away completely.

Nothing . . . the shadow steed tried to clear his thoughts in order to begin a second attempt, but the great weight of his failure made it nearly impossible to think of anything constructive.

"You have no idea how clossse you came to destroying my carefully desssigned trap. I am impressed, demon ssssteed."

Still disoriented, Darkhorse sought out the source of the voice. As he did, his surroundings shifted again. Instead of the passage, he now stood in the throne room, but a throne room not stripped of its trappings. More important, the great chair itself was no longer empty.

"My apologiesss for not rescuing you sssooner, demon steed," the Green Dragon remarked offhandedly. Despite the drake lord's seeming indifference, though, Darkhorse sensed a strong level of tension beneath. The effects of the war, no doubt. "My attention wasss focused elsewhere."

A pair of draconian guards flanked the throne and another pair watched from the entrance. All of them were very much on edge. While the eternal did not fear them, he knew that now was not the time to antagonize the warriors. He would have to control his temper, however much he might want to berate the Dragon King for leaving him trapped so long.

"A very cunning spell, Your Majesty! A new piece of work, is it not?"

"Very new. You never actually left thisss chamber; you only thought you did. A hundred sssoldiers could fill the throne room and all of them would fall victim to the same delusion that you did. They would then be sssimple prey for my ssservants, who are protected by talismans also of my creation. Extremely effective, albeit draining to create, I mussst admit. Circumstancesss demanded it, though. The . . . intrusion from the wessst hasss become more of an annoyance than previously expected. Measures were taken should the unthinkable happen."

That was not comforting news. Dragon Kings were not prone to pessimism when it came to battle. Generally they went down fighting, still certain that they could snatch victory from defeat. "That terrible?"

"They have begun burning my foressst again!" The Green Dragon nearly rose, but remembered himself at the last moment. "I have sssquelched a dozen fire wallsss of ever-increasing magnitude and I fear that sssoon I will reach my limits. In the meantime, their warriorsss, whether on foot or mount, advance through what should be an impenetrable shield of thick foliage. You were in that trap longer than you think, Darkhorssse. Sssunrise isss upon us. Within the next few hours, they will meet my firssst line of warriorsss, elves and drakes who shall be outnumbered twenty to one. Each warrior facesss the enemy knowing that all he isss meant to do isss hold them off while I further regroup my other forces and once more futilely requessst aid from my counterparts." The drake unleashed a sharp hiss of contempt. "Counterpartsss . . . only the emperor himself has clearly promised me any aid, but his meager forces will not be here in time to keep the wessstern half of my beloved forest from being rooted up or charred by thossse barbarians! Brother Blue hasss stated in principle that he will help, but much of his power is maritime, which does me little good."

The drake did not mention either Storm or Black, but Darkhorse was fully aware how little help either of them would be. In their minds, it would be better to weaken Green *and* the invaders. Only then might those two move. "What of the confederation formed by Sssaleese? Is there no aid there?"

"Sssaleese's confederation ssseems to be more interested in the lands just wessst of Gordag-Ai, landsss once belonging to Bronze. If I were a paranoid being, demon ssssteed, I would almossst wonder if thisss fledgling confederation hasss joined the invaders."

As if we do not have enough to concern us . . . Darkhorse remained silent on the subject. Sssaleese was a problem for another day. "If I may, Your Majesty, I know that events are at present demanding your attention, but I must tell you of terrible news."

A look of resignation on his face, the drake indicated that he should proceed. The shadow steed did, throwing himself into the events that had taken place since last the pair had met. He glossed over his enslavement in Zuu, especially the enchanted saddle and bridle, then focused on the details of Yureel's invasion of the Bedlams' domain. The Dragon King's expression became more and more unreadable as the eternal progressed, even when Darkhorse revealed what he knew of Yureel. The shadow steed saw no reason to keep hidden the truth about his adversary from the Green Dragon, who had ever been an ally of his friends. However, he was admittedly startled by the lack of emotion; it was almost as if the drake was not so surprised by Yureel's origins.

"A dreadful tale, demon ssssteed, and very informative. You were right to sssend my daughter to speak to the lionbird. I would prefer her far from here at the moment and she can certainly deal with the lord of Penacles." The Dragon King steepled his fingers, red eyes narrowing in thought. "You give me sssome possible options, now that I know that the real threat lies not ssso much with the horse king and his insipid Magical Order, but with sssome creature from beyond the

Dragonrealm! Yesss, I may have waysss of dealing with this
monstrosity . . ."

"Oh?" This interested Darkhorse greatly. "And what manner of artifact or spell would that be?"

The Dragon King grew evasive. "Possibilitiesss, nothing
more. There may not even be time to investigate them—"

The drake lord suddenly threw back his head and hissed.
The guards nearest him dropped their weapons and went to
his side, but he waved them off. Darkhorse's host was clearly
in pain, but was not about to give in to it.

"Your Majesty," the shadow steed called. "What is it?"

"Can you not feel it, demon ssssteed? They've moved
fassster than I thought they would! They're tearing my foressst
apart again! My firssst warriorsss already prepare to meet
them, but it will not be enough! They are hurting her, ssscar-
ring her . . . my foressst!"

One of the guards tried again to help. "My lord! You mussst
ressst! You have not ssslept sssince—"

"Away!" The lord of the Dagora Forest rose, his gaze burning. "Darkhorsssse! Attend me!"

Before the eternal could reply, the Dragon King transported
them to his personal chambers. They now stood in one of the
rooms that the drake utilized for his researches. Shelves and
shelves surrounded them. The Green Dragon's collection of
sorcerous artifacts was unparalleled in the realm as far as
Darkhorse knew. It seemed that each time the shadow steed
saw it, the collection had changed greatly, as if his host continued to add so many finds that he constantly had to move the
older ones elsewhere.

The Dragon King marched directly to a triangular, crystal
array fixed on a stand set in the center of the chamber. The
tiny emerald crystals, all identical, glittered even in the semi-
darkness of the chamber. He waved a hand over the center.
"Show me!"

The array pulsated twice, then an image formed about a
foot above it. Darkhorse was impressed by the clarity of the
vision; this latest device of the Green Dragon's, whether new
or some recent artifact uncovered, far outdid the previous
viewing devices the eternal had seen his host utilize.

Regrettably, the scene it revealed was one that made the shadow steed's fascination with the construct irrelevant. Once more magical flames overran the mighty trees but this time the flames were a brilliant golden hue. They danced around the wooded region as if almost alive. In fact—Darkhorse peered closely—some of the smaller blazes *did* move as if they knew what they were about.

Even from here, he could sense Aurim's part in the spell. Yureel had set his prize puppet to work the moment they had returned to Lanith's encampment.

"They know my warriorsss await them! That ssserpent Lanith boasts of hisss hordes, but can only fight them with sorcery! He callsss himsssself a warrior king? He isss a ssspoiled child with assspirations of greatness!"

As he spoke, however, the flames flickered out of existence, one merry blaze doing so just as it leaped for yet another defenseless tree. The Dragon King let out a weary gasp, as if the forest's reprieve physically affected him as well. He was not relieved, though.

"They come," he announced to the eternal. "Now that the morale of my warriorsss hasss been tested by their sssorcery, he sends hisss armiesss . . ."

The vision shifted, filling with row after row of armored, yellow-haired riders, each well armed. True to their tradition, the Zuu horde consisted of both men and women and many of the more capable ones that Darkhorse noted were of the latter sex. The look in the eyes of each told Darkhorse how terrible the odds were that the invaders might be turned early. The horse king, or possibly his hidden ally, had stirred them up, made them see themselves as their nomadic ancestors, whose fury even the Dragon Kings had long respected.

"They are about to meet." Without warning, the Green Dragon waved his hand over the array, eradicating the image just as the forces of Zuu reached the untouched forest.

"Why did you do that? Do you not want to see?"

"I know what will happen, jussst asss my commanders there do, too. Nevertheless, they will fight asss well as they can. The horse king will find out what it isss truly like to fight dragonsss. I have also already ssset other ssspells in motion."

The drake lord hung his head, looking exhausted. "There isss nothing more I can do and yet I ssstill feel as if I have done nothing adequate. Thanksss to this creature you mentioned, this Yureel, and his puppet sssorcerers, I am at a great disadvantage." He looked up again, eyes brighter, a thoughtful expression crossing the flat, reptilian visage half-hidden under the helm. "Perhapsss, though, perhaps, now that I have your information, I have another option. Yes, a way of dealing Lanith a crippling blow by removing the threat of this creature and dessstroying hisss cursed Magical Order all in one blow . . ."

The last words startled Darkhorse. Any aid against Yureel was welcome, but not if it meant endangering Cabe's son at the same time. He took a step toward his host, assuring that he now had the Dragon King's attention. "You cannot touch the Order until I free Aurim!"

"I will do what I mussst do, demon steed, to preserve my kingdom and my own! Lanith mussst be stopped, and the bessst way to slow him isss to deal with the true power behind him. I regret any danger that might confront Cabe and Gwendolyn's ssson, but I am facing desssperate times here!" The drake took up a defiant stance before him. "If Aurim Bedlam must die to sssave so many more, then ssso be it. I will regret hisss death, but I will not regret causssing it, not when the other choice isss worse . . ."

The Dragon King turned away, his interest now focused on a shelf containing part of his collection. Darkhorse stared at the drake's back, but was so stunned by his host's decision that he could not yet bring himself to reply to the other's cold words. The Green Dragon intended to protect his kingdom at the cost of those dearest to the eternal and Darkhorse could think of no good reason why he should prevent that from happening. The Dragon King was correct; to leave Yureel and the Order untouched was to condemn many others to their deaths. Darkhorse's monstrous twin would not cease his horrendous crusade until someone forced him to cease.

To save a continent, Cabe's son might have to die . . .

CHAPTER XV

"What're you do—?" was all that Yssa managed to blurt before her surroundings became the interior of the palace of Penacles. She clamped her mouth shut instantly, not wanting to accidentally bring every guard in the building to her.

Too late. Darkhorse had dropped her in the midst of the throne room itself and although the Gryphon was not there, sentries stood watch over the room. Four of them charged toward her, their swords ready. Yssa prepared herself, knowing that she might have to injure them.

"Stop!"

The single word acted like a thunderbolt, causing the guards to freeze where they were and the enchantress to leap in surprise. Only a few steps behind her stood the lionbird himself. Clad in the robes of state and standing much, much taller than she, the Gryphon was a sight that Yssa, who had lived among drakes, still found daunting. He was a creature of magical origin, it was said, the only one of his kind. Standing so near to him and sensing his great power, she could believe the tales.

"You are Yssa. I received notice of your coming just before you arrived." To the soldiers, he said, "This woman's no threat. Your speed is commended, but you may all return to your positions now. As for you, young woman, you will come with me."

While the guards returned to their posts, the Gryphon led

Yssa out of the throne room and down the hall. After a short walk they came to a chamber that appeared to her to have been unused for quite some time. The lionbird ushered her inside.

"This palace is far too large for my needs, even with a family. However, this was the domain of the Dragon King Purple before me and he and his predecessors for some reason chose to build this structure over the site of their former caverns. They also had a preference for large chambers, of course. You've no idea how deep down this edifice goes and so much of it is wasted space." The Gryphon chuckled. "A strange lot, the drake clan Purple."

The chamber was nearly empty, which made it look even more immense. There were chairs and tables to one side, as if on a rare occasion the room was used for gatherings, but the last such gathering had evidently taken place some time past.

"I was here already, looking out the window, when I heard Darkhorse's summons. I come here to think sometimes, especially during a rising crisis such as that which plagues my neighbor to the west. No one will disturb us here and I'll be better able to concentrate." He grunted, a somewhat feline sound. "Toos used this for various occasions, especially when he was regent during my absence. At one time, it was where he entertained his military officers—" The Gryphon cut off. "Forgive me. My mind wanders sometimes. Old wars, old friends . . . the past."

From her father and the Bedlams Yssa knew that the Gryphon was more than two hundred years old, possibly even older. It was not just because he was a spellcaster, but because of his peculiar origins. The Green Dragon had not known the truth about those origins, though, and the Bedlams had not enlightened her either. She wanted to ask him about himself, but decided it was best to wait until a better time. Darkhorse had, after all, sent her with a task in mind.

"Did he tell you why I came, Your Majesty?" The Gryphon had such a regal aura around him that she wanted to curtsy.

"Only that it was urgent . . . which was why you were able to arrive in the palace in the first place. Did you think it was this simple to enter my home?"

She had not thought about that. A good thing that her host respected the word of Darkhorse. The king of Penacles had a reputation for taking the warrior's outlook on things and that probably included unexpected visitors trying to magically pop in. "It *is* urgent, Your Majesty! Very, very urgent! The Bedlams and their people are prisoners!"

"Explain slowly and precisely," he commanded in a tone that indicated he would brook no other manner of explanation.

She did, careful not to diverge at all lest the Gryphon's gaze turn baleful. His beak was far too sharp and his hands far too strong for her not to think of his predatory nature. The monarch was neither cruel nor capricious, but Yssa could not help being a bit fearful.

By the time the Gryphon had heard all, the mixture of fur and feather lining his neck stood fully ruffled. "Bad news. Worse than I feared. So this thing is not only like Darkhorse, but has visited the Dragonrealm before? That would explain some of the tales I've heard from time past."

"If he was here before, then someone succeeded in exiling him," the enchantress reminded her host. "He wouldn't have left on his own."

"No, he wouldn't have." The Gryphon stroked the underside of his beak with the back of his hand. "Hmm . . . it appears that I must consult the libraries anew. Days wasted on research that now holds no significance . . ."

"But what about the Bedlams? Can you help them?"

He looked at her as if she had just asked him if he slept on a perch in a cage. Yssa, entirely unnerved by his fierce gaze, nearly fell back over a chair. "Of course I'll do what I can, human! Do you think I'd leave my friends trapped like that? The Bedlams are one of the few chances we've got of stopping this carnage before it spreads too far! Think, woman!"

At first Yssa resented his attitude toward her, but as she studied his movements, she saw that the Gryphon was extremely upset. The spellcasters were obviously very dear friends of the monarch. *Good! He'll do what he can for them, then!* She had been afraid that he might relegate the family's predicament to a lesser priority.

"I'll go now. I think I know what to ask for, but it may still take days to decipher the blasted answer." He ignored her look of puzzlement, adding, "My mate'll see to it that your needs are met while you wait for me to return—"

The anxiety-ridden enchantress could not believe what she had just heard. *"Wait?* Are you suggesting I simply wait? Do nothing? I can help you search for an answer!"

The lionbird shook his head vehemently. "It would take me many hours just to explain how the Libraries of Penacles work. Even I don't fully understand them, human, and I've had years and years to study them. Even the Dragon Kings who ruled this city never completely uncovered the secrets of the books . . . a fortunate thing that. If this is to be done as swiftly as possible, it must be done by me alone, I'm afraid."

"But—" Yssa gave up. If she was any judge of character, the king of Penacles was not the type to change his mind. It did not sound like the first time he had made this decision. "All right. I won't argue with you about the books. I want the Bedlams freed as soon as possible. My—the Green Dragon desperately needs help and they seem to be the only ones willing to give it."

"I won't go into that with you, spellcaster, because while I know that it's not *completely* true, it mostly is. Some help has been sent and more is on its way. I know it's insufficient, but that's all that can be done at this point." The Gryphon led her back toward the hall. "Troia will see to your needs. After your adventures, you have to be exhausted."

She was, but Yssa hardly thought it was the time to relax. She wanted to help, if not with the Gryphon's work then with something else. Letting others take chances was not the enchantress's way. Her father called her reckless, but Yssa simply thought of herself as determined and capable.

What was there left for her to do, though? Darkhorse had already visited with her father and since she knew how much he respected the shadow steed's might, it was likely that the two were already working on some sort of plan of action.

All this planning and running around and yet there still seems to be nothing for me to do! People keep sending me away from where I'm really needed! If she could not help the

Gryphon or the Bedlams, then she would return to where she would be of some use. She would return to her father. He would certainly be in need of her aid.

"Thank you, Your Majesty, but I've got somewhere else I have to be." Before the Gryphon could contradict her, Yssa summoned power and vanished from the palace.

She rematerialized by the side of the Serkadian River, far from her intended destination. The events at the Manor had sapped her strength more than Yssa had imagined. Despite the very early morning sun, the enchantress felt as if it were still the dead of night. She had rested at the home of the Bedlams, but that had not been enough.

Pausing only long enough to catch her breath, Yssa attempted another leap. She was certain that the Gryphon would be behind her at any moment. At the very least, he would not be pleased with her destination. The Dagora Forest was no place for anyone now.

No one except her.

Her second leap took her to a place where she could glimpse the ruins of the kingdom of Mito Pica. Ravaged more than two decades ago by the forces of the previous Dragon Emperor, it was a ghost that refused to be forgotten. Yssa had leaped to its vicinity only because she knew that the Gryphon would not think to immediately look here. His hesitation was all she needed. One more leap and she would be too far away for him to follow after. The king had far more pressing matters than hunting a recalcitrant young woman down simply so that he could turn her over to the safekeeping of his queen.

Her next jump took her near the Manor. As she rested briefly against a tree, the enchantress saw that Yureel's spell still held. The opaque shell still loomed over the Manor grounds. Yssa thought about trying to contact Cabe Bedlam, but realized there was nothing she could do except tell him that she had informed the Gryphon of their plight. The stress of making contact, however, would force her to rest even longer before attempting yet another leap toward her father's domain and she desperately wanted to reach the caverns as soon as possible. More and more Yssa began fearing for her sire. With Yureel to guide him, Lanith had to be making terrible inroads through the forest. Her father needed her help.

After several minutes, the enchantress decided that she was ready for the next jump. Fully rested, Yssa would have been able to make the remainder of the journey on this attempt, but she knew that it would now take her at least one more afterward. At least after this one, she would be well into the familiar forest.

Once again, Yssa summoned power. It was still somewhat of a strain, but not enough to make her think of pausing. Yssa materialized exactly where she intended, a small clearing many miles southeast of her father's caverns. It had been a favorite spot of hers when she had been growing up and one she had now and then returned to even when at odds with him.

Standing in the very center of the clearing, a weary Yssa spread her arms and looked up into the sky. It was very tempting to remain here for a time, absorbing the tranquillity of the place, but she could not. She could only relax long enough to build up her strength. The power might be drawn mostly from the world around her, but her own will and power were required as well. Yssa did not have the capacity that Aurim Bedlam did. He had leaped from one end of the continent to the other . . . such ability was *astonishing*.

Just a few minutes . . . that's all . . . just a few minutes . . .

"Well, it took some time, but I knew eventually you'd return to your special place, darling,"

Yssa whirled, unable to believe she had heard the voice. She had been careless, not thinking that another knew this place.

Exhaustion overwhelmed her. Yssa tried to remain on her feet, but the grass looked so inviting and her head felt so heavy. A part of the enchantress's mind screamed at her to defy the exhaustion, see it for the spell it was, but the rest of her was all too eager to rest. She fell to her knees.

Saress's voice floated above her. "That's right, Yssa, dear. Just relax. About time you got here; I'm supposed to be watching Lanith's kingdom for him, not hunting you down, but he seemed suddenly interested in you. Something to do with the shadow horse, I think."

Fight . . . it . . . Yssa slumped to the ground, barely able to concentrate, much less fight the spell. Had she not been so weary from jumping from location to location, Yssa was certain that she would have sensed the other woman's presence here, no matter how well shielded Saress might have been.

That did not matter now, though. Nothing mattered. Nothing but . . . sleep.

"Rest easy, Yssa. The long chase is finally over, but there's more to come for you. *Much* more."

"I cannot permit you to harm him, Your Majesty! There has to be another way!"

"If one would presssent itself, demon sssteed, then I would welcome it! Failing that, however, I mussst turn to the few options I have. There isss more at stake here. My so-called brethren have left me to my own devices. My young emperor will sssupply me with sssome aid, but it will be too little too late, as is whatever Blue *might* provide me! Now you've alssso come to tell me that the Bedlamsss are prisssoners, which leavesss me no other road upon which to travel—"

"Then help me free the Bedlams! You have all of this accumulated knowledge and power—"

"None of which I can ssspecifically make use of for your dilemma. I do not have the time to research the ssspell that Aurim and the shadow creature used to imprison them. Ssspeak to the Gryphon, if you will. I've heard preciousss little from him, demon sssteed, ssso I daresay he might have the time I do not!" The Green Dragon turned from him. "We have nothing further to discuss."

Darkhorse grew furious. "I will not be so easily dismissed, Your Majesty!"

"I think you will have to be. I have my kingdom to sssave and thisss will require doing sssomething I'd rather you did not sssee."

Darkhorse moved toward him, but before he could reach the Dragon King, the shadow steed suddenly found himself outside the caverns. Angry at the drake's disregard, Darkhorse started for the entrance, then recalled the trap. He did not want to get caught in the drake's web again.

I have to do something, though! The eternal regretted his coming here; the Dragon King's decision had only made the situation more volatile. By revealing the truth about Yureel to the drake, Darkhorse had actually endangered the younger Bedlam's life further. Aurim was possessed. He was not responsible for what he was doing and yet it appeared he would have to pay regardless.

The eternal was still contemplating his next move when he thought he sensed Yssa. It hardly seemed likely considering that she had to be in Penacles, but Darkhorse had already learned the hard way that it was best not to ignore such things. He turned around, trying to locate her. Perhaps Yssa had decided to return to her father the moment she had finished relaying the Bedlams' fates to the Gryphon.

He did not sense the young enchantress, but he did sense something else, something not at all welcome in the forest. They were fairly well veiled from sorcerer's sight, but Darkhorse still succeeded in sensing brief flashes of their presence. Soldiers . . . and not those loyal to the Green Dragon.

Focusing on their locations, Darkhorse transported himself. It was too coincidental that he would sense both Yssa and the enemy in the same area.

He arrived at the edge of a small clearing and had no trouble spotting those he sought. There were three of them, three tall, blond, armored warriors. One had her sword out and her attention on the forest around them while the two males prepared to lift up a still form on the grass. Even with the warriors' bodies blocking much of his view, he could tell that the form was Yssa's.

"What have we here? Trespassing?"

The warriors turned together, the two males pulling free their weapons. They were well trained and would have been a formidable sight to anyone other than him. One of the males joined the female in an advance toward the shadow steed. The third remained with their prey.

"I give you one warning, mortals! I am Darkhorse! Your blades will not do me any harm. You only condemn yourselves if you choose to attack rather than surrender."

They paid him no mind. Either they were fiercely loyal to

the will of Lanith or they were also puppets of Yureel. Whichever was the case, they left Darkhorse no option but to battle them. He could neither allow them to kidnap the woman nor remain unhindered in the Green Dragon's domain. If they had made it this far, it was possible that there were others.

Without warning, the two warriors advancing vanished from both his sight and his magical senses.

"Now this is an interesting trick!" Darkhorse held his ground. "My compliments to the creator of your protective spells! Nonetheless, my demand still stands. Surrender or suffer the consequences!"

He heard the swish of the blade just before it struck him. Despite his bravado, the eternal could not help tensing when the invisible weapon cut into him. Fortunately, while the warriors' defensive spell was an effective ploy, their swords were still very mundane. The blade passed through his chest and out again with barely a ripple to mark its passing.

Laughing, Darkhorse took one long step toward the invisible pair. The shadow steed was not certain of their exact locations, but he was fairly certain that both of them jumped back when he moved forward. The third warrior remained visible, his expression anything but happy. He did not flee, however.

Darkhorse took another step forward. This resulted in another attack from one of the invisible warriors. The sword thrust was aimed for the eternal's throat. Darkhorse felt the blade penetrate, then sink deep. However, this time he did not allow the warrior to free his or her weapon. Instead, the shadow steed pulled the weapon in, trying to move quickly enough that its wielder would have no opportunity to let go. The ploy failed, though, his attacker too frightened to try to hold on. It was probably the only thing that saved the warrior from a terrible fate.

However, the second of the invisible warriors chose that moment to try to leap on the shadow steed. Darkhorse felt the weight of the man—at least he thought it was the man—as the latter landed on his back. Darkhorse snorted. Without the bridle and saddle, he now had full control of his form.

He never saw the hapless warrior, only heard his scream as his seating grew nonexistent and he fell *into* the shadow steed. The scream continued on for several seconds, sounding fainter and fainter, as if the man continued to fall. The one visible soldier paled and started to back away from Yssa. The other, once more visible, quickly joined her companion.

Laughing, Darkhorse trotted toward them. The two moved a few paces behind the still woman, then held their ground. He hardly cared what they did now, his first concern being for the enchantress. If they had severely injured her, then they would have good reason to fear him.

Still she did not move. Darkhorse sought out her mind, but met resistance. He tried to check her condition, but ran against the same wall. Someone had bespelled her; that was the only answer.

The warriors watched but did not interfere as he moved close enough to touch her. With one last condescending glance at the pair, Darkhorse used a hoof to gently nudge Yssa's side.

Yssa shattered, the fragments flying into the shadow steed's face. Each fragment exploded as it struck him, not only disorienting the eternal, but momentarily blinding him. It did no good to back away from the shower; the pieces of the false image followed Darkhorse wherever he went.

"Quickly now!" called a voice he recognized as that of Saress. "Take her before he can recover! The Lords of the Dead take him! He wasn't supposed to be here!"

"Yet here I am, Saress!" Darkhorse roared, shaking his head back and forth in a futile attempt to disperse the determined pieces. "And in another moment you will learn to regret that circumstance has led me here!"

"In another moment, demon, we'll be far from here!"

Even as she finished, Darkhorse sensed her cast a spell. He tried one of his own and managed to slow if not stop the distracting shower. The fragments continued to pelt the eternal, but now at least he could see some of what was happening around him.

What Darkhorse saw was Saress, clad in her twisted version of the traditional garb of a warrior of Zuu, opening a blink hole wide enough for her two remaining underlings and their prize, the true Yssa. The sinister enchantress noticed him focus on her and nearly lost control of her spell. She recalled herself at the last moment and smiled at her adversary.

"Good-bye, demon!" She waited until the others had gone through, then, with a last wave, stepped inside.

A second later another hole opened up only a few feet from where the first had been. From it emerged the warriors, their captive, and Saress, still smiling. Her smile vanished when she saw where the hole had brought her.

"What in the—"

"Welcome back, Saress!" Darkhorse chuckled, dispersing the last of the fragments. "Did you think I would let yet another escape me so? I am not disoriented now, female! Release your captive and I may allow you to live."

Her expression turned to one of dismay. Darkhorse did not add that he had been fortunate to turn her spell around. Had he been forced to try a second time, it would have been just as likely that he would have failed. Luck was at last on his side.

"You think I am to be caught unaware this time, witch? Release Yssa and surrender!"

Saress made the warriors stand aside. Her eyes narrowed as she walked slowly but defiantly toward the eternal. "You think you've won, do you? You think I'm defenssseless, do you?"

The enchantress opened her mouth . . . and *roared*. Suddenly she began to grow, swelling larger than a bull, then larger still. Her skin changed, becoming dusky brown, and her limbs twisted. Wings burst from her back, wings that soon spread the length of the clearing and beyond. The hulking form nearly filled the clearing.

There were few of the drake clan Brown still remaining and at first Darkhorse thought that he was seeing one of them. It slowly registered, however, that had she been a female drake, he would have recognized her as such even in human form. No, Saress was much more. Small wonder that at one time she had reminded him of Yssa. Saress, too, was a half-breed, albeit of a different clan.

The revelation was so unexpected that he was not quite certain what to make of it. Saress used his surprise to her advantage, seizing Yssa from her stunned companions, who fled immediately after. This was not a secret the enchantress would have shared with many, especially her beloved monarch. Lanith tolerated her sorcery because it served his purposes well, but from what Darkhorse knew of him, the king would probably have been less than delighted to discover that he had been bedding a being half draconian. Like most of the horse people, he believed in the purity of the human race. To him, drakes, although they had once been masters of Zuu, were little more than animals.

Wings flapping, the dragon rose into the air. Near the earth, Darkhorse was swifter and stronger, but in the air dragons still held sway. Darkhorse could follow, but so high in the sky catching a dragon was difficult, if not impossible. Despite that, the shadow steed immediately leaped after her, the abandoned warriors no longer a concern. Without Saress, they would soon fall into the hands of the Green Dragon's servants. The only thing that concerned him was rescuing Saress's captive.

Darkhorse raced higher and higher, his hooves already touching the treetops. Unfortunately, Saress was already a distant form ahead of him. Whether her transformation had been planned or an act of desperation, she stood a good chance of escaping him. Even for a dragon, the half-breed sorceress was swift.

He found himself wondering how well the two women knew one another. Perhaps their similar backgrounds had drawn them to one another at one time. While rarely on excellent terms with their counterparts, the Dragon Kings did meet with one another. Perhaps that was when the two half-breeds had first met. Judging by her strength, Saress was very likely one of the Brown Dragon's offspring or at least the offspring of one of the royal line.

This may be why Yssa spent so much time in the Barren Lands! To Saress, the re-formed domain would be death. The grass would take her.

Saress continued to climb higher and higher, which made

Darkhorse's journey more difficult. He had limits as to how high he could fly and those limits were far less than that of a dragon. If she rose much higher, he might lose sight of her.

The speed with which she fled westward continued to impress him. Darkhorse soared over acre after acre of forest and yet gained little ground on his adversary. Saress was a huge but slim beast, perfectly designed to sweep across the heavens. Seldom had he seen a swifter drake.

Then . . . the landscape ahead altered in an alarming manner. Gone in many areas was the proud forest. Broken and burnt, the trees lay scattered in all directions. Smoke still drifted upward. Darkhorse could vaguely make out many tiny forms moving eastward, obviously the horsemen of Zuu and their counterparts on foot. There seemed to be a large area where the movement paused, which the shadow steed suspected had to be where the Green Dragon's warriors had finally met the invaders. The battle line resembled a madly twisted serpent, one that was unfortunately being forced east in most places.

Sorcery was also in use below, although Darkhorse could not say in what manner. Judging by how strong the trace was even at this height, some tremendous spells had been cast in the past few hours. Lanith, or perhaps Yureel, was pushing the Magical Order to its utmost. At this rate, it was very likely some of the weaker sorcerers might perish from exhaustion before the forest realm was taken, but if that meant a swift victory over the Green Dragon, the risk was no doubt worth it to the horse king and his secret ally.

So much devastation, so much chaos just for your personal entertainment, Yureel! Darkhorse turned his eyes from the earth, realizing that the distraction had enabled Saress to increase the distance between them. She seemed to be heading beyond the battlefield, most likely to Zuu. If she thought returning to Lanith's kingdom would save her from him, then she was sorely remiss.

A hole in the sky opened up ahead of the fleeing dragon.

Darkhorse cursed, picking up his pace as best he could. He had not thought that Saress would have had enough strength left to perform this feat of sorcery. If he pushed hard, though, the eternal was certain that he could reach her before she made it through.

A second hole opened directly before him. Darkhorse could neither turn nor stop in time to avoid it.

The other end opened up in a room, although what the eternal saw of it was only a flash of stone and what was possibly fire. He flew across the chamber, no more able to halt himself than he had over the Serkadian, and struck a wall reinforced by strong sorcery. Unable to shatter it or pass through, Darkhorse ricocheted off and rebounded across the chamber, crashing against the opposite side, which proved also to be reinforced. Each collision was also accompanied by a sharp jolt through his body, yet one more treat no doubt prepared for him by Yureel. Again and again, he careened against the walls, too stunned already to halt his mad flight.

By the time Darkhorse struck the floor several seconds later, he barely had the strength to even suffer the agony caused by the final jolt.

Unconsciousness prevailed. Darkhorse vaguely noted a passage of time, but how much was beyond his limited senses. He tried to gather his wits, yet every time something pushed him back toward the darkness.

What stirred him at last was a sound so terrible, the shadow steed wanted to return to his oblivion. It was a giggle. Yureel's giggle.

"A little late and a little sloppy, but all things have worked out for the best, don't you think, my dear boy?"

"Yes, Yureel," responded Aurim from nearby.

Darkhorse slowly recovered. His gaze, when he could at last focus, fixed on the source of the giggle. The shadow steed's malicious counterpart floated about four feet above the floor. Darkhorse tried to leap at him, but something held him fast. He could neither reshape himself nor cast a successful spell. Once again he sensed Aurim Bedlam's work in this.

"I hope you'll forgive the long wait, my brother, my self! It was hard to draw myself away from the delicious tableau I've been so busily concocting. I think dear Lanith can make do for now, though, even without his prize sorcerer or his oh-so-majestic steed. The drake's warriors are admirable fighters, but their defeat is inevitable, isn't it, my brother, my self? Their first lines have already been routed."

The shadow steed was startled. *Routed? How long was I unconscious?*

Yureel must have noticed something, for he added, "Didn't you know? Of course not! How could you, having been trapped here for more than half a day!"

Half a day? It seemed impossible, another of the shadow puppet's grand lies, but . . . Darkhorse believed him this time. Half a day . . . How much destruction and death had occurred? What had happened with the Bedlams? He doubted that they had escaped yet. Yureel would not have been nearly so gleeful if they had.

The tiny figure clapped his hands. "Aaah, there is so much I could tell you about present and future events, Darkhorse, but it would be rather pointless now, wouldn't it? Poor, poor Lanith will be so disappointed, but I think the crushing of his former liege will assuage him! Besides, you made for a most unruly steed, you know!" Yureel giggled. "And a very sloppy one at the moment. You really should learn to hold up better."

Darkhorse glanced quickly around the chamber. The three of them were the only ones in the place.

"This is a private discussion." Yureel's tone was no longer merry and the change chilled Darkhorse. "My grand majesty has his little war to keep him occupied. As for the female creature who has accompanied you of late, she is for the moment enjoying a reunion with the king's Saress. They are two very intriguing beings I have yet to incorporate properly into my wonderful epic, but be sure that I will soon! They both seem fond of the lad here; I think there might be something in that. Poor Saress, though, will be so disappointed when she finds that she can't keep this Yssa. They've played quite the game of cat and mouse for years, I understand."

"Saress does not know of you, does she, Yureel?"

"She will in good time. That time is not yet now. She was useful, however, although I'm sure that she's still wondering what became of you. It was very fortuitous that she chose this time to bring you to me." By his tone, it had been more than fortuitous. The malevolent figurine drifted even nearer.

"You've no idea how I missed you, my brother, my self. It was as if a piece of me had gone away . . . but that is the case, isn't it? Well, I've decided that the time's come for us to be together. No more games, no more epics, just the two of us together."

The two of us together. He could not mean what Darkhorse thought he meant. It had to be the shadow steed's overwrought imagination.

Yureel shifted closer until he was only a foot from his captive. "I should correct myself, of course. The two of us together . . . making only one."

It was true, then. He meant to reabsorb Darkhorse. Yureel intended to swallow him, make everything that the ebony stallion had been his own—and Darkhorse could think of no way to stop him. The old fear reared its horrific head, making it nearly impossible for the shadow steed to think, yet he had to or he would perish. If Yureel absorbed him, there would be nothing left.

"I so look forward to this, Darkhorse! You've lived an epic yourself, a story I could only dream of during my so lonely, so lengthy internment—"

"A sentence of your own making, Yureel! A kind punishment, considering your atrocities!"

"Kind? Kind?" For the first time, the shadow puppet nearly lost complete control. "Better would it have been if they had destroyed me! Do you understand at all my isolation, my loss? I'd intended to let you learn about helplessness a little at the erstwhile hands of Lanith, but the mortal was clumsy. Well, my brother, my self, a lesson lost is one best not remembered at all. I will just have to satisfy myself with living off of your memories." He glanced back at Aurim. "I shall begin. Be ready."

Aurim nodded, his expression blank. "Yes, Yureel."

"You're a grand, good boy." Yureel faced his prisoner again, but now his form shifted, seeming to melt. At the same time he expanded, growing more and more to encompass an area as great as that which Darkhorse filled. With each passing second, the differences between the pair lessened until even Darkhorse would have been hard-pressed to find them.

"Perhaps I'll create another self at some point when I become bored. Perhaps that one will be more *manageable* than you were, Darkhorse."

The shadow steed struggled, but Aurim held him fast. There was no sign of recognition in his steady gaze. Darkhorse could expect no help from that quarter.

The black, floating mass that was Yureel reached out—and touched Darkhorse.

The eternal felt as if needles had pierced every part of him. Darkhorse roared as Yureel began to flow over him, then quivered as his foul twin intruded into his mind. Darkhorse tried to pull away, but could not. Slowly but surely, the monster began to absorb his essence.

No! I am Darkhorse! I am my own creature! I am distinct from Yureel!

We are one that has been separated far too long, brother, returned the intruder. *The separation is now at an end. Struggle if you will, but it will not even delay what is inevitable . . .*

He was right. Darkhorse could see that. Despite his defiance, despite his strong will, he was nothing to Yureel so long as Aurim held him in place.

"Aurim! Hear me! Break his hold! Your will is powerful! He cannot hold you and still do this!"

Aurim did not respond, though, save to stare down at the shadow steed.

Nothing! I am undone!

No, brother, you've been undone all this time! Now at last, the mistake will be corrected . . .

Darkhorse felt his mind drift. Yureel was tearing him apart . . .

We are one. What you are will be mine and with it I will turn the Dragonrealm onto its head and remake this land, this world, into my own dream! What a glorious epic I will create!

I—was all that the shadow steed could think in response. Already he barely remembered himself. His sense of being was slipping away, becoming nothing more than a fragment of his twin's powerful self.

He had lost to Yureel . . . for the final time.

CHAPTER XVI

Aurim did not recall much about his time in the Manor. He remembered a struggle for control in the deep recesses of the Dagora Forest, then, for a long time, nothing. When at last he woke it was to find himself in the midst of an intricate bit of spellwork guided by the monstrous puppet master. Disoriented, he had been unable to prevent the completion of the spell that Yureel had used to trap his family.

Yureel had controlled him completely throughout the process. The creature had first marched him around the Manor's grounds like a toy soldier, then, while Aurim desperately tried to communicate with his parents, the demon had completed the spell turning the protective barrier into a prison wall. Only Darkhorse and the woman who had earlier rescued his father had escaped, although how *she* had managed to get through, he could not say. Darkhorse had been meant to follow in order that Yureel could trap him again. It had made the demon furious when, after escaping the inescapable trap, the woman had distracted his intended prey.

Still enraged, Yureel had returned him to Lanith, who had promptly called for a renewal to the torching of the forest. To Aurim, who knew the ways of the shadow puppet well by this time, it was harder and harder to tell when Lanith was himself or when he acted as spokesman for Yureel. Yureel whispered in the mind of the horse king, suggesting things and sometimes even giving outright commands through the monarch.

Only General Belfour ever questioned the commands, but he usually quieted after one glance from Lanith.

Aurim hated linking to the other sorcerers, especially when it came time to launch another terrifying assault in the name of the king of Zuu. The bond the Magical Order forged was much, much deeper than those he had created with his own family. Each and every one of the other spellcasters' personalities became known to him and with only two or three exceptions, they were not people Aurim would have wanted to meet. Hysith was harmless and two of the others, students kidnapped from Penacles, were victims like the young Bedlam. Another student from Penacles, Willar Avon, had willingly joined in return for the gold Lanith had offered. As for the rest of the Order, they were mostly ruffians who had had the dubious fortune of being born with a better than average tendency for sorcery.

The worst, other than Saress, was Ponteroy. Each time they linked, Aurim sensed the other sorcerer try, ever so subtly, to undermine the connection his successor had created between the band. Ponteroy wanted him to fail just enough that Lanith would rename the northerner second in command. From little snippets of thought Aurim had gained through the connection, he knew that Ponteroy dreamed of seizing control of Zuu, but only if he could get Saress on his side. It was a dream that the gold-haired spellcaster knew would always remain a dream. Saress was Lanith's slave.

Each time before they bonded, the Magical Order formed a geometric pattern with Aurim the center. There were seven of them this time, the others having been forced by exhaustion to abandon the spellwork. The loss was fairly negligible; those with Aurim were the strongest of the group. Losing someone such as Hysith was not a major blow to the Order.

Burn the forest! Force them to fight in a more open area like true warriors! Teach the lizards and elves what humans can do! Lanith's words did not take into account that among the defenders were many humans as well. He did not care; the horse king spoke for the benefit of his warriors, who hung on every damnable sentence.

The drakes had finally tried sending some of their number

in the form of dragons, but they had learned all too quickly the folly of doing that. It seemed that for months one of the details of the Order had been to cast spells on the arrows of the horse king's archers. The first dragons who had flown near enough had perished in a hail of remarkably accurate and deep-penetrating bolts, backed up by sudden lightning storms summoned up with ease by the sorcerers. It had not helped that many drakes had become so accustomed to humanoid form that they were actually clumsier in the ones in which they had been born.

Aurim watched the results of the spellwork. The fires raged strong, destroying all in their paths. Those who simply sought to defend their homes were perishing out there and it was *his* fault. They were dying in most part because of Aurim Bedlam's much vaunted power. All these years he had failed to reach his potential and now, when that potential had at last become realization, his abilities were the plaything of a demon.

Lanith commands that the fires be doused, Aurim Bedlam. It seems he wants to let his little soldiers play now.

The command passed along by Yureel came as both a relief and a new cause of grief. Aurim needed rest, having maintained the fires since being forced to imprison all those in the Manor. Yureel might control his body and be able to make him cast spells for hours at a time, but the weariness was ever Aurim's.

He canceled the fires, but some of the spells he and the others had cast continued to play havoc with the forest and the Green Dragon's defenses. Allowed to sit, Aurim watched with sinking hope as Lanith's forces moved ever forward through the ravaged land. Nothing the drake lord had thrown against them so far had done more than momentarily delay the horde. Lanith had lost some warriors, but not nearly enough to stem the tide.

Father, what do I do? His parents could not help him now. Anything that happened would have to be of his own doing . . . and Aurim could think of nothing he could do. His great attempt to override Yureel's control had not only failed, but had led to greater disaster. *But I can't give up! I can't!*

He was still trying to find some answer when the demon

seized control of his body again. *Come, Aurim, my friend! I've immediate need for you! An opportunity lost has suddenly arisen again!*

The invisible strings once again in place, Aurim rose to his feet against his will and turned to Ponteroy, who was watching the advance with far more satisfaction than he had. "Gather the others," Yureel commanded through him. "There is something that needs to be done."

"The king said we could rest for now," countered Ponteroy, likely more than uncomfortable in his extravagant clothing. "I, for one, follow *his* commands, not yours, boy."

Aurim's hand shot out, seizing the elegant sorcerer's arm near the shoulder. Ponteroy glared, then his face paled in pain as the hand gripping him squeezed tighter and tighter. Aurim felt Yureel pour a touch of sorcery into the grip, preventing Ponteroy from striking back.

"His Majesty'll appreciate what we're about to do, Ponteroy," Yureel added through his unwilling puppet. "Now do what I told you and make it quick!"

The hand released the other sorcerer, who nodded and hurried over to the others. Aurim heard Yureel giggle in his head.

Ponteroy soon returned to him. He was still pale, but bitterness had overcome much of his fear. "They're ready . . . well, five of them and myself. Is that enough?"

"That's enough. Oh, yes, that's enough," Yureel said, forgetting to sound like Aurim. They joined the weary but obviously cowed sorcerers, who had already formed their part of the pattern. Ponteroy took up his position. Aurim stood in the center of the group.

He comes! He comes!

Aurim's head jerked skyward. At first the ensorcelled spellcaster saw nothing, then a shocking sight materialized among the scattered clouds. A dragon. A sleek, swift one racing through the heavens. There was something familiar about it, though, and also something not quite right. It was as if there were two forms up there where only one was and neither of them radiated what passed for the magical signature of a true dragon. In fact, they reminded him more of—

There! There!

His gaze shifted to a tiny speck some distance behind the disconcerting dragon. It was as black as night and even from here he could sense who it was. *Darkhorse!*

Oh, yes, my wondrous sorcerer, it's my brother, my self! Here I thought he'd gone and found some sense, but he's come back to me after all! Now we can proceed as I intended so long ago! Grand, glorious Lanith the Conqueror will just have to make do without his perfect steed. I've other, more important plans for Darkhorse...

Unable to stop himself, Aurim formed the bond between himself and the others. Once more their wills became subordinate to his, which actually meant to Yureel's. Their power joined with his own. Aurim Bedlam felt such strength that he was certain that he could do anything... except escape his own tormentor.

Now, the demon began, *you will do the following...*

The spell trap was very simple, but very well timed. Aurim stared at the swift figure, trying somehow to contact Darkhorse or give him some other warning, but Yureel's control was insurmountable.

When the shadow steed vanished through the hole that the sorcerer had created for the demon, tears of frustration slid down Aurim's face. Darkhorse was as good as trapped. The young spellcaster had been integral in creating the holding cell where the shadow steed now resided and he knew how strong it was. Darkhorse would not soon free himself.

That was it, then. Darkhorse had been captured. There only remained the Gryphon. Yureel had managed to eliminate the other major threats to his insane campaign. Aurim had little faith in the drakes organizing themselves before the forces of Zuu laid waste most of the western half of the continent. Kyl sought for a more unified race, but even those of his kind who believed in the cause could not help bickering with one another.

The new spell left him even more exhausted. In control of his own body, Aurim Bedlam would have collapsed, but Yureel kept him standing long after the others had settled down. Three sorcerers were always on duty, working in conjunction to monitor the spells already unleashed and watching for any new magical attack by the Dragon King. The demon secretly monitored each group through carefully crafted links to one selected member of the trio. Yureel's commands came as whispers in their heads, whispers they did not realize were not thoughts of their own. Aurim had once wondered why Yureel simply did not possess all of them, but eventually realized that even his captor must have limits. Besides, it was clear to him that even the ensorcelled members were not possessed to the degree that he was. Like Lanith, they did not realize they were being influenced. Aurim Bedlam was Yureel's prize and received special attention.

A battle horn sounded, a sign that the horse king's men were beginning a new attack on the Green Dragon's domain. The battle had shifted to the mundane, with humans, drakes, elves, and others cutting one another down for what they believed. Not for the first time, Aurim wanted to throw up. He had never found war very glamorous and what little he had witnessed here from his exalted position had made it look no better.

Now you may get some rest, Aurim, my friend. There are some things to which I must attend before I visit my dear other self.

The young sorcerer barely had time to close his eyes before he blacked out. Yet again he had been reminded of how much Yureel controlled his existence. Aurim floated through a dreamless sleep, vaguely aware of things around him but not quite certain what they were. Only once did anything disturb his slumber, the voice of a young woman who called his name. He was certain that he knew her, but once the voice ceased, Aurim drifted off again, forgetting her.

Wake, Aurim Bedlam!

He nearly jumped to his feet in his attempt to obey. Blinking, Aurim looked around, only to find that he was no longer on the field of battle, but in the room set aside for him back in Zuu. The disorientation was enough to make his head spin and only by clutching it did the sorcerer prevent himself from passing out. Then he slowly realized that *he* had seized hold of his head, not Yureel. Gazing at his hands, Aurim wiggled his fingers. The minor movements thrilled him, so long had it been since this much control had been his. He took a few tentative steps from his bed—and suddenly his body began moving in a different direction.

"Well, that was a little bit of fun," Yureel commented with a giggle, suddenly floating in one corner of the room. His iceblue eyes sparkled merrily. "The time has come."

With no more explanation than that, the sinister shadow puppet whisked him to another chamber, one Aurim recognized as the cell Yureel had forced him to create. On one side of the cell lay Darkhorse, terribly misshapen. Gone were all traces of the equine form of which his friend was so fond. Darkhorse was now a shapeless, still blob that spread across a good quarter of the chamber. A pair of icy blue orbs, identical to Yureel's save that they seemed dull and lifeless, floated in the center of the unsightly mass. Once or twice in the past, Aurim had seen Darkhorse in such a shape and he had been unnerved each time. Now, though, he only felt sympathy for him.

"He really must learn to pull himself together," Yureel said, giggling again.

The laughter seemed to cause the prisoner to stir. The eyes grew more alive.

Their captor noticed this and his next words were louder, more concise, just for Darkhorse's sake. "A little late and a little sloppy, but all things have worked out for the best, don't you think, my dear boy?"

"Yes, Yureel." Although the voice was Aurim's, the response was Yureel's. Once more, all the young sorcerer could do was watch as his every action was dictated by the foul creature.

"I hope you'll forgive the long wait, my brother, my self! It was hard to draw myself away from the delicious tableau I've been so busily concocting. I think dear Lanith can make do for now, though, even without his prize sorcerer or his oh-so-majestic steed. The drake's warriors are admirable fighters, but their defeat is inevitable, isn't it, my brother, my self? Their first lines have already been routed."

Aurim desperately wanted to hear more, but then another

voice in his head caught his attention, the same female voice he had heard earlier during his enforced slumber.

Aurim Bedlam . . . can you hear me? . . . By Rheena, Mistress of the Forest, please say you do!

Someone was in his head, someone who had managed to do what Yureel had told him time and time again was impossible. *Who are you?*

Yssa . . . my name is Yssa . . . thank the Mistress that I finally got through to you! I've . . . trying to reach you ever since . . . sensed your presence! You are . . . you are Aurim Bedlam?

He acknowledged his identity to her, although it should not have been necessary considering their link. Obviously she was nearly as anxious as he was. *You . . . you're the woman who saved my father . . .*

Yes . . . my name is Yssa, but that's not important! I've tried to break through the barrier in your mind since . . . first brought here . . . listen to me . . . she thinks that I'm still under her spell. I've got to make this quick. Can you . . . anything . . . ?

He asked her to repeat her question. Their link seemed to be a tenuous one, which weakened every time Yureel made his body move or speak. The monstrous creature was saying something to Darkhorse, but Aurim paid his words no mind, wanting only to continue his conversation with Yssa. If she could break through, perhaps she could help him to escape Yureel's power.

Can you do anything at all on your own, Aurim?

He told her the sad truth in as few words as he could, finishing with *I only managed to fight him in the forest. His will is overwhelming!*

But you've got such power, such will of your own! I felt it! I've heard about it!

Something in the way she spoke to him briefly encouraged Aurim. How could Yssa believe in him if there was not truth to what she said? In all fairness, a part of the young sorcerer knew that it was also the enchantress's beauty that played games with his hopes. Nonetheless, his hopes rose. *Maybe I could do something . . .*

As if stirred by her continuing presence, Aurim's mind began to race. His father had often told him how it had been during the worst crises that his own mind had worked best. Now the same happened to the younger Bedlam. One thing in particular interested him. How had Yssa managed to breach the sorcerous walls with which their captor had enveloped his mind when no one else had? What made her different?

Whatever the reason, it was possible she offered him options that he had not had before. *Yssa! Can you help me—*

Her answer was immediate and without hope. *No . . . I can't do anything except talk . . . you. Saress doesn't know how skilled I am at . . .*

Her last words faded as Aurim found his attention forced back to Darkhorse's predicament. Yureel had him doing something. He was casting a spell to strengthen the one holding the weakened shadow steed to one place. At the same time, Yureel began to distort and expand, coming more and more to resemble the shapeless mass that was his captive brother. The floating blob immediately moved toward Darkhorse, his intention quite clear. Yureel had spoken many times about what he intended to do with his counterpart once he tired of humiliating him. Now, it was very clear that the horrific shadow man had decided the ordeal of humiliation had come to an end.

Yureel will devour him . . . Aurim knew that what he thought was not quite an accurate description, but it was close enough. Yureel would absorb Darkhorse; there would be nothing left and the monster would be far, far stronger than he had been before. The sorcerer had witnessed the amazing extent of the shadow steed's power in times past; what would Yureel be able to do with so much more strength at his beck and call?

Worse . . . what about *Darkhorse*? Such a fate went beyond horror as Aurim knew it.

What is it? What . . . happening, Aurim?

He had forgotten about Yssa. *Yureel! He plans to make Darkhorse part of him!*

The enchantress's dismay more than matched his own, but she was less inclined to simply wait for the inevitable. *You've got to save . . . Aurim! You're his only hope! You . . . the power! Use it before . . . too late!*

I can't defeat Yureel on my own. Can't you help me?

Her presence faded more. *No . . . nothing I can do. I'd hoped if I could break through . . . you . . .*

Darkhorse roared in pain and agony, a sound that nearly deafened Aurim. Already Yureel floated partially atop his captive. The process of assimilation, as the monster had sometimes called it, would soon be complete.

Aurim! I had a chance to . . . you at the Manor! Your father said that you . . . power . . .

Yssa's words no longer made much sense. She had obviously used most of her remaining strength to contact him and all she had accomplished was to discover how helpless *he* was.

To his surprise, Darkhorse suddenly called out, "Aurim! Hear me! Break his hold! Your will is powerful! He cannot hold you and still do this!"

I can't! he tried to reply. But Yureel allowed him only to watch and keep Darkhorse still.

Aurim . . . Yssa insisted, her presence momentarily stronger. With a little more concentration, he even managed to summon a vision of her. The enchantress was chained to a wall, her bonds radiating an emerald aura. Even at this dire moment, she looked beautiful.

Aurim, if there is any hope, you've got to push your will to its fullest now!

He had been saying he *couldn't* for so long, it was hard for Aurim to think otherwise, but if he did not try once again, Darkhorse would be no more.

What can I do? Fighting Yureel would be a fruitless task. There remained only one possible plan. It would enable him to avoid battling the demon directly. He had to try to send the shadow steed far, far away where Darkhorse would have the time he needed to recuperate.

Away . . . Aurim concentrated his efforts through the very spell the puppet master had forced him to maintain all this time, the one that kept Darkhorse still while Yureel devoured him. This was his link to his friend, an opening that might be turned to his favor *if* he had the will and power to do it.

Away . . . He did not know where to send Darkhorse. As far away as possible, he supposed. As far away as Aurim's will would permit.

Away . . .

Darkhorse roared—

"What is this, what is this, what is this?" Yureel cried, still formless but quivering in astonishment and swiftly rising fury. "Where is he? Where is he?"

Aurim! I felt . . . such power! . . . what did you do?

He ignored Yssa's frantic question, his efforts concentrated on doing what he could to free himself. It would not take the demon long to realize just who had been responsible for snatching his prey from his grasp. Aurim did not want to be here when that happened.

Too late. *"You!* It *had* to be you!" The massive blob turned on him. "It can't be but it has to be! What did you do, human, what did you do?"

"I sent him far away," Aurim responded against his will. He had forgotten that Yureel could simply demand answers from him. "I sent him far away."

"Where?"

"I don't know." It was true. Aurim had not consciously chosen a destination.

The blob shifted nearer, Yureel's disturbing gaze never leaving him. "You don't know *where,* my little sorcerer? You don't know where you put him?"

"I only wanted to send Darkhorse away so that you couldn't hurt him." The captive spellcaster tried to keep himself from saying anything more, but his will was not strong enough. "I don't know where."

"I heard you!" Still shapeless, the demon expanded farther, filling more than half the chamber. He floated closer, a hungry look in the inhuman eyes.

He's going to take me now! He's going to take me!

"Aurim, darling, I thought I felt—"

Saress had materialized, seduction clearly evident in her eyes. However, one look at the monstrous form hovering before them and the enchantress shrieked. Aurim could not really blame her; he wanted to scream, too. Yureel was only inches from him . . .

The demon suddenly withdrew, his form contracting and reshaping. Saress stopped shrieking and started to cast a spell, a dangerous thing for all of them considering not only how panicked she was but also how tight their quarters were.

"Grand and glorious Lanith," Yureel suddenly called. "I've need of you, O conqueror of the realm . . ."

"—Lipazar's Blade! You—" The horse king stiffened, then quickly studied those around him, finishing with the demon. Yureel had returned to his previous form and now he darted behind the monarch, as if frightened of what the sorceress could do to him. Aurim wanted to scowl; the monster was hardly in danger from Saress.

"What goes on here? Why've you brought me back here, imp? Have you found my steed?"

"Not yet, your glorious majesty! A problem arose with this sorcerer; he's proven willful when he shouldn't be! I was trying to remind him of his duty when the beautiful Saress materialized and mistook my deed for one that threatened both of their lives . . ." Yureel sounded timid.

Lanith turned to Saress. "Calm yourself. Yureel's no threat to you; he serves me . . . don't you, imp?"

"Yes, yes, I do, Lanith the Great!"

The enchantress quieted, but she was by no means convinced of the demon's complacency. Aurim prayed that she would remain suspicious; it would only serve his own chances if Saress continued to keep a wary eye on Yureel. She had seen him at his most terrible. Unless he wiped the memory from her mind, Saress would *have* to think the demon more dangerous than he now pretended to be.

"What is he, Lanith?" the sorceress demanded, thrusting a finger at Yureel.

"A servant, Saress. One who's worked hard to aid me in my conquest of the Dragonrealm."

The woman's brow arched. "Has he? I thought it was my Magical Order—and dear Aurim here—who had done so much!"

"Yes, yes, indeed," the demon cried. "They've performed marvelously, beauteous Saress! I . . . I've only done what little I could on the side."

"Why haven't I known about him, Lanith?"

"It wasn't wise to let too many know about Yureel, Saress. You can see for yourself what sort of reaction he receives. He serves me best by being unnoticed until too late." The horse king turned slightly toward the tiny demon and smiled at him. Yureel pretended to be honored.

Clearly the enchantress saw that Yureel had Lanith's ear. It did not sit well with her, but Aurim noticed that she was intelligent enough to cover her distaste before Lanith glanced her way again. The woman did not like being second to anyone or anything when it came to her beloved ruler. "You must forgive me . . . Yureel . . . but I sensed a great spell cast here, one that Aurim cast. I came to see what he might be doing down here when he should've been on the battlefield serving my dear king."

At last she had garnered Lanith's curiosity. "What spell is that, imp? Why would you drag Aurim here to cast a spell when he's needed on the field for the same reason?"

"I intended on using the aid of your precious sorcerer for a spell that would give us knowledge of the Dragon King's present position, but I discovered some . . . reluctance . . . on the lad's part, Your Majesty. As I first indicated, he seems to be having second thoughts." Yureel peered at Aurim, pupilless eyes growing colder. "Dangerous second thoughts."

"Oh?" The king also stared at Aurim. "I thought that was beyond him, imp. You said so yourself."

"I appear to have been remiss, glorious majesty! My apologies! I shall, of course, deal with the problem. Oh, I must assume that since your Saress is here, King Lanith, that she's accomplished the task you asked of her."

The horse king blinked. "Task? What task would—"

"The renegade enchantress, grand king! The woman who has danced around your city evading your Magical Order for the past several years! If Saress is here, then certainly she must've captured the woman!"

"Yes . . . I'd forgotten about that. Where is she, Saress?"

"I . . . have her in one of the dungeons, darling, but she's hardly worth the trouble to deal with now—"

The tiny figure floated away from the supposed protection of the horse king and took up a position that allowed him to gaze at both spellcasters without much effort. "I must humbly disagree, my lovely lady. More than ever she's of importance." Yureel studied Aurim closely. "Most important, indeed."

"She's nothing but a hedge witch!" Saress snapped.

"Oh, she's more than that, much, much more! Just ask her father, Lady Saress. You may have heard of him, I think."

As Aurim watched, the enchantress's visage paled. Yureel had struck a nerve. Saress actually looked frightened again. "I don't know anything about her father!"

"A great lapse in knowledge considering how long you've known *her*. One would almost think the two of you had grown up together, so familiar do you act with her."

"She's *nothing* to me."

"Enough of this babble," the horse king commanded, his expression one of increasing impatience. "I have a land and a Dragon King to conquer and this is delaying things! Bring me this woman now, Saress!"

She curtsied, managing still to display her obvious charms to the king as she bent forward. "I am ever at your command, dear Lanith."

Yureel giggled. Rising, Saress stifled what was likely a grimace. She took a deep breath, then slowly looked up at the ceiling. Power began to gather around her.

"The day is quickly waning," the shadow puppet remarked offhandedly.

The narrowing of her eyes was the only visible sign Aurim noted that indicated her bitterness with Yureel. "Come here, Yssa!"

No sooner had she finished the command when they were joined by the other enchantress. Aurim Bedlam found himself thankful that Yureel had not bothered to control his sight, for there was no one else in the chamber he would have rather stared at now than Yssa. She was even more beautiful than he recalled. Unfortunately, the blond enchantress was just as much a prisoner as he. A faint orange glow around her throat was the only evidence of the magical bonds that kept Yssa from using her own abilities, but its presence was sufficient to tell Aurim Bedlam that she would not easily escape.

King Lanith approached her, the gleam in his eye not one that Aurim cared for much. "This is her, eh?"

Evidently Saress was not pleased by her beloved monarch's interest in her rival. "She's nothing, Lanith. Not even worth trying to add to the Order. Leave her to me. I'll—"

"Be silent." The horse king's gaze drifted down, then up again. He cupped Yssa's chin, studying her face for much too long as far as Aurim was concerned. "Good form. Very healthy. Excellent breeding, I'd say."

With his back to her, Lanith could not see Saress's smoldering look.

Aurim tried to contact Yssa, but it was as if her mind had been shut away from his. He finally gave up, realizing that he could tell her nothing of value. They were both helpless.

Or were they? After his success in freeing Darkhorse, who was to say that Yureel's hold was that complete? Perhaps it had been his own distrust of himself that had made him such a pliable puppet. *I've got to try again.*

You will do nothing! commanded an enraged Yureel in his head. The confident, beguiling attitude the demon displayed for Lanith and the others was actually a mask; his fury had not abated. *Your chance is past! If you try again, my fine little human spellcaster, I shall do to your female as I intended to do to my dear twin!*

Yureel did not wait to hear if he understood. The demon vanished from the sorcerer's mind, confident, no doubt, that he had made his point. Regrettably, he had. Aurim immediately ceased his attempt. He could not risk Yssa.

"She's a fine addition, I'll admit, imp, but what best use is she? Will she join the Order?

"Her?" Saress snapped. "Never!"

"In this I must agree with your fine lady, my majestic king! No, she is no use to the Order."

Lanith seemed puzzled. "But surely you can—"

"There is a position of greater value for her to fill, oh, yes, indeed," Yureel responded quickly. "She will buy you a victory over your former liege, the dragon man!"

"Now why would she matter to him? Is she one of that green lizard's servants? I didn't know he kept human mages . . ."

The tiny puppet master giggled. "Oh, more than a servant, much more, much more . . . wouldn't you say, Lady Saress?"

Again the king's mistress grew extremely uncomfortable. She evidently knew what Yureel hinted at and it unsettled her greatly. "He values her, yes."

"So highly that he would risk surrender just for her?" the king asked, extremely skeptical.

Yureel gave a comic shrug as he drifted back to his supposed lord. "Surrender . . . possibly. Hesitate too long . . . definitely."

Growling, the horse king reached for the small, hovering figure, but Yurcel was too swift. He easily dodged aside, then took up a position nearer poor Yssa. "No more games, imp!" cried the graying conqueror. "Tell me why the damned drake would bother with a human. He's fond of them, but not that fond!"

"Aah, but with this sumptuous lass, he is!" Yureel floated next to Yssa's face. Aurim could see her trying to keep an eye on the foul monster. The tiny figure indicated her visage. "She is rather attractive, wouldn't you say, my grand emperor-to-be?"

"There's no denying that."

"Exotic, yes?"

Lanith studied her for far longer than necessary. Only when Saress cleared her throat did he finally pause. "She looks like one of my people . . . but there's definitely something else. Her blood's not pure. She's a mix."

"A mix . . ." Yet another infuriating giggle. "Oh, mixed well, indeed, wouldn't you say, Lady Saress." Using one tiny arm, he dragged Yssa even closer to Lanith. "A strong mix, your glorious majesty . . . strong, because she carries a most royal and . . . *draconian* . . . bloodline."

Saress gasped, then forcibly pushed all emotion from her countenance. Lanith eyed her, then studied the tiny demon as if the latter had completely lost his senses. "What are you saying? You sound as if you're trying to tell me that this other woman is a . . . is part . . ."

"Part *drake*, yes."

"Impossible!" The horse king seized Yssa by the shoulders and looked her over again. Had the bound enchantress been able to use her abilities, the monarch of Zuu would have been no more than a blot on the wall now. "And yet . . . maybe not . . . there's something about her . . . I've seen draconian females in human form . . ."

"She's far, far more than those little creatures, great and glorious Lanith! More so because she is also the child of the Dragon King himself."

Lanith was clearly skeptical. "How did you discover this fantastic secret?"

"Spies, searching, guesswork . . . a combination of events." The creature glanced surreptitiously at Saress.

Aurim caught the look, then the brief, frightened expression that again crossed the visage of Lanith's mistress. For the first time, Aurim noted some similarities in the women's features.

If what Yureel said was true, could that also mean that Saress was . . . that she was . . . just like Yssa?

No wonder you shake every time Yureel mentions Yssa's heritage— Aurim paused in midthought, the demon's revelation finally sinking in. Yssa was not quite human. Not *human*. It did not startle him as much as he might have expected, but then, he *had* grown up with drakes. He saw them as few others did, as a race as beautiful and terrible as any other. They were people like himself and many of them, when compared to some humans such as Lanith or even his own grandfather, Azran, were better. The Dragon Emperor's own sister, Ursa, was his sister Valea's close friend.

"Part drake . . . part *animal* . . ." Lanith released her, disgust growing. "Well, she may be of use, then, if the Dragon King will acknowledge her."

"He will, my lord, oh, he will."

"He'll not surrender his kingdom for her, though." The would-be conqueror walked around Yssa, studying her again, but his mind was clearly focused on other matters than her appearance. "No, but as you've indicated, he'll probably hesitate if he does care for her. He'll be afraid she'll be injured—"

"Or tortured," added Yureel with a giggle.

"—and that will cost him. It could cut the war down by half. Then we could turn toward Gordag-Ai as originally planned. They'll fall in half the time it'll take to conquer Dagora, especially if that drake Sssaleese can keep his pledge . . ."

Aurim did not follow the last but what he did follow made him even more anxious. He knew the Dragon King Green well enough to realize that what Yureel said was true. For someone he really cared for, especially one of his own, the drake lord *would* hesitate and that hesitation, manipulated by the horse king and the demon, might very well prove the fatal stroke.

"Magnificent!" Lanith suddenly cried. He laughed and, without warning, reached out to pet Yureel. The tiny figure remained still, although Aurim caught a hint of contempt in the inhuman eyes. "Magnificent! Once my former liege the drake has fallen, all his wondrous magical treasures will find better use in my hands! His fall will also reduce the power of his brethren, who'll realize too late that they should've aided him, the stupid lizards!"

"With Dagora yours, my great and splendid king, there will be no way they can even hope to stop you . . ."

Aurim doubted that. He still believed that Lanith could not succeed in the end; the continent would never be his. It was true, though, that if Dagora fell to him, any chance of putting an early end to the horse king's campaign would fade.

And we can't have that, now can we, little Aurim? My epic is far from complete!

Yureel's chilling voice echoing in his head was enough to make the sorcerer cringe.

I think you've had enough fun for now. Recall that her life is in your hands! She is a valuable tool against the drake, but I will sacrifice her if I have to, Aurim Bedlam! And in case you've forgotten— The spellcaster's left hand suddenly thrust itself upward, stopping only an inch or two before his face.

The fingers formed a tight fist. —*I'm still very much in control!*

"Imp! I want to return to the field! Belfour'll have the troops over the northern ridge by now, what with the Order's help. That means that we're getting damnably close to the center of the drake's domain and he'll defend it harder than any other place we've taken yet. Now's the time to remind him of his darling daughter!"

Contact between Aurim and Yureel ceased, but the hand remained where it was. A reminder. "Most definitely, Emperor Lanith, most definitely! I'll have Aurim whisk us there in but a breath! If anyone asks, you can say that he transported you here because of a matter of urgency. It would not be the first time you've made such use of your little sorcerers."

"I don't need to explain my comings and goings to anyone, imp . . . but it would be best to return before Belfour and the others get too nervous. Saress, you know the half-breed best; I want you with her for now in case she manages some trick." Without waiting for a reply, the horse king turned again to Yureel. "My mount is still missing, imp. What've you done about finding him again? I've had to commandeer one of my aide's mounts for now."

The demon did not even hesitate. "Worry not about him for the time being, my lord. Your great victory is near at hand. I'll keep an eye out for your steed, I promise you. I want to find him *nearly* as much as you do."

"All right. Then let's get back to the field. Now."

"As you command." And to Aurim, "Send them."

He could do nothing but obey Yureel. If there had been any hope before, certainly there was none now, not for him, Yssa, his family, or certainly the Green Dragon. Yureel had all of them dancing, even those who did not realize it. Only Darkhorse was free of his sinister twin's machinations.

The only question was . . . could Darkhorse return from wherever Aurim had sent him?

CHAPTER XVII

What happened to me? was Darkhorse's first question. He tried to focus, but the sudden shift in location had left him disoriented. It had certainly not been his own doing; between Yureel and Aurim, Darkhorse had been securely and efficiently imprisoned—

Aurim? It seemed the only conceivable answer. Somehow the captive sorcerer had managed to overcome Yureel's control, if momentarily, and been able to send Darkhorse away. That had to be the answer; nothing else made more sense. Perhaps with Yureel so occupied with absorbing his twin, the foul little monster had allowed his mastery of the human to slip just that precious little.

Where had Aurim sent him, though? For the first time since arriving, Darkhorse focused on his surroundings. Aurim Bedlam was a clever person. It had to be somewhere where the sorcerer trusted him to be safe.

Then again . . .

Where by the emptiness of the Void am I? It was like no place the shadow steed had ever visited either in the Dragonrealm or beyond. He *was* beyond the world of the Dragonrealm; that was immediately obvious.

Everything around him seemed unclear, as if his sight were failing him. That was not the case, though. Even up close, the peculiar plants—if they were plants—remained slightly unfocused. He shifted toward one and prodded it with a primitive appendage. The plant, a bluish, a cucumber-shaped thing with hairlike leaves, immediately quivered. A moment later a piercing bell sound shook Darkhorse so much that he immediately retreated from the alien object.

The cucumber plant's reaction set off another similar plant nearby. That, in turn, caused yet a third, then a fourth, to also peal like bells. The uproar shook Darkhorse to his very being, but there seemed to be nowhere to turn. Each direction he looked, similar plants blocked his path . . . and more and more of them were reacting to the first one.

The clamor grew maddening. Darkhorse could not have held together a form even if he had had the strength, so jarring was the noise. He finally gathered himself together as best he could, peered up at what he supposed passed for the sky but looked more like congealed fog, and flung himself upward.

The atmosphere was almost as thick as it looked, but slowly Darkhorse made headway. Somewhere above him was the way out of this peculiar realm. All he needed was a little time to locate it.

Something brown, round, and twice his size darted past him in the thick mist. Although it did not return, Darkhorse decided to push harder, not wanting to encounter any more of the strange world's inhabitants. Past experience had taught him never to assume that any creature was harmless.

The noise below grew faint, but before the eternal could relax, a second brown thing darted by. This time Darkhorse caught sight of a wicked appendage resembling a cross between a claw and a tongue. The glimpse encouraged him to yet greater effort. He did not like the notion of seeing whether or not he was immune to the dangers of this world. His friends needed him.

With what power he had at his command, Darkhorse probed the very fabric of the bizarre world, seeking any trace of a way out. Every place he had visited had some weak point that could be used to journey elsewhere. There might be an infinity of alternate realms, but they were all linked in some way. Once he escaped this one, he could begin a thorough search for the way home.

The fact that the shadow steed had never visited this world before reminded him of just how powerful Aurim was. As Cabe had always insisted, it was only the boy's will that held him back. With only minor control over his power, he had performed a feat the likes of which few master sorcerers were capable. Of course, the younger Bedlam's desperate gamble had provided Darkhorse with a new quandary. This world was unfamiliar to Darkhorse, which meant that the next one might be, too. Exactly how far from the Dragonrealm had the sorcerer thrown him? The shadow steed did not claim to know all of the infinite variety of realms, that being impossible, but he did know quite a few. This one was not remotely similar to any he had visited.

He abandoned his musings as two discoveries vied for his attention. The first concerned his path out of this realm, a tiny thread in the fabric of his present location that hinted of an escape route. Only a search would reveal the truth.

The second discovery concerned the fact that one of the winged brown things had decided *Darkhorse* was worth investigating.

He sensed it just below him, its pace far slower than that of the first one. It flew in an oval pattern that drew tighter with each circuit. Darkhorse estimated that it would likely attack after three more revolutions, which meant perhaps two, maybe three minutes at most. That gave him very little time to investigate the path ahead. If it was a false trail, he might uselessly push himself against it and waste his preciously small reserves of strength just before the thing decided to attack.

Darkhorse did not even contemplate trying to absorb the creature. Not only did the notion revolt him, but somehow he suspected that doing so would be more to his detriment. This realm was unsettling. If necessary, he might take the beast, but only as a last resort. What it might want to do with him, he did not even want to know.

Seeing beyond the thread proved more difficult a task than he anticipated. Like the sky itself, the edge of this realm felt thick and uncooperative. Darkhorse increased the intensity of his probe; the thing below him had already completed one and a half revolutions and gave signs of preparing to rise. Dark-horse did not doubt it intended to attack.

The barrier gave. Beyond the edge he sensed the hints of other worlds, other dimensions. The eternal had no time to consider which path might be best; the beast below had abruptly turned from its pattern and now rose toward him at a speed Darkhorse would not have thought possible in the thick atmosphere. He caught sight of a pair of the wicked ap-pendages focused at him. What had looked at first like a tongue now extended ahead of the beast at a rate even swifter than the creature's own speed.

Unwilling to meet it with his weakened skills, Darkhorse followed the thread out of the misty realm.

The world of the brown thing flickered, then transformed into a sunburnt, arid plain where everything held a reddish tinge. A massive crimson sun filled more than a third of the sky. There was no sign of life, past or present, and very few landmarks save the occasional worn mound of rock.

The shadow steed paused to recover. Fortunately, the path behind him had closed the moment he had passed through. Darkhorse could sense no trace of his pursuer.

An inhospitable world, he noted as he gathered his strength for the next part of the journey. So many dimensions he vis-ited were like that. A few of them even made the Void seem interesting. This one threatened to be an addition to that list.

After what might have been hours . . . the massive orb did not seem to move so it was difficult to say . . . Darkhorse fi-nally began his search for a new route. Unfortunately, al-though he soon found many threads worth following, none of the paths seemed familiar to him. The shadow steed at last chose one that resembled a world he had crossed long ago. While it was not the one he knew, sometimes similar realms were closely linked to one another. Sometimes.

Darkhorse still bore no resemblance to the animal from which he had taken his name. He had decided to conserve his energy until he managed to return to the Dragonrealm. There, the eternal knew places where he could take the time to recu-perate. Out here, where he was not even familiar with the landscape, Darkhorse did not want to trust that he could stay in one location long enough without risking himself to something like the brown, clawed creature.

Hoping for the best, the shadow steed opened the path to the next dimension and flew through. He landed this time in a world much like that of the Dragonrealm save that all the colors seemed to be wrong. The sky was light green, the clouds were pink, and the landscape itself, a wild, grassy field, was colored what could best be called golden blue. In the distance, Darkhorse could hear what sounded like birds, but he saw no trace of them, not even a tree where they might have perched.

Seems calm enough. The eternal was not lulled, though. The former lands of the Dragon King Brown were proof enough of how lethal calm could be. Nonetheless, Darkhorse needed rest.

The oddly colored field went on forever. In fact, the more Darkhorse stared, the more he was convinced that he was seeing much, much farther than should have been possible. Perhaps this was a larger world than the one he was used to. He was tempted to explore it a little, but each minute he delayed his return meant further possible danger to his friends.

He suddenly realized that he was being watched.

Unhindered yet by a set form, Darkhorse shifted his eyes to the back so that he could see his watchers. A flurry of yellow burst from the grass behind him, scattering in many directions. The creatures that had been watching him looked for all the world like huge toads with legs and wings. Some flew off, others ran away on their four gangly legs. However, one of the creatures still remained, its eyes more intent than those of its fellows.

This is not a beast. The eyes were too intelligent, too knowing.

Stretching its wings, the toadbird *transformed.*

Darkhorse caught only a glimpse of a humanoid shape wrapped in a black, obscuring cloak before the figure faded away. The shadow steed floated over to where it had stood, but there was nothing, not even a magical trace.

He noticed that the field had become deathly silent.

I had better leave. Darkhorse performed a hurried search of those paths he could sense easiest and found a single route that seemed vaguely familiar. The way was a difficult one, but not impossible. It was also the only choice he had. He gathered his strength, then opened the way.

A hooded figure, either the same one or another just like it, materialized in front of him. The general shape was humanoid, but the thing inside the black cloak was definitely not human. A pair of narrow, amber eyes stared back over what seemed a short but toothy maw. One hand was visible, a hand with only three blunt digits.

"I am departing your world, friend! There is no need to be alarmed."

The hooded figure did not respond, but suddenly a second identical creature materialized next to it.

"I mean no harm. I am simply a lost traveler. But a moment more and you shall never see me again."

A third formed on the other side of the first one. Another materialized to the shadow steed's right. In rapid succession, several more appeared, each of them twins of the first. Darkhorse realized that they were forming a circle around him.

The eternal decided to simply depart. However, when he tried to do so, a strong force pulled him back to the ground. He tried once more with no better result.

By this time, the hooded beings completely surrounded him. The first one raised its hidden hand into view, revealing a crystalline sphere. The creature spoke, but the clacking noise it made did not translate. The eternal shook his head. Whether or not the hooded creature comprehended his response, it chose to say nothing more. The crystal, though, remained in view.

"I am no threat to you! Neither have I any worth to you. Release me and you shall be bothered by my presence no more!"

The circle grew tighter as each figure took a single step toward him. The pull on him grew stronger. *If they move much closer, the force will be too great to counter . . .*

He studied his undesired companions. Raw force would not by itself free him. He needed to put them off-guard, disrupt their concentration. What could he do that would—

The answer came to him. On the surface it seemed absurd, but with creatures such as these, it had the potential. It was also a simple answer and simple answers, he had discovered, were most often the best.

Darkhorse *laughed*.

The sound shattered the silence in a way his protests had not. Startled, the hooded figures stepped back, clearly less certain of their superiority. They had probably never heard such a loud, raucous noise before.

Taking advantage of their confusion, Darkhorse again tried to depart the foreign realm. Once more he failed, but this time the force combating him proved weaker. The shadow steed scarcely paused before renewing his efforts. His would-be captors had begun to recover from their startlement. Brandishing the sphere high, the leader waved the rest forward. They were slow to obey, but obey they did. Even as Darkhorse pushed to free himself, he felt the pressure increase dramatically.

I will not be denied this time! The eternal flung himself toward the leader of the creatures, who stumbled back so quickly that it lost its footing and fell into the deep grass. The crystalline sphere went flying from its hand.

While the others moved to aid their fallen comrade, one sought after the lost artifact. At the same time, Darkhorse turned back to the path he had opened and leaped toward it.

The same force tried to seize him again, but it was not as strong as the previous attacks. Unfortunately, it did cause him to lose control of the opening and, worse, broke his link to the path itself. The eternal battled free of the spell and desperately tried to reestablish the link in time, but his concentration had been shattered and the best Darkhorse could do was seize for what he hoped was the path he had chosen.

The realm of the hooded creatures and the flying toadbirds faded behind him, but Darkhorse did not have time to revel in his triumph. His haphazard departure left him spinning out of control and unable to leave his quickly chosen route. He had only a short glimpse of a watery world before he passed through to yet another realm without slowing in the least.

Darkhorse managed to regain some control of his flight, but the second world vanished before he could even identify it.

He nearly left the third one behind as well. Only with a supreme effort did the eternal keep himself from being flung yet farther along. Finally breaking away, Darkhorse fluttered down to what proved to be gray mountaintops. Snow capped the peaks, but the cold was not a factor. Darkhorse chose the nearest and landed on a ledge.

It was a testament to his weariness that only after a long rest did Darkhorse note his surroundings. At first he could scarcely believe his luck. The eternal rose and surveyed the landscape for some miles around, but he hardly needed visual verification. This world had a familiar scent to it, a very familiar one. Not only had Darkhorse been to this place in the past, but he now knew what path he had to take to find his way back to the Dragonrealm. It was a lengthy trek, but at least a familiar one. If he set a good, steady pace, he would be able to recoup some of his strength by the time he returned home.

Home. Yes, the Dragonrealm was his home, more so than the Void had ever been. He could not allow Yureel to lay waste to his home, not even if it meant that Darkhorse had to sacrifice both of them to save it.

The sooner I depart, the better. There is no telling how much time has passed. The danger of moving from dimension to dimension was that time might pass more quickly in one world than another. It might be that only an hour had passed in the Dragonrealm . . . or it might be that *years* had.

Darkhorse rose slowly, shifting shape as he did. He would return to the Dragonrealm in the form in which he was known. In a sense, Darkhorse knew that it was his way of showing himself that Yureel had not crushed his will. The shadow steed was far from beaten; his twin would discover that soon enough.

But do I have the strength to defeat him? The shadow steed had to hope that he would have the strength by the time he confronted his monstrous counterpart. Yureel was his concern and no other's.

Fully restored to his favored form, Darkhorse took one last

look at the landscape around him. The cloud-enshrouded
mountain peaks could not be called the most attractive sight
that he had ever seen, but Darkhorse savored the image
nonetheless. It was very possible that this would be the last
peaceful sight he would see.

No time for hesitation! Tearing himself away from the
view, Darkhorse located his path to home. Yureel awaited
him, probably eager to renew contact. Darkhorse did not want
to disappoint his brother.

After all, they were family.

Realm after realm, dimension after dimension, the shadow
steed passed on, never slowing. Worlds flickered by at an incredible rate. Darkhorse could not remember the way being
this long. How many more worlds could there be? How much
time had passed in the Dragonrealm in the meantime? The
Dagora Forest could be a wasteland, its master slain, perhaps,
by Aurim Bedlam himself.

Do not think of that! The lad was strong; in the end, he
would resist Yureel. He had to. It was unthinkable that Aurim
could become, even unwillingly, a greater terror than his
grandfather had ever been.

Yet, Darkhorse knew all too well how strong Yureel's will
was.

He passed through another realm with scarcely a glimpse at
it, but as the eternal departed, he at last sensed that his final
destination was at hand. The world Darkhorse entered next
was one very near to the Dragonrealm. Darkhorse had not
come this way in some time, but if he was correct, the shadow
steed suspected that only one more realm separated him
from—

As he crossed into the next realm, a wall of water put a
shuddering halt to his journey. The darkness of the depths
welcomed him. It was not always possible to predict exactly
where a path between dimensions opened and this one had evidently opened in the midst of a body of water. In fact, as
Darkhorse finally slowed his descent, he realized that he had
fallen into a sea . . . and a very deep, cold one at that.

Recovering his equilibrium, the eternal darted upward toward the distant surface. Gradually the darkness gave way to

the first glimmers of light. Fish swam above him, dispersing wildly as he rose among them. A long, narrow shark nearly as large as Darkhorse studied the ebony form for a moment before evidently deciding that the newcomer was too much to take on.

Darkhorse broke through to the surface and although he did not need to breathe, he inhaled and exhaled deeply once in order to relieve himself of some of the anxiety that had built up within. Then, rising upward until his hooves barely touched the surface, Darkhorse looked around. However, other than water there was nothing in sight.

He was in the middle of nowhere with no immediate sense of direction to guide him, but there was at least one thing that Darkhorse knew. He *had* returned to the Dragonrealm. Despite his certainty that he had had at least one more realm to cross, Darkhorse had instead plunged his way into the dimension of his adopted home. That he had miscalculated meant nothing to him in the face of such a revelation. Darkhorse was home and that was that.

Which way *was* home, though? The cloud cover, which hinted at a quickly approaching storm, made it impossible to judge direction by the heavens and the weary traveler's incredible trek had left his mind more addled than he had realized. He *should* have been able to sense in which direction to travel.

A few minutes of rest. That is all it will take. A few minutes of rest and I shall be able to orient myself.

However, even as he thought that, Darkhorse noticed that the sea had already begun to rise and fall with increasing intensity. Darkhorse dodged one wave that threatened to wash over him. The wind picked up. He did not move, though, his attention fixed only on the task at hand.

A column of water burst up behind him. Darkhorse turned, intent on avoiding it, but halted when he saw that the column was only a thin, quickly vanishing skin over something far more imposing. The thing within the column continued to rise higher and higher until it *loomed* over the weary eternal.

The maw of the creature was large enough to swallow five Darkhorses whole. The eyes were green and glittered of their own accord. From the lower jaw, fleshy strips that gave the appearance of a beard fluttered in the wind. Its skin was a brilliant ocean blue and the scales that covered it were streamlined for swift speeds through the water, an element probably more natural to it than the land upon which it had been born.

"You are Darkhorsssse . . ." the sea dragon, a male, burbled, spraying the eternal as he spoke. "We were all told to watch for you, yet I never dreamed that you would come to be in my region. I thought it could not posssibly be true, but I invessstigated regardless. You are Darkhorsssse."

"And what if I am, leviathan?" The shadow steed readied himself. The drake's intentions were unclear, but few of his kind cared for Darkhorse.

"Then I mussst sssee to it that you are brought before my massster . . ."

Darkhorse felt the dragon's spell envelop him. The creature was a part of the clan Blue and while Blue tended to be neutral in regard to the shadow steed, he could not predict what the Dragon King might want of him. Blue had been willing enough in times past to manipulate those who might better his position. He had a peace treaty of sorts, unwritten and silent, with the Gryphon, thanks in part to the drake's son, Morgis, but that agreement did not necessarily include making peace with Darkhorse.

Despite the weakness that still plagued him, the eternal fought against the spell. "I am afraid that I have other more pressing matters, drake! I regret that your master will have to wait!"

"My massster waitsssss for nothing!"

The spell increased in intensity. Darkhorse felt a sense of displacement as he struggled to be in one location while the immense drake attempted to send him elsewhere. To his consternation, the eternal realized that after his struggle with the hooded creatures and his lengthy journey across worlds, he might not have either the will or strength to combat the dragon's sorcery.

Unless . . . if Darkhorse could not counter the spell, perhaps he could adjust it to his own needs.

A wave roared over the behemoth, but the dragon scarcely

noticed it, his concentration completely on Darkhorse. The sea now had a somewhat ghostly look to it, a sure sign that Darkhorse was losing the battle of wills. He concentrated what strength he had left to shifting the eventual destination of the spell to elsewhere. It had to be somewhere the shadow steed could recuperate. Darkhorse could barely hold his own now—and this to a *drake*.

Where? Where would I be safe? It was impossible to think. He could only hope that his own instincts would preserve him.

With one last effort, he finished altering the dragon's spell. Then, before the beast had the opportunity to realize what had happened, Darkhorse dropped his own defenses and allowed himself to be taken.

The shift struck him hard. Darkhorse fought unconsciousness throughout, but the struggle grew more difficult with each passing moment. He did not even know that he had landed elsewhere until it occurred to him that earth and not water lay beneath him. Through fading senses, the eternal realized that he lay sprawled in a field—but not just any field. If he was correct, he had transported himself to, of all places, Yssa's favored domain.

As if to verify his fears, several stalks of grass bent down and touched him lightly on the head. More of them followed suit even as Darkhorse faded into unconsciousness.

He had journeyed back from far beyond the Dragonrealm, struggled against creatures on a foreign world, battled the will of a huge drake even though greatly exhausted already . . . only to fall helpless into the Barren Lands.

Now he was *its* prisoner.

CHAPTER XVIII

Darkhorse woke to birds singing, the wind gently blowing, and the spreading realization that he felt stronger than he had in many days. He also remembered *where* he was, a bit of knowledge that destroyed any pleasure at finding himself fully recovered from his long ordeal.

Leaping to his feet, the shadow steed glared at the grass around him . . . only to find that for several yards in each direction it lay limp and, curiously, quite dead. He nosed at some of it, but the blades remained unmoving. Darkhorse probed the area around him and found not one living blade. He estimated that he stood in the center of a circle of devastation whose diameter had to be at least thirty yards, yet outside of the circle the grassland remained as pristine as ever.

What happened here? Darkhorse recalled little of his hurried departure from the sea and nothing that would have caused the destruction around him. If it had been his doing, he regretted it. While the enchanted land made him nervous, Darkhorse did not indiscriminately destroy. The grass had harmed neither him nor his companions. He held no malice against it.

Trotting to the edge of the circle, the eternal eyed the healthy blades. They did not try to reach for him as they had in the past. Curious at this shift in behavior, Darkhorse put one hoof onto the untouched portion of the field.

Blades of grass darted toward his leg. He started to remove

it, but the plants were swifter, wrapping quickly around the limb. The wary traveler hesitated, not wanting to further raise the ire of the field. It might be demanding some sort of reparation for the loss of so many. He waited, seeing what the blades would do next.

A tingle ran through him. Darkhorse felt a fresh surge of strength. He felt almost willing to take on Yureel and the entire armed force of Zuu by himself. The sensation spread. He *was* Darkhorse, after all. What creature in all the Dragonrealm was more powerful, more—

"Insane!" The ebony stallion tugged the leg away, retreating several steps at the same time. The grass around his leg fluttered to the ground, now as lifeless as that under his hooves.

But I did nothing . . . nothing . . . The tingle had died down, but the sense of growing strength did not. He felt nearly invincible. Darkhorse fought down his urge to race off and do battle with Yureel and tried to understand what had happened to make him feel so confident. The sense of growing strength had begun the moment the blades had coiled around his leg, almost as if he had been feeding off their energy.

Feeding off of their energy? But he had done no such thing! It went against his respect for life. Battle was one thing, but he was no murderous creature like his twin. He would never have done something so uncaring, so heartless. The plants had done nothing to harm him. Yet, if Darkhorse had not stolen the life force from the blades of grass, then . . . then that meant that the grass had *willingly* sacrificed itself for his recovery.

"Impossible . . ." Was it though? How else to explain his rapid recovery? He had witnessed for himself how the grass had reached out and taken hold of him. He had even sensed the power flowing from them. The plants *had* given their lives.

It must be for Yssa. The land here is fond of her. It must know that I . . . that I am her friend. The notion might have seemed outrageous to most, but Darkhorse had long ago come across evidence that the Dragonrealm itself also contained a consciousness of sorts, rumored by scholars to be the last spiritual traces of those who had founded the world. Whether that was the case, he had witnessed enough startling revelations during his lengthy life span to know that his present theory was a possibility.

It might even know that she is in danger. Cautiously, the shadow steed trotted to the edge of the circle again. He felt somewhat foolish for what he was about to attempt, but Darkhorse saw no other way. There was no one creature with which he could specifically speak.

"Hear me, grassland! I know not what force lies behind you, but whether it be the spell that restored a dying land to your present glory or whether another force entirely is to be credited, I thank you for your great sacrifice! No more must be given, though! I am well and ready, thanks to you!"

No breeze blew across the field, but the blades fluttered regardless. Darkhorse blinked, almost willing to swear that the rustling sounded like the name *Yssa*. That was nonsense, though . . . was it not?

Regardless, he could remain here no longer. Yssa, Aurim, and so many others depended on him and even if he failed in the end, Darkhorse at least had to try.

"I will do what I can for your friend and mine," he added, not wanting to chance offending the grassy region if it *had* spoken to him. "I must go now. Thank you."

The blades rustled again, but this time he made out no reply. Dipping his head once in gratitude, the shadow steed backed to the very center of the circle, then focused. There was only one person who might be able to help him. The Gryphon. He hoped nothing had happened to the king of Penacles during his absence. Yureel had to know that the Gryphon was a threat, which meant that like the Bedlams, the lionbird might be in danger, if not already a victim.

I can but hope. With one last glance at the rustling blades, Darkhorse concentrated on the throne room in the palace of Penacles. The Gryphon would help him.

A moment later, though, he found himself not inside the palace, but rather outside the gates of the city proper. The shadow steed probed and found that the defenses around Penacles had been greatly strengthened, enough so that Darkhorse doubted he could have penetrated them even at his best. The eternal sought to contact the Gryphon. Surely the king would grant him entrance once he knew who it was.

He received no response. With so many cunning spells in place, it was possible that the Gryphon was simply hidden from his probes, but Darkhorse suspected that the truth was that the inhuman ruler had departed his kingdom. It had not been uncommon in the past for the Gryphon to take personal risk in order to aid either his friends or his very kingdom, and bearing that in mind, Darkhorse could think of only one place where he might readily find the king.

A quick thought was all that was needed to send him on his way. He materialized exactly where he desired, which regrettably answered one question immediately. The opaque shell still covered the domain of the Bedlams. Darkhorse feared the worst. Whether he had been gone from the Dragonrealm for weeks, months, or even only a few hours, there was no saying what might have happened to the Bedlams and their people since his departure. Air flowed through the shell, but what if Yureel had set some other deadly trap into motion? Darkhorse tried to contact Cabe, but the wall would not allow him access of any sort.

Someone stood to the right of him.

"So, you aren't dead, Darkhorse."

Clad in plain robes that likely hid a breastplate beneath, the Gryphon nodded to him. The king of Penacles looked very weary, not a good sign at all. The Gryphon was a skilled spellcaster, one of the best and certainly one of the most knowledgeable. If he looked so defeated, circumstances had to be extremely dire. "How fare you, Your Majesty?"

He gestured at the shield. "It speaks for itself, doesn't it? I'd rather go into battle against an army of Aramites than play with this infernal trap! I've no more tricks to pull, no more forces to throw into the situation. I've been defeated at every turn . . ." The Gryphon blinked. "No, not completely. I have established contact within. They're still all right, although growing restless. Cabe thinks he knows something about how his son manipulated the field, but he still isn't certain that he can alter it without Aurim's assistance. I never dreamed that the boy was so *powerful.*"

"So the only way to free them is to bring Aurim back."

"No, eventually Cabe will find a solution. I may still have some luck, too. The trouble is we don't have the time. In the past week, the Green Dragon's all but buckled under to the damned horse king—"

"The past week?" Darkhorse thought back over his long journey. "How long since last you heard of me, Lord Gryphon?"

"It must be nearly two weeks. That's why I began to believe you dead. I didn't think you'd let things in the west go unchecked for so long, not to mention abandoning your friends. You've never been a coward, Darkhorse."

Nearly two weeks. Not as lengthy an exile as it might have been but far too long for the good of the land. Considering what he had last learned while Yureel's captive, he was amazed that things were not worse. "What was that you said about the lord of the Dagora Forest? The drake is not fighting back?"

"Delaying tactics and very weak ones. His forces nibble at the enemy but do not clamp down. As for sorcery, it's as if he's suddenly bereft of the art. I thought it might be because of Aurim Bedlam, that he might not wish to harm the boy, but I don't think the drake's that compassionate."

The Green Dragon might not be that compassionate when it came to Cabe and Gwen's children, but there was another whose presence might make him hesitate. Saress had captured Yssa and there was no reason to believe that the latter had escaped. The drake cared deeply for his half-breed daughter. It would not surprise Darkhorse that the reason for the Green Dragon's predicament was Yureel's use of the young enchantress as a bargaining chip. The cursed creature knew that he could best prolong and increase the devastation he desired by having Lanith defeat the drake. That would bring the other Dragon Kings in at last, but at the same time the resources of Dagora, including the drake lord's sorcerous collection, would be in Yureel's hands.

More important, a victory by Lanith over a Dragon King would garner him support from others who despised the drake race or saw the opportunity for advancement. A victory over Dagora meant the possibility of bringing the entire continent to war. Everything that Cabe had worked for would collapse. Kyl could not possibly keep his people from resuming their own war against humans. His race was as passionate about their beliefs and desires as Cabe's race was. In the end, there could be only one victor in such a cataclysm.

Yureel.

"Is there no hope for Dagora, then?" The eternal could not believe things had deteriorated so much.

"I was able to send some support . . . not much because my spies report that my good neighbor the Black Dragon has managed to organize his human fanatics and his clans under his heir. They're prepared to move at any moment and it'll be toward Penacles if they think I've weakened myself enough. Kyl sent some aid, too, but without the Green Dragon to co-ordinate their efforts, they can't do very much. More than half the forest has now been overrun by Zuu. I'd have never thought it possible, but it's happened . . . with the aid of sorcery, of course."

It always came down to that. Regardless of the strength of his fighting force, Lanith's true might lay in the vast reservoir of sorcery available to him through Yureel, Aurim, and the Order.

There is no other choice, then. Everything . . . the freedom of the Bedlams, the defeat of the horse king, the salvaging of Dagora, and the rescue of Aurim . . . it all demands I confront Yureel and end this. The Barren Lands had granted him as much strength as he dared command. It behooved him to see that he did not waste the gift.

Perceptive as always, the Gryphon noticed his shifting mood. "What is it, Darkhorse?"

"What will you do now, Your Majesty?"

"Return to Penacles for the time. Besides Dagora, I've got to keep an eye on Lochivar, Irillian, and Wenslis. Gordag-Ai, too, if the rumors I hear about the drake confederation are true."

It was as Darkhorse had guessed. The Gryphon had already overextended himself. Not only did he have to deal with the various kingdoms most affected by the war, but he also had to work to free his allies.

I can look to him for no aid. It would not be fair.

"Darkhorse—"

The huge stallion stepped back. "My best wishes for your success in all matters, Your Majesty. My best wishes and dearest hopes."

"Darkhorse, what are you planning? I know you, eternal! Don't do anything—"

He did not wait to hear the rest of the Gryphon's warning, mostly because Darkhorse feared that he might end up agreeing with him. For everyone's sake, he had to see this through.

However, the sight that greeted him when he materialized a moment later in Dagora nearly sent him fleeing back to the king of Penacles. Oh, the forest here still stood, but the trees were gray and leafless, clearly dead of some blight. Worse, the area was littered with dead. The Dragon King's warriors had finally confronted Lanith's horde. Most of the bloody, mangled remains were those of the defenders, but there were many blond corpses, not to mention those of dozens of horses. The half-skeletal remains of a good-sized dragon lay among several crushed trunks, testament to the futility of such might against the horse king's linked sorcerers. Dragons made easy targets.

The battlefield was days old and the only life remaining consisted of rats, carrion crows, and other scavengers. Darkhorse kicked away one overly eager rat scurrying near his hooves. He loathed them not because of what they were but because of what they represented.

This is not far from the caverns of the Green Dragon. I wonder if this time the place will be abandoned in fact, not fantasy.

He abandoned the horror of the field, choosing a destination near the eastern caverns. The western entrances had to be held by the enemy. Zuu had conquered *more* than half the forest, that was clear now.

The forest here seemed undisturbed, but it was deathly silent, a sure sign that the war raged not far away. The Gryphon had indicated that the Green Dragon had not surrendered despite the threat against his daughter, but his hesitancy had cost the drake too much already. Even if he decided to throw everything wholeheartedly into the next battle, it was possible that he would lose badly.

Darkhorse tried to contact the Dragon King, but received no response. He was disappointed but not surprised. Still, the shadow steed hoped that the drake lord would soon notice him. The longer Darkhorse had to wander the forest, the more likely that Yureel would sense him.

Blast you, Dragon King! We must speak! What could he say, though, that he had not said earlier? In the Green Dragon's eyes, Darkhorse likely appeared to be an unnecessary interruption.

A blink hole suddenly opened in front of him.

Stumbling back, the shadow steed awaited whatever threat lurked at the other end of the hole. However, instead of some new danger concocted by Yureel, a lone drake warrior stepped out. The newcomer held both hands open so that Darkhorse could see that he was unarmed.

"Pleassse, demon ssssteed! You mussst come thisss way! Quickly! Hisss Majesssty begsss you not to hesssitate!" The warrior's crimson eyes nearly pleaded with the eternal to hurry.

So the Green Dragon would see him after all. Darkhorse trotted toward the hole. From the tone of the anxious drake, the war had the clan against the wall.

The armored figure suddenly drew a blade and hissed, but he was not looking at Darkhorse. Something darted past the shadow steed, burying itself in the throat of the hapless drake. Even as his companion collapsed, already dead, Darkhorse saw more than half a dozen warriors on horseback come charging toward him. Darkhorse paused before the entrance, greatly tempted to repay them for the drake's death. Then he realized that he had detected no trace of the riders, which meant that there was at least one sorcerer nearby.

That proved to be more than correct. A trio of robed figures, one of them bearing the unmistakable stench of Yureel, materialized a short distance away. The lead sorcerer, a figure

Darkhorse recognized as once having been a student in Pena-cles, pointed at the ebony stallion.

Darkhorse leaped through the hole, hoping that the Dragon King would be quick in sealing it behind him.

The other end of the blink hole opened into the inner sanctum of the drake lord. Darkhorse whirled around as soon as he was through, prepared now to block the way if the sorcerers' spell followed. Fortunately, the blink hole had already vanished.

"You have a habit of demanding . . . my attention . . . at the worssst of times, demon sssteed."

The Dragon King slumped on a chair near the viewing artifact, his eyes fixed on the scene floating above it but his mind clearly many other places. His words were distant.

"My apologies! I have been away for quite some time and this was the first opportunity I had to contact you."

"Away?" The Green Dragon finally stared at him. "Until you materialized in the foressst, I had become certain that you had perished at the . . . handsss, isss it? . . . of your brother." He rose slowly from the chair. "He hasss my daughter, demon. He hasss my daughter, and like my foressst she isss hisss to do with asss he pleasesss!"

Darkhorse trotted up to the drake, forcing the tall figure to stare up at him. "I know that all too well! I was there when she was taken. Strange, though, I never took you or your brethren to be so fearful for the safety of your females. They were there for breeding purposes only."

The reptilian lord looked ready to strike him, but apparently thought about the consequences. Instead, he turned away and walked slowly toward one of the shelves housing his collection of artifacts. Darkhorse noted that many of the shelves were now empty.

"You do not know usss as well asss you think. In the passst I've been forced to deal with rebellious children, but that doesss not mean that I did not mourn them in quiet." He hissed. "I will admit that Yssa isss a ssspecial cassse. I cannot explain why."

Having known her for a time, Darkhorse thought he already understood. Yssa brought a sense of life to her surroundings that not all the foliage decorating the caverns could have matched. She was one of the most determined mortals he had met.

"It may—"

"I've changed my mind," the drake commented, reaching for a small box high on one shelf. "Your coming here might be the key to sssalvaging my kingdom and my daughter."

His tone did nothing to encourage the eternal. The Dragon King sounded as if he were willing to do anything. He had already threatened Aurim's life. "I will not help you kill Cabe's son, drake!"

"That isss an option I find beyond me. To attack the lad isss to attack the entire Order. The oddsss against ssssuccessfully completing that operation are great. No, I propossse inssstead a multipronged asssault that will have asss its culmination the exile of thisss monstrosity Yureel and the ressscue of my daughter."

He was mad. Darkhorse was certain of it. "You say that attacking Aurim is a futile gesture but trying to save your daughter while at the same time exiling Yureel is *not?*"

"Not with thisss!" The Green Dragon turned and held forth the artifact. It was a box, aged beyond belief, but still sturdy. There was a pattern on the lid, but time had worn away so much of it that only a wing was still identifiable. "Not with this . . ."

"Get that *away* from me!" Darkhorse reared, nearly causing the drake to back into the shelves. Fear swept over the eternal. He knew what the box was. He had seen its like before. Once, he had even been a prisoner of one.

Being trapped within the box had been worse than being lost in the Void. At least in the latter one could move. In the box, there was nothing put pain.

"Yesss, it isss of Vraad make," the Dragon King remarked, referring to the ancient race of sorcerers who were the ancestors of the humans.

"I *know* it is of Vraad make! I know what the cursed box is! By the Void, how many of the monstrous things did they create? Must they all survive the centuries?"

It had been the Vraad Dru Zeree who had led him to the

Dragonrealm, but it had been another Vraad, the militaristic clan leader Barakas Tezerenee, who had taught him fear as only his twin had before. Lord Tezerenee had used one of the boxes to break him. The box was a prison, one in which Darkhorse had been trapped, helpless. He had been forced to obey the edicts of the ruthless Vraad leader until rescued. The memory was countless centuries old but as fresh in his mind as ever.

"Destroy it! Destroy it!" The eternal backed farther away, nearly upsetting some of the shelves behind him.

Cradling the box in his hands, the Dragon King stared defiantly at him. "I will not! Thisss isss the only one I have left! Thisss is the only thing I have left that I believe will deal with the creature . . . and you will help me, demon sssteed!"

Darkhorse fought his fears down. "Help you with what?"

"To *trap* him with thisss, of courssse! I'd wondered if you, with your knowledge of Vraad wayssss, would recognize it. You do, ssso you alssso know how it worksss . . . and it ssstill doesss. With it, we shall capture the monster, ressscue my daughter . . . and perhapsss Aurim Bedlam as well."

"Exactly what do you have in mind?" Darkhorse was certain that the strain had unbalanced the drake, but his plan did have a remote possibility of success, which was more than the stallion could say for his own idea.

Seeing that he had his companion's undivided attention at last, the Green Dragon smiled. The image made Darkhorse wonder just what Yssa's mother could have seen in him. He was exotic, yes, but he was a *drake*. Darkhorse doubted he would ever understand love.

"There isss little time remaining." The reptilian monarch visibly forced himself to calm down. "I must now defend not only the west but the south asss . . . as well. The land lost to the horse king and his familiar resembles a jawbone now with the sharpest fangs just to the south of my cavernsss. Men, drakes, elves, even Ssseekers have perished by the scores, and but for the sorcery Lanith has at hisss beck and call, I could end this insufferable war in a few hours. As brave and ready as they are, the warriors of Zuu are alssso pragmatic. They'd know better than to continue if the Order wasss eliminated."

Darkhorse was not so certain about that, but he did not comment. "You said we would also try to *rescue* Aurim, not kill him."

"Yes, yesss. Hear me, then. It isss you who bear much of the responsibility for success. You will locate my daughter, who isss, I believe, far behind the lines accompanied by Lanith's witch. You must take her from the witch—"

The eternal let loose with a short, bitter laugh. "Yureel is certain to notice me!"

"So much the better. His attention will be divided. When he comes to deal with you, I will come and deal with him."

He was proposing to leap behind the lines of the enemy and face Yureel head on. The Green Dragon appeared to have a great death wish. Even if he succeeded in trapping Dark-horse's twin, the Order would make short work of him. Either Aurim or one of the other sorcerers under Yureel's spell would then release the insidious monster.

At that point, they would all turn on Darkhorse.

When he informed the Dragon King of this, the helmed drake disagreed. "The Order will not be a problem. In fact, they will be the caussse of even greater distraction for the demon."

"How so?"

The smile that now spread across the Green Dragon's half-hidden features was as grim as any Darkhorse had seen in years. "The Order—including Aurim, I hope—will be hard-pressed to aid Lanith'sss horde, much less their true master. I intend to throw everything I have at Lanith's army. *Everything*. Once the box and its contentsss are sssent far, far away, the hold the demon had on the young Bedlam will surely fade. That, then, will weaken the Order to the point where they will fall from exhaustion quite quickly. Their ssstrength without Cabe'sss son is not so great a danger."

The shadow steed nearly turned him down there and then. It was a risky plan at best. Even supposing the impossible happened and they were able to exile Yureel again, how long could the drake's defenses hold out? Lanith still had Ponteroy and the other sorcerers, and their combined powers were not so weak as the Green Dragon might think.

"I will do thisss with or without you, Darkhorssse. You'll have to admit the oddsss are better with both of usss working together. What other hope isss there?"

"The Gryphon—"

"Hasss too many concerns of hisss own! It isss either this or defeat."

It went against his better judgment to agree, but Darkhorse had found enough fault in his own judgment recently to make him uncertain. The Green Dragon had fought in wars past; he was certainly a better strategist than the eternal could claim. Besides, what other plan did they have?

"Very well. I agree."

The drake hissed in obvious relief. "Good. I had little hope for sssuccess on my own, being unable to both rescue Yssa and confront the demon. I have officers who can deal with the battle itself, but no one I could trust to aid me on this mission."

Unspoken was the fact that although the Dragon King had a male heir to his throne, he dared not risk him even for Yssa. Drakes with the markings designating them future Dragon Kings were rare and so each of the monarchs kept careful watch over their successors. The Green Dragon's heir would be helping to coordinate defensive efforts from somewhere deep within the cavern system, well away from the battle. It was a curious arrangement at times, especially considering that many Dragon Kings came into power by eliminating their progenitors.

"When do we begin this?"

Again the drake smiled grimly. "Asss they say, 'there'sss no time like the presssent,' is there?"

Death. More death. More and more death and not a thing that Aurim could do to stave off the flow. If anything, he was responsible for the rising casualties. The spells that the Order focused through him laid waste to acres of forest and hundreds of defenders. Lanith's warriors suffered losses as they pushed for the Dragon King's stronghold, but that made the matter worse, not better. The defenders had done their utmost to rout the invaders, but against sorcery that left the Green Dragon's own spells wanting, they were helpless.

Another day and we'll be pounding at the lizard's door. His head'll decorate a lance soon after—

Aurim mentally cringed at the thought. Of late, he had found himself thinking such things. Yureel's control had crept deeper into his mind, threatening to soon turn the sorcerer into a loyal, very willing servant to the monster's evil.

General Belfour rode up to him. "Any spellwork?"

"Only the protective shield," Aurim's mouth responded.

"I don't like it. Why the sudden lull? The drake's troops withdrew, too. If it wasn't for the fact that our own need the rest, we'd be after them all the way to the Dragon King's lair. This doesn't bode well."

Thankful for any respite, Aurim Bedlam hardly wanted to question the retreat, but that part of him controlled by Yureel had to ask, "Does the king want us to stir them up? We could create another fire wall."

"The king's in conference," the veteran snapped. To the sorcerer, by now familiar with the older warrior's personality, that meant that Belfour had noticed his monarch talking to himself. None of Lanith's warriors were privy to his relationship with the demon, so to them the horse king had to seem mad. Still, no one dared talk of removing him from the throne. Not only were the warriors of Zuu trapped by their own sense of tradition, but Lanith had proven he wielded great power. "We'll probably have an answer before long."

Aurim snapped to attention, his eyes suddenly darting skyward. The reaction was a combination of both parts of him in response to the sudden sensing of a familiar presence. A study of the clouds revealed nothing, though.

"What is it, spellcaster?"

He struggled with himself, trying not to reveal what he had sensed. Belfour noticed his hesitation and urged his animal nearer. The general looked ready to slap Aurim on the cheek.

Fortunately, or rather unfortunately in Aurim's eyes, the sorcerer lost his struggle to keep his secret. "Darkhorse. He's near . . . or getting near."

"Darkhorse? That beast is back?" Envy and distrust vied

within Belfour. He had not made it a secret that he would have dearly loved a steed such as his king had briefly owned. "I'd better alert His Majesty to "

The earth rumbled nearby, the sudden quake sending the three spellcasters presently on monitoring duty to their knees. Belfour's horse reared in surprise, forcing the general to concentrate his full effort on retaining control. Aurim maintained his footing, but before he could gather his wits, a heavy wind threatened to push him back into the general's anxious mount.

Ahead, a horn abruptly blared, immediately followed by several more.

"They're attacking!" Ponteroy called needlessly from nearby. The other sorcerer had been drinking some of the sickly sweet wine he transported daily from Gordag-Ai. Now he stood, a purple stain spreading across the chest of his otherwise immaculate jacket, and hurriedly began organizing the rest of the Order.

The rumble increased in intensity, spreading both to the north and the south. The magical wind matched it, blowing so hard that some of the weaker sorcerers had to be aided by their fellows. Slowly, they formed a ragged pattern, an empty spot in the middle left for Aurim.

In the midst of it all, he sensed the swiftly approaching presence of Darkhorse. The stallion was heading to the south, beyond the rear of Zuu's lines. Aurim was happy that Darkhorse had survived his haphazard exile, but bitter that now he would have to try to capture the shadow steed again.

Yssa. It was the only answer. Darkhorse had to be heading toward Yssa.

"Don't just stand there, brat!" Ponteroy snarled. "If we don't do something, the drake's attack will force our warriors back and his sorcery will scatter *us* all over the landscape, too!"

Yureel's conditioning seized hold. Unless contacted directly by the demon, Aurim had to obey the monster's primary dictate. He was to work to counter the enemy's spells, then lead the Magical Order in attempting to destroy the source of the spellwork.

Despite the dread that rose within him every time he joined

with the others to spread havoc and death among the horse king's foes, the young spellcaster now felt a shred of hope. Occupied as he was with defending the legions of Zuu, he could not immediately turn and attack his old friend. Yureel would have to face Darkhorse alone, at least for the time being.

Unfortunately, Aurim also knew that the demon had already planned for his twin's inevitable return . . . and this time the puppet master would brook no escapes.

CHAPTER XIX

There! She is there!

Darkhorse focused, opening a path to where Yssa was held prisoner. Despite the Dragon King's plan, he wanted to move in quick and be gone with the enchantress before Yureel even made his appearance. The stallion doubted he would succeed in doing so, but he had to try. He would be better able to concentrate on his foul twin if he did not also have to worry about his friend.

When he materialized a breath later, it was to the consternation of half a dozen guards and the sorceress Saress. The guards, much more used to the sudden shifts of battle, recovered before Saress. Three of them split away and tried to come around to the eternal's back. The others moved forward, spears in the hands of two, the third—a scarred woman—carrying a crimson rope. Darkhorse sensed sorcery present in all the weapons. As he had feared, Yureel had expected him to return.

"Away with all of you!" the shadow steed roared, trying to frighten them off. Beyond the three in front, Saress guarded the entrance to a tent wherein Darkhorse could sense her captive. Darkhorse contemplated leaping over the heads of the trio and charging Lanith's witch, but he suspected that Yureel had kept that notion in mind as well.

The three who had moved around him also carried spears, weapons that they seemed quite willing to use despite the rep-

utation the shadow steed had for dealing with his adversaries.
Darkhorse twisted around as no mortal horse could have and
reared at the nearest guard. The man stood his ground and
jabbed with the spear, managing to prick the shadow steed's
right foreleg. A shock briefly jolted Darkhorse, who immediately retreated a step.

He heard the swish of the rope, caught a brief glance of it
as it circled his head, then felt the noose settle around his
neck. Darkhorse started to retract his head, but the moment
the noose tightened, he lost control of his shapeshifting abilities.

"I've got him!" cried the woman.

So she did, but roping Darkhorse and keeping him under
control were two different things. He sensed the same spell
that Aurim had cast on the saddle and bridle, but thanks to the
sacrifice of the enchanted grass, the eternal now had the
strength to defy it. He reared, something the guard had not expected him to be able to do, and pulled his would-be captor
forward. The moment she was near enough, Darkhorse kicked
her soundly, sending the stunned warrior flying back into one
of her companions.

Seeing his two companions collapse was enough to make
the remaining sentry before Darkhorse lose much of his confidence in his sorcerous weapon. He started to back toward
the tent.

"Get back up there, you fool!" shouted Saress, but she
made no move to back the guard up.

The other warriors were not so reluctant. Another shock
coursed through Darkhorse as the trio attacked. Deciding to
risk further pain, the shadow steed kicked with his rear legs.
Another shock briefly assailed him, but the agony was worth
it in the end, for Darkhorse managed to stun one guard and
knock loose the weapon from another. The third met the
shadow steed's gaze and, after staring into the inhuman orbs
for but a moment, dropped his weapon and fled.

Darkhorse had no more time to waste on them. The shadow
steed reared, then planted both front hooves hard in the soil.
The earth cracked, the tremor nearly upsetting the balance of
the warriors around him. At the same time, Darkhorse created

around himself a bright green aura that crackled like lightning. "Flee before I devour you, you insignificant little worms!"

Dropping their weapons, the remaining guards fled, leaving only Saress.

Shrugging off the noose, Darkhorse confronted the sorceress. "Step aside, witch, and I may forget that you exist."

She hissed defiantly, but when the eternal took another step toward her, the sorceress quickly vanished. Darkhorse hesitated, then trotted into the tent.

Yssa stood there, arms and legs stretched outward. Thin, silky strands circled her wrists and ankles, keeping her from moving, but otherwise she looked untouched. Even Yureel knew the value of a healthy captive, it seemed. Darkhorse probed the strands, which ended in midair, and found his twin's taint on them. Disgusted, he quickly disposed of the magical bonds.

"Come with me, quickly, Yssa! Before Yureel arrives!"

She tried to say something as she approached, but no sound escaped her. The eternal detected a spell similar to the one Aurim had used to keep him silent. Annoyed that he had not noticed it earlier, the shadow steed removed it, too.

"Darkhorse! You shouldn't have come here! He's expecting you to—"

The horribly familiar giggle floated through the tent, seeming to surround the pair. Darkhorse's eyes narrowed. Even now he could not sense Yureel. The malevolent puppet had worked hard to shield himself.

"Too late! Too late, my dear sweet sorceress!" Yureel coalesced in a far corner of the tent. The miniature figure drifted toward them. "I knew that you would eventually return to me no matter where the boy sent you! Ever the hero, my brother, my self? I'd think you'd learn a new game by this time!"

"And so I have!" Using his jaws, Darkhorse seized an unsuspecting Yssa by the arm, pulling her completely off the ground. Before Yureel could react, he had carried the enchantress out of the tent.

A tall, fearsome figure blocked their path from there.

"Father!" Yssa gasped.

The drake thrust out one gauntleted hand at them. "Down, demon sssteed! Now!"

Darkhorse did not have to ask why. He could sense Yureel just behind him. Still gripping the Dragon King's daughter by the arm, he fell to the ground.

"No need to grovel, Darkhorse, it won't do you any—well, the lizard king! This is a surprise! My brother must've mentioned me to you, I see! Come to visit your offspring or come to surrender to the inevitable?"

"I've come to sssend you back where you belong, abomination!" The reptilian monarch flipped open the box.

Yureel giggled at the effrontery, no doubt thinking the Dragon King completely mad. The giggle died abruptly, though, as the floating demon's feet began stretching toward the open compartment. Snarling, the malevolent marionette tried to pull away, but his bottom half surged toward the box. Yureel began to look like an uncooked gingerbread man being stretched in two by some insane baker.

"Stop it! I command you to stop it!"

"Command all you like!" hissed the Green Dragon. "Welcome to your new home!"

With each passing moment, Darkhorse expected his twin to pull free, yet the pull of the artifact would not be denied.

"Release me! Release me or I will destroy you!" Yureel twisted and turned, ice-blue eyes wide with growing comprehension of what fate awaited him if he did not free himself quickly. Unlike Darkhorse, Yureel had never faced the boxes before.

"In, demon!" The Dragon gasped; Yureel was clearly stronger than he had expected.

There was nothing Darkhorse could do to help. If he interfered, he might find himself caught in the very same trap along with his twin. Worse, he might even accidentally free Yureel instead of assuring his imprisonment.

"You . . . will . . . stop!" Rocks burst from the ground and pelted the Green Dragon, but the attack was weak. Yureel dared not focus too much of his power on the drake; he needed everything to combat the tenacious pull of the Vraad box.

It was now only a matter of seconds.

The struggling figure stretched thinner and thinner as more of him seeped into the box. Yureel grew so sheer that it was possible to see through him. He grasped at the sky, as if trying to gain some handhold on the distant clouds.

Then, with one long howl of anger, the last of the shadow puppet vanished into the artifact.

The drake immediately shut the lid.

"Do you really have him, Father?"

"If you could feel how the box shakesss in my hand you wouldn't asssk such a question, my daughter."

Darkhorse glanced quickly around. Saress had to have warned King Lanith by now, and while by himself the lord of Zuu was little threat, he still had the power to command the sorcerers. Until the Dragon King disposed of the cursed box and its doubly cursed contents, Aurim remained a slave to Yureel. Their victory could still turn into disaster if Cabe's son gathered the Order and confronted them. "Dispose of the box, now, Dragon King! We do not have much time remaining to us."

"I . . . am . . . trying!" The Green Dragon clutched the artifact with both hands, as if trying to squeeze it out of existence. "It is . . . resisting my attempts to cast it out of our world."

Even without the use of a probe, Darkhorse could sense the tremendous force with which Yureel sought to free himself of the Vraad device. For the first time, the eternal wondered if the ancient box would hold out against the might of his vile counterpart. Perhaps time had taken a toll on the Vraad artifact after all.

"Darkhorsssse, I think it may require both of usss—"

Whatever else the Dragon King said, the eternal did not hear. Sorcery was at play around them, familiar sorcery.

"I think you've got something that belongs to me, lizard."

The horse king suddenly confronted them, but he was hardly alone. Not only did a now-smiling Saress lean on his shoulder, but Aurim, the oily Ponteroy, and two other sorcerers flanked the pair. The younger Bedlam still stared at Darkhorse as if recognizing him only as an enemy of his master.

"Keep back, vassal, unless you'd care to lossse your precious ally!"

Lanith's expression shifted to mild confusion. "I'm talking about your dear, sweet daughter, lizard. She's my special guest and I'm here to see that she'll stay that way. Come here, woman."

Before the Dragon King could retort, Aurim Bedlam interjected, "He has Yureel in that box, Your Majesty. That's what he meant."

"Does he? That box?" Fascination and indignation clashed as the horse king squinted at the artifact. "Now that's clever." He extended a hand. "Give it to me and I'll at least let your half-breed child live, lizard. Oh . . . and your death'll be relatively quick and painless, I suppose."

"Are you not leaving your warriors and your remaining spellcasters to face a storm of death, Your Majesty?" Darkhorse asked, trying to shake King Lanith's confidence a little. "They might be wondering where you are even now."

"My people are dedicated to me. They're warriors of *Zuu*, horse. The finest in the land and willing to prove it to any who disbelieve. If it costs some of them their lives, so be it. In the end, Dagora will be mine. After that, Gordag-Ai, then probably Talak."

"You fool!" The drake lord hissed, struggling more and more with the box. "Even with your spellcastersss you will eventually lossse! Can't you sssee that the demon isss playing you like a puppet?"

It was the wrong thing to say. The horse king pointed at the box. "Take it from him, Aurim. Feel free to hurt him while you do it."

But at that moment the Vraad artifact suddenly blazed with light. The Green Dragon snapped one gauntleted hand away, the palm already a fiery red. However, he refused to release the box, though his other hand must be suffering terrible pain.

Yssa started toward her father, but Darkhorse used his power to drag her back, knowing it was already too late to help the Dragon King. There was nothing either of them could do.

The box exploded.

The explosion hurtled the Green Dragon back toward the tent, whether dead or not, Darkhorse had no time to discover. A pitch black cloud rose above the cracked remnants of the foul device, a cloud with icy blue eyes. It surveyed those assembled, at last fixing its murderous glare on the scorched form of the drake.

"I'll burn him, I'll tear his limbs off one at a time, I'll spread his body across every land in the continent!" Yureel reshaped himself, but now he was larger, less cohesive. "I'll kill him, then kill him again!"

Focused as he was on Yureel's horrific return, Darkhorse forgot about Yssa until it was too late. The blond enchantress suddenly darted away from her companion, trying to reach her father.

"Yes, yes, yes!" Yureel ranted, eyes glittering in swelling anticipation. "You'll do even better, dear one! I hope your father survives long enough to hear your cries!"

"You'll do nothing!" roared Darkhorse, but as he moved to intercept his twin's spells, he found something holding him back.

"You won't do anything, Darkhorse," Aurim stared blankly at him.

"Very good," commended the horse king. "Hold him there." Lanith took a step toward his shadowy ally. "Don't harm her, imp! She's got too much potential. We can use her to strengthen the Order, make her help conquer her father's own land! Just do with her as you did with Bedlam here."

"Her mind's all wrong, you fool!" Yureel seemed to no longer care about pretending he was servant to Lanith. "Just like that witch of yours!"

Lanith clearly did not understand, but Darkhorse thought *he* did. Yureel could not control either half-breed the way he could humans. Something in the half-breeds' minds must differ from the minds of true humans. He wished he had the time to discover just what. Any advantage was welcome.

A brief, low moan escaped the Green Dragon. Yureel turned toward him again, his interest in his former captor renewed.

"Leave him be, damn you!" The Dragon King's daughter

seemed not to care that Yureel had the power to tear her limb from limb.

A brave and impetuous young woman . . . and one about to die horribly because of those traits. Darkhorse struggled to help her, but Aurim held him at bay. The shadow steed stared at his young friend. Aurim stared back, expression still indifferent.

Gathering his will, Darkhorse tried to contact the mind held prisoner within the sorcerer's body. He knew that some part of Aurim had to be there; it had revealed itself in time to save him before. Perhaps there was a chance Darkhorse could stir the true Aurim to action.

In his mind, he called the human's name over and over. The sorcerer's expression tightened, as if he was not at all at peace with himself. Darkhorse took the change as a sign and pushed harder to reach his friend. *Aurim Bedlam! This is not you! You have the power to shift the balance here! You must!*

As the ebony stallion fought to reach the sorcerer's mind, Yureel looked down upon the drake's defiant offspring. "Yes, you're absolutely right! I should leave him alone . . . at least for now! I *should* play with you first! I'll make your death an epic in itself!"

Standing her ground, Yssa cast a spell. A cloud formed around Yureel, but the shadowy figure shrugged it off with scarcely any effort. He moved nearer, reshaping and solidifying into a massive, dark figure very reminiscent in outline of an armored warrior, a drake to be precise. Even the eyes seemed half-hidden now by a pitch-black helm. The dark knight stood at least a full foot taller than Darkhorse.

"Kaplo's Charger!" gasped the horse king. Darkhorse suspected he had never seen his ally in anything but the most minute of forms. "Imp—"

"Why don't you change, too, little witch?" Yureel taunted the defiant woman. *"She* can do it"—Saress blanched and quickly retreated a few steps behind Lanith— "you can certainly do it, too."

Yssa's response came in the form of another spell, this one a score of bright flashes that burst into and out of existence accompanied by a loud explosion. Briefly startled, the shadow knight backed up a step . . . and walked into a cage formed from the earth. As the entrance of the cage sealed itself, the enchantress fell to one knee, gasping.

"The box could not hold me," Yureel casually remarked, putting one massive hand against the front of his cage, "and it was your only hope, dragonspawn." The cage shattered, pelting all of them with bits of earth. He stalked toward Yssa, each step leaving small craters. "Now, how shall we begin with you?"

As he reached for her, his hand swelled, growing all out of proportion to the rest of his form. Yssa tried to vanish, but Darkhorse sensed Yureel counter her attempt. She was still trying to transport herself away when the fearsome knight lifted her up by the waist.

"Perhaps I'll squeeze you apart first, then absorb the leftovers . . . "

Try as he might, Darkhorse could do nothing to free her. Aurim kept his powers in check. He stared again at the young sorcerer. *Aurim! Do not let this happen!*

Yureel tightened his grip. The enchantress first gasped, then moaned as the shadowy knight started to squeeze the life out of her.

A silver scythe formed between Yureel and Yssa and without pause *sliced* clean the hand that held her.

Hand and enchantress dropped the short distance to the ground. The severed appendage immediately released her and scurried back to its master, who absorbed it and formed a new hand to take the original's place.

Aurim stepped in front of the king, eyeing the monstrous shadow with new and growing defiance. "I've . . . killed for you. I've ravaged . . . a land . . . for you. I've seen more . . . death . . . than is right for . . . any one person . . . to want or have to witness!"

"Return to your place!" commanded Lanith, reaching for him.

The younger Bedlam glared at the horse king, who suddenly thought better of touching a powerful spellcaster in anger. "I am."

"You little whining traitor!" Ponteroy raised his staff, but

Aurim blinked and the staff suddenly burst into flames. Gasping, the other sorcerer dropped his fiery weapon and kicked it away. A slight wave of Aurim's hand sent the burning staff flying in the direction of Lanith's advancing warriors. A breath later, they heard it explode.

"Go home, Ponteroy," Aurim added. "I know your former liege in Gordag-Ai will be pleased to see you. You've told me that often enough."

"No—" was all the arrogant spellcaster managed to spout before vanishing. If Aurim *had* sent him back to Gordag-Ai, it was doubtful he would be returning soon, if at all. The kingdom's spies likely knew every traitorous action the overdressed sorcerer had been involved with since his arrival in Zuu and without his staff, Ponteroy was not as much a threat.

The two remaining sorcerers retreated to Saress, who still watched Lanith nervously. Her own fear that he would realize what she was kept her paralyzed.

Not so Yureel. "Naughty boy! Behave yourself or I'll just have to strike you from my epic!"

Aurim's expression instantly slackened. He started back to the other spellcasters.

"Fight it, lad!" Darkhorse roared. Belatedly he realized that Aurim had dropped the spell holding him prisoner, probably at the same time the sorcerer had turned on his foul master. Now nothing prevented him from using his power. The ebony stallion immediately focused on Yureel, trying to strike between the eyes. If he could distract his murderous brother—

Yureel easily deflected his spell, but as Darkhorse had hoped, the attack gave Aurim the reprieve he needed to recover control of himself. The young sorcerer gritted his teeth and stared at his former master. Aurim was frightened, but doing his best to face the source of his fears.

Two of the spears dropped by the sentries rose into the air and darted past Aurim. Behind him, the king of Zuu, sword drawn, tried to protect himself from the unexpected attack. Lanith had clearly intended on stabbing the spellcaster from behind, realizing, perhaps, that without Yureel, his own dreams of victory would remain just that. If it meant sacrificing even so valuable a pawn as Aurim had been, so be it.

The treacherous monarch managed to deflect the first missile with his sword, but the second came too fast. Lanith tried but failed to raise his weapon in time. The head of the spear buried itself in his shoulder. Grunting, the horse king dropped his weapon and stumbled back.

Hissing, Saress went to his side. She pulled the weapon free, passed her hand over the wound, then signaled the other spellcasters to come to her aid. "I've stopped the bleeding, but more needs doing! Get him away from here and see that he's healed completely or you'll face me later! Go now!"

The two immediately took hold of the king and carried him away. Saress stood and glared at the source of his agony, the Dragon King's daughter. Yssa, though, had already forgotten the murderous king, her concern once again for her injured father. She did not even notice the other woman start toward her.

Knowing that the drake lord's daughter was too distracted to be of good use, anyway, Darkhorse called out, "Take him away from here, Yssa! Somewhere safe! Do it now!"

Looking relieved yet guilty, Yssa carefully scooped up her father. The drake's hand was a burnt ruin, probably unsalvageable even through high sorcery. The Dragon King breathed in short gasps. Yssa hurriedly opened a path of escape, clearly aware of how weak the drake had already become.

With an inhuman roar, Saress flung herself after her disappearing rival. Occupied with Yureel, Darkhorse could do nothing to stop the furious sorceress. Saress vanished only seconds after Yssa and her father did.

Yureel continued to prove more resilient than the stallion had hoped. The dread knight had so far fought Darkhorse and his companion to a standstill, something that should not have been possible. True, Yureel had always maintained greater reserves of strength due to his horrific habit of eventually devouring any source of power he came across, but Darkhorse was at his peak and Aurim was possibly the greatest spellcaster in generations. Even Yureel with his parasitic link to the other spellcasters of the Order should not have been able to stand against the pair, unless . . . Aurim was unconsciously holding back because his confidence had begun to erode again.

"We have him, lad! Keep at him!" He hoped he sounded encouraging. Aurim needed to believe in himself.

The human did not respond and his face was horribly pale. He still worked alongside the shadow steed, but it was clear that he recalled too much of his enslavement. Fear made him hesitant, something that threatened to be fatal for both of them.

Aurim! He cannot harm you anymore! You have proven your will superior to his! Darkhorse repeated himself, uncertain as to whether the boy paid any attention to his plea.

He made me . . . I couldn't do a thing, Darkhorse . . . he made me kill for him! I thought I was strong enough, but now I don't know . . .

But you saved Yssa and the drake! You broke free, Aurim! You broke free!

At first Darkhorse believed that his words had had no impact on Cabe's son, but then he sensed a new onrush of power behind the spell that Aurim cast next. Yureel certainly felt something, too, for although the spellwork itself was invisible, the shadow knight's reaction was anything but. Yureel's form glowed crimson and he stumbled back, crushing the tent.

"You are ours, Yureel!" Darkhorse meant his cry not only for his twin but for Aurim, too. The young mage needed more encouragement if the pair of them had any hope of victory. Aurim had finally freed himself of Yureel's control and now had the insidious demon at the disadvantage, but events had a habit of changing quickly in such dire situations. "Your epic will have to remain incomplete!"

The monstrous creature regained his footing. "I'm very disappointed in both of you, brother! You've misbehaved! I will just have to absorb you . . . but not before I teach you your place."

"Your power is not enough to withstand both of us, Yureel. That should be obvious even to you!"

He expected Yureel to retort again, but instead the shadow knight did something that caught both Darkhorse and Aurim completely off-guard. He flung himself into the air and flew off toward the east, his speed so great that he was little more than a speck by the time either of his adversaries realized what had happened.

"Darkhorse—"

"Aurim! Mount quickly!" Darkhorse waited only long enough for the sorcerer to obey, then leaped into the air after their foe. Yureel had already flown halfway to the battlefield, a destination dangerous even for so deadly a creature. What he planned, Darkhorse could only guess.

Still behind the Zuu lines, Yureel began to descend. The shadow steed could not readily detect who or what Yureel flew toward, but he thought he sensed sorcery there. A sudden suspicion started to gnaw at him.

"Hold tight, Aurim! We must reach him before it is too late!"

The sorcerer had already wrapped his arms around his friend's throat, but he tightened his grip. Sorcery was in play all over the battlefield despite the fact that both armed forces had come together, and it was likely difficult for the spellcasters to separate friend from foe. Even one stray spell might be enough to slow Darkhorse and possibly brutally injure the human astride him.

Yureel disappeared from sight, but Darkhorse still sensed his presence below. He now also sensed the presence of several sorcerers: the remnants of the Magical Order. Without Aurim, Saress, and Ponteroy, the Order was severely weakened, but the potential for danger still existed. If anyone knew best how to exploit that potential, it was Yureel.

"Be ready, Aurim. I fear the worst."

They were suddenly buffeted by earsplitting shrieks from every direction. Aurim screamed, and it was all the eternal could do to keep from following suit. The shadow steed spiraled toward the ground, just barely able to maintain control. In the distance, he caught sight of at least half a dozen figures positioned in a recognizable geometric pattern.

In the center stood the huge, shadowy figure of Yureel.

Darkhorse touched the earth still facing the group. A quick probe verified his fear; Yureel had taken Aurim's place as the

Order's focus. Worse, he had thrown off the mask of independence under which they had operated. Now he controlled each and every one of them.

"Darkhorse! He's made them like me!"

"I know that, Aurim! We cannot allow that to dissuade us, though."

"You don't understand, Darkhorse." The sorcerer gripped his companion's mane tight. "In a link of that complexity, they become so much more than a group of low-level mages."

Darkhorse understood that also, but before he could say so, Yureel and the Order struck again. Tremendous pressure threatened to flatten the eternal to the ground. Next to him, Aurim fell first to his knees, then on his face.

"We—must—work together! Give me your mind!" The moment he said the words, the eternal realized his grave mistake. Animal fear overwhelmed his friend, fear based deeply in the human's recent captivity. Aurim saw Darkhorse as too much like his twin.

The pressure continued to build, but now the ground changed, liquefying. Sorcerer and shadow steed quickly sank. It was all either of them could do just to keep their heads above the surface.

"Aurim! I am not Yureel! I will not seize control of your mind and body! We will work *together*. It is the one weapon we have that he can never understand well enough to use himself. We must link and become one together, not one held by the will of the other!"

The spellcaster shook his head. "I can't! Not again!"

"If you do not, then we have no hope. I must intertwine our powers so well that whatever Yureel attempts, he will be unable to separate them. Divided we are two against many. Together . . . we have the power to see to it that he will never cause such devastation and terror again."

Aurim nodded. His mind opened up to Darkhorse and although the eternal still sensed some lingering fear, he also noted building resolve. This time, Aurim Bedlam would not falter.

It was nearly too late. Darkhorse bound his power with that

of the sorcerer just as Aurim's mouth sank below the surface. The human's eyes widened, but he did not give in to panic.

It is done! We are one in our strength now. The binding briefly gave Darkhorse a sense of double thought, but he immediately sorted out his own mind from that of his young companion. With the stallion to guide them along, the pair lifted themselves from the earth.

Yureel forced his thralls to attack again, but this time the pair shrugged off the spell. With Aurim once more atop him, Darkhorse closed in on his counterpart. Neither he nor his companion attacked in turn; the spells they cast simply acted to deflect those of the Order toward the forces of Zuu. Each time Yureel attacked, he dealt damage to his own cause.

At last, only a few yards separated Darkhorse and his brother. Yureel looked slightly smaller and less fierce; controlling so many during so relentless a struggle had taken a toll even on him. The spellcasters looked even more bedraggled, but they had no choice.

"You are wasting your weapons, Yureel," taunted the shadow steed. "You can never make use of their full power while their spirits are trapped. Your very desire to control means that full control can *never* be yours."

"Still you preach, my brother, my self. Still you preach and no one listens!"

"Look around you! The power you threw against us has instead fallen upon the warriors of your supposed ally! Do you call that control? In the past few minutes, you have probably done more damage to the legions of Zuu than the Dragon King's own forces have."

Yureel hesitated, icy orbs shifting momentarily in the direction of the two battling armies. Like Darkhorse, he could sense that the horse king's warriors no longer had the advantage; the deadly spells the shadow steed and Aurim had redirected had struck Lanith's army at its most vulnerable points. The power that the dark knight had thrown at his foes had caused such damage that in some places the defenders were now pushing westward.

"My epic . . ." Yureel glared at the duo. "All my lovely work . . ."

"Worry not about your epic so much as yourself, Yureel. The box might not have been able to hold you, but there are other cages. The Void awaits your return."

"I will not go back there! I will not! I will not! Never again!" Arms burst from the shadowy giant's body, enough arms with which to seize the defenseless sorcerers around him. The arms retracted the moment each had hold of its prey. Darkhorse tried to sever the limbs as Aurim had earlier, but Yureel was too swift. The unmoving mages disappeared into the recesses of the knight's monstrous torso without so much as the slightest scream.

"God!" Aurim nearly slipped from his back. Darkhorse could not help shivering. He never ceased to be amazed at Yureel's complete lack of respect for life. The sorcerers had meant no more to him than a blade of grass or a fly.

Yureel no longer seemed weary, pushed to the edge of defeat. He looked stronger now, stronger and larger. The ebony knight had threatened to absorb his twin and make all that Darkhorse had been a part of him. He had done exactly that with the mages. Their lives and especially their *power* were his.

By themselves, they had not been spellcasters of great ability. As part of the Order, their combined might had made them strong, but not impossibly so. As a part of Yureel, though, a part of his very essence . . . Darkhorse feared that once more his brother had snatched victory from him.

Only the two original arms remained, and now the shadow knight held a pitch-black mace. Yureel, already more than twice the height of his brother, raised the sorcerous weapon high. He moved as if fully revitalized.

"I've enjoyed our game so very much, my brother!" the murky titan bellowed. "But now the game ends, Dark-horse . . ."

CHAPTER XX

Yssa propped her father against the tree. Her guilt at leaving Darkhorse and Aurim behind had been countered by the Dragon King's serious condition. She hoped that she had the time and power left to stabilize him before it was too late.

Darkhorse . . . Aurim . . . forgive me for not being there to help you.

She already knew that healing the drake's hand was beyond the scope of her capabilities. Had it occurred because of a normal fire, she might have been able to repair it. Unfortunately, the potent energy wielded by Yureel had caused the damage and true to the monster's parasitic nature, it continued to ravage the limb even now. As much as she hated to think it, the enchantress knew that a good part of the arm would have to be removed in order to save her father. Taking a deep breath, Yssa knelt on the grass and prepared herself for the inevitable.

A shadow fell across her.

"You hurt my Lanith, you little hedge witch!" A strong blow against Yssa's cheek sent the blond woman falling against her patient. Through teary eyes she looked up at her attacker.

"I think I'll give him your head asss a presssent," Saress hissed, expression anything but human. "After I'm through with it . . ."

* * *

General Belfour noticed the two sorcerers first, then the weary form between them. His brow, already furrowed in worry from the way the battle had suddenly turned, formed deeper valleys when he recognized the somewhat bedraggled figure. The general turned the reins of battle over to his second in command, then urged his mount toward the newcomers.

"Your Majesty!" Lanith's eyes flashed open at the sound of his voice, searching the area around him as if expecting something. Belfour, who had seen that look before, nearly clamped his mouth shut, but his curiosity got the better of him. "Your Majesty, what happened to you?"

The monarch looked down at the wound near his shoulder. Belfour had never seen a wound so—*blue*—but when he started to repeat his question, King Lanith cut him off with a wave of his hand.

"Your Highness," one of the sorcerers began, trying desperately to keep the wound covered at the same time. "We've only just begun. Neither of us are as powerful as Saress—"

"Saress . . ." Lanith looked up at his general. His tone seemed almost clinical. "She's a half-breed, drake abomination, Belfour. Kill her when she returns."

While removing the influence of the enchantress from his king had always been high on the veteran warrior's list of goals, the revelation of her origins nearly left him speechless. "A . . . *drake*, my lord?"

Lanith ignored him, eyes on Belfour's mount. "Give me your horse, General." He reached out to touch the bow and quiver hanging on the saddle. "Leave everything."

"My horse?" Meridian had been the warrior's favored battle mount for years, trained to obey a variety of signals and defend his master at all costs. There were times when he was fonder of the animal than he was some of his family.

"Your *horse*, General."

"Majesty, your wounds—" the same spellcaster began, cutting off Belfour before he could lodge a protest.

With speed that belied his injuries, Lanith drew a knife from his belt and thrust the blade into the sorcerer's stomach. Gasping, the man collapsed as his life quickly fled. The lord of Zuu pulled the blade free, wiping it off on the dead man's robes, then glanced at the remaining spellcaster. The other mage blanched, then scurried off in full panic.

"Worthless trash. When this is over, I'll rebuild the Order anew." The king stared at Belfour, who immediately dismounted and handed the reins to him. Lanith climbed up and, without another word, rode off.

The general watched Lanith vanish into the distance, then belatedly noticed that something was happening far ahead of the king. It seemed to be some sort of panic, as if they did not have enough trouble with the chaos spreading from the middle of their lines. The entire tenor of the war had shifted, just as General Belfour had feared from the start. Deep inside, he had known that this entire campaign had been madness, but as an officer of Zuu, he had been bound by his post to obey his monarch.

What would happen now, when it could no longer be denied that the king had not only led them to ruin but was insane as well?

Frowning at his own thoughts on the subject, the aging warrior quickly began searching for a new mount.

The mace struck the ground, causing tremors and opening a crevice wide enough to swallow a man. Sorcerous energy from the monstrous weapon scattered over the area, most of it in the direction of Darkhorse and his companion.

Yureel obviously did not care that they had moved closer to the battle. If some of Lanith's warriors were too slow-witted to get out of his way, he simply crushed them. All the gargantuan shadow desired was the destruction of his foes. He gave them no time to think, striking again and again without pause. The pair could do nothing but back away and defend.

This is madness! Darkhorse knew that at the rate they were retreating, he and Aurim would very soon be in the midst of the Zuu army. Already Yureel had scattered several riders, killing two in the process, and while that benefited the Green Dragon's defenders, it did nothing for the shadow steed. It was not that the link between Darkhorse and his human friend had grown any weaker, just that Yureel's vicious, rapid attacks kept the eternal and his companion at constant bay. Worse, the memories of his imprisonment in Zuu and the fate he had nearly suffered there had begun to return each time Yureel neared him. Yureel had almost swallowed him and still would again if given the opportunity. The deaths of the sorcerers had reminded him too much of the probability of that. Try as he might, the shadowy stallion could not forget.

"Darkhorse! We have to take the offensive!"

He heard Aurim and agreed with him, but the mace, as much a part of Yureel as the hand that wielded it, crashed into the ground only a few yards away. Darkhorse felt a slight pull from it, as if it sought to draw him into it. He knew then that if Yureel struck him even lightly, he would be absorbed.

The shadow knight giggled again, icy blue eyes bright beneath the helm. "You were always the lesser of the two of us, my brother, my self! Let me end your miserable existence so that you can live on in my own glory! I'll even preserve a little place in my story for you, Aurim Bedlam, perhaps a little tale of a boy who sought but never found his full potential . . ."

The mace came down again. Darkhorse moved almost too late. Yureel missed him by less than a yard, but energy released by the strike threw stallion and rider several feet into the air. Aurim slipped from the shadow steed's back, falling some distance away.

"I'm tempted to take you first as you've slipped from me far too many times, brother, but I think I'll start with your little mage friend first as an appetizer and savor you as the main dish! Since you two are linked, I know you'll fully enjoy his agony."

Yureel kept the mace pointed toward Darkhorse as he reached for Aurim. Darkhorse eyed the ebony weapon, then Cabe's son.

Rearing, he charged the huge figure. Yureel reacted, but too slowly. Darkhorse ducked below the mace, not that he would have cared at this moment if it had hit him. All he intended to do was grant the sorcerer time to escape. Even with the power bequeathed to him from the Barren Lands, Darkhorse knew that Yureel had the advantage. The shadow steed's own deeply rooted fear, a fear as great as that which Aurim had suffered earlier, worked against him. He did not want to be engulfed by Yureel.

The shadow knight fell back as they collided, but recovered quickly. Seizing Darkhorse by the throat, he shook the shadow steed hard. "So eager to rejoin me as all that? Very well, I'll be happy to grant your desire."

Darkhorse! The link! Our power together, remember?

Aurim's words made perfect sense, mirroring as they did his own earlier ones, but for some reason he could not take them to heart. This was *Yureel.* Darkhorse of all creatures knew his twin best. Yureel had been first. Yureel had always been stronger.

You said that together we could beat him, Aurim reminded him, sounding more like Cabe Bedlam. *Together. One.*

Aurim—

Let me take over. I'll do it. You said I could.

He felt Aurim take control of the link between them. The shadow steed wanted to warn him about the dangers, but to his surprise, the human manipulated it as if he had done so all his life.

With a shriek, Yureel dropped him. Darkhorse fell to his knees, then stared up at his twin. The shadow knight held his head in his hands and howled. His form became less defined and he seemed to shrivel a bit.

Aurim Bedlam, eyes closed and back straight, pointed one hand at their adversary. His control of their combined might was flawless; Darkhorse could not have done better. Yureel had only himself to blame; in the process of utilizing the lad as a pawn, he had shown Aurim what he could do. The boy remembered everything, it seemed.

We're still not one, Darkhorse. You've got to join me completely in order to let this work.

The student had to remind the teacher of his own lesson. Another time Darkhorse would have laughed. Now he could only hope that he would be able to give Aurim what the sorcerer needed.

He opened himself up, giving all that he could to the effort. As if struck, Yureel fell to one knee. He was only vaguely humanoid now and much smaller than he had been a moment before. The shadow man finally tore his hands away from his head and tried to reach for his attackers. However, he moved as if the very air around him had solidified. Yureel managed one step closer, but the effort caused him to shrink more.

Through their connection, Darkhorse knew what Aurim planned. It was justice of a sort, the same kind of trap Yureel himself had had the sorcerers set in Adderly. The pressure on each side of Yureel increased tenfold, pushing him into a smaller and smaller place. Like Yssa, Aurim had built a cage; but unlike the enchantress, he had the power and skill to make it inescapable.

It was in your mind, Darkhorse. I hope it was all right to use it.

Darkhorse said nothing, allowing Aurim to control the situation. All that mattered was finishing with Yureel, and the spellcaster seemed to know exactly what had to be done.

Yureel abruptly shrank to a foot tall, trying, perhaps to escape the trap through some sort of trickery. Aurim matched him immediately, though, giving the monster no extra room in which to move. He did not want Yureel coming back to plague them again.

"Don't send me back!" the tiny figure suddenly cried, the icy eyes wide and pleading. All trace of the fearsome monster had vanished. Yureel sounded like a frightened child. "Destroy me, but don't send me back!"

For the first time, Darkhorse sensed Aurim falter. If they exiled him, they could never be certain that Yureel might not return. On the other hand, the shadow steed knew that Aurim had been sickened by all those his sorcery had injured or killed in the name of the king of Zuu, even if he had not truly been responsible. Even destroying Yureel might prove too much for the lad's mental state.

"Darkhorse, what should I do? I don't think I can kill him!"

The shadow steed himself did not know how to answer. To be rid forever of the fear of Yureel had always been his dream, but to dispose of him in a manner so . . . so . . . much like what his twin himself might have chosen . . . did not sit well with Darkhorse either.

"I know a place," he finally said "a place far, far away from which I doubt even Yureel can escape . . . especially if we work together to fashion this cage into one stronger than the last."

Aurim stared at the imprisoned figure. "I wanted to . . . after all he's made me do . . . after all those whose deaths he caused . . . I wanted to make him suffer for all of them . . . but I can't."

Recalling his own fears of eternal imprisonment in the box, Darkhorse replied, "He will suffer, Aurim. Sending him to exile in his cage will be a far more effective punishment."

"You can't, you can't, you *can't!*" Yureel roared. "Don't send me away! I was so *lonely!* I couldn't bear it again, Darkhorse!"

"You will have to bear it, Yureel! For all that you are responsible for, you will just have to bear it. After all, you really have no choice, do you?"

The tiny figure's eyes dulled. All the fight appeared to have drained out of Yureel now that he was a helpless prisoner. "No choice. Yes, my dear brother, my self, I've no choice . . ."

Ice-blue eyes met ice-blue eyes.

Yurcel began to swell.

"Aurim!" Darkhorse flung himself between the sorcerer and the cage.

The cage held the forces unleashed by the shadow puppet for only a breath, maybe two. Not even the combined might of Aurim Bedlam and Darkhorse could contain it any longer. The burst of energy rose ten, twenty, even thirty feet into the sky and even farther along the ground. Raw power raged over the shadow steed, who now completely covered his human friend.

Darkhorse was on fire, but he did what he could to protect Aurim, if not himself. The agony became so great that the eternal screamed loud and long. Still the murderous wave washed over him, threatening more and more to tear him apart.

At last, the level of pain decreased. Darkhorse shivered, astonished—no, unable to *believe*—that he still lived. He remained where he was until the last vestiges of the terrible assault had faded, then, with each movement still agony, the shadow steed slipped off of Aurim.

Despite the protection Darkhorse had given to his companion, he saw that the spellcaster, too, had suffered. Deathly white, Aurim could not even rise at first. Only after several anxious minutes did he manage to sit up.

"What . . . what happened?" Color began to seep back into the human's face.

Still in the process of refining his form, Darkhorse indicated the ravaged area where the cage had stood. A gaping, blackened hole marked it. The words came harder than Darkhorse would have imagined. It was not as if anything related to the notion of love had ever existed between the ebony stallion and his darker half. "Yureel could not stand the thought of returning to exile."

The battered mage paled again. "Do you mean that he *destroyed* himself?"

"It was that or face a fate he feared more." Darkhorse snorted. "I had not thought he feared exile so *much,* even knowing how terrifying it was to him. I did not know he would choose this last path until I saw the death in his eyes."

Aurim buried his head in his hands. "I killed him. In the end, I killed him after all."

"No! Yureel's end was his own doing and one that should not be wept over! Too many died for his madness for you to even consider taking some blame! You tried to be humane; Yureel did not even know the word *existed.*" Darkhorse glanced again at the devastated area. "Do not pity him, Aurim. If there was ever one creature not deserving of pity, it was Yureel."

The sorcerer looked at him, finally shaking his head. "I think that no matter what he was and what he did, I'm going to pity him a little, Darkhorse. I didn't know he hated imprisonment so much he would do this."

Too weary to argue, the eternal simply shook his head. He would never completely understand humans.

A hissing sound made the shadow steed stiffen.

Aurim cried out. A long shaft was buried in his thigh. Darkhorse looked for the source, wondering who had recklessly chosen to remain behind when all the other warriors had fled from the vicinity of the deadly duel. He saw in the distance the lone figure of King Lanith, mounted, preparing another arrow. Even without attempting a probe the shadow steed knew that the arrows were all enchanted. They were the same bolts used to penetrate the hides of dragons and magical shields. The sorcerer was fortunate that it had not completely pierced his leg.

"I'm all . . . right . . . Darkhorse," Aurim Bedlam called through clenched teeth. "I can deal with the arrow. I can."

Gratified by the news, the shadow steed refocused on the would-be assassin. Fury at the human's continued audacity fueled Darkhorse to renewed effort. Lanith might have been a pawn in many ways to Yureel, but he was hardly without guilt in matters. Yureel would not have chosen him otherwise. The blame for much of the destruction and death that had occurred and *would* have occurred lay at the feet of the horse king.

Darkhorse reared, daring Lanith to try for him. He doubted that the enchanted arrow would harm him, but even if it did, it would not be sufficient to keep him from stripping the human from his mount.

The horse king aimed, his target Darkhorse's head. Another breath or two and the shadow steed would find out exactly how deadly the arrow could be.

Lanith jerked straight in the saddle. His arrow shot harmless into the air, landing far to the warrior's right. The king dropped the bow and gripped his mount's mane. He weaved back and forth, glaring at the shadow steed, who was mere moments from reaching him.

King Lanith, ruler of Zuu, the horse king, tumbled to the ground, an arrow in his back.

Slowing to a trot, Darkhorse approached the sprawled figure. As he did, he noted a second rider approaching from behind the horse king; General Belfour. A sword hung from the man's side and he wore a bow looped around his shoulder, but the veteran warrior's hands were empty.

"That will be close enough, General," the shadow steed called when Belfour had come within a few yards of his king.

"I intend no trouble, Darkhorse." Belfour showed him open

palms. "I only came in search of my liege." The warrior peered down at the limp form. Blood pooled beneath the king's body; Lanith was clearly dead. "A perfect strike. I warned him that he shouldn't count on that magic shield around him. Sooner or later, it would fail him. The Dragon King has many fine archers and we're certainly near enough to the lines to be in danger." He shook his head. "I *did* warn him."

"Against normal weapons his shield might have held, General, but both wounds he received were from ensorcelled shafts." The eternal probed the arrow. Not only had it been enchanted, but he was fairly certain that the Magical Order had done the enchanting.

General Belfour leaned forward, one hand resting on the quiver. Surreptitiously studying the shafts within the quiver, Darkhorse knew that he did not have to look far to find the horse king's assassin.

"If you've no qualms, demon steed, I'd like to take my lord and my horse, which he borrowed, and depart."

He eyed the officer. "What will happen now, General Belfour? What about his war, his dreams of conquest?"

The human straightened, his face a perfect mask. No one who met him later would realize that he had murdered his own monarch. "This war was wrong, and *I* am certain that the king had just come to believe that. All that would've been accomplished in the end was tearing apart the Dragonrealm, something we don't need. We had no right to start this in the first place. As senior officer, it's my duty to withdraw our forces from Dagora and return to Zuu. A royal funeral must be prepared. Then, since the king had no direct heir and his brothers are all long dead, one of his nearest kin must be chosen to take his place."

"You are his cousin, are you not, General?"

Belfour actually looked surprised. "Yes . . . I am . . . and I suppose if they ask, I'd take the throne, if only to prevent anarchy."

"I believe you would make a good monarch, General. You look to be a man who believes in peace, not conquest, a man who would realize how rich his kingdom is already. Rich enough, in fact, to aid those whose lives have been ruined by this futile war."

"Yes . . . yes, I'll do what I can."

The shadow steed nodded. "See that you do." He paused, then added, "His brother Blane was a good man."

Belfour dismounted. "Aye. He would've been a good king."

One last thought occurred to Darkhorse before he could take his leave. "What of Saress and the Order?"

"My king's last command was to kill the witch if I saw her again. Something about her disgusted him. It's a command I'll fulfill if the opportunity comes. Sorceress or not, I'll see it done." Belfour removed the shaft from Lanith, studied it, then tossed it aside. He wrestled the king's corpse onto the back of the horse he himself had just ridden, then reclaimed his own. "As for the Magical Order, Zuu prospered for centuries without mages and the like, and what's worked so well for so long is just fine with me."

"That will be good news to many." Darkhorse turned. "Fare you well, General Belfour, and good luck with your future."

"A moment," the warrior said. "Two things I'd tell you still. The first is to watch out for the drake Sssaleese in the north. The king might not have liked his kind, but he was more than willing to deal with them in order to advance things. Watch the north."

It only verified facts that Darkhorse already knew, but he nodded his thanks, nonetheless. "Sssaleese will be watched. The second part?"

Looking somewhat uncomfortable, the general finished, "If you should ever come to Zuu again, you will be welcome. I promise that. It is owed to you and yours."

Darkhorse turned and departed without a word in response. It would be a long time before he would consider returning to the kingdom of the horse people. First he would wait and see how the new monarch fared.

Aurim waited where Darkhorse had left him. The sorcerer had removed the arrow from his thigh and not only stopped the bleeding, but healed the wound, too. The shadow steed was impressed. Even for Cabe, wounds of a sorcerous nature took more time. Some wounds, like the one that had taken the Gryphon's fingers, could never be completely healed.

"I heard your conversation with the general through our link, Darkhorse." Aurim was pale but otherwise in reasonable condition, all things considered. "I heard everything."

"We can sever the link now, Aurim." Darkhorse chose not to speak further about Belfour and his friend did not press.

"No, if you don't mind, we still have a few more things to do." The young human stood, looking stronger by the moment. "And they can't wait any longer."

Darkhorse nodded. Linked to Aurim, he knew exactly where his friend wanted to go.

The Manor.

"Mount, then. There is nothing more to keep us here any longer." The eternal could not help glancing at the scorched area that marked the last of Yureel. "Nothing at all."

CHAPTER XXI

When at last the Bedlams had been freed and Darkhorse had been able to verify that General Belfour had kept true to his word by withdrawing the forces of Zuu from Dagora, the shadow steed made a visit to the forest kingdom. No word had come as to the Dragon King's condition. There were even rumors that he was dead, rumors that some of his fellow monarchs seemed eager to believe.

Darkhorse might not have worried save that he had not heard from Yssa since she had fled from the battle with her injured father. That Saress had been not far behind made the matter more vexsome.

The eternal materialized before one of the entrances to the drake's caverns and waited. He knew that they were aware of his presence from the beginning, so it came as no surprise when a dark-skinned human appeared from behind a tree. The middle-aged human, clad in evergreen robes that marked him as one of the reptilian monarch's senior aides, bowed before Darkhorse.

"Is there something I can do for you, demon steed?"

"I would speak to your king."

The news did not please the aide. "His Majesty is very occupied at the moment—"

"It's all right, Gyman," interjected a female voice.

Yssa stood near the cavern, her clothing and demeanor a tremendous contrast to the vital enchantress Darkhorse had come to know. While the brown and tan gown still hinted of Zuu, it covered her far more than the dresses she had worn in the past. More important, her features were devoid of all traces of pleasure at seeing her friend again.

"Yssa! You do live, then!"

His remark brought a faint smile to her face. "That should be obvious."

"And your father?"

The smile vanished. "Come see for yourself."

Darkhorse found himself standing in the chambers of the Dragon King, the enchantress beside him. On a bed formed entirely by plants of a thousand varieties, the master of the Dagora Forest lay sleeping. His chest rose slowly, with intermittent hesitations, and occasionally he twitched as if in pain.

His left forearm was gone, the stump bound with white cloths.

"He'll recover in a few weeks, but until then, I don't dare leave him." She looked over her shoulder where two sentries, one human, one not, watched. "My bro—his *son* and heir almost ordered him put to death, a drake tendency I've never cared for. I convinced him in the end that our father would still be able to rule well. He believed me."

"And is that so?"

"Yes."

The shadow steed turned away from the unconscious Dragon King. "What happened to Saress, Yssa?"

She looked down. "She followed us. I brought Father to the first place I could think of where I might be able to help him. I hadn't even begun before she appeared and struck me. I thought we were both dead."

"But you are not. How did you defeat her?"

"I didn't. You see, I took my father to the Barren Lands." Yssa looked again at the drake. "She knocked me to the ground and reached for Father. That was when the grass took her."

The grass? It took Darkhorse a moment. The grass had taken Saress— "Her father *was* of the drake clan Brown."

"Yes. You know how Cabe's spell worked. The grass knew her bloodline despite her human appearance. There was noth-

ing I could do." She shivered. "It was over in little more than
a minute."

That would save the new king of Zuu the duty of fulfilling
his predecessor's last command. Darkhorse was not entirely
dismayed at the fate of the sorceress.

"I really need to see to him, Darkhorse," Yssa added, indicating her parent.

He was being asked to leave already. The shadow steed saw
no reason not to oblige her. When the Green Dragon was better, Darkhorse would visit Yssa again. "Very well. I am glad
that you are well, Yssa."

"Wait . . ." She reached up and briefly hugged him around
the neck. In a quieter yet still tense voice, she said, "I know
most of what's happened. I know you and Aurim dealt with
Yureel and that the two of you also freed everyone trapped at
the Manor, but I just wanted to find out if everyone is . . . feeling well."

Knowing exactly who in particular she meant, he responded, "Everyone is well. Cabe provided food and there
was water and air aplenty. As for Aurim . . ." He noted the
way her interest grew at mention of the lad's name. "He will
never forget what Yureel put him through, but he is doing
fine. His skills and confidence have grown tremendously. You
should visit sometime. I think he would enjoy that."

"I doubt his mother would, though." She smiled as she said
it, a sign to Darkhorse that the enchantress *would* be visiting
soon.

"I will go now, Yssa, but I hope to see you before long."

"You will. All of you. You've my gratitude for many things,
Darkhorse."

With a dip of his head, the ebony stallion returned to the
surface. He started to open the path to the Manor, but at the
last moment chose to turn west.

A brief run brought him to the site of the battlefield. Most
of the dead had been removed, but the devastation remained.
No spell would restore the Dagora Forest this time. The burnt
and shattered trees would have to be cleared, then new ones
would be planted. Darkhorse knew the Green Dragon well
enough to understand that despite the immensity of the pro-

ject, the drake would see that it was done. The shadow steed wished him the very best of luck. He would try to assist. After all, it had been his brother who had caused all of this.

His brother . . . Their origins might have been linked, but from then on he and Yureel had been two entirely different creatures. There had been no love, no kinship, no sense of family. In the end, they had only existed as enemies.

"Family . . ." he whispered. In the physical sense, the eternal had no family, especially now that Yureel had destroyed himself. Still . . . he thought about the times he had shared with first Cabe, then Cabe's children. There had also been Queen Erini of Talak and her daughter. He had even shared good times with Melicard, Erini's dour husband, and the Gryphon. Even now, the Bedlams awaited his return to the Manor. Lady Bedlam had decided that a holiday festival was in order to revive everyone's spirits. She had made a special point of reminding Darkhorse to be there. Coming from Cabe's wife, that meant much.

Family . . . The shadow steed turned from the ruined forest. Come the morrow, he would do what he could to assist the inhabitants of Dagora in resurrecting the western half of their realm, but today . . . today . . .

Today he needed to be with family.